Love and Sexuality in Modern Arabic Literature

Love and Sexuality in Modern Arabic Literature

Edited by

Roger Allen, Hilary Kilpatrick and Ed de Moor

Saqi Books

In-house editor: Jana Gough

British Library Cataloguing-in-Publication Data
A catalogue record for this book is available from
the British Library

ISBN 0 86356 062 8 Hb
ISBN 0 86356 075 X Pbk

This edition first published 1995 by
Saqi Books
26 Westbourne Grove
London W2 5RH

Typeset by Group E, London

Contents

List of Contributors

Roger Allen, *University of Pennsylvania, Philadelphia*
Miriam Cooke, *Duke University, Durham (US)*
Rosella Dorigo Ceccato, *University of Venice*
Susanne Enderwitz, *Free University of Berlin*
Hartmut Fähndrich, *Polytechnic, Zurich*
Stephan Guth, *Institute of the German Oriental Society, Istanbul*
Sabry Hafez, *School of Oriental and African Studies, London*
Boutros Hallaq, *University of Paris III, Sceaux*
As'ad E. Khairallah, *University of Freiburg*
Hilary Kilpatrick, *Lausanne*
Richard van Leeuwen, *University of Amsterdam*
Ed de Moor, *University of Nijmegen*
Cornelis Nijland, *Dutch Institute for the Near East, Leiden*
Robin Ostle, *University of Oxford*
Mattityahu Peled, *Tel Aviv University*
Angelika Rahmer, *University of Münster*
Paul Starkey, *University of Durham (UK)*
Wiebke Walther, *University of Frankfurt*
Stefan Wild, *University of Bonn*

The editors acknowledge help from the University of Nijmegen and a grant from the European Meeting of Teachers of Arabic Literature in the publication of this book.

Introduction

On Love and Sexuality in Modern Arabic Literature

Hilary Kilpatrick

If the subject of this volume is love and sexuality in modern Arabic poetry, prose and drama, that does not mean that these themes do not have a long history in Arabic, as in other, literatures. From time immemorial they have fascinated poets and tellers of tales, as can be seen from Greek myths, the *Ramayana*, the *Shih Ching* and parts of the Old Testament. In the earliest known texts of Arabic literature, the *qaṣīdas* (polythematic poems) place the evocation of a past love at the very beginning, and while the poem may develop in a number of ways, its initial theme is fixed.

Because of the *qaṣīda*'s prestige, the image of the poet weeping at the memory of his lost love is considered the main expression of pre-Islamic literature's concern with matters of love and sexuality. It is by no means the only one. The frank evocation of playful eroticism, for instance in the *Mu'allaqa* of Imru' al-Qays, belongs to the repertoire of the poet's boasts about his prowess in various areas of life, as do descriptions of the poet's nagging wife, complaining that her husband squanders all his resources on entertaining guests without a thought for the consequent privations he is inflicting on his dependants.

More profound, even bordering on tragedy, are those stories and fragments of poetry which record a woman's decision to abandon the man who has acquired her as booty from a raid and the children she has borne him and to return to her original tribe. The couple's love for each other is not proof against the constant humiliations to which the woman is subjected by her husband's tribe because she is a prisoner-of-war and thus a slave.

Later Arabic literature developed the subjects of love, sex and marriage in several ways. The unfulfilled longing of lovers kept apart by family opposition, a theme first encountered independently in Umayyad literature, occurs in all periods of pre-modern Arabic poetry and prose, in both élite and popular expressions. The frequency of this theme is connected with its capacity to convey criticism of social norms and constraints, and to express the individual's longing for freedom. Erotic poetry developed in the pleasure-loving circles of the Hijazi aristocracy before moving to the 'Abbasid court in Baghdad. Depending on the poet's temperament and his (or occasionally her) milieu, this poetry could be witty, delicate or obscene. The early 'Abbasid period also saw the beginning of Islamic mystical poetry. The first to have composed in the genre is traditionally considered to be the poetess Rābi'a al-'Adawiyya, but the most sublime exploration of mystical love in Arabic is to be found several centuries later in the poetry of Ibn al-Fāriḍ and Ibn 'Arabī.

In prose literature the many anecdotes about highly cultivated slave girls and their admirers reflect a society where the expression of love and sexuality had become a refined art practised by both men and women. Love stories abound, not only around ill-starred couples, often poets and their beloveds, but also around luckier young people whose adventures end happily, as the weddings which round off stories in the *Arabian Nights* show. Divorce, too, is not unknown in the anecdotal literature, though it tends to be a sudden occurrence, the husband simply being portrayed in the act of repudiating his wife. The increasing domestic disharmony which must often have preceded this moment is seldom represented, except in the telescoped and caricatural form of the lampoon. Only very rarely can the reality of married life be glimpsed, and then thanks to writers such as al-Jāḥiẓ, whose interests extended beyond court circles to the urban middle class and who sought to explore the social reality they perceived around them. But indirect evidence that some profound attachments existed is provided by the stories of Nā'ila bint al-Farāfiṣa throwing herself between her husband, the caliph 'Uthmān, and his murderers, and Maḥbūba risking her life for refusing to sing before the assassins of her master, al-Mutawakkil.

A series of treatises expresses the intellectual reflection in Arab-Islamic culture on the emotion that is so frequently at the heart of both poetry and narrative prose. Some treat it within the framework of the behaviour appropriate to those possessed of elegance and refinement; others—among them Ibn Ḥazm, whose *Ṭawq al-ḥamāma* [The Neck-ring of the Dove] is perhaps the only work of classical Arabic *belles-lettres* to have been widely translated into European languages—are much concerned with psychological, moral or religious aspects of love. Others again, such as the first half of Ibn

Dāwūd's *Kitāb al-zahra* [Book of the Flower], are essentially anthologies of fragments of love poetry.

It might have seemed natural for modern Arabic literature to use this rich indigenous heritage of writing on love as a starting-point for new explorations. But the élite literary tradition developed little during the Mamluk and Ottoman periods, creative vitality being channelled essentially into popular literature. It is only with the cultural contacts between Europe and the Arab world, which started in the seventeenth century and increased markedly in the nineteenth, that Arab intellectuals acquired the impetus to reformulate the foundation on which their literature should be constructed.

The first essay in this volume, by Boutros Hallaq, shows clearly the theoretical positions which informed the writing of four early, and crucial, reformers—al-Ṭahṭāwī, al-Shidyāq, Jibrān and al-Manfalūṭī—and demonstrates the close connection between their attitude to literature and their portrayal of love. Hallaq also suggests an analogy between these pioneers and the Jena Romantics.

Rosella Dorigo Ceccato's essay is a useful reminder that while the early Arab Romantics were striving to create a new literature, popular theatre was continuing a much older tradition. This theatre is characterized by a frankness of expression and a concentration on the physical which can also be found in some élite classical literature but has been very rare in modern Arabic literature until recently. The reticence, and in some cases prudishness, of much writing about love and sexuality in the modern Arab world has generally been ascribed to the influence of Victorian England, but one may wonder whether such an explanation is sufficient, given that British influence was not felt everywhere in the Middle East, and also that a phenomenon as complex as changes in the literary representation of sexuality is unlikely to be due to one factor alone.

The first decades of the twentieth century saw powerful movements for political and social reform, including the emancipation of women and the triumph of Romanticism in literature. Robin Ostle's essay traces this evolution in Egypt, one of the centres of Arabic culture, concentrating particularly on poetry.

Cornelis Nijland discusses the representation of love in the periphery, among some Arab writers in North and South America. Interestingly, his choice of authors demonstrates how women and members of the religious minorities, long excluded from contributing to élite literature, early on rejoined the mainstream of literary activity.

But Romanticism was not the only influence at work in the portrayal of love and sexuality in fiction, as the two essays on Egyptian fiction in the first half of the twentieth century prove. In analysing love and sexuality in

Tawfīq al-Ḥakīm's novels, Paul Starkey shows a leading writer and thinker grappling with the dilemmas created for society and the (male) individual by the movement for women's emancipation. Ed de Moor's presentation of shorter fiction by writers of the Modern School and Yaḥyā Ḥaqqī makes clear that these early writers, who were familiar with the works of the French realists and naturalists and the Russian psychological realists, produced some far from idealized pictures of sexuality and eroticism. Indeed, one cannot help wondering whether there are not traces of the earthy humour of the shadow plays in some Modern School stories.

The short story has established itself as a major genre in modern Arabic literature, and since the Second World War it has become widespread all over the Arab world. Roger Allen draws on the immense variety of experiences portrayed by men and women from North Africa to the Gulf in his survey of the roles played by women in literature, from granddaughter to civil servant, and from mother without sons to wife abandoned during a civil war; these roles apparently cannot be separated from women's sexuality, at least in society's eyes. Allen stresses the importance of the innovations—both in theme and in technique—introduced into the genre by women writers.

Love as a revolt against social constraints and oppression, which is discussed in connection with the Romantic writers treated at the beginning of this volume, returns in Richard van Leeuwen's analysis of two major Egyptian works of fiction, Najīb Maḥfūẓ's *Trilogy* and Jamāl al-Ghīṭānī's *al-Zaynī Barakāt*. Despite the differences between these books, they both portray love as incompatible with injustice and moral corruption, as a path to intellectual liberation and as an escape into a world where relations of power do not exist.

In the *Trilogy* it is the father, the patriarch, who embodies the system of power, and Hartmut Fähndrich examines other examples of mainly Egyptian and North African fiction where the father/husband represents authority within the family. Noting the tendency among Egyptian authors to portray family relationships as much warmer and more humane, and the fathers as less savagely authoritarian, than do their North African counterparts, Fähndrich asks whether this is evidence of two distinct regional traditions or styles, or whether different social and political conditions or individual visions lie behind the divergences.

The issue of regional distinctions is also raised by Susanne Enderwitz in her essay on the European woman in North African novels written in French. North African Francophone literature is the only significant body of texts produced in a foreign language in the Arab world and it differs from literature written in Arabic in several respects. Enderwitz notes an evolution in the portrayal of the European woman by North African writers and shows that these women are generally more convincing than those who appear in Arabic fiction from the Mashreq dealing with relations between Europe and the Arab world.

The violence and repulsive imagery which at least one of Enderwitz's authors employs when writing of sex are paralleled by certain passages in Egyptian fiction of the 1980s. Stephan Guth relates this phenomenon, and also the treatment of formerly taboo subjects such as incest and paedophilia, to a new understanding of realism among Egyptian writers. Perverted forms of sex in their work represent situations of emotional frustration, and they can also be read as an accusation levelled against a harsh, economically oppressive society that does not permit its members a normal life.

In modern Iraqi literature, the association of sex with violence—and in particular the theme of cleansing a family's honour through the killing of any woman member who transgresses the code of relations between the sexes—goes back much earlier, as Wiebke Walther's contribution indicates. The recurrence of the theme may be connected with the influence exerted by tribal values in Iraqi society. But Walther's discussion of Fu'ād al-Tikirlī's work shows how a leading Iraqi author has evolved from simply criticizing social attitudes to sexuality, especially women's sexuality, to using the portrayal of relations between the sexes as a means of expressing rejection of paralysing traditions and political injustice. Al-Tikirlī's most recent work shares the same aims as the texts discussed by Guth.

Another example of the centrality of sexuality is provided by a recent novel of a leading Palestinian writer, Jabrā Ibrāhīm Jabrā. Though sexuality here exhibits none of the abnormalities noted by Guth and Walther, Mattityahu Peled's analysis shows that it is also being employed to reveal weaknesses in a society which the novel's author considers gravely flawed. In addition, the radical change in the hero's sexual behaviour reflects the transition in his life from Palestine to the prosperous milieu of the Baghdad bourgeoisie.

As already noted, one of the characteristics of modern Arabic literature is that it is an enterprise to which, in principle, both men and women can contribute. Sabry Hafez's discussion of the development of women's writing from feminine through feminist to female uses insights derived from the study of women's writing in Europe to trace the different stages in the evolution of a specific consciousness among women of their role in creating Arabic literature.

One of the authors he refers to, Laylā al-'Uthmān, is the subject of the following essay: Angelika Rahmer focuses on the themes of this Kuwaiti author's fiction and shows that her strongly developed sense of women's oppression goes hand in hand with a deep concern for the direction in which modern Kuwaiti society is developing and an awareness of the injustice meted out to other disadvantaged groups, such as the Palestinians.

Much of Miriam Cooke's essay on Iraqi war literature is also devoted to the discussion of the work of a woman writer, Luṭfiyya al-Dulaymī. The texts which Cooke analyses all portray sexuality against the background of a country at war, where death is ever-present; they put sexuality in a new perspective.

The last two essays focus on poets and poetry. Nizār Qabbānī is one of the most important and popular Arab poets today, and he owes his reputation in the first place to his love poetry. Stefan Wild analyses his autobiography for the light it sheds on his attitudes to love and sexuality, discerning in it a genuine sympathy for the plight of many Arab women and a certain machismo, both inseparable from the process of poetic creation.

Finally, in a contribution inspired by a profound familiarity with Arabic poetry since the Second World War, As'ad Khairallah argues that physical love and the body have acquired a new prominence in the work of recent Arab poets, who have used such themes to express the rejection of socialist ideologies and to convey metaphysical, even mystical, aspirations. If this essay is juxtaposed with the two introductory ones, it will become clear what enormous changes have occurred in sensibility and literary expression in the last hundred years of Arabic literature.

The authors of the essays in this volume had at their disposal a number of earlier studies devoted largely to love and sexuality in modern Arabic literature, such as the Egyptian critic Ghālī Shukrī's pioneering *Azmat al-jins fī 'l-qiṣṣa al-'arabiyya* [The Crisis of Sex in the Arabic Short Story], the Lebanese Jūrj Ṭarābīshī's inquiries into the symbolism of women and femininity, Charles Vial's and Ṭāhā Wādī's analyses of the representation of women in Egyptian fiction and Miriam Cooke's *War's Other Voices: Women Writers on the Lebanese Civil War.*[1] *Love and Sexuality in Modern Arabic Literature* is intended as a further contribution to the investigations first undertaken by these scholars.

As will have become clear, however, the essays presented here do not cover the whole range of modern Arabic literature. Fiction, in particular from the very recent past, receives preferential treatment compared with poetry and especially drama. Popular literature has not been given the attention it deserves. Certain countries, for instance Sudan, with a fascinating author like al-Ṭayyib Ṣāliḥ, or the states of the Arabian peninsula, have been mentioned little, if at all. To some extent this is the result of chance, but it also seems to reflect tendencies in the research now being carried out in

Europe to concentrate on certain countries and genres. An awareness of this fact may encourage researchers to move out into less familiar territory—a development which would be very welcome.

But while this book does not pretend to offer a complete survey of love and sexuality in modern Arabic literature, it indicates certain constants in their treatment. The search for love is intimately connected with the individual's desire for freedom and fulfilment, while the frank affirmation of sexuality, of whatever kind, represents a challenge to a rigid and hypocritical social order. In both cases the act itself cannot be separated from its expression, and innovative attitudes to love and sexuality are bound up with literary renewal. Above all, the writer who takes up these issues knows that his or her handling of them is a social act, implicating the whole community. Much more than in most West European literatures, discussions of love and sexuality in modern Arabic literature are intricately connected with ideas about society and the individual's place in it. They are central to contemporary Arabic culture.

1

Love and the Birth of Modern Arabic Literature

Boutros Hallaq

It is now accepted that the idea of literature, as presently understood, emerged in the West with the Romantic movement of Jena,[1] which was elaborated and given a theoretical basis by Friedrich Schlegel and Novalis in particular. This idea of literature replaces the notions of *belles-lettres* or genres such as the drama, epic, fable, story or ballad.

In the Romantic thought of Jena, literature is conceived of as ontological in nature. This conception is part of a crisis of philosophy brought about by Kantian criticism, since it springs from the metaphysical question: what is Being? and from the recognition that philosophy and theology are incapable of expressing this Being. A daring plan then takes shape: to substitute aesthetics for philosophy, and consequently theology, in order to express Being. For this school of thought, aesthetics is limited to poetics, which, paradoxically, is embodied essentially in what the movement calls the novel, the prototype of all literature, including poetry. In both the practice and the theory of the members of the Jena school, literature, understood in its ontological sense, is inseparable from the subject of love, or, more generally, of the relations between men and women.[2]

It is astonishing to observe how the same approach was at work in the Arab world too. I use the word 'approach' because it is obvious that an enormous cultural divide separates the nineteenth century there from the intellectual context of the Romantic movement of Jena, while the education and philosophical reflection of a Schlegel and those of the writers of the *nahḍa* are several generations apart. It is true none the less that reflection on the nature of man went hand in hand with the development of the new literature and the creation of the very term of *adab*,[3] which conveyed a quite different meaning in classical Arabic literature.[4] At the same time, in this new literature, this reflection on man was bound, in the first place, to be pursued in the domain of love.

We shall try, then, to indicate briefly this evolution in the development of modern Arabic literature, referring first to al-Ṭahṭāwī before considering at greater length al-Shidyāq and especially Jibrān, and concluding with some remarks about al-Manfalūṭī.

Al-Ṭahṭāwī

Rifā'ah al-Ṭahṭāwī's first book, *Takhlīṣ al-ibrīz fī talkhīṣ Bārīz* [The Gold of Paris],[5] although regarded as one of the first fruits of modern Arabic literature, resembles rather the travel books known in classical Arabic culture and also, perhaps even more appropriately, those accounts of travel and exploration produced in Europe in the sixteenth and seventeenth centuries to which the generic term *relations indiennes* is sometimes applied.[6] In both cases the chief aim is to stimulate reflection on the Self with the help of elements drawn from the world of the Other.

What lies at the basis of al-Ṭahṭāwī's account is an anxious, ambiguous, even paradoxical questioning of the nature of man. Is he a social being essentially governed by his ancestral heritage, both political and religious, or an individual possessing his own will and sensibility? It is here that the work acquires its profound significance and its purpose; the naive descriptions of everyday life, the interest in the social behaviour or personal convictions of individuals, the reporting of debates between adherents of different philosophical and theological movements, in addition to the discussion of the major political and social institutions of the country, only serve to sustain this reflection.

Al-Shidyāq

With the famous Aḥmad Fāris al-Shidyāq's *al-Sāq 'alā 'l-sāq fī mā huwa 'l-faryāq* [Crossed Legs],[7] we have reached literature at last. In my view, this work represents the first real approach to fiction in modern Arabic literature. A fictionalized autobiography, it is occupied with the same inquiry as is al-Ṭahṭāwī's book mentioned above, the status of man between ancestral heritage and individual destiny (one could translate part of the title, *mā huwa 'l-faryāq*, freely as 'what man is'). It adopts the same register, the Other and the Same, and develops the identical main theme, wanderings between East and West, though with the significant difference that for al-Shidyāq there is more than one form of both East and West. For the literary critic, however, what gives this reflection its specific character is first and foremost the fictional quality, closely bound up with the account of the journey, which runs through the major part of the book. This fiction relies on disjunction, a disjunction evident in the nouns and names themselves, man/woman and Faryāq/Faryāqa.

These two characters represent the two symbolic poles of humanity. To employ the language of semiotics, we may say that they make up a semiotic category in which each of the two contrary terms exerts influence over its opposite so as to structure the fictional universe.[8] These two characters, moreover, establish themselves as agents continually exchanging their roles of subject and anti-subject. Each in turn represents good and evil, reason and feeling, truth and falsehood, freedom and bondage, and they alternate these roles indefinitely, as illustrated by the various dialogues between them.[9]

Fiction thus makes its entry into literature not in posing the fateful and, in the last analysis, banal problem of women, but in putting women face to face with men, or more precisely presenting women as the subject of fictional reality. This confrontation offers a basis for a genuine literary creation, whereas Buṭrus al-Bustānī's and al-Ṭahṭāwī's method, in preaching the need for women's education, only offered a basis for reflection on society; the semiotic roles it assigned to women were usually object or at best inert, even passive, subject.

Connected with the internal opposition between the two methods is the presence or absence of an erotic charge. Entirely lacking in the work of the two reforming teachers, al-Bustānī and al-Ṭahṭāwī, who preferred an asexual, almost theoretical view of women, it runs through al-Shidyāq's writings like a live wire, though with the discretion imposed by the constraints of the time and perhaps also of the author's temperament.

Another distinctive trait of al-Shidyāq's work, highly indicative of the close interpenetration of women and literature, is that the emergence of woman as the subject of a fictional universe coincides with a questioning of the nature of literature. This occurs not in theoretical terms but by means of irony, which is at work in different guises: through the detached use of the *maqāma*,[10] the choice of themes and the levels of language employed, not to mention the unconsciously subjective utterances and the authorial intrusions referring to the idea of literature.[11] This all betrays a calling into question of the status of language and literary genre, and even an implicit reflection on the very status of literature. Such a reflection only becomes explicit half a century later.

A corollary of this second distinctive trait is the relative eroticism in the use of language, which is here charged with an almost sensual luxuriousness. The relationship of the narrator to the language is marked by the same eroticism as the relation of Faryāq to Faryāqa. It is enough to refer to the play on words,[12] the effusiveness and the interminably diffuse passages which punctuate the text and are far from being merely a product of a schoolmasterly desire to instruct the reader in the language. In al-Shidyāq's work literature and womanhood go hand in hand, combine and could be said even to embrace each other.

The decisive period in the emergence of a literature that is connected in a real sense with love is, however, introduced by Jibrān and to a lesser extent by al-Manfalūṭī. Jibrān's work represents an important break, with regard both to the definition of literature and to the practice of it.

Jibrān's Definition of Literature

Although not obviously theoretical or even thoroughly thought out, Jibrān Khalil Jibrān's vision situates this inquiry in a domain that is quite unheard-of in Arabic literature and on quite another plane from the attempts of Amīn al-Rayḥānī[13] or Khalīl Muṭrān[14] which precede or are contemporary with it. Already present at the start of his career in his first book, *al-Mūsīqā* [Music], this vision can be found scattered through many subsequent texts of a theoretical nature.[15] Apart from its unique place in Arabic literature, both modern and classical (since as far as I know it is the only work which discusses music from this point of view), this deceptively simple text can still surprise us today, and for more than one reason, because it recalls the main lines of Jena Romanticism.

On the one hand, it includes in the idea of music the notions of poetry and narrative prose, or more broadly, the novel. The literary phenomenon thus appears in a totality, single and pluriform at the same time, as the representative of aesthetics as a whole, the Genre as such, which encompasses all literary genres and is thus in opposition to the classical definition of distinct literary categories arranged hierarchically. This cannot but recall Schlegel's definition of the novel or poetry—which come down to the same thing, according to him—as opposed to classical poetry and the Aristotelian genres.[16]

On the other hand, this vision of Jibrān's entrusts literature with the mission of expressing Being. And that includes not only man but the entire universe, both the physical world and that other, invisible world of the hereafter which is closely bound up with it. Jibrān's vision, then, can hardly be said to involve a definition, but it springs from an aesthetic and metaphysical approach, the very terms generally employed to define Jena

Romanticism. The only difference between the two approaches—but it is considerable—is that Jibrān's terminology is inspired by the Platonic concept of Ideas, expressed in the Myth of the Cave or Avicenna's symbolic poem,[17] whereas the School of Jena is operating in Kant's conceptual universe.

This vision endowes the poet—or musician, or novelist; it all comes down to the same thing in this context—with a specific, superhuman quality, that of the mediator, the prophet, perhaps even the creator of a new world. This quality is affirmed by the practice of writing fiction to be discussed below. The literature issuing from this theory is designed to express love, whatever the character of the Beloved in the original story, Siren, Goddess, Fiancée or Bride. Thus the new definition of literature turns on the image of love.

Jibrān's Practice of Fiction

It is commonplace to recall that the starting-point of Jibrān's fictional universe is an invasion of the Ego, an Ego ontologically based on the heart in opposition to the mind.[18] The literary break he initiates thus proceeds in turn from another, ontological break. After centuries of man's being subjected to the rationalizing processes of religion or society, Jibrān thus inverts the equation, so endowing himself with a legitimacy that can hold its own against the time-honoured one.

But beyond this familiar observation, it is the structuring of Jibrān's fictional world which is important for us. This world is not, in the first place, based on a sociological or even stylistic order, but on the use of allegory, an allegory which in turn is reflected on the levels just mentioned.

Let us turn briefly to the example of his short story "Maḍja' al-'arūs" [The Bride's Bed] in the collection *al-Arwāḥ al-mutamarrida* [Spirits Rebellious]. This story can be regarded as containing the seeds of *al-Ajniḥa al-mutakassira* [Broken Wings], Jibrān's best work of fiction. It thus throws light on the whole of his *œuvre*. The narrative itinerary of the subject in this story traces the familiar semiotic diagram.

It starts off from *love* (since Salīm and Laylā love each other) and passes through the contrary pole of *non-love* (the two lovers separate, thanks to the action of a counter-manipulator) to reach the contrary pole of *tradition* or *anti-love* (in other words, social tradition which the lovers bow to in accepting a 'social marriage'). But it moves away from *tradition* towards *non-tradition* (when a new revolt against the social order makes its appearance) to arrive again at *love* at the end of the journey. This journey finds its systematic fulfilment when the protagonists undergo the essential test of *death*, which occurs during the progression from *non-tradition* to *love*.

This narrative itinerary may be expressed in the following diagram:

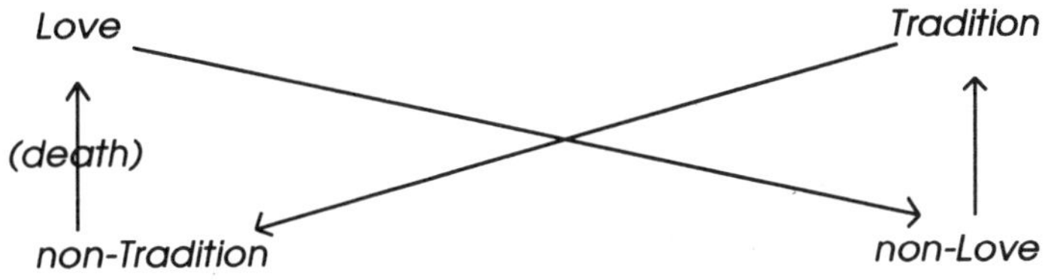

The narrator goes out of his way to represent this obligatory transition as necessary and justifiable although he fails to explain it by means of probable events or the internal logic of the story (the lovers insist on rejecting any other plausible alternative to death). As a result, all the attempts to avoid death appear arbitrary, clumsy and far-fetched. How could it be otherwise, when death appears from the start to be established as an essential premise for the coherence of the whole? This requirement, which is external to the dynamics of the fictional world, places the work fairly and squarely in the realm of allegory, where the conflict between love and tradition can only be resolved outside time and space, that is, in the world of the spirit, as opposed to that of matter. It is this, and this alone, which justifies the obligatory passing through death.

Allegory brings us back to the Romanticism of Jena,[19] where literature has a particular connection with this technique—a technique which, transcending the limits of its name, appears to be the basis of much of Goethe's writing too, even if he prefers the term symbol, which covers essentially the same reality.

Thanks to allegory, then, Jibrān lays the foundation of the new practice of literature. And it is against this background that the stylistic register should be seen, borrowed as it is from that of the archetypal, founding scriptures, both Old and New Testament, and Greek as well as Near Eastern mythology. The lexical, symbolic and stylistic registers chosen are permeated with biblical and mythological references. Jibrān's writing exhibits a generalized transtextuality.[20] The language of the origins seems here to be the only one capable of expressing Origin and Totality. Jibrān's fictional discourse would be abstruse and incomprehensible if this overwhelming transtextuality were ignored.

As we have seen, love is the linchpin of this literary edifice. To return to the idea of the narrative itinerary, we may note that this applies equally to both the lovers, the man and the woman, who are simply two roles belonging to the same subject. And what is at stake in the action, or in semiotic terms the object, is the encounter of these two subject-roles.

Al-Manfalūṭī

Although he appears as a poor relation in the emergence of the Arabic novel, Muṣṭafā Luṭfī al-Manfalūṭī, the second writer whose work testifies to the newly founded literature, played a vital part in popularizing the new dynamics set in motion by Jibrān. He did it in his own way, that is, painfully simplistically and superficially, but he was effective all the same. To realize this, one need only refer to the statements of his contemporaries, even those who held him in utter contempt, such as 'Abbās Maḥmūd al-'Aqqād, Aḥmad Ḥasan al-Zayyāt and Ṭāhā Ḥusayn.[21]

In the definition of literature which he attempts in the introduction to *al-Naẓarāt* [Views],[22] al-Manfalūṭī stipulates that it has its origin in *raḥma* (compassion), a quality which in his view enables the writer to approach the Other, perhaps even to share his heartbeats. The point is to enable the writer's self to express itself *vis-à-vis* the world, which he has decided once and for all is a world of desolation. We may say it is a pretext for the outpouring of the self. This outpouring is achieved in two ways and in successive stages: first *bukā'* (weeping) before the misery of the world and then the solitary act of writing. This is how al-Manfalūṭī sees the birth of literature.

We may ignore this blatantly naive formulation. In the last resort, what determines this vision of things is Romanticism, even if in an astonishingly impoverished and degraded form. This founding Romanticism is part of the opposition to the old order right from the start, for it creates a new authority which regulates both literature and the ontological concept of man. On the one hand, the style of the new literature is totally at odds with that governing the classical style defended by al-Azhar. Himself a product of al-Azhar and a disciple of Muḥammad 'Abduh, al-Manfalūṭī was rejected and violently attacked by his fellows. On the other hand, the new writing conceives of man no longer as primarily a religious being, but as a being of feeling, which represents an unheard-of ontological change of attitude. These two mini-revolutions are expressed in al-Manfalūṭī's famous slogan, *sulṭān al-wijdān wa lā sulṭān al-adyān* (the domination of the heart, rather than that of religion)—a truly revolutionary slogan on the lips of a former Azhar student.

The arguments al-Manfalūṭī uses to justify revolt—and consequently his conception of man and literature—are connected with three social phenomena, distorted and simplified in the extreme: the relationship of alienation which oriental society has with its Western counterpart; social relations built on hypocrisy and petty self-interest; and woman as a simple object of desire, to be raped with impunity or rejected after she has been seduced. In fact, although they are painfully simplistic, these phenomena pertain to three thoroughly Romantic themes. First, the relationship between civilizations comes under the heading of the relation to the Other, and thus poses the problem of human nature, in other words man's metaphysical status. Second, the connection between the individual and society implies the inauguration of new ontological values founded on the individual self and not on the collective. Finally, the relationship of man to woman is what provides a basis for love—the heart opposed to reason—as the driving force of all human life.

In al-Manfalūṭī's work, this last theme takes precedence over the first two. The author's own fiction, as distinct from his translations, bears the mark of it when it centres the action almost exclusively on the female characters. Furthermore, he structures this universe where women predominate according to an allegorical scheme, though a much poorer one than Jibrān's. Love thus remains the theme best fitted to serve as a basis for the new literature. A certain parallelism between the two approaches can thus be discerned, and if al-Manfalūṭī's is on a far less ambitious scale than Jibrān's, it belongs to the same dynamic trend.

The foregoing has attempted to show the connection between love and the birth of modern Arabic literature, a connection situated as much on the level of theoretical reflection as on that of the structuring of the fictional world. The parallelism established between the approach of these early modern Arab authors and that of the Romantic movement of Jena is not a comparison as such, but an indication of the relationship that exists between Arab and Western thought. It is a relationship that a certain policy of domination in favour today in the Western world rejects, in the most archaic fashion possible, by waging war even against the symbols which constitute the basis of the other's culture.[23]

2

The Figure of the Lover in Popular Arabic Drama of the Early Twentieth Century

Rosella Dorigo Ceccato

Popular theatrical performances based on mime and farce, with live actors or puppets, were widespread not just in the Arab world but all over the Near East until a few decades ago. Based on relatively simple dramatic stories, they were lacking in codified literary support; they came into being spontaneously among the people as a way to liven up their spare time or communal occasions, fairs and public holidays.[1]

Humour and Licentiousness

The erotic element was always present in these usually comic plays, to such an extent that it aroused in the first European travellers who saw them[2] ill-hidden feelings of indignation at their vulgarity. On the other hand, marked obscenity was also common in the Western Commedia dell'Arte, just as lack of morality was a feature of European burlesque literature. The leading figures in popular comedies, whether real or mythical, were very earthy and knew only too well that normal bodily functions had always proved to be an inexhaustible source of amusement for simple folk.[3] The relationship between humour and obscenity was well known in classical literature; indeed, it was noticeable right from the earliest sources of Greek comedy.[4]

In the Arab world other factors were added to these elements of a general nature found in the popular literature of all countries: factors particularly linked to local culture and traditions. Public representation of the most comic side of human beings when they are at their weakest and most intimate, both through puppet shows and with actors and mime, meant that the simplest and least educated strata of the population could challenge a literature which was often too serious and normative and in any case inaccessible to the masses. By freely using dialect, with all its rich nuances, in public performances, the populace could thus overcome the laws imposed by the cultured world, which wanted the *fuṣḥā* (formal, standardized Arabic) as its own exclusive means of literary communication.[5] In that sense, therefore, the satirical performances in a humorous, erotic and colloquial language which toured in the Near East could be taken as an affirmation of the freedom of the people to express themselves uninhibitedly in all their imaginative independence during their free time or festivals.[6]

However, these shows were not always just simple entertainment for the masses, but took on a deeper meaning when performed at traditional festivals or at religious ones such as Ramaḍān or *mawlids*.[7] The European travellers' indignation at the vulgarity which enlivened the performances was therefore even greater due to the religious-sexual connection: to Western eyes, this seemed to be indecent if not actually sacrilegious.[8] However, bearing in mind that the Islamic world of the imagination contained traces of previous civilizations,[9] in which divine love and human love did not know the opposition which came later with monotheism, the natural tendency of the populace to use erotic-sexual elements even during religious festivals is not surprising. On the contrary, at private gatherings with sexual overtones, such as marriages or circumcisions, some forms of rudimentary theatrical performance with an erotic theme could even appear to be propitiatory and auspicious.[10] The marked eroticism in Arab and Near Eastern popular shows in general could also be due to the survival of older cults in the spirit of the people, such as the fertility rites associated with the cult of Goddess-Mother, which held the sexual act as being the basis of life.[11]

The erotic element found in popular drama was naturally present in the comic antics of clowns, who also amused the people in the Near East regions until the nineteenth century. With obviously sexually inspired dances and songs, their role was to make the crowd laugh by transmitting intense eroticism through mimicry clearly inspired by an amorous dance or the sexual act.[12] One of these clowns, Abū 'Ajjūr—whose name alone ('the one endowed with the cucumber') already has clear phallic implications—is said to have used his *farqala* (whip) a great deal, gripping the long wooden handle and moving it in a very lascivious way;[13] another, 'Alī Kākā, actually wore an object shaped like a large penis hanging from his belt.[14]

Although popular theatre could make use either of the animation of inanimate figures or of live actors, the first type was perhaps better at satisfying the desire for comedy of the simple man in the street. It has been pointed out that the most popular puppet theatres, above all those for adults, tended to become comic theatres *par excellence*. In fact, the audience at this type of comedy was amused not only by the humorous text, whether recited or improvised, but above all because the movements and stance of the puppets, although imitating those of everyday life, could not be an absolutely true resemblance and took on far-fetched connotations which stimulated the imagination and freed inhibitions. In addition, if the puppet theatre was performed with the shadows technique the effect on the public could be very powerful. The contrasts intrinsic to shadow plays, which were at the same time highly realistic yet mysteriously magic, gave rise to a primitive and fascinating comicality.[15]

It was precisely because the puppets could not and were not intended to be simple copies of human beings that they were also bound to be exaggerated; this exaggeration showed up and accentuated everything that normally existed, even if only potentially.[16] The physical characteristics such as facial features, height and corpulence of the persons represented on stage were sometimes exaggerated so as to make the figures grotesquely comic and to highlight the nature of the various personages.[17] The sexual organs could therefore also be used in the same way:[18] in Turkish shadow plays for example, it seems that Karagöz, a rather licentious hero, was often portrayed with a conspicuous male sexual organ rearing up like a sword.[19]

Shadow Plays in the Arab World

The shadow play was a widespread form of entertainment in the Arab world until about fifty years ago. Its comedies, called *fuṣūl* (plays) or *lu'ab* (games), offer a rich field of analysis for those who wish to study certain typical aspects of social life in the nineteenth century and the first decades of the twentieth, seen through the eyes of the common folk and through texts which, however rudimentary, formed part of the repertoire of the animators/puppet masters. They were either very short comedies, almost sketches, or alternatively so long and complicated that they had to be performed 'in instalments', in several successive performances; we have evidence of this through the research and collections of Arab theatre-lovers who saw them when they were children,[20] and through the work of European scholars who have devoted long hours of research to this sector.[21]

Much has already been written about the origin, history and diffusion of shadow plays in the Near and Middle East. The present essay aims instead to draw attention to a few types of characters and situations typical of these comedies in the Arab world and which truly enter into the general context of marked sexuality found in Near and Middle Eastern popular entertainment. Texts handed down orally will not be taken into consideration, only written ones, whether officially published or in the form of manuscripts or typewritten pages. Most reference material dates back to the repertoire of several famous animators of the nineteenth century.[22] The authors are generally anonymous, the texts having been passed down from master to disciple over the years.[23]

We shall concentrate on the nineteenth century, when shadow plays were widespread throughout the Mediterranean basin and enjoyed great popularity not only in Egypt and Turkey, but also in Syria, Greece and North Africa.[24] Egypt appears to be the only Arab country that can boast of an uninterrupted theatrical tradition of this type, going back to at least the Fatimid period,[25] while evidence of such entertainment in other geographical areas is much more recent.[26]

The satirical vein which ran through most of the comedies with shadow puppets throughout the Mediterranean area, and which dealt principally with social aspects, also took on distinct nationalistic implications in certain circumstances and periods. In Greece, for example, after mobilization in 1880 it was ennobled by patriotic aims and, cleansed of many obscenities, was used as a revolutionary weapon against the Turks.[27] In Algeria it was used for a similar purpose—to express the anti-French feeling of the population during the fight for independence—so that the authorities had to forbid performances.[28] Generally, however, satire portrayed through shadow plays had social overtones and underlined—often in an extremely crude way—the stupidity of some aspects of human behaviour, the moral weakness of many categories of people and, last but not least, the incongruous attitudes in relationships between the two sexes. Several types of licentious places, topics and situations can be recognized: as well as the numerous comedies situated in the public baths, many were in brothels, both extremely suitable places for intertwining witty remarks and equivocal situations, which the street public in the various geographical areas greatly enjoyed.

In the nineteenth century in Syria and Tunisia, where Turkish shadow plays were very popular, the leading characters were generally Karākūz and ʻAywāẓ—Arab versions of the two Turkish heroes Karagöz and Haçivad; this type of art is still known by the name *masraḥ Karākūz*.[29] A reading of the texts of Syrian or Tunisian comedies reveals numerous other Turkish elements that survived even after the end of Ottoman domination, from praise of the sultan, to the names of many characters, to the abundance of beatings.[30] Indeed, in Tunisia, for many years the plays were given in Turkish, and Tunisian dialect only began to be used as French domination was consolidated.[31]

Differences nevetheless emerge between the two types of works: first, a perhaps milder licentiousness in Arab shadow plays compared to Turkish ones;[32] and second, the former's particularly varied way of dealing with the subject of relationships between men and women.[33] It is true that in both Tunisian and Syrian shadow comedy texts the comic element was almost always based on ambiguous situations, coarse jokes and behaviour bordering on the limits of decency,[34] and that physical love, understood as a natural and necessary pleasure, dominated the majority of amusing scenes. However, an analysis of the relationships between the sexes as they appear in these plays gives rise to some interesting points. Two themes are basically developed around the amorous motif (a constant in such plays): one is physical love, often represented in a coarse way and laced with obscene, witty remarks; and the other is desire, whether appeased or not, laced with skirmishing, laments and more or less licentious jokes. In a strongly male-oriented society such as the Arab one, the role of the lover had to be assigned basically to the man. The woman could appear either as a defenceless victim of male desire, or alternatively, she could be presented as the clever instigator of his desire, the astute dominator of his naive mind, the enemy to be fought. She rarely appeared in an actively sexual function.

An example of woman dominated by male desire and the source of his physical pleasure appears in the Tunisian comedy *La'bat al-Hindāwī* [Hindāwī's Play] (1889)[35] in which the heroine Fāṭima, wife of al-Hindāwī, is kidnapped by Karākūz who wants to amuse himself with her.[36] No hint is given of the woman's reaction to such abuse, nor to the later abuse by another character, an Algerian sent by the husband to save her, but who instead is also ready to take advantage of her, thus making a fool of al-Hindāwī. In the play it therefore seems that no autonomy is attributed to Fāṭima; she has no power of decision and displays no rebellion against male abuse. The same observation can be made regarding a later Tunisian comedy, *Faṣl al-ḥammām* [The Bath-house Play] (1927),[37] in which violence is shown towards a defenceless woman by 'Aywāẓ. At the end of a long argument about money with an old woman in front of the public baths, the man throws her daughter over his shoulder and departs, exclaiming, 'You'll repay me with this lovely girl!' Here again,[38] no mention is made of the woman's reaction to the sexual violence of the man.

By contrast, where the female comic characters are presented as astute and conniving, a woman's potential role in society is completely different. A perfect example of a clever and flirtatious woman, capable of confounding the naive male before her, can be found in a dialogue between 'Aywāẓ and a pretty girl in the Syrian comedy *'Urs Karākūz* [Karākūz's Wedding].[39] In order to obtain the man's help against her mother, who does not want her to marry, the girl maliciously draws the attention of her interlocutor towards her main physical features, taking advantage of the power her body has over the male intellect:

> My height, isn't it a little displeasing?
> No!
> My physique . . .
> It's like a bamboo cane!
> And my forehead?
> It's like the half moon in the month of Sha'bān!
> And my eyes?
> Like the eyes of a gazelle!
> And my breast?
> Oh my God! It's a square as big as a battlefield!
> And my belly?
> Ah, it drives one mad! It makes one rise like the baker's yeast!
> Don't I therefore deserve a piece of man who goes in and out of my house?[40]

Another example of an astute woman is provided by the wife of Karākūz in the Tunisian comedy *La'bat al-'arūsa* [The Bride's Play] (1880).[41] Here the naivety of the popular hero is portrayed as real gullibility, giving rise to many comical scenes. 'Aywāẓ and his daughter make a fool of Karākūz, convincing him to marry a woman who, although single, is in an advanced state of pregnancy. On their wedding night, the bride convinces her husband that she has been hit by a 'lightning pregnancy' and is on the point of giving birth. The artist–animator's wish to show up male weakness when confronted with feminine wiles is clear in such a plot. Within the domestic walls, the figure of the woman/wife in some shadow plays is portrayed as the ferocious jailer of her husband. One example is the wife of 'Aywāẓ in the Syrian play *Faṣl sarāyat 'Aywāẓ* [The Play of 'Aywāẓ's Palace].[42] She continuously threatens the poor man, demanding he give her an expensive gold necklace consisting of fifty coins attached to a chain so as not to cut a poor figure in society, despite the fact that the family has serious financial problems. 'Aywāẓ's desperation and fear of his wife are clear from the first words he speaks to his friend Karākūz: 'She has thrown me out of the house and told me not to return without it [the necklace]!'[43]

A strong-willed, dominating woman, therefore, or a downtrodden, dominated one? It seems that in Egyptian shadow plays, too, there were examples of female protagonists who revealed a stronger character than the man's. For example, Aḥmad Taymūr in his study of the nineteenth-century Egyptian *Khayāl al-ẓill* [Shadow Play] mentions a comedy entitled *La'bat al-*

Shaykh Sumaysim [Shaykh Sumaysim's Play],[44] in which a woman appears who is determined to marry a man at all costs, even though he is against it. Taymūr only gives the plot, but the picture of the woman's character is clear enough.

Just from these few examples two distinct and almost opposing types of relationship between a man and a woman seem to emerge. Social and personal relations between husband and wife within the family are exemplified in the second type. Here, the man is almost always dominated by the woman, whether in an obvious way when she is capricious or domineering, or in an indirect way when she is cunning and astute. In popular comedies, social situations of this type were a source of hilarity as they revealed, in an often exaggerated and licentious way, the secrets of the protagonists' domestic life, probably mirroring, not infrequently, real situations of female tyranny in the home. The first type, however, dwells on the erotic-sentimental relations between the male protagonists and other women outside the family. The most scurrilous themes and obscene dialogues were developed around these situations of extra-marital or pre-marital relations. The man almost always took the role of male lover whose attitude towards the opposite sex was simply one of desire and possession. The comic side of these stories stemmed mostly from the strong sexual desire expressed by the male characters and the practical jokes that friends played on each other in connection with amorous matters.[45]

As well as the erotic-humorous element, social satire, which was always latent in these shows, made itself more strongly felt in some texts than others. Whether ironic self-derision, clever caricature of general vices or acute observation of social immorality, in one way or another the wit of the people was a constant element, even where the most rudimentary farcical situations or reasons seemed to reign supreme.[46] In the Tunisian play known as *La'bat al-ḥōta* [The Fish Play],[47] for example, the humour is extremely simple and immediate as it derives above all from the rhythmic repetition of the same gestures and words by the two protagonists in the boat: Karākūz, who wants to fish; and his black servant, who has to row. The erotic element is contained in the dialogue between them, stimulated by the servant's continual questions about sexual relations with women; the social satire, however, makes itself clearly felt in the obvious spiritual poverty of the black man and his physical isolation within a society which has evidently not yet given him the opportunity to know a woman.

Conclusions

Overall, society as portrayed in many shadow plays seems to revolve around the figure of the woman, pole of attraction of both man's physical desires and his marital fears. The man/lover is therefore the domineering protagonist in the traditional popular theatre, but it is above all the woman—lover or loved one—who directs the amorous game, whether she is the direct instigator or just the unconscious, defenceless inspirer. Artist-animators seem to pay great attention to her, despite the prevalence of the male element among the public. Or perhaps it is due to the essentially male chauvinist character of Arab society at that time that the female figure is inevitably the constant antagonist in conflicts represented on stage, the eternal 'enemy' to understand, conquer, fight, dominate and, if necessary, even flee from.

Thus the role of the woman in the family and society, as portrayed in the popular theatre comedies, would seem to be a very important one. Further confirmation of this has emerged in a study by J. M. Landau[48] of some Egyptian manuscripts from 1909 in which several women with a strong character and quick intellect, capable of consciously tackling and discussing the most delicate aspects of relations between men and women, stand out among the characters of a group of comedies.

This is the case for example in *Riwāyat ibn al-balad* [The Native Son], in the conversation between two women, Laṭīfa and Ḥanīfa, about the faults of their respective husbands and the merits of Western women; or the dialogue in the same play where there is an interesting series of comments on feminine virginity.[49] In another of the texts quoted by Landau, *Riwāyat al-Shaykh al-Ṭuruqī wa 'l-mar'a wa zawjihā* [The Tale of the Shaykh of the Order, the Woman and her Husband],[50] mention is made of a conversation between the female lead, Faṭūma, and her mother, in which they express their views on marriage. A third text actually outlines a society which protects the physical rights of women: when the protagonist Aḥmad al-Fār has his genitals amputated, leaving him sexually impaired, his wife does not hesitate to ask for divorce, conscious that as a wife she has been cheated of her rights to important property.[51]

The figure of the lover is rarely romantic in the popular theatre, particularly in shadow plays, and love is looked upon as a purely platonic feeling. The Egyptian comedy *La'bat al-dayr* [The Cloister Play],[52] which Taymūr describes as based on a sentimental theme of romantic love, in reality proves to be different from many other shadow plays regarding the amorous theme; this is not so much due to a different and more noble conception of love, but for religious reasons. In fact the comedy is a representation, although in popular dramatic tones, of the triumph of Islam over the Coptic Church.

In conclusion, it is clear that the popular theatre exercised a strong erotic influence on its audiences through the presentation of themes, dialogues and behaviour which found in sexuality their main erotic and satirical inspiration. However, the heterogeneity of the elements that helped form the Arab world of the popular imagination, and, by reflection, the development of this form of art that was so strongly attached to daily life, must always be borne in mind. In a social context that was culturally simple but extremely complex in its formation, in which the comic theatre acted as a safety valve for expressing the weaknesses, conflicts and delusions of the people, Eros was one of the most important objects of interest for the production of an often provocative, even obscene literature, but one always profoundly tied to the most natural elements of life.

3

The Romantic Imagination and the Female Ideal

Robin Ostle

It is no accident that the rise of the Romantic imagination in Arabic literature coincided with a period of convulsive change which was to shape the lives of many Arab countries for most of the twentieth century.[1] After the First World War, the Ottoman Empire, which had been the most successful political system in the history of Islam, no longer existed. In the course of the 1920s, new nation states arose in Egypt and the Levant, even though Anglo-French domination remained very much in place when in 1922 the League of Nations approved the mandate system for Syria, Lebanon, and Palestine with Transjordan. Although both Egypt (in 1923) and Iraq (in 1924) were declared independent sovereign states, these new versions of national independence were harshly circumscribed by the continuing reality of European power, while in North Africa the French colonial system had a depressingly permanent air. Yet in spite of all the underlying deceptions, these were heady days in Cairo, Damascus and Baghdad. The final downfall of the Ottoman system gave great new impetus to the forces of Arab nationalism, which had to some extent been held in check during the war years, and the appearance of these new national political forms was accompanied by waves of strong, sincere emotions on the part of Arab populations and their leaders. On occasion, these forces of patriotic emotion and the resistance which they encountered from one or other of the Western powers developed into full-scale revolution, as was the case in Egypt in 1919 and Iraq in 1920.

The concept of national freedom, whether it be from the Ottoman system or from the British occupation, was an intoxicating notion which excited strong emotions at many levels of the population. But the single most significant message which came to the Arab world from the perceived wisdom of the European Enlightenment was that of the sanctity of the individual. Among *avant-garde* intellectuals, particularly in Egypt in the early decades of the twentieth century, it was a commonplace idea that the individual, whether humble or great, male or female, could and should expect to play a part in the destiny of the community as a whole. This was the strange new idea which generated great excitement, as well as confusion, bewilderment and above all fierce debate.

Egypt was at the very centre of the Romantic movement in modern Arabic literature and art: in the nineteenth century the social transformations linked with the development of the cotton economy led to the emergence of a bourgeoisie. Groups of landowners and *'umdas* (village headmen) took full advantage of the secular educational opportunities which had been created during the reign of the Khedive Ismā'īl (1863–79), the impatient Europeanizer, and many of the representatives of this class completed their intellectual development in the capital cities of Europe. Typical of them were the pioneers of the intellectual and artistic life of modern Egypt: the political theorist Aḥmad Luṭfī al-Sayyid (1872–1963), the sculptor Maḥmūd Mukhtār (1891–1934), the painter Muḥammad Nājī (1888–1956), the novelist and journalist Muḥammad Ḥusayn Haykal (1888–1956), the dramatist and novelist Tawfīq al-Ḥakīm (1898–1987) and the educational reformer and social thinker Ṭāhā Ḥusayn (1889-1973). Most of them stood firmly on the side of the feminist reformer Qāsim Amīn (1865–1908): in both *Taḥrīr al-mar'a* [Women's Emancipation] and *al-Mar'a al-jadīda* [The New Woman], Amīn had made no secret of his opinion that one reason for the superiority of societies such as the British and the French was their evolution from despotism to democracy, and the progress they were making in the field of women's rights. Such progress, in his view, was both a precondition for and an accompaniment to development and modernization.[2]

Thus it was that the theme of female emancipation became one of the *causes célèbres* espoused by Egypt's liberal reformers in the early decades of the twentieth century, for the stand taken on the sensitive issue of the position of women in society was one of the touchstones by which someone's position in relation to tradition and modernity was defined. Yet it was only as the century advanced into its second and third decades that women themselves began to become involved: Ḥāfiẓ Ibrāhīm wrote a poem on the occasion in 1919 when women demonstrated in Cairo against the arrest and exile of the nationalist leader Sa'd Zaghlūl.[3] The periodical *al-Sufūr* was founded during the First World War and feminist issues were naturally one of its most frequent topics. Hudā Sha'rāwī created the first Women's Union in the country in 1923 and on 15 March 1924, when the first Wafdist parliament opened, some of the delegations who flocked to honour the occasion consisted of women demanding the right to vote.[4] Women were admitted to Cairo University in the 1930s, and throughout the 1920s legal measures were introduced to protect women from some of the worst abuses of *sharī'a* law. While polygamy could not be abolished, its practice became more and more restricted. Welcome as all these measures were, however, their effects were restricted to small sectors of Egyptian womanhood in the period between the two world wars; it was not until the 1950s that women gained significant rights such as those of suffrage and the holding of elected office.

The rise of the Romantic imagination was an integral part of the Romantic nationalism which gripped Egypt and the Levant during the inter-war period. It was as though the sentimental and emotional liberation of individuals would accompany the processes of political liberation as a matter of course, but in the end both the individuals and the nation states became a prey to ambiguity, contradiction and bitter disillusion. Not surprisingly, much of the discourse of nationalist politics was expressed in black and white terms. The slogans adopted as the rallying cries of the 1919 Revolution or which accompanied Sa'd Zaghlūl and his delegation to London and Paris had no room for self-doubt or ambiguity, but the human, intellectual and emotional realities behind such revolutionary situations were never so simple and clear-cut. The writers and intellectuals of the Romantic period in the Arab world developed artistic and personal ideals which were difficult to fulfil in their own societies. While nationalist politicians might look to the future in terms of one-dimensional optimism and a clearly defined struggle for emancipation from imperialism, sensitive individuals faced the impossible task of reconciling dreams and aspirations with stubborn social realities which were wracked by cultural polarities. Nowhere was this more true than in the context of women's emancipation.

Much of the inspiration for the age of Romantic nationalism in the Arab world came ultimately from the European Enlightenment and the French Revolution which was the climax of many of its ideals. Here one can discern certain parallels in the field of women's rights, particularly in relation to the Egyptian situation. The early years of the French Revolution had not been without hope for women: debates had taken place about female suffrage, marriage had been made into a civil contract and prostitution had been attacked. The overall egalitarian atmosphere and nomenclatures of *citoyen/ citoyenne* and general *tutoiement* all raised the profile of women, the process being helped by their participation in key events such as the Versailles bread march of 1789.[5] This role of women in the early years of the Revolution, combined with the general effects of the eighteenth-century philosophy of Sentimentalism, led to a significant emotional liberation for upper-middle-class and aristocratic women, trends which were reinforced by the literary manifestations of Sentimentalism such as Rousseau's *Émile* and *La nouvelle Héloïse*. In the European context, these individual emotional liberations preceded by many generations genuine emancipation of a political, economic or social nature.

Thus there are close and relevant parallels with the Egyptian situation in the first half of the twentieth century. The Romantic imagination which arose along with the birth of the new nation state encouraged an intense concentration on individual sensibility, but the individual emotional liberations which this fostered were not accompanied by widespread liberalizing tendencies in society as a whole. Those who benefited most from such emotional liberations were small circles of *avant-garde* writers and intellectuals among whom women were scarcely if ever represented.

The powerful new 'structures of feeling'[6] which accompanied the birth of the new nation state in Egypt inevitably had a dramatic effect on literary and artistic creation. The pre-modern literary forms and conventions could no longer encompass the new range of themes and experiences, and one obvious result of this was the rise of the novel. Another was the development of Romantic poetry, which saw some of its most impressive achievements in Egypt in the 1920s and 1930s and which provides an intriguing commentary on the ambiguities and contradictions surrounding the portrayal of the female *persona* in literature and in art.

The Lebanese poet Khalīl Muṭrān (1872–1949), who adopted Egypt as his home country, was a significant innovator in the early development of Romantic poetry: as early as 1908 in the preface to his first published collection of poetry (*Dīwān al-Khalīl*, Cairo), he shows an interest in breaking the old moulds of poetry and rhetoric. He wants to write poetry in his own fashion, to relieve his soul when in solitude, and the demands of metre and rhyme will not sway him from his objective. The rhetoric of poetry will henceforth serve the emotions and needs of the individual artist, and it is the firm declaration of this principle that sets Muṭrān apart from his neo-classical contemporaries and makes him the precursor of Romantic poetry proper. He put this principle into practice in famous poems such as "al-Masā'" [Evening], "al-Asad al-bākī" [The Weeping Lion] and "al-'Azla fī 'l-ṣaḥrā'" [Solitude in the Desert], in which the burgeoning power of his subjective emotions dominates the language and the imagery. But in spite of the significance of his innovations in the early development of Romantic poetry, in the realm of love he is unsure of himself. Most of his amatory verse has a highly classical flavour to it, and he resigns himself to enduring the pangs of separation from his beloved in terms which derive directly from old Arabic poetry. In his poem "Tadhkār" [Remembrance], Muṭrān is moved to nostalgic reminiscence as he passes by the scene of a former love-affair, very much in the manner of a *jāhilī* poet singing over the *diman* (ruins) of an old encampment.[7]

The history of such amatory poetry extends back to pre-Islamic Arabia, and much of the time it celebrates the physical attributes of the female character rather than her spiritual or psychological qualities—with the honourable exception of the *'udhrī* poetry of the Umayyad period. This tradition was still represented in the more anachronistic sections of the neo-classical poets, such as the *nasīb* (erotic prelude) which Aḥmad Shawqī wrote to his poem on the Milner Plan, where the women are likened to wild cows with eyes like the narcissus and buttocks like sand dunes.[8] This alleged tendency to concentrate on the physical attributes of the female character was taken by the Egyptian Romantics to apply to the majority of classical Arabic poetry, and perceived as a literary convention against which they rebelled. Although this does less than justice to the subtlety and variety of the representations of the female personality in pre-modern poetry, most of the Romantics nevertheless seized on this element of the classical Arabic literary imagination as an integral part of a wider mentality which had reduced women to the subordinate, degraded status that Qāsim Amīn and his disciples sought to reform.

An important pioneering role in the development of Romantic poetry was played by the '*Dīwān* poets', 'Abd al-Raḥmān Shukrī (1886–1958) and his two colleagues Ibrāhīm al-Māzinī (1890–1949) and 'Abbas Maḥmūd al-'Aqqād (1889–1964), who set out to attack the existing canons of taste and style in neo-classical poetry. A typical reaction against the heavily physical conventions of old Arabic amatory poetry was a process of idealization which derived from the European Romantic tendency to confuse the human and the divine in the transmuting experience of love. In the preface to his fourth *dīwān* Shukrī seeks to explain the dominance of this theme in his work:

> By love poetry I do not mean the poetry of lust or sexual passion, but that of spiritual love which rises above all descriptions of the body except those which reveal the working of the soul. The love poetry I have in mind is caused by the passion which enables man to feel keenly Beauty in all its manifestations, whether in a beautiful face, a body, a flower or a river, in the beauty of lightning in the clouds, the beauty of night and stars, morning and its breeze, or the beauty of the soul or character, an

attribute or an event, or the beauty of the images created by the human mind. The love of one human being for another is only one aspect of this extensive passion which embraces all visible beauty in life.[9]

In the light of such remarks it is hardly surprising that much of Shukrī's love poetry is suffused with powerful strains which are both spiritual and pantheistic:

Would that I were a breeze, and you a flower for me,
I would love you, and you me, with no rebuke or separation.
Would that I were the rain-watered meadow, and you the shower of rain . . .
Would that I were an ocean, and you a drop within me.
Would that I were a horizon, and you the radiant star.[10]

But for all his thirsting after the immortal ideal of love, Shukrī ultimately became obsessed by what he perceived as the constant conflict between physical and spiritual needs. Allied with his feelings of deception caused by the dual nature of love are strong hints of misogyny, which appear in such poems as "al-Ḥasnā' al-ghādira" [Deceitful Beauty] and "Qublat al-zawja al-khā'ina" [Kiss of the Treacherous Wife].[11] Unfortunately this darker side of Shukrī's psychology came to dominate the vast majority of his love poetry.

The high priest of the Romantic movement in Egypt was Aḥmad Zakī Abū Shādī (1892–1955). The periodical *Apollo* which he founded and edited from 1932 to 1934 was an inspirational publication for young writers and artists in Egypt and other Arab countries, and Abū Shādī and his associates became known as the '*Apollo* group'.[12] He spent the years 1912–22 studying medicine in England, and on his return to Egypt in 1922 became one of the most distinguished members of the new Egyptian intelligentsia. He identified wholeheartedly with the renaissance of the new nation state and he himself was a truly remarkable version of the modern Egyptian renaissance man: the moving spirit behind a number of scientific and agricultural societies, he was appointed to the chair of bacteriology at the University of Alexandria in 1942, and was the author of at least nineteen collections of poetry, to say nothing of several opera librettos and a number of translations and literary studies. His most vital contribution to the national culture was in acting as a source of constant inspiration and encouragement to a group of younger poets who became the core of the Romantic movement in Egypt, in particular 'Alī Maḥmūd Ṭāhā (1902–49) and Ibrāhīm Nājī (1898–1953). Abū Shādī's earliest major *dīwān* was published in 1910 under the title *Andā' al-fajr* [Dewdrops of Dawn]. This was reprinted in 1934 with some additions; the dedication to this second edition is to the mysterious woman Zaynab who became the leitmotiv of much of his later poetry:

> Twenty-five years have passed away, and the flame of my love still leaps and flickers.
> I am still that maddened youth with pounding heart.
> Love's memories and its frenzied visions parade before me sleeping and awake.
> She is part of me, so how can I forsake her? O welcome imagination, which lets me hold and touch.[13]

The reference in the first line is to an unhappy love-affair which traumatized the poet in late adolescence but which remained one of the most consistent sources of inspiration throughout his career. The *dīwān* which he published after his return from England also had the title *Zaynab* (1924) and the sub-title 'breaths of lyrical poetry chosen from the verse of youth'. It is above all through his love poetry that Abū Shādī made his most important contribution to the overall development of the Romantic movement. As mentioned above, most of the amatory poetry written by Muṭrān and the *Dīwān* poets (with the exception of some of Shukrī's work) was not distinguished by any great originality. The theme of unrequited love predominated and it did so in a manner which rarely departed from the pattern of the rhetoric of old Arabic amatory verse. Unrequited love was also the basis of most of Abū Shādī's love poetry, but his simple and relatively unaffected poetic diction, and the intense and subtle analysis of all the finer shades of his emotional states, marked a genuine new departure, putting aside the conventional imagery associated with this age-old theme. In *Zaynab* he surrounds his beloved with an atmosphere of sacred adoration as his emotions rise to heights of platonic intensity:

> Be, O my angel, an ideal of purity which brings me close to your God . . .
> My feelings, my passion, my all, are pledged to that which is most perfect and beautiful in you.[14]

Although some of the amatory verse by Abū Shādī certainly contains powerful erotic overtones (see especially his poem "al-Jamāl al-'arbīd" [Wanton Beauty]),[15] much of his love poetry published in the 1920s in the collections *Zaynab* (1924) and *al-Shafaq al-bākī* [Weeping Twilight] (1926–7) shows a tendency to produce the idealized, almost disembodied images of womankind which were becoming typical of the female ideal in the new Romantic imagination. Similarly ethereal visions of women are apparent in many of the statuettes produced by Maḥmūd Mukhtār in the 1920s and which are on display in his museum in Cairo. They are remote madonna-type figures whose effect is anything but erotic. They are the three-dimensional equivalent of the nude goddess figures which illustrate many of the series of *dīwāns* by Abū Shādī, usually depicting personalities or events from Ancient Greek or Egyptian mythology (see the illustrations in the original editions of *al-Shu'la* [The Flame] (1933), *Aṭyāf al-rabī'* [Visions of Springtime] (1933) and *al-Yanbū'* [The Well] (1934)). The sculpture of Mukhtār and the love poems of Shukrī and Abū Shādī created idealized and platonic representations of female figures, emphasizing the fact that relations between the sexes prior to marriage had more to do with flights of the imagination than with any tangible physical contact. Romantic love is played out in the realms of fantasy, both blissful and anguished. Thus Abū Shādī composed the poem "Yā Ilāhī" [O My God] in which it is clear that the woman who is the object of his adoration has a divine, unattainable quality which makes it impossible for him to gain her in his lifetime. The poet protests bitterly at this hopeless prospect and makes passionate declarations of his love in his appeal for mercy and clemency:

> She is my desire, my passion and faith; my disturbance
> And my madness when departure removes you
> From a pure, distressed, lowly heart
> Whose sin is to keep my secret like your secret.[16]

Outside the Egyptian scene, the Romantic poet who made the strongest and most unambiguous disavowal of the traditional view of women in Arab-Islamic culture was the Tunisian Abū 'l-Qāsim al-Shābbī (1909–34), who was a corresponding member of the *Apollo* group and whose poems were published in the review:

> The attitude of Arabic literature to woman is base and ignoble and sinks to the lowest depths of materialism. It only sees in woman a body to be desired and one of the basest pleasures in life to be enjoyed . . . Have you ever heard anyone among them [the Arab poets] talk about woman, who is the altar of love in this universe, in the way a devout worshipper talks about the house of God?[17]

True to his principles, al-Shābbī reacted against the heavily physical conventions of old Arabic poetry with an excess of platonic spiritualism, taking as his model the idealized representations of love and woman which had become the hallmark of the new Romantic poetry. The most complete statement of this in his poetry occurs in *Ṣalawāt fī haykal al-ḥubb* [Prayers in the Temple of Love]:

> You . . . You are life in its heavenly holiness, in its unique pleasant enchantment.
> You . . . You are life in the delicacy of the dawn, in the splendour of new-born spring.
> You . . . You are life at all times in a new freshness of youth.
> You . . . You are life. In you and in your eyes are signs of its spreading magic.[18]

It would be misleading to imply that the poetry of platonic adoration was the only form of love poetry practised by the Arab Romantics, although it could fairly be described as a dominant mode. Sensuality and downright eroticism are also represented in full measure. Although both these themes have a long history in the Arabic tradition, the Romantics transformed them with their own particular style. Ibrāhīm Nājī (1898–1953), vice-president of the *Apollo* society, in many ways conforms to the typical pattern of the new Egyptian intelligentsia who had risen to prominence since the First World War.[19] He came from a comfortable, educated family background, was reasonably well acquainted with English, French and German literature and was a qualified doctor. The most outstanding element in his work is his love poetry, but his are not the spiritual, ethereal, platonic visions of love which informed the work of most of his contemporaries in the Romantic movement. To be sure, his love poems are full of frustration and unrequited passion: in common with most of his fellow Egyptians, both male and female, if Nājī fell in love he had to worship from afar, but the general inaccessibility of the beloved did not lead him to seek solace in the realms of the spirit. On the contrary, his poetry sees a revival of that powerful sensuality which existed in much of the amatory verse of the classical Arabic tradition. Indeed, there are clear signs in some of Nājī's major poems that he has adapted for his own purposes the *dhikr al-diyār* (reminiscence of deserted dwellings) and *raḥīl* (journey) elements of the classical *qaṣīda*. In one poem entitled "al-Aṭlāl" [The Ruins], the ruins referred to are not the remains of some desert encampment which was the site of a former love-affair; they are the symbolic ruins of a relationship which collapsed and left the poet desolate:

> I have seen creation like a narrow tomb, in which reigned silence and despair.

My eye saw the deceptions of love, as flimsy as spiders' webs.
You used to lament for me and know my pain, if ever a silent statue could lament for tears.
At your feet a world ends. At your door hopes die.[20]

In Nājī's longer love poems, in particular, the pleasures of love are frequently suffused with suffering and endurance, and a sense of lack of fulfilment. For him, the device of the old *raḥīl* seems to be a symbol that he adapts with conscious irony to the predicament of the modern Romantic poet's quest for fulfilment in the pursuit of love, which in most cases remains unrequited. The desert, with its aridity, lack of resources and physical comforts, is the most apt scene to throw into relief the poet's exhausted frustration and emotional sufferings:

The mirage which deceives; the desert; thirsting, bewildered fugitives.
Night after night after night. One year of bleakness, and others of emptiness.
Nothing to sustain me. The water has run out. Friends and faithful ones have gone.
How can I fly to my far-off love on wings of disease and distress?[21]

A considerable number of Nājī's short love-lyrics, however, form a complete contrast to his sufferings in the desert of life or amidst the symbolic ruins of past love-affairs. They concentrate on some moment of joyful amorous dalliance, or some aspect of the pleasurable experience of love. They have much in common with the uninhibited sensuality of the classical tradition, and in form they are reminiscent of the old *qiṭ'a* (fragment). They avoid the pained metaphysical speculation which was a hallmark of so much Romantic poetry at this time. But it is in his longer love poems that Nājī achieves a remarkable fusion between the strong echoes of classical Arabic poetry and the spirit of modern Romanticism. "Al-'Awda" [The Return] has all the qualities of a *dhikr al-diyār*, but the site is no longer that of a ruined desert encampment but a deserted house in Cairo's Qaṣr al-'Aynī Street.[22] The house had once belonged to friends of Nājī and in it he had enjoyed the presence of love, beauty and happiness: the poet now laments its emptiness and loneliness. The entire poem is a delicate mix of time-honoured vocabulary with the images and sensibility of an Egyptian poet in the avant-garde of his culture in the 1930s. One of Nājī's most creative qualities is his strong sense of irony, which on occasion appears as an open sense of humour in his work; perhaps this is what enabled him to achieve such a successful symbiosis between the Arabic tradition and modern

Romanticism. One of the weaknesses of neo-classical poetry was an inability to play with or improvise on the tradition: elements of the *nasīb* which appear in the work of Ḥāfiẓ Ibrāhīm or Shawqī often appear as ludicrous anachronisms which can no longer cope with the thematic demands which were being made of poetry. The politics of culture in the neo-classical period dictated that tradition was still a hallowed heritage with which poets tampered at their peril. Nājī did not have to bear the same burdens as the previous generation. His fusion of both the spirit and the motifs of old amatory verse with the modern Arabic Romantic mode was eloquently symbolic of much of the ambiguity which surrounded the whole area of sexual relations and women's emancipation in Egypt in the 1930s and 1940s.

The major cult figure of Romantic poetry in the period under discussion was not in fact Nājī, or indeed Abū Shādī, but their colleague in the *Apollo* group, 'Alī Maḥmūd Ṭāhā (1902–49). Like Nājī, his family circumstances were reasonably comfortable and his professional career was also non-literary in that he qualified as a construction engineer in 1924.[23] After Abū Shādī himself, Ṭāhā was perhaps the most complete representative of all that the *Apollo* group stood for: the sources of his cultural inspiration were largely English and French, he was attracted by artistic experimentation and innovation, and he sought to widen the scope of conventions both in art and in life. As an individual he found considerable liberation in the frequent trips to Europe which he began to make from 1938 onwards and which he celebrates in his second volume of verse, *Layālī 'l-mallāḥ al-tā'ih* [Nights of the Lost Mariner], published in 1940. This collection abounds in descriptions of Venice, Lake Como, Zurich and the Rhine, which serve as attractive impressionistic scenes for the pursuit of pleasure, which is relatively uncomplicated by ambiguous feelings of guilt or remorse. In this new mood of liberated hedonism, Ṭāhā began to write love poetry of powerful, exciting sensuality. Some of his shorter amatory pieces can be compared with the brief love lyrics of Ibrāhīm Nājī; they are equally concrete and immediate, leaving little to vague suggestive effect or mystery to tease the imagination. Such poems are often set in an atmosphere of alcoholic intoxication, a trend which was emphasized even more in *Zahr wa Khamr* [Flowers and Wine], published in 1943. This collection develops still further the air of carefree hedonism which was apparent in *Layālī 'l-mallāḥ al-tā'ih*: showing all his talent for brilliant impressionistic description, Ṭāhā creates vivid scenes of night-long revels in taverns with wine, dancing girls and drinking companions.

The nature of 'Alī Maḥmūd Ṭāhā's life and his art struck many chords among his Arab contemporaries, not only in Egypt. He had a bohemian attitude to the prevailing manners and customs of the majority of people in his own society, and this he was able to indulge through his frequent visits to Europe and his own life in the cosmopolitan centres of Cairo and Alexandria. Ṭāhā's poetry is a celebration of all the fantasy and exoticism which his generation associated with Western Europe. The scenes of Venice, Switzerland, France and the Italian lakes are magical visions of luxury, beauty and sexual liberation. The opening poem of *Layālī 'l-mallāh al-tā'ih* is entitled "al-Gandūl" [The Gondola] and describes a trip on the Venetian canals during carnival time:[24] set to music and sung by Muḥammad 'Abd al-Wahhāb, it enjoyed enormous popularity during the 1940s. One of Ṭāhā's greatest gifts as a poet was an ability to create through his language that sense of musical delight which has been rivalled by only a few poets in the twentieth century, such as Aḥmad Shawqī or the Syrian Nizār Qabbānī. This combination of the entrancing musicality of the verse and the often excitingly erotic subject-matter had a powerful effect on the youth of Ṭāhā's generation for whom sexual repression remained very much the norm outside marriage. His poem "al-Qamar al-'āshiq" [The Amorous Moon] is an exquisite example of the fevered masculine imagination which is jealous of the ability of moonbeams to penetrate inaccessible feminine spaces:

> When the thin light of the moon wanders around the balcony
> And shimmers over you like a dream or the ray of a thought.
> Whilst you lie on the bed of purity like a slumbering lily,
> Then enfold your naked body and guard your beauty . . .
> I am jealous, I am jealous if it kisses this mouth or enfolds it,
> And softly envelops the bosom, and clasps the supple body.
> Its light has a heart, and its charm has an eye,
> Which hunts the virgin ripple from its depths by night.[25]

It is fair to conclude that a general feature of life in Egypt in the 1920s and 1930s was that there was little direct organic relationship between theory and practice, or between the proclaimed ideals and the realities of life for the population at large. This applied to numerous different aspects of the life of the nation: the country was now independent, and yet certain continuing facts of British imperial power and influence inside Egypt called into question the very basis of that independence. Democratic processes were supposed to apply, but the monarchy and the lack of good faith of many politicians themselves constantly conspired to undermine these processes. Certain leaders of society, both men and women, called for greater equality and emancipation for women, but the numbers who derived genuine benefit from this remained pitifully small and insignificant. The Romantic imagination which arose along with the birth of the new nation state encouraged an intense concentration on the individual sensibility, but the individual emotional liberations which this fostered were not paralleled by widespread liberalizing tendencies in society as a whole. The Romantic love poetry of the period oscillates between remote, platonic adoration of the female ideal and varying shades of sensuality and eroticism. As such, it provides an intriguing commentary on the dislocations between theory and practice, and on the contradictions and ambiguities of its age.

4

Love and Beyond in *Mahjar* Literature

Cornelis Nijland

In this essay we shall concentrate on love relations and some of their social and other implications as treated by Arab authors who lived and worked in North and South America and who wrote in Arabic. They do not cover every kind of love relation one can think of, but only heterosexual love relations between adults. They fall under three headings: relations within the law; breaking the law; and prostitution. Two female and four male authors have been selected, two of them writing in North America and the others in South America.[1]

Relations within the Law

Mīkhā'īl Nu'ayma wrote about love, marriage and sex in various contexts. He composed poems, wrote a play and two novels on the subject and gave it a great deal of attention in his biography of Jibrān and in his own autobiography, *Sab'ūn* [Seventy]. The play *al-Abā' wa 'l-banūn* [Parents and Children][2] (1917) is the only text which unequivocally comes under the heading 'relations within the law', however. It is the story of Zayna, daughter of the late Buṭrus Bek Samāha, whom her mother has destined for a man of 40, called Naṣīf Bek 'Arkūsh, who drinks, gambles and composes second-rate poetry. Zayna is obedient and docile, much to the annoyance of her brother Ilyās. It is only when her fiancé tells her to obey that she becomes self-assertive and throws her engagement ring in his face. Her brother's friend Da'ūd and his sister Shahīd are on Zayna's side. Zayna and

Da'ūd fall in love with each other, but Da'ūd is a poor schoolteacher and an agnostic. Zayna's mother does not want her daughter to marry this son of a nobody but finally she gives in after her daughter's suicide attempt and after Nasīf Bek turns out to be heavily indebted.

Anjal 'Awn[3] writes about love, marriage and divorce, as can be seen from the titles of some of her articles: "al-Zawāj" [Marriage], "Naẓra fī 'l-ṭalāq" [A View on Repudiation] and "Wājibāt al-zawja" [Duties of the Married Woman]. In the first of the articles she writes that love is generally judged as the best, most stable and most secure basis for marital bliss, whereas reason is considered sterile. However, she maintains, reality is different. Reason is a better basis than love, which inevitably fades over time.

In "Rabī' al-mar'a" [Woman's Spring-time], she writes that every girl is waiting to be married and is therefore naturally disposed to preserve her beauty and her youth for her future husband. After she has given her husband her most precious possession, she has the right to demand anything from him. She may ask too much and that is where the trouble starts.

The question of divorce is treated in a separate article, "Naẓra fī 'l-ṭalāq", which again stresses that love alone is not a sufficient basis for a marriage and that other factors must be taken into account. 'Awn argues that second marriages are more successful since people have learned from their mistakes. However, since not everybody is fit for marriage, it should be made more difficult to marry and easier to divorce. Furthermore, the large increase in divorce is no reason for alarm since it indicates that people take life seriously, especially those whose marriage has ended in failure or those who were married against their will. 'Awn comments that the Christian religion does not allow divorce, although many people want it. How many couples live in a permanent hell? What can save them from it but divorce?

Breaking the Law

Most of Jibrān Khalīl Jibrān's stories about love relations come under the heading of 'breaking the law'. The theme of "Martā al-Bāniyya" [Martā, the Girl from Bān][4] is well known in the genre of sentimental literature. A poor orphan girl is seduced by a wealthy man. He brings her from the countryside to the city, she becomes pregnant and has to prostitute herself to earn her living. She dies of tuberculosis and is denied a burial in sacred ground.

A very different story is "Warda al-Hānī" published in 1908 in *al-Arwāḥ al-mutamarrida* [Spirits Rebellious].[5] The narrator's rich friend has complained that his wife has deserted him to live in poverty with another man. A few days later the narrator meets the wife, Warda al-Hānī, living in a humble house surrounded by trees and flowers, and hears her singing. The narrator asks himself, 'Could this woman be bad? Is it possible for this open face to conceal a depraved soul and a criminal heart? Is this the unfaithful wife?' Warda tells the narrator that she has heard about him and that she recognizes him as a reliable, trustworthy and understanding person. She then tells him her life story:

> I was 18 years old when fate led me into the arms of Rashīd Bek, who was already 40. He married me and gave me jewels. This all happened before I awoke from the deep sleep of youth and before the goddess had ignited the flame of love in my heart. I felt a sacred fire scorching my breast and a spiritual starvation knawing at my soul. I knew that a woman's happiness is not dependent on a man's fame, his domination or his generosity . . . but in love binding her spirit and his together. I knew that every day I spent near him was a terrible lie.

Warda says that she stayed two years with her husband and then met a young man living among his papers and books in a humble house and that she had tried to turn away from him. She concludes her story with the following words:

> I was whoring and deceitful in the house of Rashīd Na'mān because he made me his bed companion through the rules of custom and tradition before heaven made me his wife by the ruling of the spirit and affection. I was vile and lowly before myself and before God because I satisfied myself with his gifts to satisfy his physical desires.

Jibrān's story is innovative. It challenges time-honoured morality by declaring that the woman who has left her husband to live with somebody else is chaste and pure, whereas she sees herself as unfaithful and whoring when living in lawful wedlock. The story, however, is not without commonplace elements: rich is wrong and poor is right. This may be seen as a standard motif in Jibrān's writings.

The novel *al-Ajniḥa al-mutakassira* [Broken Wings][6] tells the story of a girl named Salmā who is married against her will while in love with somebody else. The story is told by a young man, who, as the son of a close friend of the girl's father, is welcomed in the house as a son and brother. He falls in love with the girl. However, the bishop intervenes for his nephew, so that the latter may get hold of the girl's fortune. The wedding takes place, but Salmā continues to meet the narrrator secretly to console and be consoled. Their meetings are filled with conversations. Salmā speaks about the marital relations of her time and the ills and wrongs that surround it:

> Writers and poets try to grasp the essence of woman but until now they have not understood the secrets of her heart, because they look at her from behind the veil of lust and see nothing but the shape of her body.

Elsewhere she says:

> Limited love seeks to possess the beloved but endless love seeks nothing but itself. Love which comes between the awakening of youth and numbness of the senses is satisfied with meeting and grows when nourished with kisses and embraces; but love born in the bosom of eternity, descending with the secrets of the night, is satisfied with nothing but eternity and is not impressed by anything but by divinity.

The bishop becomes suspicious of Salmā's outings and tells his nephew not to allow her to leave the house. The dénouement is that Salmā dies in childbirth together with her baby, unmourned by her husband.

The commonplace elements are easily recognizable: the girl being married against her will, the frustrated lover, the opposition between physical and spiritual love and the death of the unhappy girl. A new element is the vicious bishop, who, while appearing to be a good servant of the church, is in private quite the opposite. The corruption of clergymen and monks is a stock motif in Jibrān's writings in Arabic.

Most of Nu'ayma's narratives about love relations concern those outside the law or breaking the law in various ways or breaking the law of nature. In his autobiography *Sab'ūn* he has written about his affairs with married women in Ukraine and the United States. In 1908 Nu'ayma met Varya, the sister of a friend, and her husband Kutya in a village in Ukraine. He describes Kutya as a strange kind of man: he is tall and slim; his green eyes have a bewildered expression as if there is an endless void behind them; he has a sparse blond beard; and he resembles a child whose intellectual faculties are not yet fully developed, rather than an adult man. Elsewhere Nu'ayma speaks of Kutya as an incomplete man with a deficient intellect (*rajul ghayr muktamil al-rujūla wa ghayr muktamil al-'aql*) and as 'that infant in his thirties'. He writes about his relation with Varya in a sort of soliloquy:

> What fault was she committing when she took hold of me as a drowning person grasps at a rope? What fault does a lover commit by loving? Where is the blame when the man who is her husband by law is

physically and mentally retarded? If I respected the feelings of the husband I would wrong the wife in her dearest possession: the right to love and to live by that love during a limited period of time.

During his stay in New York Nu'ayma had a relationship with his landlady Bella who was married to Harry; it began in 1919 and lasted for five years. Bella is about 30, beautiful and with good taste, whereas her husband Harry is rude and uncouth, a simpleton in his speech, about 40 and an alcoholic. Bella tells Nu'ayma that she was only 16 when Harry's mother convinced her guardian that it would make his life easier to marry her to Harry. Bella tells the author, 'I could live with a blind man, a man with one eye or someone who was dumb, but not with a quarrelsome drunkard with bad manners and a foul tongue.'

Nu'ayma dedicated a poem to Bella entitled "Yā rafīqī" [My Companion].[7] He opens the poem thus:

My companion, companion of my body and my spirit
My partner in well-being and in adversity
My friend, friend in knowing and in ignorance
My confidante in misery and opulence
When the Lord of heaven calls us to Him
For reckoning, beware of make-believe
My love, before the Lord.

Tell Him that we did not know of any prohibition
And that we went each day our way
That we allowed the soul its wish
And that we quenched our thirsty heart.
When we looked at the world with the eye
Which heaven had made our guide,
An eye we had not chosen, nor
Taken part in its creation,
We saw the creator after we had seen
That everything he had created was excellent
And wonderful and pure and beautiful.

He ends with the following lines:

Tell Him we saw purity and beauty
Not wickedness in what the Lord of heaven made
And we allowed the soul all its wishes

And left the prohibitions to those who know the law.

Nu'ayma ended his relationship when Harry came home drunk one night after he had abstained from drinking for some time. Guessing that his affair with Bella had caused Harry to relapse into his drinking habits, Nu'ayma left the house.

In 1929 Nu'ayma met Njonja with whom he had a relationship until 1932. This love-affair ended rather suddenly, however, when Nu'ayma discovered that he was not the lover of a married woman who had a difficult time with her husband and was in need of a comforting hand, but that she had a good relationship with her husband and had another lover as well. Shortly after he had broken off with her, he returned to Lebanon and adopted an ascetic life-style. From then on he exalted spiritual love as opposed to physical love. This change of attitude found expression in the novels *Liqā'* [Encounter] (1946) and *Mudhakkirāt al-arqash* [Memoirs of a Pitted Face] (1949).

Liqā' tells the story of Leonardo and Bahā'. Bahā' lies unconscious in bed, probably in a coma, having been enchanted by Leonardo's playing of the violin. She is on the verge of death. Leonardo has withdrawn into a cave where, in seclusion, he tries to free himself of all sexual passions to be able to achieve spiritual union with Bahā'. When he has reached the desired state of purity, he remembers and plays the sacred melody. The spiritual union is achieved, leaving their bodily remains behind.

Mudhakkirāt al-arqash is the story of a man who worked as a waiter in a New York café and evidently had some kind of secret. The narrator tells us that the man disappeared one day leaving behind a diary. It turns out that he suffered from amnesia after killing his new bride. A newspaper article about the murder quotes the line the man had written on a small scrap of paper: 'I killed my love with my own hand because it was more than my body could sustain and less than my spirit longed for.'

The difference between Jibrān and Nu'ayma is obvious. For Jibrān love involves both the body and the spirit, whereas for Nu'ayma, in later life, the ideal stage of love is spiritual only. Moreover, Jibrān tries to interpret the feelings of the woman whereas Nu'ayma's heroes are predominantly male.

As regards spiritual and physical love, Jibrān's Warda al-Hānī prefers to live with the man she loves and not only to have a spiritual relationship with him, as does the heroine of *al-Ajniha al-mutakassira*. The difference between the two is that the first defies public opinion and takes a decisive step whereas the second does not want to trangress the laws. Nu'ayma's Leonardo seeks spiritual love and so, in fact, does the hero of *Mudhakkirāt al-arqash*. It is worth mentioning that Nu'ayma published parts of this novel in 1917 and 1918 in the arts magazine *al-Funūn*, published in New York between 1911 and 1918 with intervals. It remained incomplete until Nu'ayma returned to it in 1949 and invented the story of the murdered bride. There is a deep rift between the poem "Yā rafīqī", in which he exalts his relationship with a married woman, and the *Mudhakkirāt*.

As regards the female voice which is to be heard in Jibrān's stories and novels, Nu'ayma has no room for it with the exception of *al-Abā' wa 'l-banūn*, a play for both male and female actors. "Yā rafīqī" is in one voice, as most poems are. The novel *Liqā'* displays the peak of male activity and female inactivity. Leonardo has to free himself from lustful thoughts whereas Bahā' is declared pure and unsoiled, being a virgin in her teens. What happens when a man tries to withstand his lust but is unable to do so is related in the *Mudhakkirāt*.

Najīb Qusṭanṭīn Ḥaddād's sentimental novel *Badī'a Nu'mān aw nafathāt masḍūra* [Badī'a Nu'mān or the Outpourings of a Woman with Tuberculosis] consists of letters written by a dying mother to her emigrant son and in which she describes her life. Her mother was approached by a wealthy woman who wanted the girl (who was 12 years old) as a bride for her son. The engagement contract, drawn up with five monks as witnesses, provided for an indemnity to be paid if any of the parties annulled the contract. It was then discovered that the woman was a procuress who wanted the girl to work for her as a prostitute when she reached the proper age. The girl wanted the contract annulled but the five monks declared it valid and reminded her of the indemnity clause. The future mother-in-law was then killed in a road accident and the girl was free again.

The girl's life then took a turn for the better when she fell in love with a young man who was studying medicine. He wanted to marry her but suddenly went away. (It is later discovered that his family did not want him to marry a poor girl and a priest told him that his parents would disinherit him. The church does not allow this marriage because she does not belong to our church, was the next argument. Finally somebody told the boy that if he persisted in his wish to marry the girl his family would take steps to have her killed.) She was then married by her uncle to a 60-year-old man. She accepted this marriage because it would protect her from criticism. The attentive reader knows by then that she was pregnant and needed a husband to protect herself and the child from being ostracized. Her husband was hard and harsh on her and she ran away. She says that the law permitted her to leave her husband but not to find a new partner to take care of her. She did fall in love with another man but had to put an end to this relationship lest people discovered and defiled her name. In one of the letters she writes that a neighbour of hers said that every wife living apart from her husband is regarded as a fallen woman. In one of her last letters she tells her son that the medical student is his father, not the man to whom she was married.

The tone of this novel is somewhat different from that in Jibrān's writings. Although the 'author' of the letters writes that she loathes traditional opinion which does not allow lovers to live together, she also believes that the greatest crime a man can commit is to deflower a girl before the proper time: 'Mothers leave their daughters alone with their fiancés thinking that they have to do so, not knowing that it is bad and that the result is fatal. He soils the honour of the girl and walks away.'

We shall now turn to the great poet Shafīq Ma'lūf, who not only composed short poems but also a long poem, "'Abqar" [The Realm of the Jinn].[8] It describes the poet's visit to the realm of the jinn, the genies, the 'Abqaris. One of the songs is that of the Queen of the Jinn who complains that, as an immortal spirit, she envies mortal man. She would love to sacrifice her immortality to be able to enjoy love as man does.

Alas, who satisfies my appetite?
Whenever spirits lie down in my arms
And then my lips come near
They fade away, All I kiss
Or hold is utter nothingness.[9]

According to the critics, this was physical love and nothing more, a poem from the *jāhiliyya*.[10]

The poet, however, also meets the sons of Iblīs (the Devil) in hell. Among these sons is 'Awar, the Devil of Lust, who sings:

I am the protector of foul language
Of whoring and of lust.
A spark of mine in the eye
Sets fire to the blood.
I stir up frenzy
Mouth upon mouth.
Lovers do not lie down
But in my arms.

In the end he sings:

Let lovers know
When eyelids close
In hazy bliss,

It is only a trick

To prepare the eyes
For everlasting sleep.

It should be noticed that the song of the Queen of the Jinn gives space to a female voice although it is a man who invented the actual words said and the feelings expressed in these lines. There is a refreshing wit in these lines. Ma'lūf's Devil of Lust seems to be the least devilish of the sons of Iblīs.

Prostitution

Shafīq Ma'lūf included five stories in this long poem "'Abqar" of which the story of Anāhīd, the girl who was changed into the star Venus, comes under the heading prostitution. Anāhīd falls in love with one of her visitors, a horseman. He spends three nights with her and then she hears him go. She follows his trail until, exhausted, she falls down. The rider appears and tells her to go away, saying, 'I am the great Hubal,' the main deity of the Arab tribes. Hubal tells her, 'This is the punishment for prostitution.' She weeps and asks him to forgive her. She begs God humbly to cleanse her future of her past, so that love will be eternal and the unseemly will be hidden in her heart. God takes pity on her, believes that she is sincere and changes her into the star, saying that the heart of heaven is more worthy of her love than he. This story should not be taken to mean that Ma'lūf supports the double standard of morality, one for men and another for women. The tale is part of Arab lore, not the author's invention.

Prostitution also plays a role in "Ya'qūb al-Sharrāṭ" [Jack the Ripper], a short story by Salwā Salāma Atlas[11] which appears in the volume *Amām al-mawqid* [In Front of the Stove]. It concerns an unknown killer who ravages London, every day leaving a female corpse somewhere in the city. A famous detective comes from America to help the London police solve the riddle. On one of his tours through the city he comes across Nelly Nelson in the company of a man. The two rent a room for the night and so does the detective. On hearing Nelly's screams, he enters her room to find her dying from her wounds. The murderer, named Ya'qūb, is apprehended and turns out to be from an upper-class background. In court he reveals that Nelly was hired by him and his wife, fell in love with him and, to free the way, poisened his wife. Since her death he had sought Nelly everywhere. Hearing that she was a prostitute, he had taken revenge on every prostitute he had met since then, killing hundreds of them until at last he had found her. Now he is satisfied and only wishes to die in order to be reunited with his beloved wife. The people in court are so moved by Ya'qūb's story that they demand his acquittal. Even the judge declares that if the law did not say otherwise he would have demanded an acquittal. The law, however, stipulates that such an act is punishable by death and so the death sentence is pronounced. The execution itself is described as a kind of apotheosis with a great light shining from the roof and two spirits embracing each other.

5

The Four Ages of Ḥusayn Tawfīq: Love and Sexuality in the Novels of Tawfīq al-Ḥakīm

Paul Starkey

The present essay discusses the four major novels of Tawfīq al-Ḥakīm as they relate to love, marriage and sexuality in a segregated society. We shall ignore a fifth novel, *Ḥimār al-Ḥakīm* [al-Ḥakīm's Donkey], although it contains material relevant to this theme, since unlike *'Awdat al-rūḥ* [The Return of the Spirit], *'Uṣfūr min al-sharq* [Bird from the East], *Yawmiyyāt nā'ib fī 'l-aryāf* [Maze of Justice] and *al-Ribāṭ al-muqaddas* [The Sacred Bond], it has no claim to be considered a major work and is of little importance either in Tawfīq al-Ḥakīm's development as an author or in the development of modern Egyptian literature in general. The novels will be examined against the background of the commonly held picture of the author (to some extent self-propagated) as a misogynist ivory-tower dweller,[1] and we shall ask whether or not this view can be justified on the basis of the novels themselves.

As many critics have remarked,[2] each of these four novels contains a strong autobiographical element, each being based on a different stage of the author's life and reflecting experiences in a variety of social contexts. They thus provide an ideal backcloth for reflecting on the social, emotional and intellectual development of one of the most important of the twentieth century's Egyptian men of letters.

'Awdat al-Rūḥ

The first of these novels, *'Awdat al-rūḥ*, published in 1933, is in some respects the most complex, being capable of analysis on a number of different levels. We may ignore for our present purpose the nationalistic aspects of the work (which inspired, among others, Jamāl 'Abd al-Nāṣir),[3] to concentrate on what one critic has described as 'a wonderful picture of the torturing love of adolescence'.[4] The shy Muḥsin, a sensitive adolescent of 15 or so and easily embarrassed, awakes to the charms of the girl next door, whom he meets a few times for an exchange of piano and singing lessons before being separated from her by his trip to the country. He dreams of her, in expectation of her letter, but has already realized his own inadequacy—an inadequacy which is confirmed when Saniyya, his idol, turns her affections to a more mature suitor, Muṣṭafā, who finally asks for her hand.

Thus far, as a pen-picture of a failed adolescent romance largely based on fantasy, *'Awdat al-rūḥ* may be regarded as an expression of adolescent love equally appropriate to a European setting. But there is more to it than that. For the social context in which Muḥsin's romance is played out—a far from wealthy Cairene household—might almost be seen as a paradigm of the 'segregated society'. Before the events of the novel itself, 'the only time he had ever seen her . . . was when he had peeked through cracks in the door, along with his uncles, when she came one day to visit [his aunt] Zanūba'.[5] Muḥsin himself is at a delicate age, not only emotionally but also socially: straddling the dividing-line between child and man, he is just able to be admitted to Saniyya's presence without a scandal—but not before Saniyya's mother (in a first hint of evolving morality) has protested that it would not have been done in her day.[6] More importantly, Muḥsin's uncles—grown men all—appear themselves to suffer from much the same adolescent fantasies as the genuinely adolescent Muḥsin, contriving any excuse to visit the neighbours' house; indeed, Muḥsin's realization that he stands no chance in competition with their superior physique is an important stage in his coming to terms with the reality of his own position.

By the second half of the novel, the emphasis of the narrative has changed from Muḥsin's relationship with Saniyya to Muṣṭafā's courtship of her. And love, of course, will always find a way. In what seems at times like a grotesque parody of a Shakespearian balcony scene, the courtship of Muṣṭafā and Saniyya, and the attempts of the jealous Zanūba to wreck it, are played out before our eyes under the light of the moon and a hail of cucumber peelings. Not for the last time has the dramatist in al-Ḥakīm surfaced, temporarily to oust the novelist. But love is not all fun. A serious romance implies some thinking about the future, and in Saniyya's discussions with Muṣṭafā about his plans for a career we can see a first attempt on al-Ḥakīm's part, at least in novelistic form, to work out some ideas on marriage and the relationship between the sexes—ideas which are treated at greater length in *al-Ribāṭ al-muqaddas*.

Love itself is seen in *'Awdat al-rūḥ* first and foremost as a transforming experience. Muḥsin returns to school, his face beaming with happiness after his encounter with Saniyya, convinced that tomorrow he will be able to express 'what is in the heart of the whole people'.[7] More surprisingly, his uncles 'Abduh and Salīm are equally transformed—despite their less idealistic view of Saniyya, who for Salīm is chiefly remarkable for possessing breasts like 'small, sweet oranges hanging on the tree'.[8] Like the characters in al-Ḥakīm's play *Shahrazād*, written at about the same time as *'Awdat al-rūḥ*, the characters of the household view Saniyya in different ways which reflect their own natures; but they are united by the sexual frustration which is the standard lot of the unmarried male, whose previous sexual experience—if any—has been confined to prostitutes and, in Salīm's case, a flirtation with a Syrian woman which has led to his suspension from the police force. All now, however, return from their experiences at their neighbours' house yearning for privacy and loathing the communal life which is their normal daily lot. Nor is this transforming power of love a male prerogative. On the contrary, Saniyya also experiences it in much the same terms: receiving Muṣṭafā's declaration of love, she reads and rereads the letter, proof that 'heart speaks to heart', as she says. The letter has 'been able to provide her, by day and night, [with] the most beautiful happiness she ha[s] known throughout her life'.[9]

If 'heart speaking to heart' sounds like a union of equals, however, the limits of al-Ḥakīm's liberalism are soon marked out fairly explicitly. Describing Saniyya's argument with her mother that she should be allowed to follow her future husband to al-Maḥalla al-Kubrā, al-Ḥakīm remarks (as though this was the highest aspiration of a feminist) that 'Saniyya was not an old-fashioned girl. She wanted to take an interest in her husband's work and to encourage him in it.'[10] Though the author pays Saniyya the compliment of attempting to analyse her feelings with the same seriousness he gives to Muḥsin and Muṣṭafā, and though there are hints of changing social customs in Saniyya's conversations with her mother, it is difficult to read the novel as much of a plea for social change.

'Uṣfūr min al-Sharq

With *'Uṣfūr min al-sharq*, first published in 1938, we enter a different environment, the Paris of the 1920s—an intellectually exciting world in which there is so much to occupy Muḥsin artistically that the thought of studying for his degree appears to have gone out of his head. We have now left the segregated society with a vengeance: with nothing better to do, the young Muḥsin can sit all day in a café in Montmartre, eyeing the girls at the next table. For the most part, however, the serious young man that Muḥsin has now become shows a preference for Wagner and Beethoven, and for intellectual discussions with the Russian émigré Ivan on the differences between East and West; but, like *'Awdat al-rūḥ*, the novel is also a record of a failed romance, and as such, of relevance to our present theme.

Although Muḥsin has left the segregated society physically, he has brought with him the emotional baggage of his past. Indeed, in his initial shyness and hesitancy he seems scarcely to have developed from the Muḥsin of suburban Cairo. His initial conversations with his future girlfriend Suzy (who works at the box office of a cinema) are confined entirely to 'hallo' and 'goodbye', the two words being separated by an extended interval in which the strange Egyptian simply stares. It is only under the prompting of his friend and landlord André and his wife Germaine that Muḥsin is moved to exchange dreaming for action—to find out where she lives, to buy her a present and to ask her out. So begins their short-lived and tortuous affair, an affair which ends when Suzy is reunited with the Frenchman whom she really loves.

In the contrast between the practical André and the dreamy Muḥsin, al-Ḥakīm has given us one aspect of the theme (fashionable at the time) of the dichotomy between East and West[11]—a gesture in the direction of artistic unity, linking the love-affair with Muḥsin's discussions with Ivan. This theme is expanded in Muḥsin's letter to Suzy after he has been ditched, where he contrasts the selfishness of the European girl with the devotion of the Indian girl who throws herself on the pyre after the death of her lover.[12] Interestingly, al-Ḥakīm makes no comparison between European and Egyptian women at this point, which might well not have suited his purpose. When such a comparison is made in *'Awdat al-rūḥ*, for example, it is hard to tell who is flattered least. The Egyptian woman, says the narrator:

> does not look much at the person with whom she is speaking: she does not glance idly or randomly as daring, frivolous, European women do. Instead, she keeps track of her glances and holds them between her languid lashes . . . then raises her head and releases a single, devastating look.[13]

Compared with Saniyya, whose personality is explored by the author in some detail, the Suzy of *'Uṣfūr min al-sharq* comes across as a rather flat character. Indeed, disappointingly, since she is the only European girl to appear in al-Ḥakīm's major novels, little attempt is made to provide her with a personality at all. To the end we remain unclear quite what Muḥsin sees in her—apart, presumably, from her availability. The routine of their days together (inevitably structured around Suzy's work schedule) is described in some detail, but there is little passion, apart from a few kisses. In a book so obviously largely autobiographical, this is perhaps not surprising, but the whole affair has an element of artificiality about it. The parrot in a cage shrieking 'I love you, I love you'[14] to the bewildered box-office girl is symbolic perhaps not only of Muḥsin's own 'cage'[15] (as the book makes explicit) but also of the insincerity of his own position. The parrot's words are mouthed but not understood; they have, admittedly, some purpose, but they express no genuine feeling.

Yawmiyyāt Nā'ib fī 'l-Aryāf

Muḥsin's choice of a box-office girl as his lover is a further indication of the overriding importance of art in his life, even if the link is a good deal more tenuous than Saniyya's love of music, or that of the popular artiste Madame Shakhla' who visits Muḥsin's family in a flashback in *'Awdat al-rūḥ* and who seems to have aroused vague erotic feelings in the pre-adolescent Muḥsin—an interesting attempt on al-Ḥakīm's part to trace the awakening of sexuality back to childhood itself.[16] Marooned in a small town in the Egyptian countryside, the narrator of *Yawmiyyāt nā'ib fī 'l-aryāf* (published before *'Uṣfūr min al-sharq* in 1937, but relating to a later period of al-Ḥakīm's life) is denied access both to sex and to music, or indeed, to any other form of what he would regard as civilization apart from his own diaries. No longer awakened by the kisses of his French girlfriend, he is more likely to be roused from his bed by a telephone message telling him that someone has put a piece of metal on the railway line.[17] A posting in the Delta is, perhaps, marginally preferable to Upper Egypt, where the narrator and his colleagues used to spy from windows for articles of women's clothing in order to convince themselves that women still existed in the village.[18] There is, in fact, an unbridgeable gulf between the assumptions and mentality of the narrator, charged with applying a Western legal code, and the peasants to whom it is to be applied. Beside this gulf, the segregation of the sexes pales into insignificance. Marriage and prostitutes are held up as possible solutions to the problem of sexual frustration, but are not thought very attractive; sexual frustration, one feels, is but a minor symptom of a general discontent with the wretched lot of the *nā'ib* (prosecutor).

In this situation, the narrator and his colleagues are driven to clutch at straws. The 'straw' in this case is the peasant girl Rīm, who not only plays a crucial role in the construction of the story, but is possessed of a quite stunning beauty: the most beautiful girl that the narrator has set eyes on since he arrived in the *rīf* (countryside), her eyelashes seem to cover a whole feddan.[19] Although no more articulate than the rest of the villagers, her appearance has an instant effect on all those connected with the case of the murdered man, Qamar al-Dawla, their normal lethargy being temporarily replaced by enthusiasm for their work under her influence. When she is found dead, boredom returns with a vengeance. The *qamar* (moon) of Qamar al-Dawla's case has disappeared for ever, and as a tribute to her beauty the routine post-mortem is cancelled, despite new suspicions aroused by the mysterious Shaykh 'Uṣfūr's allusive songs.[20]

Despite her importance for the plot, Rīm herself is a symbolic rather than a fully drawn character. This is hardly surprising, since al-Ḥakīm's purpose is to expose the ridiculous nature of the legal system rather than to explore the Egyptian peasant mentality. Like Shahrazād in al-Ḥakīm's play, she remains an enigma to the end. Admittedly, the narrator does entertain thoughts of marriage for her, but it is marriage not to himself (unthinkable, given their respective social situations), but to Shaykh 'Uṣfūr, as an inducement to him to cooperate with the inquiry. It is interesting that, despite the narrator's blameless character and moral scruples about many aspects of his work, he never appears to suffer any doubts about using the institution of marriage for the purposes of manipulation in this way.[21]

Al-Ribāṭ al-Muqaddas

If love and marriage are incidental to the narrative of *Yawmiyyāt nā'ib fī 'l-aryāf*, they are central to the last novel to be discussed, *al-Ribāṭ al-muqaddas*. By the time of its publication in 1944, al-Ḥakīm had abandoned his official career as prosecutor to devote himself to his art, and the writer appears in the novel as a bookish and infatuated bachelor called Rāhib al-Fikr, who seems to epitomize the popular notion of al-Ḥakīm, the ivory-tower dweller. The most consistently intellectual of al-Ḥakīm's novels, its plot seems to take place almost entirely in the writer's head, despite a physical setting which swings back and forth between Cairo and Ḥelwān with the development of the story.

The Cairo of this novel is, however, far removed from that of *'Awdat al-rūh*. We are here in a different social structure, whose members have the money to indulge most of their whims and whose women have a fair, if circumscribed, degree of freedom. In part, this change may reflect the passage of time; but the change of class is more important. In the young lady of *al-Ribāṭ al-muqaddas*, al-Ḥakīm has given us a picture of the 'modern Egyptian woman' as he conceives her, of a kind which will also be familiar from a number of his plays in *Masraḥ al-mujtama'* [Social Theatre] and elsewhere.[22] The woman is superficial, flippant and fickle; she is almost certainly a liar, quite certainly a manipulator. But there is more to al-Ḥakīm's portrayal of her than that. For in her 'confessions', be they fact or fiction, he has given us an impassioned, at times eloquent, defence of a woman's right to freedom, love and equality with men in the realm of the emotions. Moreover, as in his portrayal of Saniyya in *'Awdat al-rūḥ*, he has deliberately set out to present part of the narrative from the woman's point of view. The use of the 'confessions', a 'fiction within a fiction' which mirrors his liking for the dramatic 'play within a play',[23] may be a somewhat transparent strategy for achieving this end; but the seduction scene, as the woman surrenders to the charm of her actor lover, is undoubtedly the more powerful for its being narrated by the woman herself.[24]

But of course, there are limits. As in *'Awdat al-rūḥ*, woman's happiness is seen partly, even by the young wife, in terms of her submission to men. More importantly, the writer, in his subsequent reflections and discussions with the woman, tries vigorously to dilute her plea. Challenged as a writer enjoying freedom of thought to grant woman a comparable freedom, he concedes that she may have this freedom so long as she remains unmarried, but insists that the contract of marriage must be respected absolutely on the woman's part once she is no longer single. For the writer, the essential nature of marriage is a contractual one:

> I want to draw your attention [he tells her] to the fact that marriage is first and foremost a contract, not a fetter—a contract between two parties, each of which has rights and each of which has duties. No one is shackling you; you are simply being asked to implement a contract.

When the woman objects that contracts cannot be built on the basis of changing emotions, the writer makes the startling suggestion that if her emotions change, she is entitled to go to her husband and ask for a divorce. But this seemingly forward-looking suggestion is soon thrown into focus by the traditionalist arguments which the writer then puts forward for the acceptability of unfaithfulness on the husband's part, but not the wife's—arguments which are in part financial, in part connected with purity of descent.[25]

Conclusion

To what extent, then, does Tawfīq al-Ḥakīm emerge from these novels—and from *al-Ribāṭ al-muqaddas* in particular—as *'aduw al-mar'a* (the enemy of women)? There is no clear-cut answer to this question. It is not difficult to find examples of apparently gratuitous rudeness about women in *al-Ribāṭ al-muqaddas*, as elsewhere in al-Ḥakīm's work. But these lapses need not perhaps be taken too seriously in the present context, for even the most ardent feminist could hardly argue that the young lady of *al-Ribāṭ al-muqaddas* is a saint, or even a model for their cause. More important is the distinction that the writer draws, in his final reflections on the events of the novel, between two different kinds of love: the base, sensual kind of love which has its origins in woman, the temptress; and the pure, chaste love which is here—though not always—linked especially with religion. This general dichotomy, of course, is not peculiar to al-Ḥakīm: it is a common feature of Egyptian and other Arab writers of the period.

What then of the arguments themselves? Here, too, it seems hard on the basis of this last-mentioned novel to regard al-Ḥakīm as a misogynist ogre; he was, rather, a spokesman for his contemporaries on the issues of the day. The arguments in the last part of the novel provide a vivid illustration of the extent to which the theory of individual liberation (including women's liberation) had been accepted by Egyptian intellectuals of the period, while society itself remained largely unchanged. If the writer of *al-Ribāṭ al-muqaddas* fails in his attempt to square the circle at this point, he should not, perhaps, be judged too harshly. It is equally significant that, here as elsewhere, he has been generous and perceptive in his exposition of the young wife's views and has drawn her character, flawed as it is, with sympathy and sensitivity. The same sympathy and sensitivity are also in evidence elsewhere—for example, in the portrayal of the ageing spinster Zanūba in *'Awdat al-rūḥ*.

With *al-Ribāṭ al-muqaddas*, al-Ḥakīm's career as a novelist came to an abrupt end. He married, produced two children, appears to have led a conventional domestic life and confined his literary activities to plays, essays, short stories and the kind of journalistic activities in which most Egyptian authors have to engage in order to eke out a living. For some reason, the novel form was pushed aside. One view might be that, after the tortured introspection of *al-Ribāṭ al-muqaddas*, this was no bad thing. How could an author who wrote a novel as good as *Yawmiyyāt nā'ib fī 'l-aryāf*, runs this argument, go on to write one as bad as *al-Ribāṭ al-muqaddas*?[26]

On rereading these novels recently, I am inclined to the view that this judgement is too harsh. Admittedly, al-Ḥakīm does not always make it easy for us to appreciate his novels. To introduce one's main character as *'rāhib al-fikr'* (the monk–philosopher) and leave most of the others nameless is not a promising start. But if the reader can avoid the temptation to take al-Ḥakīm as seriously as al-Ḥakīm takes himself, even *al-Ribāṭ al-muqaddas* begins to reveal its merits, as al-Ḥakīm gently pokes fun at the writer for knowing nothing of what goes on in the real world and allowing himself to be all but seduced before being ludicrously saved by a telephone call.

Above all, we should resist the temptation to regard these novels as no more than a footnote to the author's dramatic activities. Each one of these books is an important work in its own right, and together, they reflect many of the social and intellectual preoccupations of the Egypt of the period.

6

Erotic Awareness in the Early Egyptian Short Story

Ed de Moor

The third chapter of Yaḥyā Ḥaqqī's famous novella, *Qindīl Umm Hāshim* [Umm Hāshim's Lamp] (1943),[1] offers a marvellous, well-written passage about the young Ismā'īl at the onset of puberty. It tells us how the young adolescent becomes 'the prey of relentless contending forces pulling in opposite directions. He shunned the company of other people and yet his loneliness nearly drove him mad.'[2] It goes on to explain how Ismā'īl begins to find a strange pleasure in mixing with the women who visit the mosque: 'Surrounded by these bodies he experienced the pleasure of someone bathing in a flowing stream not caring whether the water was clean or not.'[3]

This passage offers a convincing description of awakening sexual awareness and also serves to explain the presence of the prostitutes in the mosque, especially one named Na'ima. In the novella, Na'ima is one of the female characters with whom Ismā'īl will have to deal, although he does not exchange a single word with her. For Ismā'īl she represents a female persona who in no way corresponds with her true profession. In his eyes she is an example of beauty and sincerity, not a woman who sells her body.

Qindīl Umm Hāshim contains a number of motifs that might be discussed in the context of this book. However, since the novella is well known, I shall only mention some elements that might be termed 'exemplary' for modern Arabic literature and which have certainly influenced other writers afterwards: first, the inauguration into the sexual experience of a young Arab Muslim by prostitutes or non-Muslim women, in this case represented by Mary, Ismā'īl's English colleague; second, the dream woman who cannot be reached—here the young prostitute who is saved by the grace of Umm Hāshim, the patron saint of the mosque; and last, the bride, Fāṭima al-Nabawiyya, chosen by the bridegroom's family. The first woman provides sex, the second provokes erotic feelings and the third is the object of care and responsibility.

Ḥaqqī's novella can be considered a key work between the New or Modern School of the inter-war period and the post-war novel tradition of the fifties. I shall not try to show here whether or not this work may be considered as the start of the post-war novel tradition. That it can be seen as a convincing and concluding example of the *adab qawmī* (national literature) movement of the twenties and thirties, however, should be obvious to anyone who is familiar with the aims of the Modern School, which emphasized such concepts as *miṣriyya* (Egyptianness), *maḥalliyya* (local colour), *ḥaqīqiyya* (realism) and *'aṣriyya* or *ḥadātha* (modernity).

Erotic awareness is part of any sexual experience in its infancy and will be found in most descriptions of the love theme. What is interesting is to see how writers approach this aspect of the love theme in their narratives, especially in a society like that of Egypt at the beginning of the century which considered it indecent to write or speak openly about erotic themes and preferred the poetic allusion or the romantic story in which lovers dreamed of each other in terms of spiritual relationships and chastity. An example of this kind of approach can be found in the work of Muṣṭafā Luṭfī al-Manfalūṭī (1876–1924) who, in his volume of tales *al-'Abarāt* [Tears] (1910), offered examples of excessive romanticism, 'not indebted to psychological insight' (to paraphrase Gibb's still readable analysis of early Egyptian literature),[4] but extremely popular among the Egyptian readership of the time. Al-Manfalūṭī's approach to the love theme was certainly influenced by his readings (in translation) of the great French Romantics like Bernardin de Saint-Pierre whose *Paul et Virginie* he adapted for an Egyptian readership, Alexandre Dumas père, Edmond Rostand, François de Coppée, Victor Hugo and Alphonse Karr, to mention only those writers whose work was adapted by the Azhar-trained al-Manfalūṭī.[5] In his stories he demonstrated a predilection for sad tales and impossible love relationships, as in "al-Yatīm" [The Orphan] in which a young man falls in love with his cousin, but, because they cannot meet, they die, to be united only in the grave. In another story, "al-Ḥijāb" [The Veil], al-Manfalūṭī attacks reformist ideas on unveiling. The male character in the story, a visitor from Europe, lets his wife take off her veil, go out and meet other people. One night the police inform him that his wife has been imprisoned along with her lover. The husband has a heart attack and dies, after admitting that he is responsible for his wife's behaviour.[6]

Another author who took an important step towards realistic description was Muḥammad Luṭfī Jum'a (1886–1953), who preferred the realism of Balzac and Zola to the romanticism of Sir Walter Scott's *Ivanhoe* and the French Romantics. With his collection of stories, *Fī buyūt al-nās* [In People's Houses] (1904) and his novel, *Fī wādī al-humūm* [In the Vale of Anxieties] (1905), Jum'a made a deliberate transition from romanticism to realism. In his novel he shows the miserable lot of an Egyptian prostitute and, considering woman as a victim of social circumstance, he puts the blame on society just as French naturalists might have done. More than Jum'a, however, it was al-Manfalūṭī who dominated the Egyptian literary scene at the beginning of the First World War. His work was the object of admiration and discussion in the circle of young men who would start the literary movement of the New School and still later the Modern School.

In the treatment of the erotic theme one cannot overlook the touching scenes found in Muḥammad Ḥusayn Haykal's novel, *Zaynab*. These were still painted from a strong idealizing point of view, although the work also contains convincing realistic and sentimental elements and is far removed from al-Manfalūṭī's repressive attitude towards women.[7] On the contrary, Haykal suggests that the segregation of the sexes leads to an unrealistic idealization of the other sex, making it impossible for young people to find suitable partners or to have a realistic understanding of each other.

Since the novel remained a neglected field of literary appreciation until the thirties, it was the short story that flourished between 1915 and 1927. The main impetus for that development came from Muḥammad Taymūr and his friends in the *Sufūr* and *Fajr* group. We shall now discuss some examples of short stories by authors from this circle in greater detail.

In January 1925 Aḥmad Khayrī Sa'īd, a medical student, and Maḥmūd Ṭāhir Lāshīn, a civil engineer, realized an old dream by launching the literary magazine, *al-Fajr*. In it they published a large number of what were labelled *qiṣaṣ miṣriyya* (Egyptian stories), mainly written by themselves and authors such as Maḥmūd Taymūr (the brother of Muḥammad) and Ḥusayn Fawzī. In *al-Fajr*'s second year of publication, Yaḥyā Ḥaqqī also contributed to these *qiṣaṣ miṣriyya*. The members of the *Fajr* group specialized in the modern method of story-telling, something they had learned from French realists like Maupassant and Zola and from Russian psycho-realists such as Turgenev, Pushkin, Chekhov and Dostoevsky. From these European models they learned that human behaviour was determined by all kinds of social and hereditary factors; like their models, these

Egyptian writers tended to portray extreme situations and marginal personalities in society. In her marvellous book about the early stories of Maḥmūd Taymūr, to which the reader is referred, Rotraud Wielandt has provided a wealth of material to prove this point.[8]

Muḥammad Taymūr: between Romantic Tradition and Naturalism

We shall first discuss erotic awareness in the stories of Muḥammad Taymūr, the predecessor of the Modern School. In his stories erotic awareness is mostly described from the point of view of the adolescent or young adult who wishes to meet women. This is the case, for instance, in "'Aṭfat al . . . raqm manzil 22" [Narrow Lane No. 22] in which a man has an affair with the wife of his colleague without knowing who she is. The discussion between the two friends which precedes the adventure—concerning what kind of women are the most attractive: those who are veiled in the traditional way or those who show their body in a Western manner—places the story in a reformist context. At the end, the message is that a woman should not veil since veiling leads to mistrust between friends. The most revealing passage in the story is the discovery of the woman's real identity. The narrator is keen to discover who she is, and this leads to his misfortune. The description of the characters, however, is not profound; psychological touches are added through an ironic description of the characters and also by means of vivid dialogue, as, for example, when the bachelor and the married woman meet on Bulaq Street:

> [Man:] 'We should slow down. Why are you in such a hurry?'
> She looked at me without giving an answer and continued on her way. Her look encouraged me.
> 'Where are you going, pretty angel?' I asked. 'Take your time!'
> Again she turned in my direction, and this time, she smiled. She slowed down, too, so that I could walk beside her and talk to her.
> 'Why are you following me?' she asked.
> 'Because I need to hear a single word from you,' I replied.
> 'Well, now you've heard a number of them,' she said, 'so leave me alone and go where you have to go!'
> 'But we're going the same way,' I said.
> 'You silly man!' she replied with a laugh.
> We then spent a long time chatting.

In Taymūr's novel, *al-Shabāb al-ḍā'i'* [Lost Youth], we meet a young man who tries to be in control of his own life but falls in love with his neighbour's daughter. This is how the love-story begins:

> It was, as we have noted, sunset. The sun had disappeared, and on the horizon only the red afterglow was visible. At that moment Ḥasan decided to look at the window. In the house on the other side of the street he saw a girl staring out of the window; as she admired the rosy sky she was clearly relishing the sheer beauty of nature. Ḥasan looked at her indirectly [*naẓra lam tu'arriha iltifātan*]. It was as though she had come to the window without any intention of meeting him; in any case, as we all know, coyness is a part of the feminine temperament. Ḥasan called out to her with the sound of love and anxiety in his voice. She gave a start, as frightened as an antelope that has just heard the hunter's footsteps. When she saw it was him, she calmed down. He gave her a gesture of greeting, which she returned gracefully. He followed it with a kiss sent in her direction from his fingertips.[9]

This passage reveals a strange blend of 'Manfalūṭīan' and realistic description. We find the same romantic vein in the story "Rabbī li-man khalaqt hādhā 'l-na'īm?" [Lord, for Whom did Thou Create this Paradise?][10] in which traditional *ghazal* elements are mixed with a modern situation. The girl who is to be married is said to resemble 'a beautiful narcissus in the garden of poetry'. When she meets her lover in the garden at night, they swear a pure love for each other until the very grave itself; the young man leaves after kissing his beloved on the forehead. The girl's father, a traditional Muslim figure who treats his daughter harshly when she refuses to marry the man he has chosen for her, behaves in an unusual way. When he discovers his daughter's clandestine meeting with her chaste lover, he does not rush to attack his disobedient daughter and the shameless intruder, but remains hidden behind a tree. Watching the couple he recalls his own juvenile love-affairs and declares that the beauty of the night has been made for lovers. Back in the reality of daytime he declares that his daughter will marry her lover, a solution that was certainly not applauded by the defenders of traditional marital customs.

The description of the young Maḥjūb and his nanny in Taymūr's most titillating story, "Kāna ṭiflan fa-ṣāra shābban" [He Was a Child, but He Grew Up], is rather naturalistic.[11] In the final section of the story, only published in the author's collected works, we have a rare example of erotic awareness turning into sexual behaviour. To summarize briefly, a young Egyptian with rich but absent parents has been brought up by a nanny who is more than twenty years older than he and who has cherished him like a mother. At the age of 20 the young man begins to show signs of interest in the neighbour's daughter, just as Ḥasan did in *al-Shabāb al-dā'i'*. This affects his relationship with the nanny. She forbids him to indulge in this kind of behaviour, whereupon he locks the door to his room. One day she catches him again and warns him that she will tell the whole story to his father. At that moment Maḥjūb gets angry and tries to leave the room, but she stops him and offers him her body. The seduction scene, which is very well written, is no doubt inspired by a short story by Maupassant, "La patronne" [The Landlady], in which a student is seduced by his landlady with whom he has a kind of mother–child relationship. The predominant feature of the final scene is the body language. Not a word is said. The physical need to make love becomes apparent when the two bodies touch accidentally. But the most beautiful aspect of the passage is the use of the glance as an instrument of communication and discovery. Both Maḥjūb and his nanny realize that they are ending their mother–child relationship in order to become lovers:

> As he looked at her, he noticed on that face, that he had known so well ever since childhood, a strange trait of desire he had never seen before. For a moment he stood there staring at her, while she stared back at him. In spite of her forty-five years there was still a touch of beauty to be seen on her skin. Maḥjūb was a young man whose passion could be aroused by the smallest trifle. He kept staring at her, and so did she at him. He heard her breath heaving in her bosom as she stared at the strand of hair dangling from his forehead. She kissed him on the mouth and he kissed her back. They embraced and their bodies clung together. He could feel her breasts against his body . . .

That the author regarded this story as an example of Egyptian naturalism can be concluded from the narrator's final words: 'Oh how wonderful is that which the eyes behold in the darkness of life!'[12]

We do not need to investigate here the large amount of juvenile erotic description found in Taymūr's poetry and drama. We shall concentrate instead on the short story and the Modern School, that mixture of imitation of the West and authentic Egyptian creation, and move from Muḥammad Taymūr to later representatives of the group which called itself *al-madrasa al-ḥadītha*, the Modern School. The most important writers in this group are undoubtedly Maḥmūd Ṭāhir Lāshīn, Maḥmūd Taymūr and Yaḥyā Ḥaqqī, who brings the adventure to a close just as Muḥammad Taymūr began it. We shall now turn to examples by Lāshīn and Maḥmūd Taymūr, finishing with a story by Ḥusayn Fawzī, who, of all these writers, might be considered as showing the most acute psychological insight but whose output as a short-story writer is confined to half a dozen titles.

Maḥmūd Ṭāhir Lāshīn on Marriage: "Yuḥkā anna . . ."

Between January 1925 and September 1926 Maḥmūd Ṭāhir Lāshīn published sixteen stories under the title *qiṣaṣ miṣriyya* and a large number of *ṣuwar waṣfiyya* (sketches). Both types of text fitted well into the main purpose of the Modern School: to create a new type of narrative description.

The short story "Yuḥkā anna . . ." [It is Told that . . .] was published on 7 November 1925 and has been discussed by a number of critics.[13] It is an example of the cynical approach to marriage common in French naturalism and English *fin de siècle* literature. Lāshīn shows a certain preoccupation with this theme. His first-published story, "Ṣaḥḥ" [It's True], treats the unequal marriage conditions in the relationship between a young woman (Dawlat) and an older man who, following the death of his brother, marries his sister-in-law who already has a young son. Some years later, after the widow has died, he marries again, this time a young woman (Dawlat) of the same age as his nephew. An affair develops between the young woman and the young man. When the older man discovers what has happened, he concludes that 'young people are made for each other, that's the law of the times' (*al-shābb lil-shābb . . . dhālik qānūn al-fatra*).[14]

In another story, "Zawājuhu ma'a Su'ād" [His Marriage to Suad],[15] age difference and sexual frustration also lead to the breakdown of a marriage. The social problem highlighted here is a loveless marriage imposed by the system in which it is the family that decides on the choice of partner. In "Bayt al-ṭā'a" [House of Obedience] marriage becomes a prison for a young woman who is married off to a domineering Turkish efendi. The man forbids her any contact with the world outside the home. She revolts against these regulations and leaves the house. As a result her husband forces her to return to the 'house of obedience'. However, she revolts once again by holding secret assignations with a younger man on the roof and getting pregnant by him. In spite of appearances, she then manages to live her own life. In yet another story, "Fī qarār al-hāwiya" [At the Bottom of the Abyss], the same kind of behaviour on the woman's part leads into prostitution as an extreme consequence of her determination to be liberated from her husband.

"Yuḥkā anna . . ." has been interpreted as an illustration of the old adage, 'Look before you leap.'[16] That, of course, is partially true. However, it can also be viewed as a story about marriage and thus is typical of Lāshīn's output. It also serves to illustrate the Modern School's vision of short-story writing.

The story is situated in three locations, thus giving it a clear structure. The first is the house of a well-to-do but fragmented family and is somewhat provocative. We find a young lady, Ni'māt (Nini), lying in bed at breakfast-time. Through an interior monologue she takes us back to the previous evening, which she spent on a boat with her lover, Rashād. The narrator tells us about a matchmaker's proposal to marry Nini to a decent man named Mabrūk Efendi Darwīsh. Once again the text moves back to Ni'māt's interior monologue. We discover that Rashād, the lover, has even suggested the night before that she marry this Mabrūk, in view of her stable relationship with him. Ni'māt's reflections are interrupted by the arrival of her mother, who expresses anger at her daughter's evening out with Rashād. Realizing that attack is the best form of defence, Nini starts crying, saying she wants to die. Her mother then declares that her daughter will indeed marry Mabrūk Efendi Darwīsh.

The second part of the story opens with a description of Mabrūk in his office; he proves to be a simpleton, despised both by his colleagues and by his boss. Here again an interior monologue is used, this time to show us Mabrūk Efendi's spiritual preoccupations, which seem to rule out any kind of sexual aspirations. The only purpose of his forthcoming marriage is to become rich and attain some social standing as Ni'māt's husband. When he gets home, the matchmaker arrives and the marriage with Ni'māt is arranged.

In the third section the location is the home of the young couple, Makky (i.e. Mabrūk Efendi) and Nini. Nini is about to go out. The narrator informs us that Rashād has not disappeared from her life; on the contrary, he hangs around the house all day as though he were a member of the family. Makky is furious about this, whereupon Nini promises to keep Rashād away. She starts visiting friends in the afternoon, clearly a ruse to allow her to meet her lover again. At this point in the story, Makky declares that, since his mother is ill, he is going to spend the night at her house. He asks his wife to stay at home. In a single sentence, the narrator now brings us to the epilogue: 'The curtain falls on the scene of a wife kissing her husband, then, after an entr'acte, it goes up again to reveal a lover kissing her beloved.' The lovers meet, but in the middle of the night the husband returns home. Surprise and bewilderment. What should they do? The devil suggests the answer to Rashād. When Makky knocks at his own front door, the maid tells him that she will not allow 'Sī Rashād' to come in. She admits that the voice of the person outside sounds very similar to that of her master, but still refuses to give in. The husband is thus sent away from his own home and conjugal rights. The story ends just as it started: with a reference to a fable from the *Kalīla wa Dimnā* collection about the gazelle that went down to a stream and the fox that looked at it and then said: 'Why didn't you think before going down to the water?' This helps to explain the social significance of "Yuḥkā anna . . .", which is not only a sophisticated tale about a woman who marries a simpleton in order to continue her love-affair but also a story about a middle-class man who thinks that marriage to a girl from a higher class will help him socially. It can also be seen as a comment on a mother who is prepared to use a wedding as a way of taking revenge on her unfaithful and absent husband. What gives the text a wonderfully spontaneous effect is the skilful use of the Egyptian colloquial in the dialogue.

Maḥmūd Taymūr on Money and Sex

Let us now consider Maḥmūd Taymūr's "al-Ustā Shaḥāta yuṭālib bi-ujratihi" [Ustā Shaḥāta Demands his Fare]. In this short story a poor coachman named Shaḥāta endeavours to get his fare from a middle-class widow named Iqbāl; in the end he is paid 'in kind'. At the beginning of the story, Iqbāl has made use of Shaḥāta's coach to visit her friends but up to now she has not paid. He has had to come back several times to ask for his money. The text opens with the coachman once again asking for his fare and getting angry when he is yet again refused. He will have to come back again in the afternoon. The discourse moves to a discussion of Madame Iqbāl, who is in her late thirties and bears the traces of a turbulent and promiscuous life in which she has been morally degraded by a husband who has led her into prostitution, gambling, drugs and alcohol. The husband died young, but has left his widow with all the negative consequences of their married life. Having lost her beauty, Iqbāl has become a matchmaker.

The historical flashback prepares us for what is to happen when the coachman returns and again asks for his fare. When he knocks on the door of the house, no one answers. He forces his way into the apartment of Madame Iqbāl, who, confronted with his presence, invites him to take his money and leads him into her bedroom. Here the narrative is interrupted by a second description in which the reader learns why the coachman accepts Madame Iqbāl's offer. For him she is an incarnation of all the beautiful women who have sat in his coach with their boyfriends, while at home he has to cope with a cantankerous wife. Like Iqbāl, his past has determined how he behaves in the present.

As in Muḥammad Taymūr's story about the young man and his nanny, we notice the way glances are used, this time combined with the sense of smell:

> He sniffed the scent of powder and perfume that filled the room. It made him feel calm, and his eyes lost their fierce appearance as he watched Madame Iqbāl moving around the room searching for the key to her cash-box. Finally she opened it up and made as though to give him the money . . . Had he ever seen such soft white skin, such a well made-up face, such bewitching black eyes? Before now, had he ever beheld such a slim body, scarcely covered by a transparent nightdress that revealed a smart pair of legs? No indeed, Shaḥāta had never seen naked feet, loosened hair and provocative breasts to rival these.

The text insists on the fact that this observation is subjective and that Shaḥāta only sees the girls of his dreams, not the real Iqbāl. When she tells him that she is penniless, he is quickly brought back to reality. When he makes it clear that he is attracted by her, she pounces on him. Ignoring his dirtiness and the stench of his body, she embraces him and gives him his due. If seduction in Muḥammad Taymūr's story was used to express a real sexual feeling, the same process in his brother's story here serves only to resolve a financial problem. The coachman's sexual needs help bring about the solution.

Ḥusayn Fawzī on Sexual Greed and Erotic Feeling

Of the stories published by Ḥusayn Fawzī in *al-Fajr,* there is one that resembles "al-Ustā Shaḥāta . . .". It is entitled "al-Shaykh 'Awda" [Shaykh 'Awda]. The main character is once again an older woman, Zannūba, who overwhelms a man. This time, however, the motive is not money but sexual desire. With her husband out of town, she dismisses all her servants so that she can be alone with the blind Qur'anic reciter, Shaykh 'Awda, who has his fixed place in the *salamlik* (men's reception room). In order to meet him, she disguises herself as the maid who always serves him his coffee. In a well-written scene full of ironic comment, she seduces the shaykh; on the days when her husband and servants are away and she is alone, this seduction scene becomes a habit. However, the real maid becomes a victim of her mistress's behaviour. When she brings the shaykh his daily coffee, she is assaulted by him; he, of course, cannot understand why the maid is so unwilling this time. When the girl starts screaming, the shaykh defends himself by shouting loudly and accusing the girl of insolence. Zannūba makes good use of the occasion to dismiss the maid before the true story can be revealed.

In Fawzī's other stories we find a quite different tone as far as erotic feelings are concerned. Fawzī had made an intensive study of French literature and with Muḥammad Taymūr and his friends had read the stories of Maupassant and other authors. Before leaving for France in the summer of 1925, he had trained as a physician, and some of his stories may be considered an expression of his own experiences as a doctor at a clinic in Ṭanṭā where he worked after getting his diploma in 1923.

It is no wonder, then, that we find a preoccupation with illness and death intermingled with erotic awareness which is so much a part of the writings of al-Manfalūṭī whom both Muḥammad Taymūr and Fawzī admired. For Fawzī, however, his medical practice provided him with a direct motive for writing. Although we shall not here explore Fawzī's specific style, it should be stressed that his stories require close reading in that, more than any other writer in the Modern School (with the possible exception of Ḥaqqī), he developed a strong sense of the psychological details of human behaviour.

In his writing about the confused relationship between the young doctor and the dying girl in "Qiṣṣat marīḍa" [Story of a Sick Girl] one can detect an autobiographical element, whereas his story about a friend who falls in love with a spoilt actress and goes to pieces when she leaves him might well have been written by a Russian psycho-realist or by Maupassant in his final years. In both this story, "Ḥikāya qadīma" [An Old Story] and another, "Nustāljiyā" [Nostalgia], women are seen from a man's viewpoint: they are insatiable and their behaviour is ruled by the emotions. Men struggle in vain to get a grip on their female partners. The adored actress in "Qiṣṣat marīḍa" and Sonya in "Nustāljiyā" dream of love and long for freedom even at the expense of their own social situation. The image they present fits well with the heroines of the French naturalists such as Madame Bovary and Marguerite in *La dame aux camélias*. For such women marriage is a cage from which they must try to escape.

Conclusion

The stories presented here—somewhat at random, but in a roughly chronological order—have several points in common. First, they concentrate on exemplary situations, and as a result the authors set up characters in opposition to each other, such as the flirtatious Nini and the dull simpleton, Makky; the older woman in search of sexual satisfaction and her victim, be it a young adolescent, a poor coachman or a blind shaykh; the young woman and her older husband; the doctor and his patient; the technician and the actress; and so on. Second, no character is innocent from a moral perspective. Even in the victims there is a kind of concupiscence that makes possible the things that happen. Everything can be justified by historical causality: characters are victims of their fate and find therein an excuse to legitimize their own actions. Third, women are often represented with sympathy, but they are also seen as dangerous. Men are dolts and simpletons, except for the narrator who represents the intellectual élite and considers the female characters from a reformist point of view. Fourth, marriage is viewed as an institution by which men can suppress women: it is something that women can only survive through trickery.

As far as erotic awareness is concerned, the descriptions serve the moral judgement of the writer, but also the desire for lust. In their descriptions of sexual behaviour, the writers of the Modern School made great progress, even if they chose for their characters marginal personalities on the fringes of society. One wonders, however, whether these so-called realistic representations of Egyptian life were really so Egyptian; and, if they were, then one is drawn to the conclusion that, even as early as the twenties, there was already a considerable gap between the world of fiction for the élite and the realities of life for the Egyptian people.

In Yaḥyā Ḥaqqī's *Qindīl Umm Hāshim*, written fifteen years later, the main character is not a person on the margins of society, but rather a genuine Egyptian adolescent. Although Ḥaqqī's approach is completely in line with the main purpose of the writers of the New School, we find in his novella a reflection of the autobiographical novel of the thirties. The description of character is not restricted to incidental observation, as in the writing of authors in the Modern School that fits well with the general purposes of the short story, but focuses on the whole of its psychological evolution throughout a person's life. And there is another major difference: Islam, which was not a major theme in the writing of authors in the Modern School, becomes a central issue in *Qindīl Umm Hāshim*. Here we can also observe the influence of a growing interest in Islamic themes in the Egyptian literary tradition of the thirties. As far as erotic awareness and description are concerned, the novella is marked by Ḥaqqī's personal tendency always to write about sex in a discreet and restrained manner, emphasizing psychological rather than physiological detail. This serves to remind us that, in analysing the works of a particular period or a so-called school, we must always be ready to hear the individual voice of the author rather than to indulge in undue generalization. This holds especially true when the subject concerns the most intimate workings of body and soul.

7

The Arabic Short Story and the Status of Women

Roger Allen

This essay will attempt to link the theme of women in society to a particular genre in modern Arabic literature, what in English is termed the short story. The initial focus will be on the way that changes in the status of women in Middle Eastern societies have been reflected in the development of the short story, as seen in the themes and techniques that writers have selected to express their creative vision of this general topic. A second section will examine the narrative voice in a sampling of contemporary Arabic short stories, concentrating in particular on those in which the genders of author and narrator are different.

The short story in Arabic, as developed at the hands of its early exponents, managed to make full use of its generic characteristics to explore particulars while alluding to the wider implications that were often examined in early Arabic novels with a certain lack of subtlety or specificity, as, for example, in Muḥammad Ḥusayn Haykal's *Zaynab* and 'Abbās Maḥmūd al-'Aqqād's *Sāra*. What is remarkable about the Arabic short story, however, is not only the number of examples that deal with issues associated with women in society, but also the fact that the comparatively short chronological divide between the development of the short story in Arabic and its European precedents seems in part to account for the emergence of a truly mature literary genre in Arabic within a remarkably short time-frame.

Roger Allen

The Status of Women in the Modern Arabic Short Story

The Individual Within the Traditional Family Structure: From the earliest stages in the development of the Arabic short story, a good deal of attention has focused on the status of women in society. The traditional perspective of that predominantly male society has been that the primary aspiration of its female members is marriage. From the very beginnings of the short-story tradition in modern Arabic literature, writers have cast a mostly critical eye on the institution of marriage—its precedents, rituals and consequences—using the gradual and often confrontational processes of change within it as one of their most frequent themes. The depiction of the sequence from young girl, to adolescent woman, to wife, to mother, has continued to provide the short-story writer with a plethora of opportunities for the exploration of the conventions that govern the lives of women in the Arab world.

The short story often chooses to describe the position of the young girl within the protective cocoon of the family through portraying a relationship with one particular family member. Especially characteristic of the extended family that still survives as a Mediterranean institution is the role of the young girl as granddaughter.[1] In the Lebanese writer Ḥanān al-Shaykh's (b. 1945) story, "Ḥammām al-niswān" [Women's Bath], the girl's mother has died and it is the older generation, with its traditional and completely different values, that has to assume the responsibility for taking the young daughter of a Shi'ite family to a newly opened swimming pool for women in the capital city of Beirut.[2] Among the poorer segments of society, young girls are often part of the workforce. In "Naẓra" [A Glance], a typical vignette from the Egyptian Yūsuf Idrīs's (1927–91) earliest creative period, we see a young girl deftly weaving her way through the chaos of the city traffic carrying a tray of food; there is presumably a lesson in the fact that it is the narrator who is almost knocked down in trying to observe her progress.[3] Another of Idrīs's insightful portraits, albeit from a different class, "La'bat al-bayt" [Household Game], provides a somewhat sardonic commentary on sex roles in family life to be gleaned from the postures adopted by two young children. Fātin, the young girl, leaves in tears when Samīḥ, her young playmate, adopts an aggressively male role in their enactment of grown-up married life.[4]

With the onset of puberty and adolescence, the protective cocoon of the family comes to be seen in an entirely different light. Customs, rituals, etiquette and taboos combine to make this particular phase in the life of the majority of women into one of familial and societal constraint. The Arabic short story provides us with very few 'boy meets girl' fairy-tales where women manage within the context of societal convention to find the person of their own choice and, in the time-honoured phrase, 'live happily ever after'. The Tunisian writer Muṣṭafā al-Fārisī's (b. 1931) story, "Man yadrī . . .? Rubbamā" [Who knows . . . ? Maybe], manages to bring two young lovers together in marital bliss after some preliminary jealousies and suspicions have been averted, but the point of the tale is not in the ending—the couple living happily in a new apartment, the kind of terminal prize that Henry James finds so unsatisfactory[5]—but in the narrator's wonderfully sardonic intrusions into the reader's encounter with the text.

Pursuing this somewhat illusory theme of fairy-tale romance one stage further, the Egyptian story-teller Salwā Bakr (b. *c.* 1950) provides a carefully drawn picture of contemporary 'marital bliss'. In the title story of her collection, "'An al-rūḥ allatī suriqat tadrījiyyan" [The Spirit that Was Stolen Step by Step], we follow the life of a married couple who not only have a flat with plants and a cat, but also respond to the communal pressures to purchase all the gadgets that modern life offers. It is the gradual process implied by the title—the disenchantment with evening excursions to the cinema, the first signs of a middle-aged paunch and, unkindest cut of all, the reliance on television soap-operas—that comes to symbolize the meaninglessness of a marriage dominated by the demoralizing routines of modern life.[6]

Still within the family structure, the figure of the brother often assumes authoritative dimensions. In the Egyptian Yaḥyā Ḥaqqī's (b. 1905) "Kunnā thalātha aytām" [We Were Three Orphans], the first-person narrator is a brother who finds the tables turned on him; or, as he himself expresses it in a proverb at the conclusion of the story, '*rāḥ yaṣṭād . . . iṣṭādūhu*' (He went hunting but they hunted him).[7] Left as an orphan with two attractive sisters and made fully aware of his brotherly responsibilities, the narrator moves with them into a flat in Cairo's Garden City district that they cannot really afford, so as to provide them with better 'prospects'. In the end, it is he who finds a match in the much idealized person of Saniyya.[8]

Such apparent fraternal neglect seems positively benevolent, however, in the context of other narratives involving brothers and sisters, ones in which the familial authority vested in the brother figure leads to sheer violence. In "al-Thalj ākhir al-layl" [Snow at the End of the Night], the Syrian Zakariyyā Tāmir (b. 1931), one of the most accomplished writers of symbolic stories, brilliantly captures the atmosphere of blind hatred that the norms of the society can arouse in a tyrannical father (whose daughter has run away from home) and transfer them to the son; it is only when the girl's brother envisages the act of slitting her throat that memories of their childhood together come flooding back to temper and then curb his relish at the thought of carrying out such communally condoned murder.[9] Tāmir's story is a complex picture of the mind of a young man tortured by the incompatibilities of societal convention. The Iraqi writer May Muẓaffar's (b. 1948) story, "Awrāq khāṣṣa" [Private Papers], takes the convention still further, in that the brother, self-appointed guardian of the family honour, shoots his sister dead on the street as she walks hand in hand with her beloved.[10]

The didactic purpose of many early short-story writers makes the 'one slip' theme a popular choice, 'a fate,' if you will, 'worse than death'. One of the earliest stories of all, the Lebanese Khalīl Jibrān's (1883–1931) "Martā al-Bāniyya" [Martā, the Girl from Bān], is an example of this, as is the Iraqi Dhū al-Nūn Ayyūb's (b. 1908) "Sāqiṭa" [The Harlot].[11] The heroines of both these tales have fallen into a life of prostitution, abandoned to their fate by their families. The vigorous didactic purpose implied by this notion of irretrievable loss of honour and family acceptability finds a more forgiving voice in the Egyptian Maḥmūd Taymūr's (1894–1973) story, "Najiyya ibnat al-shaykh" [Najiyya the Shaykh's Daughter], in which a father who has thrown his daughter out for making 'one slip' is reconciled with her on her death-bed and then rails at a preacher in the mosque who consigns whores and adulterers to hell-fire.[12]

The tragedies represented in these narratives and their didactic motives represent the extreme end of a spectrum that is used by short-story writers to reflect a situation fraught with both potential and actual tension. In an early example of a less tragic variety, "Fatāt al-jīrān" [The Girl Next Door], Maḥmūd Taymūr explores (with the obvious didactic purpose characteristic of the period) the ridiculous aspect of parental attitudes, as a young man's interest in the daughter of Greek neighbours is only aroused when he overhears his mother talking about his moral probity.[13] Much more psychologically penetrating is another story by Zakariyyā Tāmir, "Wajh al-qamar" [The Face of the Moon], in which the narrator tells us the story of Samīḥa, who was raped as a child and has recently been divorced by her husband. She has failed to make the required transition from a cloistered girl slapped by her father for revealing too much leg to a passionate lover endeavouring as best she can to imitate the movements and groans of the sexual act that have been rapidly taught to her by her female relatives in anticipation of her marriage.[14]

The fishbowl atmosphere within which so many of these surreptitious relationships are supposed to occur, and the suspicions and conspiracies that arise as a result, are well captured by Yūsuf Idrīs in "Ḥādithat sharaf" [A Case of Honour], a story that begins with the narrator informing his readers, 'I think they still refer to love over there [i.e. in the provinces] as "the shame".'[15] An entire community, that of a country estate—with all its jealousies and complex relationships—is possessed by the idea that 'something may have happened' between Fāṭima and Gharīb, its two most beautiful young people. In fact, it is proved that nothing has happened, but at the end of the story the narrator makes it clear that what has been lost is a sense of innocence.

In contrast with all these stories in which young people do manage to meet, whatever the consequences, we may cite examples from the Arabian peninsula in which the situation is portrayed in even more restrictive terms. Ḥanān al-Shaykh's "Bint ismuha Tuffāḥa" [A Girl Named Apple] tells the story of an oasis woman who, while hoping for the prospect of marriage, continuously resists the communal means of advertising her availability, namely putting a coloured flag on the roof of the house—the colour depending on the age of the prospective bride.[16] It is hardly surprising that, as the tradition of fiction has developed in the Arabian peninsula, the frustrations resulting from society's attitudes towards the status of unmarried women has been one of the most prevalent themes.[17]

From the outset, the institution of marriage itself has been the focus of a large number of narratives. The convention of arranged marriage and the modes of coercion frequently involved aroused Khalīl Jibrān into homiletic ire in both "Warda al-Hānī" and "Maḍja' al-'arūs" [The Bridal Couch].[18] More recently, the entire process of marriage between cousins and the repulsiveness of marital rape and infidelity are explored in terse reminiscence by the Egyptian Alīfa Rif'at in "Fī layl al-shitā' al-ṭawīl" [In the Long Winter Night], a story whose impact is heightened by the fact that the heroine's mother informs her that the situation described is simply the way things are: 'All men are like that.'[19] While these stories lay heavy stress on the intolerable situation in which these married couples live, dysfunctional marriage appears in a variety of guises. In "Zawjatuhu" [His Wife], Dhū al-Nūn Ayyūb allows his narrator to provide a very male-oriented picture of a curious relationship. Two friends walking down the street bump into a woman (who, we are obligingly told, is 'unusual').[20] It emerges that she is the wife of one of the two men and has married him after a bet with a girlfriend. He has left her in disgust, but she has grown to love him. They remain married, but only in name.

The *locus classicus* for the dysfunctional marriage within the tradition of the Arabic short story, however, must surely be the miniature masterpiece of Yūsuf Idrīs, "al-Martaba al-muqa''ara" [The Hollow Mattress], where the expectations of the opening sentences are dashed in a nihilistic parable of life in general as seen through the minimal communications of a married couple.[21] Some stories portray attempts to bring about change in the marital situation. An example of this is Maḥmūd Taymūr's story, "Inqilāb"

[Revolution], where a letter from a wife to a woman friend informs her that she has transformed her marriage by deliberately making her husband jealous.[22] On a more psychological plane, Yūsuf Idrīs' "'Alā waraq sīlūfān" [In Cellophane Wrapping] takes the pampered wife of a paediatric surgeon into the operating theatre to show her an aspect of her husband's personality that she had never realized existed. By the conclusion, the husband has emerged as a powerful tyrant in his professional life whose apparent submissiveness to his wife in their domestic situation is a reflection of his wish to meet her every need. It is, however, presumably a male narrator who comments on her sexy appearance at the story's outset, and the adulation that she feels towards her husband at the end seems somewhat overdrawn.[23]

With the role of the wife frequently comes that of the mother.[24] The traditional craving for male heirs is reflected in dire form in the Lebanese writer Mīkhā'īl Nu'ayma's well-known story, "Sanatuhā 'l-jadīda" [Her New Year], in which a village frame is placed around the dark secrets in the household of Shaykh Abū Nāṣīf. After giving birth to seven daughters, the shaykh's wife is pregnant again; the newborn child is a girl, but this time the shaykh buries it alive, announcing to the world that it was a stillborn son.[25] In short stories dealing with marriage and the family, children are frequently present, although their presence is often implicit. Stories that focus on children tend to be about them and their world, rather than on their role within the larger family structure. Where children do seem to be a factor is when they are the cause of a problem. In the Kuwaiti Laylā al-'Uthmān's story, "al-Raḥīl" [Departure], a couple about to leave for an extended stay abroad sift through their belongings and come across a doll belonging to their dead child.[26] The Lebanese Laylā Ba'albakkī's (b. 1936) "Safīnat ḥinān ilā 'l-qamar" [Ship of Tenderness to the Moon] is also about a couple with no children, but, while the sexual allusions in the story are controversial enough, what is even more so in societal terms is that the female narrator is refusing her husband's desire to have children.[27] If the homes in these last two stories are childless, the opposite is the case in "al-Wāfida" [The Newcomer] by the Iraqi Daisy al-Amīr (b. 1935).[28] The daughter of a family with nine children and struggling to make ends meet is desperately afraid that her mother is pregnant again, but, when she confronts her, it is to discover that her father's overriding will has been expressed in another way: her sister is to be married off.

In a society in which women's functions are a reflection of the presence of men in one role or another, the status of the widow is often problematic. This ranges from the brutal murder of Haniyya by her male relatives in the Egyptian writer Edwār al-Kharrāṭ's "Ḥīṭān 'āliya" [High Walls] to the sweet reminiscences of Helena, the recently widowed woman in the Lebanese Tawfīq Yūsuf 'Awwād's "al-Armala" [The Widow].[29] Once again, however, it is Yūsuf Idrīs—in "Bayt min laḥm" [House of Flesh], an almost tactile portrait in words of loneliness and sexual deprivation in the home of a widow with three daughters and no male presence—who best captures the frustrations aroused by social convention.[30]

The Individual Outside the Family Structure: Within the stories surveyed thus far, the family and its members are clearly seen as one of society's most cogent repositories of traditional mores. The changes that occur in the larger framework of society as a whole are shown in their impact on the family structure but through its individual members. That process of change, however, inevitably involves a far greater transformation in societal attitudes, as women have begun to move out of the confines of the familial environment and into society at large, into educational institutions and eventually into the workplace itself.

It is hardly surprising that the process of representing the complexities of this social transformation in fictional form is intimately connected with the growth of educational opportunities and the raising of women's consciousness on the issue of their rights. In Egypt—for which we appear to have the most available information—Hudā Sha'rāwī's foundation of the Egyptian feminist movement in 1923 was followed by a proliferation of periodicals that addressed women's issues; the availability of such publications provided increased opportunities for expression in fictional form. The year 1935 saw the appearance in the public domain of the first collection of short stories by a woman, *Aḥādīth jaddatī* [Stories by my Grandmother] by the Egyptian Suhayr al-Qalamāwī (b. 1911), a pioneer here as in the academic sphere. As women writers have begun to join their male colleagues in giving fictional expression to their ideas and emotions, they have brought new perspectives and voices to the depiction of the social reality they witness. Al-Qalamāwī herself clearly suggests her views regarding these changing roles in a story entitled "Imra'a nājiḥa" [A Successful Woman]. Her readers are given a portrait of a young woman, Na'īma, who seems to have let all the 'right' opportunities pass her by: the attraction she feels for her hairdresser boss is thwarted when he marries a richer woman; when she returns with her mother to their village, it is only to find that her cousin has married too. In the end, however, we are led to believe that she is the winner. She opens her own hairdressing salon and is highly successful. Meeting her former boss in the street one day, she is struck by how much he has changed; but she cannot pause for long, since she has to collect the day's takings from her business.[31]

In the period since the Second World War, the pace of social change has quickened. In particular, the revolutionary decade of the 1950s had a major impact on every country and society in the Arab world, and in several societies that provided a conducive context for a further expansion of woman's role in society. The almost inevitable tensions that arose as women began to enter the workplace in Egypt are well portrayed in several of the vignettes in the Egyptian Najīb Maḥfūẓ's interesting work, *al-Marāyā* [Mirrors]. In fact, the narrator himself draws a specific contrast between the arrival in his office of 'Abda Sulayman in 1944 (the first woman to be appointed a civil servant in the secretarial department) and Camelia Zahran in 1965 ('old faces . . . had all disappeared, and a new wave of civil servants, half of them members of the fair sex, had invaded the scene').[32] These societal transformations, and a gradual but palpable increase in publication opportunities, have both been reflected in the output of short stories by female authors that take up the subject of the changing role of women in contemporary Arab society.

The situation described by Maḥfūẓ in *al-Marāyā* is seen in an entirely different light in the Egyptian Nawāl al-Sa'dāwī's *Mawt ma'ālī al-wazīr sābiqan* [Death of an ex-Minister].[33] A minister, who believes that a woman's place is in the home, narrates a sequence of events as he finds himself confronted with a female employee who, while punctilious in her duties, stares him straight in the eye and steadfastly refuses to be overawed by his masculine presence. The situation obsesses him to such an extent that he loses his concentration during an important meeting and is fired. In this story not only do we find a woman serving as a professional in the workplace, but we also learn the details concerning this clash of traditional male expectations and more modern professional norms from a male narrator. Many other short stories depict women in professional roles from a female perspective. The narrator in Daisy al-Amīr's "Marāyā al-'uyūn" [Mirrors of the Eyes] is annoyed and defiant. A professional woman attending a conference, she is the only female in a mirror-lined hotel restaurant. Withstanding the barrage of stares while she waits for her food to arrive, she eventually returns to her room in disgust.[34] For the air-stewardess narrator of the Egyptian Zaynab Rushdī's "Taṭābuq al-muwāṣafāt" [Congruence of Specifications], an encounter with a male passenger on a flight from Cairo to Paris brings childhood memories flooding back, but she is frustrated when, upon arrival in the French capital, the man prefers to visit the Louvre on his own.[35]

Stories such as these depict the wide variety of situations and reactions as women enter the professional workplace within the urban business environment. It should, of course, be emphasized that the traditional norms among the poorer classes of society and in the countryside have always permitted, indeed expected, women to work alongside their male counterparts. Such venues have not in general been the favourite topics of writers of modern Arabic fiction, most of whom by both background and predilection have preferred to focus on the urban middle class and its multi-faceted problems. Among notable recent portraits of the struggles and aspirations of poorer women is Salwā Bakr's deliciously ironic narrative, "Zīnāt fī janāzat al-ra'īs" [Zīnāt at the President's Funeral], in which the protagonist succeeds in extending her small hovel and expanding the scope of her 'business' with the local schoolchildren against a backdrop of attempts to communicate with the president by letter, initiatives that come to an abrupt end when the president dies.[36]

In those societies where traditional norms are prevalent, the process of change has begun relatively later. In Saudi Arabia, for example, the short story is fulfilling its illustrative and didactic function through a number of interesting insights into the lives and aspirations of women, and at the hands of both male and female authors. A primary focus of developments in the lives of women has been that of education. The Saudi writer Khayriyya al-Saqqāf, for example, writes about a girl who is called home from her boarding school in the middle of term to learn from her parents that they have arranged her marriage. The title, "Ightiyāl al-nūr fī majrā al-nahr" [Assassination of Light at the River's Flow], may be somewhat melodramatic, but it says a great deal about the way in which one contemporary Saudi writer regards this way of destroying a woman's aspirations for an education and possibly a career.[37]

War is one effective vehicle for challenging and often destroying prevailing societal values. Civil war, in particular, may radically dislocate traditional norms; the aftermath of such tragic conflicts rarely, if ever, permits a return to the *status quo ante*. Women writers of fiction in Lebanon have clearly viewed the civil war in their homeland as such a transforming event; their literary contributions have of necessity placed them in the vanguard of discussions concerning the changing role of women within Arab society and the depiction of it in fictional genres. Ghāda al-Sammān (b. 1942) and Emily Naṣrallāh (b. 1938), from Syria and Lebanon respectively, have written short stories and longer works that provide graphic illustration of the horrors involved and reflect on the crucial anchoring force that women try to provide in such circumstances, often in the face of insuperable odds.[38] In two separate studies of Lebanese women's fiction, Miriam Cooke and Evelyn Accad have shown clearly the way in which the utterly inhuman and illogical behaviour engendered by the civil war has forced women into a more self-assertive and aggressive role that challenges many of the givens of that particular society and, at least by implication, of others in the region as well.[39]

As these writers have addressed themselves in their fiction to the unspeakable, endeavouring at the same time to prepare the way for a more logical tomorrow; several of them posit a society in which their own role and rights will be different. The protagonist in the Palestinian Nuhā Samāra's "Wajhān lī imra'a" [Woman with Two Faces] is a schoolteacher who is left to care for her ailing father on her own when her businessman husband decides to accept his company's offer of a posting to Paris. Musing about the drudgery of her married life against the backdrop of the daily destruction of Beirut, she decides to liberate herself. She cuts her luxuriant head of hair (that her husband adores) very short and makes contact with Munaḥ, the handsome leader of a guerrilla cell who is also a friend of her husband. She gives clear voice to the view that, if she has been left by her husband to cope with the insanity of the Lebanese civil war, then the initiative to act in the present so as to prepare for the future is hers; in making that decision she feels no obligation to act on her own or to lead the cloistered life of a dutiful wife to an absent husband.[40]

The Narrative Voice

The emergence of the female voice in the short story in a more individualized and even revolutionary light is, needless to say, a gradual process, and one that is directly connected with the increase in the number of women who have had the interest, not to say the opportunity, to become creative writers. It has often proved frustrating; as Marilyn Booth observes, their reality has tended to be 'shaped and usually constrained by the rigid social expectations surrounding home management and childbearing in marriage as women's prescribed roles'.[41] In other words, a decision to embark upon a writing career has, more often than not, implied adding an extra dimension to the obligations, professional and/or familial, that already exist.

Against this background those women writers who wish to assert their individuality through a new kind of fictional voice have clearly had to seek for different narrative modes of expression. In the realm of the novel, the appearance of Laylā Ba'albakkī's *Anā aḥyā* [I Am Alive] in 1958 is viewed by many critics as a landmark in that process. The very title presents a forceful statement, a challenge. The account of family relationships and feelings is no longer given within the framework of a distanced, omniscient third-person narrative, but shifts to a direct first-person experiential montage. As a French commentator notes, 'What particularly shocked some Arab readers is the frankness with which this young woman tackles the problems involved in family and sexual relationships.'[42] In the early 1960s, the Syrian Colette Khūrī renewed the challenge implied in the title of Ba'albakkī's novel by publishing *Ayyām ma'ahu* [Days with Him] and *Layla wāḥida* [One Night].[43] When Ghāda al-Sammān's collection of short stories, *'Aynāka qadarī* [Your Eyes, My Fate], appeared in 1962, some people assumed that yet another voice was being added to what were often regarded as fictional confessions by women writers. Al-Sammān herself, described by Miriam Cooke as 'someone who seems to treat the whole of life as an absurdist stage, with herself as the main character playing out whatever role suits her at the moment', seems to have been at some pains to cultivate such a persona by publishing some juvenilia in a still later collection, entitled *Ḥubb* [Love]. Here readers find themselves confronted with titles such as "Li-annī uḥibbuka" [Because I Love You], "Ataḥaddāka bi-ḥubbī" [I Defy You with My Love], "Li-mādhā ayyuhā 'l-shaqī?" [Why, Wretch?] and "Kuntu atamannā yā zawjahā" [I Wished, O Husband of Hers].[44] The aim of these writers, as Ḥalīm Barakāt has suggested, is 'to shock and defy society', while, from a more detached historical perspective, Ḥanān 'Awwād notes that the works 'generated heated discussion in literary, social and legal circles'.[45] As late as 1964, in the famous legal case against Ba'albakkī in which she was charged with public obscenity, attempts in Lebanon to put a stop to this confrontational process through court action failed. Following Anwar al-Sādāt's assassination in 1981, Nawāl al-Sa'dāwī emerged from prison more forthright than ever, to write her memoirs of the experience.[46]

But what has been the effect of these efforts on the development of the short story as a literary genre? In a laudatory introduction to Laylā al-'Uthmān's short-story collection, *Fī 'l-layl ta'tī 'l-'uyūn* [In the Night the Eyes Arrive], Ḥannā Mīna finds a difference between the voice in al-'Uthmān's stories and those of 'the many women writers in the Arab world in the second half of this century'. She is not interested, he says:

> in writing for sheer fame, in telling stories that will get some gripe off her chest or present women's matters completely divorced from their social motivation . . . tales confined to the kind of sexual titbits which have bored us to death in the works of some women writers; the volume of cheap animal thrills in them has disgusted us all.[47]

Mīna clearly belongs to a group of writers who have been so shocked by the forthrightness of these contributions to the short story that they would deny them any role in bringing about changes in narrative strategy or, equally significant, in readership.

In the introduction to a collection of short stories by Egyptian women, Yūsuf al-Shārūnī discusses what he regards as one of the major problems associated with the issue of narrative voice. He notes that, in the case of women writers, too many critics confound the difference between author and narrator, assuming the two to be one and the same. In the context of the kind of narrative approach represented by some of the women writers that we have just mentioned, it is interesting to note that al-Shārūnī goes on to attribute this tendency on the part of critics to the fact that:

> the majority of our women writers make use of the first-person narrative voice, the voice of confession, thus giving the impression that they are talking about some personal experience. As a result, the reader does not want to believe that the pronoun only refers to the character in the story and not to the author.[48]

We seem to have some kind of double standard at work here, at least if al-Shārūnī's assessment of the reader's attitude is valid, particularly those readers who are critics. A good deal of modern criticism posits the disappearance of the author. Harold Bloom notes that the current vogue for making authors disappear may be due to what he terms 'Parisian preferences' and that, like shorter skirts, they will certainly reappear.[49] One assumes, however, that he does not envision such a reappearance as taking place within some process of revalidating the intentional fallacy! In the light of the current expansion of women's writing in Arabic literature, it seems particularly important to apply similar critical techniques and standards to writings by authors of either gender and thus to allow Laylā Ba'albakkī, Ghāda al-Sammān and others the right of authorial detachment from the statements and reflections of their fictional protagonists. In retrospect, it seems reasonable to suggest that writers such as Ba'albakkī, al-Sammān and al-Sa'dāwī, whatever one's verdict may be about the literary merits of their fiction, have considerably expanded the creative space within which contemporary writers of both sexes may portray their worlds. In other words, the fictions that they create and the narrative strategies that they employ to bring them into existence are to be regarded as contributions to the technical repertoire of Arabic fiction, quite apart from whatever kind of adjustment of balance or advocacy of change they may be effecting in the broader societal frame.[50]

Turning to the issue of the creative use of gender ambiguity in the narrative voice, one can, of course, cite many well-known examples of the multi-faceted potential of the interplay between the various categories of narrator and protagonist(s) where genders differ. Two pioneers of the short story, the Egyptians 'Isā 'Ubayd and Maḥmūd Taymūr, both make use of the obvious and well-tested strategy of the letter as a means of permitting a female narrator–protagonist to recount her experiences in marriage.[51] But as narrative techniques become less overt and more subtle, the narrative contract is not always satisfactorily concluded. In Yūsuf Idrīs's "Bayt min laḥm", for example, the description of the widow and her three daughters fully matches the title in its emphasis on the corporeal, a depiction that strongly suggests a male narrative voice, and yet at one point the story also contains the following sentence: 'Poor dears! They had yet to learn about the world of men. How could they know that you don't rate a man by his eyesight?'[52]

One might argue that this represents an interpolation of an authorial comment into the narrative, something that occasionally interrupts and even disrupts the fictions of Idrīs, a writer who was often anxious to include within his stories references to the narrative act itself. It might also be suggested that the voice in question is that of the widowed mother. But, if that is the case, it is a unique instance in the story. Here, then, we do not find ambiguity but rather inconsistency. The same may be said of Nawāl al-Sa'dāwī's *Mawt ma'ālī al-wazīr sābiqan*, although it has to be admitted that the narrative artifice is of a more complex variety in that the reader is confronted with a male narrator–protagonist who addresses his story to his mother in the first person.[53] The resulting story provides a telling commentary on the effects of woman's emergence into the workplace on the psychology of male authority figures, but the incorporation of such a large burden of feminist societal content into a short story in which the male protagonist is the teller of the tale produces an inconsistency between narrative voice and character.

One of the more subtle exploiters of the narrative voice in the contemporary Arabic short story is Laylā al-'Uthmān. While one may disagree with Mīna's comments about the motivation of other Arab women writers, his verdict concerning al-'Uthmān's acomplishments is certainly justified in terms of the variety of techniques that she uses. Certain stories seem almost to tease the reader concerning the narrative voice. In "al-Maqhā" [The Café], for example, the first-person narrator is sitting in a crowded café in a state of considerable disillusionment and loneliness. His/her self-reflections proceed to tantalize us: there are comments about the male customers' gleaming shoes that have obviously been shined by their wives while the women's shoes are scruffier, but it is not until we are well into the story that a flashback provides us with a female name and identity to assign to our narrator.[54] In "al-Ru'ūs ilā asfal" [Heads Downwards], we are immediately thrust into the protagonist–narrator's bitter musings: 'I left prison without delay.'[55] If we wonder about the narrator's gender, it cannot be for long, in that we soon discover that he has been imprisoned for eighteen years for murdering his wife. The story consists of the narrator's rediscovery of the outside world mingled with memories of his dysfunctional marriage, an experience which leads him to conclude that, for him at least, life was freer inside prison.

As noted at the beginning of this essay, the roles that women play in society have been a constant, indeed inevitable, topic of the short story in Arabic. The examples mentioned above, a tiny fraction of the output across the Arab world, have attempted to show that women writers are not only contributing new perspectives to the topical corpus of the genre but are participating vigorously in that experimentation in technique that guarantees an interesting future for the genre and its critics. It is one of the short story's most accomplished recent practitioners, Salwā Bakr, who points out that women's writing has an important role in converting and enlightening and that men stand to be the beneficiaries of that process as much as women.[56]

8

Love and the Mechanisms of Power: Kamāl 'Abd al-Jawwād and Sa'īd al-Juhaynī

Richard van Leeuwen

It is well known that the Egyptian author Jamāl al-Ghīṭānī has always maintained close relations with the Nestor of the Arabic novel, Najīb Maḥfūẓ. In the years of his apprenticeship as a writer, al-Ghīṭānī used to frequent the coffee-house gatherings of Maḥfūẓ and his circle and he has never concealed his admiration for the great master. However, although he acknowledges the importance of Maḥfūẓ's work as a source of inspiration for his own writings, he also stresses the difference between them. After all, Maḥfūẓ belongs to an older generation; social circumstances have changed and literature has changed accordingly.[1] Thus, in the eyes of al-Ghīṭānī, the development of literature should at least partly be explained by external factors and the social context.

At first sight, both the lives and the works of Maḥfūẓ and al-Ghīṭānī provide interesting material for comparison, derived partly from the socio-political context. Both authors grew up in revolutionary periods in which Egypt experienced far-reaching transformations. Whereas Maḥfūẓ witnessed the emergence of the Wafdist nationalist movement, al-Ghīṭānī grew up with the slogans of the Nasserist regime and its efforts to build a strong, independent, modern Egypt. Both authors also saw the revolutionary movements' failure to attain their goals, and the subsequent preponderance of the cynical practicalities of everyday politics over idealism and revolutionary euphoria. In the 1930s just as in the 1960s, visions of a radiant future were shattered by the confrontation with reality and the politics of power.

Since both Maḥfūẓ and al-Ghīṭānī have always emphasized their social commitment and the influence of political developments on their work, it is not surprising that these circumstances have left their mark on the *œuvre* of both authors. Apart from these external influences, similarities can also be perceived in more direct forms of intertextuality. Even a superficial glance at al-Ghīṭānī's work shows that he has never been reluctant to draw upon textual sources to incorporate themes, motifs, images and stylistic elements into his novels, and in some of his works echoes of classical Arabic texts and the novels of Maḥfūẓ can easily be traced.[2] Thus, both 'circumstantial evidence' and a close reading of the texts suggest that a study of similarities and differences in the works of Maḥfūẓ and al-Ghīṭānī may be rewarding.

This essay concentrates on two prominent characters in novels which enjoy a central place in the *œuvres* of Maḥfūẓ and al-Ghīṭānī: Kamāl 'Abd al-Jawwād in the *Trilogy*,[3] in particular the second part, *Qaṣr al-shawq* [Palace of Desire]; and Sa'īd al-Juhaynī in *al-Zaynī Barakāt*.[4] The main theme which directly links these two characters is love.

First, the two novels will be briefly discussed and placed in their historical and literary context. Next, the theme of love as it is depicted by both authors with regard to the two characters will be analysed in the context of the representation of the mechanisms of power. As far as the definition of 'power' and the 'mechanisms of power' is concerned, the point of reference has been Michel Foucault's study *Discipline and Punish: the Birth of the Prison*,[5] which is not only a history of the emergence of the penitentiary institutions in Europe but also, and perhaps primarily, an analysis of the mechanisms of the exertion of power and the way they determine social relations, or, in other words, a study of the functioning of power strategies. As various forms of authority, power and visions of liberty play a prominent role in both novels, Foucault's approach may serve as a convenient framework.

The Trilogy *and* al-Zaynī Barakāt

The novels *Bayn al-qaṣrayn* [Palace Walk], *Qaṣr al-shawq* and *al-Sukkariyya* [Sugar Street]—together better known as the *Trilogy*—were first published in the 1950s and completed a series of ambitious, naturalistic novels, situated in Cairo and focusing on the complex interaction of psychological, social and political issues in a changing society. The *Trilogy* covers a fairly long period beginning shortly before the Revolution of 1919, and portrays life in the old Mamluk quarter of Cairo as seen through the eyes of a fairly well-to-do merchant family.

Within this setting a wide range of themes are explored: the political upheavals and intrigues connected with the struggle against the British occupation; the erosion of traditional social structures; the ambiguous cultural attitude towards Europe; the psychological tension deriving from individual and collective quests for freedom; the position of intellectuals; and the friction between emotion and reason, religion and science. In general, the novels analyse the process of social transformation and the relentless march of time, which undermines familiar structures and leaves the characters tentatively searching for new ones. The final episode ends in the 1940s, on the eve of the Free Officers' coup in 1952, which marked the beginning of a new phase in the history of Egypt.

Al-Ghīṭānī's novel *al-Zaynī Barakāt* is also concerned with the tension between continuity and change. The story is situated against the background of the collapsing Mamluk Sultanate in the years 1507–18. The process of disintegration of the state is recorded in the accounts of several characters, grouped around the powerful figure of al-Zaynī Barakāt, who, as an unknown official, is unexpectedly appointed *muḥtasib* (chief inspector of commerce and public morality). Zaynī subsequently acquires enormous power by carefully combining Machiavellian and populist methods. His opposite number is Zakariyā ibn Rāḍī, the head of the intelligence service, who is responsible for the safety and stability of the empire. He eventually helps Zaynī survive the fall of the Mamluk throne and join the ranks of the new rulers, after the Ottoman conquest of Cairo in 1517. *Al-Zaynī Barakāt* was written in 1970–1, shortly after Egypt's catastrophic defeat against Israel (1967) and the death of the revolutionary leader Jamāl 'Abd al-Nāṣir (1970).

Considering their dates of appearance and their main themes, it is not surprising that both the *Trilogy* and *al-Zaynī Barakāt* have been seen as evaluations of the turbulent periods preceding their publication. Hence, the *Trilogy* has become the saga of the birth of modern Egypt, its characters representing various social groups and its psychology reflecting the growth of the Egyptian national identity and intellectual self-awareness. Taken in this sense, the story mainly represents a call for national unity, democracy and reason, as opposed to political discord, repression, authoritarian traditions and obscurantism. The novel treats all these issues as elements in Egypt's struggle to achieve independence and political stability. However, the depth of psychological insight and the care for even the smallest details ensure that the discussion of these broad issues does not remain abstract, but is connected to the innermost feelings of several sharply portrayed individuals.

Likewise, *al-Zaynī Barakāt* has been analysed as an assessment of the

Nasserist era. This seems a logical approach, since the description of the revolutionary *élan* created by the ascendancy of Zaynī, his promises of a better future for the poor segments of the society, his subsequent reluctance to confront a corrupt bourgeoisie and his alliance with the repressive apparatus headed by Zakariyā are among the standard criticisms of Nāṣir by leftist intellectuals. Moreover, Zaynī's preoccupation with internal security and his neglect of the external threat, resulting in the catastrophe of 1517, show a striking resemblance to Egypt's unpreparedness to ward off the Israeli attack in 1967. In both cases, the main exponents of political authority, Nāṣir and Zaynī, remained in power in spite of the failure of their policies.[6]

When seen as 'historical' evaluations, the assessment of both the *Trilogy* and *al-Zaynī Barakāt* is unequivocally negative: the idealism of the Wafd is shattered by political intrigues and repression, and any sense of unity is broken by internal strife; the idealism of Zaynī is corrupted by the mechanisms of political power and opportunism; seemingly bright futures are turned into nightmares, hope is replaced by cynism and despair. In the two novels this cycle from hope to despair is personified by, respectively, Kamāl 'Abd al-Jawwād and Sa'īd al-Juhaynī, whose development is not only determined by external circumstances, but also reflects the psychological attitudes associated with these circumstances. An outline of the main features of both characters seems appropriate here.

First, both Kamāl and Sa'īd are portrayed in particular during their adolescence, that is to say, in one of the formative phases of their personality. Of course, this means that they can be represented as susceptible to ideas structuring their behaviour and thought, responsive to the exertion of authority and the dilemmas it entails in contrast to calls for liberation, and perceptive of processes of change. Both characters more or less embody a phase of transition, which should be seen in the perspective of the periods of uncertainty experienced by Egypt in the 1930s and 1960s. Hence, they are not only often seen as *alter egos* of the authors, but also as a personification of the dilemmas of their time. Their personalities are receptacles in which impressions of the upheavals, atmosphere and intellectual dilemmas are collected.

Second, both Kamāl and Sa'īd are influenced by political idealism and are responsive to revolutionary calls for national liberation, the eradication of injustice and the creation of a new, ideal society. They project their idealism onto one figure, respectively Sa'd Zaghlūl, the foremost leader of the Wafd movement, and al-Zaynī Barakāt. These two represent the hope of the future and an escape from the frustrations suffered by Kamāl and Sa'īd.

Third, both characters are conscious of a far-reaching moral responsibility towards humanity. This partly derives from their religious background, Kamāl having grown up in a particularly rigid religious environment, and Sa'īd as an Azhar student and a disciple of the mystic Shaykh Abū al-Su'ūd. Their moral consciousness and their idealism awaken in them a sense of revolt against the representatives of authority, who seem to foster various forms of injustice and appear as the antithesis to freedom and social harmony.

Finally, both Kamāl and Sa'īd are passionately in love. This love pervades their being, consumes their emotions and is one of the main factors determining the course of their lives.

The following sections will examine these elements, which constitute the essential similarities between the two characters, in the context of the power structures as they are depicted in the two novels. We shall focus on the way in which the representations of love are fitted into these structures of power or, rather, how the exertion of power 'structures' the experience of love. Finally, the consequences of this examination for the possible interpretation of the novels will be discussed.

The Mechanisms of Power

The main argument put forward by Foucault in his study *Discipline and Punish* is that the apparatus which is created to exert power and reproduce power relations is not separated from society, but is rather an integral part of it, manifesting itself in all systems that regulate the functioning of society. The formation of society is thus an exact reflection of the power relations and is, in fact, produced by the exertion of power. It is not only society that is shaped by the power system; individuals, too, are affected as they tend to accommodate their thought and behaviour according to prevailing modes.

In Foucault's view, three mechanisms constitute the fundamental elements of power strategies:

Punishment: In the course of time, the focus of punishment has shifted from the body to the mind. Corporal punishment, common in the Middle Ages, has been transformed into 'corrective' detention, aimed at the mental 'improvement' of the delinquent. This does not mean that the body gradually escaped from the surveillance of the power apparatus. On the contrary, it was incorporated into a more refined system by subjecting it to various forms of discipline and confinement, to suit every individual's role in society. Punishment, as a means of exerting control over the body, was not only for those involved in criminal behaviour, but also came to regulate social behaviour. The body was submitted to a complex set of training programmes, restrictions and regulations, in order to maximize its capabilities as a source of labour.

Hierarchy: The various forms of discipline regulating the body and the mind serve to preserve a hierarchical organization of society, which involves a categorization and division of individuals and groups into ranks, functions, classes, etc. This hierarchy is expressed in social relations, but also in the organization of time and space. In Renaissance Europe, for instance, an awareness of time was gradually introduced which involved an efficient division and use of the 'working day', and the idea that the advancement of time should be equivalent to 'progress' and an organic process of successive events. Of course, since it emphasizes a structural continuity of chronology, this concept of time not only envisages progress as an aim, but also sees tradition as a source of authority.

Surveillance: The power apparatus can only function through an elaborate system of surveillance, observation and registration. All individuals should have their 'duplicate' kept in a file, a textual replica of themselves, preserved in the appropriate section. Each life is scrutinized in order to spot deviant behaviour and threats to the preservation of the social structure, but also to maximize the efficient exploitation of every individual's capabilities for the benefit of society. Again, the surveillance apparatus is not a 'tool' manipulated from above, but rather something impregnated in the individual's consciousness, the mechanisms of social control and moral and social codes, and forms an integral part of everyday life.

It should be kept in mind that, in Foucault's view, power is not in the first instance characterized by its aspects as a repressive apparatus, but rather as the sum of strategies which have developed with the rise to power of certain social classes and which are part of a continuous process of transformation. The power mechanisms have not been 'invented' or preconceived as such, but have grown as the dominant groups sought to control the power relations which already existed and to refine the organization of social relations and labour. Moreover, Foucault's concept is a representation of this power apparatus and an analysis of social relations as deriving from the exertion of power. As such, it can be related to other representations.[7]

In *al-Zaynī Barakāt* the power system is personified by Zakariyā ibn Rāḍī, the head of the intelligence service, and, to a lesser extent, by Zaynī himself. Together they constitute the almost invisible, anonymous power apparatus which manipulates not only the population, but also the visible power structure consisting of the sultan, the Mamluk emirs, the *ulema* and the guilds. For the population, their methods are so impenetrable that a precarious balance between fear and hope emerges and a suggestion of all-embracing power, which facilitates a tight control over the society. Zakariyā and Zaynī see everything and everyone without being seen themselves.

Zakariyā is an extremely proficient and intelligent official who is permanently devising means of enhancing the efficiency of his intelligence apparatus, eventually with the help of Zaynī. To achieve this, Zakariyā conceives four basic methods, which fit neatly into Foucault's representation of power. First, power for Zakariyā is to a certain extent synonymous with the control over one's own body and the bodies of others. It is significant that new inventions in the field of torture are introduced which clearly show a shift from physical to psychological torture, from real pain to a suggestion of pain, from mutilation of the body to mental disfigurement that leaves no physical traces. The aim of these methods is to secure total control over the body and mind of the victims, to preserve their apparent integrity, send them back to their usual environment and manipulate them. Of course, in the eyes of Zakariyā, this 'modernization' represents a major step forward in the history of the power apparatus.[8]

Second, Zakariyā's system is based on a huge secret archive, which contains detailed information on every citizen in the sultanate. These files are kept not only to scrutinize people's behaviour and activities but, more specifically, to register their origins, class, professional status and human preferences. They divide the population into categories, designed to facilitate the choice of methods for their manipulation. Nothing is more threatening to social stability than a person who transgresses the hierarchical boundaries, as Zaynī did when first appointed.

Third, Zakariyā's organization consists of a vast number of spies, recruited from all strata of society and bound by a rigid discipline. This organization stands in the service of truth, knowledge and stability. It also enables Zakariyā to know the weak spots of every individual, which subsequently allows him to conquer and manipulate the person's soul. The ultimate goal of which Zakariyā longingly dreams is that every citizen will be transformed into a docile spy and informer under his control, and that new methods will enable him to look into the souls of people, to know their future and to rival the perfect methods utilized by God, the All-knowing.[9]

In Maḥfūẓ's *Trilogy* authority is embodied in the forceful figure of Sayyid Aḥmad 'Abd al-Jawwād, Kamāl's father. He is a paragon of physical power and beauty, rigorously dividing his life between responsibilities and pleasure, and imposing a rigid discipline upon his family. He is conscious of a strict hierarchical division concerning the subordination and discipline of women and children, and of the importance of class and social status. Moreover, he is omnipresent in the conscience of all, only slightly relieving the pressure during his absence. His punishments include beatings, scolding and seclusion. The pillars of his authority are religion, in both its rigid and more tolerant forms, and tradition, which legitimizes the continuation of hierarchical divisions. Of course, Sayyid Aḥmad does not represent an organized apparatus, such as Zakariyā's; he rather represents a model in which both the psychological and the institutionalized aspects of power are reflected.[10]

Thus both the *Trilogy* and *al-Zaynī Barakāt* provide a description of the power apparatus that is largely compatible with that of Foucault's study. In all these novels, the mechanisms of power are not merely mentioned, but form an essential element of the story and are carefully elaborated to pervade the tale in all its layers and themes. Their importance is only balanced by one other force: love.

Love and Power

Neither Kamāl 'Abd al-Jawwād's love for 'Ayida nor Sa'īd al-Juhaynī's love for Samāḥ can be dissociated from the context of the power systems as represented by the figures of Sayyid Aḥmad, Zakariyā and Zaynī. Their passions should primarily be seen in relation to their urge to revolt against the authority imposed upon them. Sa'īd looks upon Zakariyā and his service as the ultimate incarnation of repression and arbitrariness, while his beloved is associated with visions of a future world without injustice or tyranny. In the case of Kamāl, the experience of love is embedded in a complex process, which is set in motion by his efforts to define his personality *vis-à-vis* his father's authority. His urge to revolt is thus connected to the broader set of father–son relations.

It is no coincidence that both Kamāl and Sa'īd's 'love-affairs' remain platonic. Both men swoon even at the thought of a touch from their beloved, if only indirectly, through an object which has been touched by her, the air that she has breathed or a glance in their direction. The existence of the beloved is spiritual rather than physical; the lovers are incapable of imagining her naked body or associating her with the physical aspects of love. In connection with her, the act of love seems infinitely vulgar and incompatible with the sincerity of the turbulent emotions that their love stirs.

This attitude is not due merely to the social codes imposing the seclusion of women and the segregation of the sexes. After all, Kamāl and Sa'īd are surrounded by friends who indulge in the physical pleasures of love. Moreover, 'Ayida is not inhibited by moral conventions or restrictions and mingles freely with her brother's friends. This relative accessibility of his beloved in fact increases Kamāl's agony. Thus, it is not only the beloved's unattainability as a woman that is tantalizing, but rather the suggestion that she belongs to another world which cannot be affected by anything material or human. 'Ayida and Samāḥ are angels rather than human beings.[11]

This notion can be related to the lovers' image of their own body as it is shaped by the structure of power: they do not own their bodies, since they are the product of external forces and cannot be identified as an integral part of their person. Kamāl is 'owned' by his father, and any use of his body outside the range of his surveillance and discipline lies in the realm of taboos and prohibitions. These taboos are reflected in his repugnance at his own physical appearance and his aversion to sex as something associated with squalor and unpleasant smells. For Sa'īd, too, sex is a symptom of evil, which is incompatible with moral integrity. Kamāl is only able to overcome his aversion when several parts of his life and personality are incorporated into a more or less mechanical schedule, modelled on the example of his father: a separation between love and sex, and between responsibilities and pleasure. Still, he longs for the day when man will be freed from physical yearnings.[12]

The fact that in both cases the beloved belongs largely to the world of fantasy is obviously of major importance, both in the field of psychology and concerning the relations with the power systems. Sa'īd and Kamāl are both involved in a search for their identity and a definition of their relations with their environment. This search entails a vision of reality which embraces love as well as politics, or rather, which is built on idealized concepts of love and social relations. In their efforts to define their personalities as separate human beings, detached from the systems of power, they clasp to themselves the images of the beloved, which in the first instance are more properly self-images, or reflections of narcissism. This corresponds with a process of psychological evolution towards the building of an ego, which presupposes a distortion of the perception of reality in order to establish controllable relations with the environment and to formulate the nature of these relations. In this sense, the beloved should by definition be unattainable in order to preserve the 'construction' of the ego. However, the fixation on this image is a tragic force which tends increasingly to alienate the lovers from reality and eventually leads to a form of self-destruction.[13]

The essentially imaginary nature of Kamāl's and Sa'īd's loves does not imply that they are not affected by the forces of reality, even in the characters' own perception. Both lovers are aware of the social hierarchy which impedes their contacts with their beloved and renders her beyond their reach even if she were seen as a part of reality. Class differences, as depicted in the *Trilogy* and *al-Zaynī Barakāt*, involve various aspects such as social prestige and wealth, but also cultural orientation and political outlook. It is significant that in both novels the family of the beloved is, at least initially, rising to social prominence, while Kamāl and Sa'īd experience a deep sense of stagnancy. The beloved is identified with 'progress', upward social mobility and incorporation into the power systems, while the lovers remain marginal, excluded from the main upward streams and unable to catch up with time. Partly due to his past passion, Kamāl eventually sees himself as an anachronism, stuck somewhere between the past and the present, living on his memories or, indeed, not living at all. Sa'īd finally loses his consciousness of time as a result of the torture to which he has been subjected by Zakariyā.[14]

Even if the two lovers refuse fully to acknowledge the all-powerful role of social reality, it is unequivocally demonstrated by the course of events. 'Ayida eventually marries one of Kamāl's friends, Ḥasan Salīm, a diligent and intelligent student from a prosperous background, who has a brilliant career in front of him. Samāḥ is likewise married to a promising young official. Sa'īd's former idol, al-Zaynī Barakāt, is prominently present at the wedding. Both Kamāl and Sa'īd are tempted to challenge the exponents embodying their defeat, Kamāl by physically threatening Ḥasan, Sa'īd by denouncing Zaynī in a public display of revolt.

Surveillance and observation play a crucial role in the two love-stories and their inevitable dénouement. Kamāl's disillusionment is exacerbated when he hears that his secret love has been known by all for a long time, that he has been laughed at by 'Ayida and her family, and that his shy and clumsy behaviour has been observed by his friends. Having previously been watched by his father, his inner life is now transparent to his friends, who represent various constituents of the power system. Moreover, he notices that he has been manipulated as a powerless object in 'Ayida's schemes to arouse the jealousy of the arrogant Ḥasan Salīm. His only refuge from this humiliation is to humiliate and torture himself still further, conceding to his voyeuristic curiosity and hiding in the dark to observe the bridal chamber in 'Ayida's villa on the wedding night.

Observation becomes the tool of his destruction, since it reveals his powerlessness *vis-à-vis* reality and shatters his illusionary ego. In the end Kamāl uses it himself to bring about his final collapse.[15]

The story of Sa'īd follows much the same line. Of course, Zakariyā watches Sa'īd carefully as a potentially rebellious element among the Azhar students. He immediately realizes that Sa'īd's love for Samāḥ is his fundamental weakness, which makes him vulnerable to various forms of manipulation and mental pressure. When the confrontation finally occurs, it is suggested that Sa'īd is forced to watch a violent act of love-making between his beloved and her husband, a scene which drains all his will-power and turns him into an automaton who is completely under Zakariyā's control. Again, the act of observation is not only a strategic weapon of the power apparatus; it also seals the destruction of the self-image of the victim.[16]

It is noticeable that, in the mind of the two lovers, Samāḥ and 'Ayida are not individual women, but rather symbols of womanhood. As such, they are in no way affected by the trivialities of the power mechanisms. They are immune to the manifold dilemmas that frequently throw both Kamāl and Sa'īd into despair. As paragons of perfection, they symbolize the lovers' own craving for a harmonious personality, a coherent ego, that is not subservient and fettered by the mechanisms of control. They are the symbols of freedom, unaffected by the restrictions of reality and of the power systems. They are the symbols of the ideal world, in which the realization of love is intimately related to the extermination of injustice and moral corruption. They are the symbols of mental liberation, in the case of Kamāl connected with the discovery of rational philosophy as opposed to religion and in the case of Sa'īd through the submersion in mystical experiences. Finally, they are the symbols of the escape from power relations into a world where all power systems are effaced by the force of love.

Two Concepts of History

In the foregoing, a structural congruity has been noticed between the characters of Kamāl and Sa'īd as far as they are shaped by their loves and by the mechanisms of power as they are represented in the novels. When such significant similarities can be perceived, the differences between the two figures become the more interesting. Here we shall discuss some of the most important differences and their impact on the possible interpretations of the novels.

The first noticeable difference between the characters of Kamāl and

Sa'īd is that Kamāl is much more 'organically' incorporated into his environment than Sa'īd, especially with regard to his psychological development. It is no coincidence, of course, that the main exponent of the power system is Kamāl's father. This means not only that the analysis of the relations between Kamāl and the power system becomes more complex, but also that these relations are placed in a framework of historical continuity. Sayyid Aḥmad is not only the model of the power apparatus which shapes Kamāl's psychological evolution; as a father, he also has a decisive influence on Kamāl's search for an identity. This identity is embedded in the wider framework of Kamāl's relations with his mother and his brothers and sisters, which serves as a set of premises that can explain the successive phases of Kamāl's development in a more or less naturalistic, or even Freudian fashion. Thus, Kamāl's psychological growth is deeply rooted in his environment and is seen as part of a process of evolution which corresponds to a notion of historical continuity.

In the case of Sa'īd, no such relationships or psychological evolution are described. Whereas Kamāl's evolution reflects an internalization of the complex mechanisms of the power system, Sa'īd seems to stand apart from his environment as an individual who is shaped mainly by external influences. He represents the individual who is not integrated into an evolutionary process, but stands alone in the confrontation with a merciless power apparatus. There is little effort to explain the course of this confrontation as deriving from a historical process or the logic of psychological growth.

Second, as in the description of individual psychology, the development of the power structure is represented in the *Trilogy* as a process which basically reflects a structural historical continuity. Changes are carefully placed into the chains of cause and effect, and not treated as the coincidental result of events or individual choices. The process of transformation is analysed in its successive phases, from the power monopoly of Sayyid Aḥmad, the gradual erosion of his authority, the struggle of Kamāl's friends to become part of the new power system and, finally, the appropriation of the power monopoly by the state. This description is intended as a reconstruction of Egypt's evolution as part of a historical reality.[17]

In the case of Sa'īd, no 'natural' evolution is suggested. The course of events seems to be determined by the personal ambitions and schemes of Zakariyā and Zaynī, and even by supernatural forces, rather than by a meticulously reconstructed chain of cause and effect. There is no structural evolution of history, but only a 'structure' of power, which survives in all ages. Sa'īd's development is not part of an evolution, but is one of the fields for the eternal battle between the individual and the power apparatus.

Of course, this difference in approach has a bearing upon the interpretation of the love experiences of the two characters. Kamāl's love for 'Ayida is in the first instance described as an element of his psychological growth and his search for identity. It is set within the framework of time and place and is identifiable as a product of the environment of both Kamāl and 'Ayida, and of the inner transformation of Kamāl. In a metaphorical sense, 'Ayida is easily recognizable as a covetable symbol of a new 'social order' and a certain vision of Egypt, free of the inhibitions imposed by tradition, fostering a rational, secular philosophy and unrestrictedly oriented towards Europe. This metaphorical quality is further extended in the third part of the *Trilogy*, when 'Ayida has divorced her 'captor' and has fallen back into poverty and triviality. In both cases, Kamāl's love-story is connected with a certain era in the development of Egypt and as such is part of a reconstruction of historical reality.

Although Samāḥ, Sa'īd's beloved, can be seen as a metaphor for Egypt, her metaphorical meaning is much more abstract. Sa'īd's love is not placed within the chain of historical developments or within a psychological evolution, and is not elaborately integrated into its historical setting. Samāḥ is rather a 'meta-historical' metaphor of a just society, which is corrupted and subsequently destroyed by the power apparatus. She is not part of a reconstructed historical reality, but rather one of the constituents of the mechanisms of power as they may occur in any time, in any place. Whereas the *Trilogy* primarily deals with love as a psychological phenomenon of which the mechanism of power is only a part, *al-Zaynī Barakāt* should be seen as an analysis of the mechanisms and psychology of the exertion of power, of which love is only a part.

The difference noted above is particularly apparent when the separate narrative elements and their relationship—Kamāl and Sa'īd, love and power—are seen in their narrative context. It can essentially be ascribed to two different concepts of history, or at least to a different way of integrating history into the story. At first sight, both stories follow the methods of the historical novel: they give a detailed description of a certain period; they include historical events, historical figures and even historical texts to enhance the suggestion of reality; and they both offer an interpretation of an era from a contemporary perspective. In general, this genre is connected with the formative phases of nation states—the definition of a collective identity, the ascendancy of certain classes and the reassessment of the meaning of certain historical events—and serves to present a basically ideological reinterpretation of historical transformations.[18]

Since the *Trilogy* concerns the growth of independent Egypt, it can easily be identified as an exponent of the classical concept of the historical novel. It aims to reconstruct and explain an evolutionary process through the eyes of its main characters and by complementing historical facts with fictional elements to achieve a comprehensive view. It is concerned with the search for a national identity which is enclosed in the folds of history. Although in *al-Zaynī Barakāt* the care for detailed description and historical accuracy may suggest that a resuscitation of a past era is intended, the way in which the historical material is incorporated into the story suggests the contrary. Whereas Maḥfūẓ traces events and links them to the individual lives of the characters to constitute a coherent, organic whole, al-Ghīṭānī puts the elements of his story together in a much more fragmented way. No evolutionary process can be discerned explaining the course of events in a coherent fashion. Whereas Maḥfūẓ moulds his story to make it conform to the historical process, al-Ghīṭānī moulds history to make it fit into his story.

Al-Ghīṭānī's apparent intention was not to reconstruct a bygone era, or to offer a reinterpretation of past events, but to use the representation of a past era to illustrate a theme. This theme is not bound to any historical period, although it is associated more with some periods than with others, and historical evidence can thus be useful to expose the essence of the theme in question. In the case of *al-Zaynī Barakāt*, the Mamluk era is represented as a paramount example of the way in which the mechanisms of power functioned; it serves to depict these mechanisms and the psychology of the oppressor and its victims in their essence. However, it is not oppression in history which interests al-Ghīṭānī, but oppression as a meta-historical phenomenon, occurring in all ages. Paradoxically perhaps, this sense of timelessness is enhanced by the use of historical material in a way which rejects any direct link of the theme with only the past, or only the present.

Conclusion

Of course, it is impossible fully to explore such a complex subject as the theme of love and power in the *Trilogy* and *al-Zaynī Barakāt* in the scope of one essay. Nevertheless some tentative conclusions can be formulated.

First, a structural congruity can be perceived between the characters of Kamāl in the *Trilogy* and Sa'īd in *al-Zaynī Barakāt*, as far as their love for 'Ayida and Samāḥ respectively is concerned. This congruity becomes more prominent when related to the representation of the power mechanisms in both novels. In both cases, the interrelationship between love and power seems to be the main factor determining the characters' evolution and eventual downfall.

Second, the way in which this interrelationship is embedded in the narrative framework indicates a different perception of history, or at least a different fashion of integrating history and fictional writing. In the *Trilogy* the main love-story is a significant element in the description of the evolutionary process experienced by Kamāl and by Egypt in a defined period; in *al-Zaynī Barakāt* historical material is used to create a collage which elucidates the theme of the confrontation of the individual with the mechanisms of power.

These observations lead to a final remark. Whereas it seems plausible to see the *Trilogy* as an evaluation of Egypt's history in the inter-war period, especially in the light of Maḥfūẓ's treatment of history, the argument seems less strong in the case of *al-Zaynī Barakāt*. Here, the interpretation of the novel as an assessment of the Nasserist regime should be supplemented with at least one more layer: an analysis of the functioning and psychology of power at all times and in all places.

9

Fathers and Husbands: Tyrants and Victims in some Autobiographical and Semi-Autobiographical Works from the Arab World

Hartmut Fähndrich

Some time ago, Edwār al-Kharrāṭ, today one of the most eminent literary figures in the Arab world, was asked what might seem a strange question, to which he gave what might seem a surprising answer.[1] The famous Egyptian novelist was asked whether 'the Arabic novel' exists or, to put it differently, whether one may justly talk about 'the Arabic novel'. Edwār al-Kharrāṭ's reply was in the negative. No, he said, it is no longer justified to subsume all novels written in the area between the Gulf and the Atlantic under the same label—except, of course, if one wants to talk about nothing but the fact of these works' being written in the Arabic language. This, however, would force us to omit an important number of novels, particularly from north-west Africa, written in French. But language, argues al-Kharrāṭ (and his reasoning is now accepted by many others), is not the only criterion for the classification or grouping of literary works. Style, imagery, themes, and so on, must also be taken into consideration.

On the basis of these criteria it seems reasonable, and even necessary, to differentiate between all the literature produced in the Arab world according to region and/or country. This is something that other Arab critics[2] apart from al-Kharrāṭ and also Western Arabists have been proposing, even when acknowledging similarities between Arabic novels in terms of problems treated, prevailing moods and ways of thinking. An interesting attempt in this direction—that of pinning down the regional literary particularities of Arabic literature—was presented in an article by

Hilary Kilpatrick[3] some years ago. Basing her argument on three modern Arabic novels from three different regions, the author shows that 'these three novels chosen at random from the same period bring out the variety in the contemporary Arabic novel in form, subject and style' and that they 'reflect specific aspects of the countries which have produced them'.[4]

To continue in this line, one could, for example, go further back in the history of modern Arabic prose and compare the two short stories that have been considered the point of departure for the modern Arabic short story: "Sanatuhā 'l-jadīda" [Her New Year] by the Lebanese Mīkhā'īl Nu'ayma,[5] originally published in 1914, and "Fī 'l-qiṭār" [In the Train] by the Egyptian Muḥammad Taymūr,[6] originally published in 1917. These two stories, while both treating essentially socio-political problems, are profoundly different from each other. Nu'ayma deals with family problems: the relationship between husband and wife, the lack of importance given to daughters as opposed to sons, and so on. Muḥammad Ṭaymūr, on the other hand, deals in the framework of an exclusively male group with problems that are more immediately related to the welfare of the country as a whole, especially the question of the education of the masses. There are also stylistic differences: whereas Nu'ayma's language is poetic with a touch of gentle irony, that of Ṭaymūr is much more sober and matter-of-fact.

Two caveats may conclude this brief introduction, for the debate about orientalism has taught us to be aware of orientalists' fallacies and misdeeds. First, there are inevitably certain political implications or consequences inherent in the particular argument developed in the present essay. The purpose, however, is not to divide up the body of Arab[7] literature but only to examine to what extent literary expression varies within the Arab world. Second, it remains to be seen to what extent possible differences are derived from outside the realm of literature or, in other words, do not belong to the stuff of which literature is made.

In the following pages I shall present one thematic and stylistic feature that would support the idea of a regional differentiation of Arab literature. The point of departure is an idea that occurred to me when reading the novel *Le chemin des ordalies* [published in English as *Rue du retour*][8] by the Moroccan poet and critic Abdellatif Laābi. Laābi was born in 1942 into a middle-class family in Fez. He studied French in Rabat and then worked as a secondary school teacher from 1965 until 1972. Beginning in 1966 and until it was forbidden in 1972, he, together with some friends, published *Souffles*, a literary and later a more generally cultural magazine, the purpose of which was formulated by Laābi himself as follows: 'It was absolutely essential to get away from the folkloric, ethnographic image that people wanted to give to life in the Maghreb. We had to stop writing for an audience in the ex-mother country.'[9] In 1973 he was sentenced to ten years in prison for 'disturbance of the public order'. Released in 1980 as a consequence of international pressure, he left Morocco shortly after and has since been living in Paris. His literary work consists of poetry, prose and also plays.

In *Le chemin des ordalies*, a novel which may justly be called largely autobiographical, Laābi has one phrase relevant to the topic of this essay. He makes the narrator remember his childhood and then remark that he cannot boast of a ruthless and brutal father whom he had to hate or even to kill. His father, he continues, was a peaceful man, quiet, modest, industrious and pious:

> Since when had you not obeyed? From circle to circle you reach back to your childhood. You rummage through your memory and paradoxically you don't find anything. Obedience? Unknown. Your father was not one of those paterfamilias who haunt many stories set around the edge of the Mediterranean and the Arab world. The dictator in his room, the indestructible kernel of the family and solid unit around which gravitate all economic activity, the dominant ideology, arranged marriages, divorce by decree, religious rituals and festivals. The trunk of a genealogical tree and the hand of Providence in everything. He was a good-natured small craftsman who left each day to go to work at six o'clock in the morning and came back at eight in the evening. Except on Fridays. A highly precise machine at work in our own apparently drifting and lethargic society, turning its back on productive work. This small artisan had managed to send all his children to the 'French-Muslim' school so that they might learn the language of power of those days and understand the mystery of that power.[10]

This is obviously not the kind of man of despicable character fit to represent, or even to personify, a despicable culture and a despicable society as presented by other North African authors, to whom the passage seems to make a silent reference. This silent reference develops into a scream when viewed within the framework of recent Maghrebi literature from the mid-fifties onwards.

It was in 1954 that a book was published which was to become a model for not a few authors: in it we find the prototype of a father against whom the sons revolt or whom they leave if they are not killed by him.[11] When first published in Morocco, *Le passé simple* [The Simple Past][12] by

Driss Chraïbi caused a scandal.[13] Chraïbi was born in 1926 in al-Djadida, Morocco. He first went to a Qur'anic school, then to the Lycée Lyautey in Casablanca. In 1945 he left for Paris to study medicine, then chemistry. He travelled all over Europe earning his living by taking a variety of jobs. For a long time he has been working as a free-lance writer, living mostly in France, sometimes in Morocco. His literary output so far consists of twelve novels.

Le passé simple, a rather conventional linear narrative in the first person singular, is a markedly autobiographical novel presenting a family triangle that consists of a father, a mother and a son. All other figures of the novel are but extensions of these three, employed here to analyse an essential part of the traditional social structure, as the author sees it.[14]

The father, called 'Seigneur' (and here we recall the 'Sayyid' of Najīb Maḥfūẓ's *Trilogy*, who, however, possesses more humane traits), is not merely a father, but the spokesman for a whole social order, divinely sanctified; he is the embodiment of power, force, ruthlessness and ignorance and thus represents traditional Islamic society, a society considered to be patriarchal and repressive. This society as represented by the father becomes the son's obsession, leading to delirious outbursts. The mother, on the other hand, is weakness and submissiveness personified. She has neither name nor will and is completely at her master's/husband's whim; thus she becomes the victim of a tradition depicted as dreadful and even murderous.[15] The son observes this situation with horror and suffers from it. He develops a profound hatred of his father and a certain disgust in relation to his mother, feelings that he also has for his uncle and his aunt, whom he conceives of as extensions of his parents.

The father, however, takes a far-reaching decision, which (from his point of view) may even be called a mistake. He sends his son to a French lycée where the boy learns to understand and judge his own society; this increases his feelings of hatred towards his father, whom he reproaches for his hypocrisy. At the same time, Driss, the son, develops a sense of alienation, being torn between the environment of his origin and the French culture then dominant in Morocco which offers the means for individual liberation. In the end, he sets off for France, leaving the final revolt 'for tomorrow', as he puts it. The father stays behind—a tyrant turned victim of his despotic behaviour, which was, after all, nothing but the performance of his social duty: to be the one almighty master on earth, as there is only one Almighty Master in heaven. It never occurred to him to question this set-up—a devastating criticism by the author of traditional Islamic Moroccan society, which is seen as petrified and thus incapable of change or development/progress by itself.

The main theme of *Le passé simple*—the father as a personification of a rotten tradition, as an obstacle to the development of his sons (to say nothing of his daughters) and as a brutal animal towards his wife—has been formulated and reformulated in numerous variations in Maghrebi literature ever since. For example, Driss Chraïbi himself continued along these lines in *Succession ouverte* [Open Succession][16] and *La civilisation, ma mère!* [Civilization, Mother!][17] Two novels by another Moroccan, Abdelhak Serhane, *Messaouda* and *Les enfants des rues étroites* [Children of the Narrow Streets],[18] deal extensively with the father-as-brute theme. A particularly famous (or notorious) example of this kind of novel that settles accounts with the tradition in which the narrator grew up (Islamic Maghrebi) is *La répudiation* [The Repudiation],[19] the first novel by the Algerian writer Rachid Boudjedra.

Boudjedra[20] was born in 1941 in the Algerian village of Ain Beïda near Constantine where he went to a Qur'anic school. He actively participated in the anti-colonial struggle, then in 1962 began his studies in Algiers, and later continued them in Paris. He lives in Algiers. Though he wrote his first novels in French, Boudjedra has used Arabic as his language of literary expression since 1981. In *La répudiation*, Rachid, the narrator, tells the story or, rather, the drama of his life to his French girlfriend, thus showing his alienation from the civilization of his origin and his orientation towards France, the colonial power that, in spite of everything, offers the intellectual tools for emancipation. And emancipation seems necessary from a society marked in the novel by blood, which carries a variety of meanings. At times, it is the symbol of life, mixed frequently with milk in the narrator's visions or nightmares; at other times, it symbolizes pain, torture or victimization, the foremost victim being a 15-year-old girl taken by the 50-year-old father as a second wife.

Nowhere in the book is there an open rebellion by the humiliated against their oppressor, for the father derives the justification for his behaviour from religion, which thus proves to be a repressive system, the ideological arm of patriarchal claims to power. And the fact that the narrator ends up in a mental asylum is meant to prove that fathers who abandon their paternal responsibilities but retain their private and public power are responsible for their children's neuroses and, ultimately, for the sickness of their society.

There is another group of literary works that are even more immediately autobiographical than the ones mentioned so far. This group has been called *littérature de Tanger* (Tangier literature), due to its place of origin, or *littérature au magnétophone* (tape-recorder literature), due to its strongly oral nature.[21] One of its most characteristic works is the novel by the Moroccan Mohamed Choukrī, *al-Khubz al-ḥāfī* [For Bread Alone].[22] It shows the childhood and adolescence of a boy whose whole life in traditional society consists of hunger, violence (frequently inflicted by his father or his mother's husband), drugs and sex in the form of prostitution. The narrator here learns about his society through hunger, just as Driss in *Le passé simple* learns about his society by going to a French school.[23]

In all these novels, the father is well-embedded in the traditional society; he is considered its personification, its representative. The mother, on the other hand, is only its victim, just as are the children. The children, however, and the sons in particular, are given the possibility of breaking out of this society by revolting, openly or covertly, against their father and by leaving their family and their society, in other words, their original cultural environment. It is the familiar topic of the revolt of sons against fathers, turned into a metaphor for cultural change in north-west African Islamic society. And whenever the target of the author/narrator is not the traditional society but rather, for example, a foreign occupation force, we do not find a father. The most striking example here is Mohamed Dīb's *Trilogy*,[24] where the father is conspicuous by his absence. In the novel, traditional society is depicted as wretched, but the narrator's criticism is not immediately directed at this society. In other words, the author does not find fault primarily with traditional Islamic values but with the occupier's impact on society. The mother is very similar to those creatures found in the other novels—oppressed, wretched and suffering—but here she is a victim not of the father but of the situation created by foreign intervention.

Thus it appears that a description like Laābi's of the father as peaceful, quiet, modest, industrious and pious signifies a less hate-ridden attitude on the part of the narrator/author towards the environment of his/her origin.

Turning our attention away from the Maghreb to the Mashreq, and more specifically to Egypt, we immediately notice a remarkable difference, at least as far as autobiographical works written by male authors are concerned. Taking two classic Egyptian autobiographies as examples, Ṭāhā Ḥusayn's *al-Ayyām* [The Days], volumes 1 and 2,[25] and Tawfīq al-Ḥakīm's *Sijn al-'umr* [Prison of Life],[26] we find father-figures who might well be considered personifications of sections of the traditional society but who differ considerably from the fathers in the above-mentioned works by Chraïbi, Boudjedra, Choukrī and others.

In both works, we find fathers performing their social role or duty: to introduce their children (sons, more exactly) to the demands society places on them, and to their future role in a society that the fathers strive to preserve the way it is. To succeed in their task, the fathers may use anything from persuasion and authority to physical punishment. In contrast to the Maghrebi works, however, the general atmosphere is never gloomy or unfriendly, and certainly not inhuman; the language is never harsh or hostile, and certainly not vulgar. Thus, even the relationship between father and mother is not based on absolute despotism on the one hand and absolute submissiveness on the other. There is, to be sure, a gap between the different functions which men and women, husbands and wives, are demanded or forced by their environment to perform, but we look in vain for the outright hostility, the completely shattered relationship between husband and wife, that is so conspicuous in Maghrebi literature.

The first volume of *al-Ayyām*, Ṭāhā Ḥusayn's (1889–1973) autobiography (covering the blind narrator's childhood in an Egyptian village), is interesting in this context. There are recollections in it of a time when, as a little boy, he could still see. There are also descriptions of a number of embarrassing situations when, already blind, he did not behave 'properly'. However, it is only 'physical blindness' that the narrator suffers from in his native village. The phenomenon of 'social blindness'[27] is hardly experienced before the boy leaves to take up his studies in Cairo. The reason for this comparatively happy childhood lies in the family situation and the boy's positive relationship with both his father and his mother.

The father, while certainly a patriarchal figure, is without the horrifying and almost mythical dimensions of his Maghrebi counterparts. The mother, on the other hand, although certainly not a prominent figure, is not as subdued as her Maghrebi counterparts. There is hardly a word of a human relationship between the father and the mother, yet, to the boy, both were sources of warmth and tenderness as well as of harshness and severity, leaving him room to develop without that permanent hostile confrontation or feeling of disgust found, for instance, in *Le passé simple* or in *La répudiation*. Finally, the fact that this fairly acceptable family arrangement is situated in the village and described without any reference to either the big city or Western influence may suggest a certain nostalgia for the author's rural origin including the family pattern.

In *Sijn al-'umr*, Tawfīq al-Ḥakīm (1898–1987) advances several steps in the attempt to understand and analyse his family background. He tells the story of his childhood and youth, starting from his very first day and the traits he inherited from both his father and his mother, and concluding with his departure for Paris in 1926. And here, in the Egyptian bourgeois milieu, which may well be contrasted with the Moroccan milieu presented by Driss Chraïbi, the gap between the father's and the mother's positions is much less wide than in all the other works mentioned so far. There is a mutual understanding and a cooperation—even in financial matters—between the two, and the father is presented as possessing the very human trait of admitting to faults or injustices committed.

As will be seen, the social atmosphere symbolized by the personalities of the father and the mother, and by their relationship with each other, differs radically in the works mentioned from the Maghreb and the Mashreq. This means that the ending has to be interpreted differently in *Le passé simple*, *al-Ayyām* and *Sijn al-'umr*, even though it describes the same phenomenon in each case: the son's departure for Europe.

In *Le passé simple*, it is the father, the 'Seigneur', who sends his son to a modern educational institution so that he will be intellectually equipped to face the modern world as the father envisages it. But the son's French education leads to ever fiercer confrontations with his father which, in the end, exhaust them both. The son's setting off for France has to be understood as a departure from the battleground in which the father has given in.

In the two Egyptian autobiographies referred to, by contrast, the traditional culture is, by and large, not experienced as something hostile by the son (the family relationships make this clear). Thus he is able to see the weaknesses of the society—particularly in the intellectual and literary, but also in the moral field—and try to change things. Ṭāhā Ḥusayn gradually leaves al-Azhar to continue his education at the newly founded Cairo University. And when both Ṭāhā Ḥusayn and Tawfīq al-Ḥakīm, at the end of their early autobiographies, leave Egypt for Europe, it is not to flee from a hated and despised (because despotic) society personified by a father figure, but to widen their intellectual horizons and, after their return, to contribute to the development of their society.

Even more striking than the presentation of the father in Ṭāhā Ḥusayn's and Tawfīq al-Ḥakīm's autobiographies is that given by another Egyptian, Edwār al-Kharrāṭ, in his *Turābuhā za'farān* [City of Saffron].[28] Al-Kharrāṭ was born in 1926 in Alexandria, where he also grew up and later studied law. He spent two years in prison (1948–50) for his participation in nationalist activities. In the fifties, he had various administrative and clerical jobs before accepting, in 1959, the position of Second Secretary-General at the Afro-Asian Peoples' Solidarity Organization, a post he held until his retirement in 1983. He now lives in Cairo.

Turābuhā za'farān tells the story of a childhood in Alexandria during the thirties and forties. In spite of the author's claim to the contrary, it is a strongly autobiographical novel. Here we find a father who is the exact opposite to the 'Seigneur' in *Le passé simple*. This is a man who is often unemployed and living in dire material straits (and for whom the narrator, the son, shows great sympathy); a man who weeps in desperation in front of the crucifix because, time and again, he is unable to support his family. In contrast to, for example, Moḥamed Choukrī's autobiography, material need does not lead to violence and brutality in *Turābuhā za'farān*. The father, here, resembles the sort of man Abdellatif Laābi's narrator describes his father to be—peaceful, quiet, modest, industrious and pious.

And so, too, is the father of Mīkhā'īl Nu'ayma,[29] the Lebanese Christian writer. In his autobiography, *Sab'ūn—ḥikāyat 'umr* [Seventy. The Story of a Life],[30] Nu'ayma remembers and describes his father as one of the victims whom the situation in Lebanon forced to emigrate but who stayed in the memory of those whom he left behind right next to God the Father: the mother of the little boy mentions in her evening prayer the Father in heaven alongside the father in America.

Conclusion

As literary critics of the genre have frequently remarked,[31] modern autobiographical works are based on an ever more acute awareness of the value and importance of the individual human being. At the same time, there seems to be an increasing awareness of a crisis of values (in a very wide sense) that encourages an author to write an autobiography or an autobiographical novel. The reactions, however, to this awareness of the self and of the crisis of values may differ widely. To show these different reactions, authors have used the presentation and interpretation of family relationships or, in particular, of the father figure, who best represents the varying degrees of power exerted by society upon the individual.

The question that concerns us here is whether the interpretations of, or reactions to, these changing circumstances show true regional differences between one part of the Arab world and another. The simplest answer would be to see all differences as merely the result of individual interpretation and style, any regional differentiation then being due to mere chance. There may, on the other hand, be different regional styles, literary traditions or influences that could account for varying treatments of the same subject-matter, for different presentations of the same or a similar reality. The era—and thus a certain political and social mood—may also account for varying attitudes towards the traditional family structure, and towards the father's and mother's roles therein. Finally, differences in the presentation of a social reality may be due to differences in this very reality, the political history, the educational structure, and so on. On the evidence of the very limited number of works examined in this essay, there do appear to be regional differences between the Maghreb and the Mashreq in how family relationships are presented. It would be interesting to explore this point further on the basis of a wider sample.

10

The Foreign Woman in the Francophone North African Novel

Susanne Enderwitz

In Wielandt's study of the image of the European in modern Arabic literature, one chapter is devoted to the European woman.[1] Its conclusions can be summarized as follows: without exception the authors are male, their topic is the sexual relationship between an Arab man and a European woman, and the presentation of the woman (frequently a blue-eyed blonde with libertarian attitudes) corresponds with the author's wishful thinking.

Déjeux's study of the image of the European woman in Arabic literature written in French[2] comes to the same conclusion: here also the beautiful, blonde, feminine woman dominates the scene. Notwithstanding their similarities, the two literatures seem to differ from each other in at least one important aspect. While Arabic prose in the Middle East after the Second World War concentrates mainly on the *sexual* encounter of the Arab-European couple,[3] the Francophone Arabic novel from its beginnings in the twenties focuses on the possibility of a true *love* developing between the partners.[4] Thus the European woman, in spite of all the clichés, sometimes gains a face, a shape and a personality of her own, as the following three examples will illustrate.[5]

We shall concentrate on three works from North Africa: *La terre et le sang* [Earth and Blood] (1950) by the Algerian Mouloud Feraoun (1913–62), *Agar* [Hagar] (1955) by the Tunisian Albert Memmi (b. 1920) and *La répudiation* [The Repudiation] (1969) by the Algerian Rachid Boudjedra (b. 1941). The reasons for this choice are not only the authors' reputations,[6] their different social backgrounds[7] and the publishing dates of their novels,[8] but also the variety of ways in which they treat their subject. Feraoun depicts a marriage that succeeds because of the woman's willingness to adapt to the living conditions of the Algerian peasants.[9] Memmi describes a marriage that fails because of the woman's inability to accept Tunisian social mores. Finally, Boudjedra portrays a love-affair that ends when the balance of mutual benefit to the two partners is disturbed.

La Terre et le Sang

The novel *La terre et le sang*, the second part of a trilogy written by Mouloud Feraoun in the early 1950s, is considered as belonging to the so-called ethnographic branch of Algerian literature. This refers to Feraoun's aim of depicting, with photographic exactness, the way of life in his Kabyle homeland before it is destroyed by modernity.

The leading male character Amer, having worked for many years in a French coal-mine, returns to Algeria. He is accompanied by his young French wife Marie, who is probably his cousin, or rather the illegitimate daughter of his uncle Rabah and a French hotel-owner. While the reader is expecting a clash between the two cultures, Marie, who was brought up in miserable conditions and had several humiliating experiences, now counts herself lucky to have left France and displays a remarkable adaptability right from the beginning:

> Little by little she acquired a taste for her new companions; she lived intensely with these women, who forced her to understand, to make herself understood and to discuss matters. She managed with gestures and mime, which evoked peals of amused laughter. She no longer felt bored and learned the language from everyday life. The words imprinted themselves on her memory, which had no chance to resist, since most words had the same existential importance as the air for breathing: take, give, good, bad, yes, no . . . and then all those polite phrases which express beauty and admiration.[10]

When a catastrophe occurs at the end, it is not Marie who is to blame but a jealous husband who sets off a bomb without warning Amer. On the contrary, Marie becomes the only hope for Amer's family after his death, since she is pregnant with a son, who is the hero of the last part of the trilogy.

Agar

Albert Memmi was born neither Algerian nor Muslim, he is a Tunisian Jew; but in spite of their different backgrounds his novel *Agar* exhibits many similarities with Feraoun's *La terre et le sang*. Both leading male characters have spent many years in France before returning to their native lands, accompanied by their French wives. In neither case is there a serious conflict between the son and his patriarchal father.[11] (Amer's father is already dead at the time of his son's return, while the father in Memmi's novel gives in almost completely to his son's needs.) It is the mothers who tend to be the source of quarrels, since they more or less openly demand that their sons divorce their seemingly sterile wives.[12] A fourth similarity, however, also reveals a fundamental difference between the two novels: at the end of *La terre et le sang*, Marie's pregnancy ensures continuity in spite of Amer's death, while *Agar* ends with an abortion which confirms the wife's return to France.

Memmi's narration, like that of Feraoun, is conventional and linear, although he does not look upon his figures from a bird's-eye view like the omniscient Feraoun, but uses the semi-autobiographical form of the first person, modified by dialogue and reflections. His novel centres on the destiny of a marriage that is condemned to failure from the beginning, since both partners have unrealistic expectations of each other.

After having passed his examination in medicine in Paris, the narrator returns to Tunis, accompanied by his French wife (as in Feraoun's novel, named Marie). He is ambivalent in his attitude towards East and West and feverishly occupied by his search for identity. On the one hand, he needs Marie as an outsider who represents the living example of his ability to make conquests, for this will exempt him once and for all from the necessity to grapple with the conditions he meets with:

> When I remembered my former protests and decisions, I sometimes had a sensation of doubt and defeat. At these moments I used to look at my wife and loved her all the more. Wasn't she there as the living proof of my audacity? Without her, my return would perhaps have been an escape; in marrying her, I came back with my hands full of that strange fruit from faraway countries. Wasn't I now entitled to return to my homeland, after having gone away in anger, and indulgently to accept some gestures and customs that I had refused in former times?[13]

On the other hand, Memmi's narrator needs Marie's willingness to adapt to (and therefore accept) his country, for this will silence his own gnawing doubts and make him feel more at home:

> Returning as an adult to the land which I had left as an adolescent, I felt both amazement and discomfort. Perhaps I could not have done for long without Marie, but I blamed my wife for revealing my incapacities to me as well as for embodying them. Could I have found a better symbol when I discovered that I had been a traitor?[14]

Not only does Memmi's narrator differ from Feraoun's Amer, but so does his Marie from Amer's Marie. Brought up in a Catholic middle-class family from Alsace, she suffers with regard to many things, the Tunisian climate, the food, the noise, the smells, the Tunisian way of life and especially social customs, which are opposed to her own idea of a self-sufficient love:

> She suffered from the heat and the cold, from the humidity and the crude light which dazzled her, from the incessant noise of radios and the all-pervading smells . . . She could neither comprehend nor excuse our Mediterranean muddling on . . . I asked my relatives not to speak dialect in her presence. It was perhaps at these moments, when they all started to speak at the same time while shouting to make themselves heard, that the solitude of my wife with her frozen smile—the smile of the dumb—struck me most. But I admit that I didn't insist; my mother only understood a little French, and why should she be excluded from the conversation just so that Marie could somehow feel less lost?[15]

After building a house in a suburb of Tunis, the couple move away from the husband's family, have a baby and try to make a new start, but in vain. When Marie discovers that she is pregnant again, she has an abortion and they decide to separate.

La Répudiation

Whereas the novels of Feraoun and Memmi show some similarities, although they take place in different surroundings (countryside and city), refer to different communities (Muslim and Jewish) and differ in prospects and outlook (hope and despair), Rachid Boudjedra's first novel *La répudiation* can in no way be compared with them. The most recent of the three books, it is unique, not only with regard to its language, an Arabic-structured French full of repetitions and neologisms, but also with regard to its technique, a strange mixture of realism and hallucination, as well as to the narrated reality itself. The European woman is no longer an obedient wife who seeks protection from her husband, but an independent schoolteacher.[16] Nor does the father stand back in favour of his son, but violates Islamic law by marrying a 15-year-old girl and terrorizing his family all the more from a distance. Finally, the mother has ceased to be content with her role as her daughter-in-law's subtle enemy, and through her weakness as a divorced woman threatens her own son, who is afraid of being overwhelmed by her love.

Although Boudjedra has published a great deal during the last twenty years, his first novel is still considered to be his masterpiece. While the book caused a sensation when it came out in France, it was censored in Algeria until 1980, the reason being its political criticism rather than its shocking love-scenes. Céline, the narrator's French lover, appears right at the beginning of the novel. With his outspoken tendency to invent repulsive details, Boudjedra depicts her genitals as if they were a monstrosity. But Céline is not only the narrator's lover; more important is her role as his patient listener, to whom he exhibits his wounded soul in almost the same way as he uncovers her body to the reader. She acts as if she were a real therapist, forcing him to verbalize his immense suffering caused by himself, his family and the ruling class in his country:

> She insisted again and again (go on with your report!) that I should explain myself and finally I stopped talking altogether, thus rejecting her absurd idea of a therapeutic catharsis which would help me to overcome this phase of groping in the dark of which she kept reminding me when she got nervous and angry because of my silence, although moments before she had yearned for that very silence. Our mutual distrust increased to an unbearable degree, especially in these moments when she considered herself beaten and gave up trying to get me to speak. Now it was she who retreated into complete silence and thereby forced me to speak again. When she kept silent, my own silence no longer made any sense; hurt, I waited for my lover to beseech me, but I waited in vain all day long, until I collapsed. I was then irrevocably at Céline's mercy and fell back into the state of a helpless child that is going to suffocate because of some shameful secret. I had to recover my sense of direction and start anew with many difficulties and interruptions.[17]

Nevertheless the psychoanalytic process fails, for no identification with Céline takes place. On the contrary, the narrator realizes the fundamental difference between himself and his lover, who is a stranger in the double sense of being French and a woman. In the end it is not Céline who cures the author's obsessions. Rather, it is he who destroys her illusions of Algeria as an earthly paradise and so she finally leaves him to go back to France.

Conclusion

With their different backgrounds, upbringing and life-style, the European women in the three novels discussed are all convincing figures. What is also convincing is their behaviour in set circumstances: for example, Marie's grateful indulgence for Amer, who ensures her a respected position; the second Marie's romantic love for her husband, which cannot but come into conflict with reality; and Céline's identification with Rachid, which proves to be nothing but a weariness with Europe. All three women feel, speak and act as individuals. This fact is all the more important because Maghrebi novels—reflecting reality—in the past allotted *indigenous* women nothing but the mother's role.[18] Several authors commented upon this, complaining that the segregation of the sexes did not give them any idea of the female psyche or allow them to portray a woman other than one who was repressed, and no realistic love-story could be devised.[19]

By the end of the sixties and the beginning of the seventies, however, things had begun to change. Women writers like the Algerian Assia Djebar and others had, as early as the beginning of the sixties, written about Maghrebi women, showing the rise of a new and self-confident generation, and the end of colonialism as strengthening young people's interest in their own society, culture and past. These features are clearly discernible in the work of Boudjedra: in the early seventies, he was already choosing Algerian women as his leading female characters;[20] and in the early eighties he started to write his novels in Arabic, being his own translator for the French editions. From the very beginning of his career, Boudjedra has dealt with the effect of colonialism on his people—this is why he could finally consider certain topics such as the European woman as no longer of interest.

This leads us back to the fact that there is a clear difference between Maghrebi literature written in French and Middle Eastern literature written in Arabic, at least with regard to the way the European woman is dealt with. Why is it that the first seems to depict her more as an individual than the second? The answer must be that the authors had a better understanding of Europeans, they were brought up with European languages and there was a greater need to cope with European culture. The French were in the Maghreb much longer than in other Arab countries, and being a part of the everyday life of many North Africans they exerted a deeper influence than elsewhere. France was always more concerned than the British to encourage the use of its language, thus systematically spreading French throughout the Maghreb. Hundreds of Maghrebi intellectuals spent years studying in France before returning to their native countries. Since they were more familiar with European than with Arab culture and literature, French became their preferred language. Lastly, since most of their books were first published in Paris, they almost always wrote for a French audience as well.

11

The Function of Sexual Passages in some Egyptian Novels of the 1980s

Stephan Guth

> Some people hold that sexuality and fantasy are closely linked with human existence . . . And it is perhaps for this reason that a large number of literary works give special prominence to sex in order to keep the reader interested . . . Sometimes, however, sex is also used as a means of escaping the prison of a novel's character in which the author himself is trapped. Third, sex may be used in an attempt to convey an idea with a certain implication [i.e. in a metaphorical sense].

These sentences are part of the introductory passage of a newspaper article[1] in which Muḥammad al-Qalyūbī sums up the statements of four contemporary Egyptian writers whose opinions he had asked about the relation between sexuality and literature, in their works and in general. He goes on to tell his readers that very few modern Arabic authors have dared to touch upon sex and sexuality in their work, an amazing statement for anyone familiar with modern Arabic literature were it not evident from the context that he does not mean the traditional way of tackling sexuality but a new, less allusive and much more direct approach.

Indeed, the appearance of an article like this seems to be the reaction of a literary critic to a new trend of treating sexual themes, a trend which is characterized by the breaking of taboos. This trend can also be observed with some writers of the older generation in their latest works. It is, for instance, no longer the 'old' Najīb Maḥfūẓ of his realistic novels of the 1950s or even his 'existentialist' ones of the 1960s that we find in the opening passage of his novella *al-Ḥubb fawqa hadbat al-haram* [Love on the Pyramids' Plateau][2] where the reader is confronted, without any preliminaries, with a young Egyptian man's cry of sexual frustration:

> I want a woman. Any woman . . . Sex has become the axis of my life and its only aim, a wild beast with claws and fangs . . . It has made out of me a pure sex creature, with senses only for sex, with sex fantasies, sex hopes, sex dreams . . .[3]

Compared to the style of younger authors, however, Maḥfūẓ's approach remains very moderate. It does not seem to have aroused the protest of those narrow-minded religious circles whom Yūsuf al-Qa'īd, one of the younger writers interviewed by al-Qalyūbī, calls '*salafīs*' (literally, 'followers of the path of the ancestors', 'traditionalists', but here meant in the sense of 'reactionaries'). For them, the passages quoted in this essay are to be condemned as *mashāhid ibāḥiyya* (licentious scenes), an accusation which would correspond to that of 'pornography' in the West. Al-Qa'īd has some interesting stories to tell about what happened when the *salafīs* started to interfere.[4]

As an example of these '*mashāhid ibāḥiyya*', we might take a novel by Ṣun'allāh Ibrāhīm entitled *al-Lajna* [The Committee] and first published in 1981.[5] The first chapter has the famous scene where the hero is asked by the members of the committee to undress the lower part of his body to enable them to find out if he is really homosexual or impotent (as their reports tell them). The examination is then carried out, under the reader's eyes, by a member of the committee who introduces his finger into the hero's rectum. Two other passages revolve around the testicles and penis of the hero's guard, himself a member of the committee, whom they have left behind at the hero's home to supervise his activities. Also in *al-Lajna* we find the description of a rude giant rubbing his body against that of a woman while riding on a public bus.

In 'Abduh Jubayr's novel *Taḥrīk al-qalb* [The Moving of the Heart],[6] which deals with the decay on all levels of a typical middle-class family in the 1970s, we see the younger characters, in a kind of interior monologue, talk about, think of or comment on a number of biological or psychological facts on which society would normally keep silent, such as menstruation, or an adolescent youth's Oedipal desire to see his mother's underwear. In addition, one of the daughters eventually remembers being raped by an acquaintance when she was still a child. This explains her schizophrenic attitude towards men, of which the reader is given some vivid descriptions, including some strikingly direct allusions to performances of hard sex.

Risālat al-baṣā'ir fī 'l-maṣā'ir [The Epistle of Insights into the Fates] by Jamāl al-Ghīṭānī, published in book form in 1989,[7] has at least three masturbating young men and also a large number of homosexual and/or paedophile Arab shaykhs from the Gulf who assault Egyptian young men or children. We also encounter some tourists making love on a minaret and an Egyptian father who was forced to emigrate in search of a better livelihood and, as a result of the long separation from his family, has become so alienated from his children that one day he is shocked to find himself sexually stimulated when looking at his own daughter.

It is clear that neither the novels nor the extracts just cited belong to what may be called 'erotic literature'. Their purpose is surely not that of advocating a liberation from sexual taboos in order to allow hitherto suppressed feelings towards the other sex to develop spontaneously and to legitimize what is seen by the authors as only natural, but is condemned by society as immoral or shameless. That kind of erotic literature as we know it from, say, the Marquis de Sade, D. H. Lawrence or Henry Miller is only scarcely, if ever, to be found in modern Arabic literature. Moreover, if there are attempts in this direction they seem to be almost exclusively a women's domain, as, for example, the works of Alīfa Rif'at.

Yet although there is a significant difference between erotic literature and the passages we are dealing with here, in so far as they do not propagate 'freer' relations between men and women and an emancipation from the values of society—note that the authors themselves would by no means find those scenes examples of a beautiful ideal of sexual relations!—there are, on the other hand, some aspects which those '*mashāhid ibāḥiyya*' have in common with erotic literature.

The first is closely connected with the concept of realism in literature. The writers whom Edwār al-Kharrāṭ would group under the heading of 'The New Sensitivity' (*al-ḥassāsiyya al-jadīda*), i.e. the so-called 'generation of the sixties' and after, would always describe themselves as 'realists', as did Maḥfūẓ and Yūsuf Idrīs before them; but their realism is of a different nature to that of the previous generations.[8] The scope of reality has been considerably widened, and so has the concept of man. Being an integral (if not the most important[9]) part of human existence, sexuality, with *all* its aspects, must not be excluded from literature because otherwise 'real' realism would not be fully achieved.[10] The literary portrait of a personality, according to 'Abduh Jubayr, 'has to come from reality lived naturally and spontaneously'. He hastens to add that, with regard to sexual passages, this concept is completely different from that of less able writers who are eager to 'sexualize' their writings in order to produce best-sellers. In his opinion, this is pure *ibtidhāl* (triviality) and these authors are like 'fourth-class dancers' who think that the more naked their body, the more admirable they are, 'without caring about the human body's sacredness' (*dūna . . . 'l-ta'āmul bi-qudsiyya ma'a 'l-jasad al-insānī*).[11]

In post-1967 Egypt, and especially since Sādāt's *infitāḥ* policy (i.e. the policy of 'opening the gates' to the West and re-privatization), the consequences of official policies have become evident in almost all areas of life. Man's reality has come to be conceived of as, among other things, essentially cruel and ugly by Egyptian writers; so anyone who wants to translate this reality into adequate literary forms can no longer do this in 'decent' ways. This function of the sexual passages can be observed, for instance, in 'Abduh Jubayr's novel where the author does not want to do more than give a description of 'normal', average everyday life in the seventies. Yet he wants to cover life in all its aspects, depicting everything people do and think, even if their deeds and thoughts are cruel or disgusting. To ensure genuine realism, an author has to resort, in those cases, to what in traditional eyes may appear as an 'aesthetics of the ugly'.[12]

This conception of reality shares with erotic literature not the content but the form: it involves breaking taboos by speaking about subjects that are not supposed to be discussed openly. Ṣun'allāh Ibrāhīm views this as necessary because 'if we were able to face ourselves exactly as we are, this would help us to lead a better life'.[13]

In the novels of the post-sixties, human existence is essentially seen as involving suffering. How far this suffering goes and how deep it reaches is, in many cases, obviously best demonstrated in terms of unfulfilled sexuality, because sexuality is one of the most fundamental aspects of human existence. Al-Ghīṭānī's masturbating young men are just one example. Their tragedy seems to be condensed in these pictures because they are particularly appropriate to what the author wants to say, namely that the age of Sādāt's *infitāḥ* deprived the youth of something basically human: as long as they cannot afford to pay the *mahr* (dowry) and rent a flat (because of rapid inflation and the illegal practices of housing agents), they will not be able to enjoy what the author sees as a 'human right' to marriage and legitimate sexual intercourse. Of course, to express this idea the author could have described his heroes' suffering in more 'decent' terms, letting them roam around aimlessly or heave helpless sighs. But by letting them masturbate before the reader, he illustrates the suffering in a much more conspicuous manner, appealing to the reader's emotions more successfully than, for example, Najīb Maḥfūẓ when he handles similar problems (as in *al-Ḥubb fawqa hadbat al-haram*). It is clear that for al-Ghīṭānī, the basic concept of realism underlying his writing is the very same as for 'Abduh Jubayr: writing in a realistic way implies telling the *whole* truth, whatever the aesthetic taboos in the minds of the recipients.

Ṣun'allāh Ibrāhīm, with his young man riding a bus and rubbing his body against that of a woman in the crowd, describes a kind of 'sport' which is very common among today's Egyptian youth. It is a result of the miserable conditions that do not allow young people to marry; accordingly, the narrator explicitly approves of this kind of activity provided that the women signal that they are willing to take part themselves. But in other cases Ibrāhīm goes much deeper. In all his novels he is concerned with the crisis of the intellectual. Again, sexual themes are used because they are the most able to convey the message, this time metaphorically.

In his first novel(la), *Tilka 'l-rā'iḥa* [The Smell of It], written in the mid-sixties, Ibrāhīm shows the hero masturbating in such a realistic fashion that Yaḥyā Ḥaqqī was disgusted by this picture[14] and the novel could not be published in its original version for twenty years. The author had chosen a symbol for his character's state of mind, by which he intended to underline the isolation of an oppositional writer just released from prison but still under observation. This isolation is forced upon him by political and social circumstances, but also by literary conventions; it is an isolation which is not only physical seclusion or lack of sexual fulfilment, but the most important trait of his very existence. Masturbating here, on the one hand, symbolizes the hero's strong desire for life and his wish to create something. At the same time, it shows that being free after years of imprisonment has not changed anything: life itself, for him, is still an overall prison, and so are the literary conventions—notice that the masturbation is done in a chair in front of the narrator's desk, just after an unsuccessful attempt to write something down.

In *Tilka 'l-rā'iḥa*, there is also a scene where the hero is unable to have sexual intercourse with a woman. On cases of impotence, which occur quite frequently in his other novels as well, Ibrāhīm comments:

> The overwhelming majority of Egyptians and Arabs are sick—full of complexes, lack of sexual fulfilment, and double moral standards. Everybody talks about his conquests and victories, in the sexual as well as the political and military fields. What Arabs have to learn, however, is to confess their defeats, too.

It should be noted that Ibrāhīm is here drawing parallels between the kind of propaganda boasting of successes before the 1967 *naksa* (defeat) on the one hand, and the boasting of sexual conquests and masculine potency on the other. For him, both seem to be merely different aspects of the same psychological defect.

In Ibrāhīm's *al-Lajna*, the famous homosexuality or impotence examination is again meant to express a number of aspects of reality in a way which might be described as 'naming names by translating emotional data into the language of sexual metaphor'. The frustrated leftist intellectuals of the seventies whom the hero represents have not *really* been summoned before an obscure committee and asked to bend down to allow someone to put his finger into their rectum. When Ibrāhīm creates such a situation, it is to underline his hero's frustration and loss of self-esteem, which, in the author's opinion, has reached such an extreme degree that it can only be communicated to the reader by the language of monstrous sexual acts.

All the novels considered so far seem to show that the 1970s and 1980s in Egypt must have been, for these writers, an era of polarization, an age of extremes. The very explicit sexual passages in question are evidently to be looked on as a surface phenomenon of this discourse of polarization. On one side, that of the victims, there is extreme suffering. On the other, there are those who are the cause of this suffering, and whom the authors tend to 'sexualize'. 'Naming names', as I called it above, here means 'making them obscene' and thereby showing their power and brutality or, more generally speaking, their inhumanity or even animality, in terms of 'pornographic' scenes. In *al-Lajna*, the committee who make the hero take off his clothes and, after the examination, enjoy the announcement of his impotence or homosexuality is just one example. Another is the amusing description of the area between the legs of the hero's guard who, when staying overnight, shares the same bed with him. The hero first notices that his guard's testicles seem to be of an extraordinary size; in bed at night, he feels something very large and hard touching his legs which he—and, of course, the reader—takes for the guard's penis. Apparently not satisfied with these satirical allusions, the author decides to take the scene further: the next morning, the hero catches a glimpse of the guard when he is using the toilet. Here, by accident, something drops from where the hero had assumed were the voluminous testicles: it turns out that the reason for the bulge was neither the testicles nor the penis but a large revolver hidden in the guard's underwear. In this way Ibrāhīm manages successfully to characterize the power of the ruling classes by combining obscenity with aggression and brutality. Giving a hint as to the level of meaning on which we have to take this episode, the narrator says that he could hardly stop himself from laughing when it became clear that, out of fear, he had reversed Freud's famous saying that the revolver symbolizes the penis.

Al-Ghīṭānī's aim is similar: to turn into obscene figures the mighty and powerful who are dangerous to his middle-class heroes and cause their suffering. For al-Ghīṭānī, the main target are the rich Arabs of the Gulf states. Many of his heroes are forced by the situation of Egypt in the seventies to leave their country in order to earn their living abroad. In the Gulf, their residence and work permits depend entirely on good relations with the native contractors who are their official guarantors with the authorities. But this institution of *kafāla* (guarantee) is often abused by the local shaykhs who, in al-Ghīṭānī's novels at least, are mostly homosexuals and/or pederasts. Here, therefore, sexual abnormality—another instance of 'obscenizing'—is again paralleled, or made almost synonymous with, an abuse of power by the mighty, exercised against poor innocent Egyptians and their children.

In conclusion, while some Egyptian novels of the seventies and eighties tend to make use of 'pornographic' elements, these passages should be read as a surface phenomenon of a discourse of extreme polarization in Egyptian society. This polarization has reached a point where the *whole* truth must be told. Implicit in that is a concept of reality and realism that no longer permits one to be silent on aspects of human existence which became a basic experience of life during these two decades: until now, such aspects were not supposed to be expressed publicly and were considered taboo. The main purpose of this direct and outspoken approach is to shock the reader by breaking those taboos because, in a situation where people resign themselves to their fate, nothing else will reach them emotionally. The taboos which are broken, however, are only aesthetic taboos, taboos on a linguistic level. It must be permissible to *talk* about what is going on in the surrounding reality—but that does not mean calling for a system of ethical values which is really new. On the contrary: in terms of traditional sexual mores even the 'pornographic' passages are nothing but affirmative. Thus, in those scenes traditional morality is, for the time being, not questioned but only radicalized. Looking only at the surface of what is written, the *salafīs* have obviously failed to notice that, in the end, the targets of the authors' critique may be nearly the same as their own! The writers try to provoke a readers' rebellion against an atmosphere which they themselves find cruel, ugly, disgusting and therefore unbearable, an atmosphere which they think will be perpetuated unless the facts are named and discussed openly (while the *salafīs* prefer to keep silent and call for the *sharī'a* to be introduced instead).

12

Distant Echoes of Love in the Narrative Work of Fu'ād al-Tikirlī

Wiebke Walther

As early as 1930, the Iraqi Jewish author Anwar Shā'ūl (b. 1904 in Hilla) had written in the preface to his first collection of short stories entitled *al-Ḥiṣād al-awwal* [The First Harvest]:

> The short story is not based on the ardent kisses exchanged by a couple of lovers or the glowing of passion they kindle, but it has its roots in the society, its customs, its traditions, its moral standards and its manners, as in its shortcomings, in the decline, in the confusions existing in it, which attract the author's attention and require him urgently to work hard for its reformation.[1]

Shā'ūl contradicted his fellow Iraqis who claimed that a modern narrative prose could not be developed in Iraq because the tradition-bound society did not permit either freer relations between the sexes or more liberal love relations. He states:

> It is not unknown that our society is still moving between narrow limits, that intellectual freedom is still suspended far off on a dark horizon, and that the mass of people is not accustomed to hearing the strong blame and bitter criticism that writers make the backbone of their short stories.[2]

Anwar Shā'ūl, like other Iraqi authors before and after him—for example, Maḥmūd Aḥmad al-Sayyid (1903–37) to mention one of the earliest and 'Abd al-Malik Nūrī (b. 1921) to mention one of the best—have tried to combine both principles, in other words, to depict in their short stories male–female relations in a strongly male-dominated Arab society and to show women's suffering under patriarchal social structures and ethical standards. They describe the psychological pain of women and men in a society where, for the sake of the family's reputation, women must be punished by their nearest male relative for male sexual assault; a society whose traditions prevent, rather than encourage, natural love relationships between men and women. Thus in Iraq, as in other Arab countries, modern narrative literature from its very beginning focused upon gender problems. With the development of modern narrative literature in Iraq since the 1950s, the depiction of these problems has become increasingly sensitive and varied.

Fu'ād al-Tikirlī was born in 1927 in Ba'qūba, a small town to the north-east of Baghdad. A judge by profession, he is regarded as one of the outstanding authors of his generation. His short stories have been published in various literary journals since the early 1950s. They were brought out in one volume in 1961, entitled *al-Wajh al-ākhar* [The Other Face].[3] A new edition was published in Baghdad in 1982, with eight additional stories, most of them written after 1961. A heavily adapted stage version of the title story was performed as *al-Rahn* [The Pledge][4] in November 1984, during the first Gulf War: perhaps the government regarded it as a 'suitable' text or, even more likely, official government institutions may have ordered the creation of an Iraqi folk theatre. At that time, novels and stories by other Iraqi authors were also performed on stage as comedies, obviously to entertain a wide public, even when the works were not originally written in a humorous vein. Al-Tikirlī's only novel, *al-Raj' al-ba'īd* [The Distant Echo],[5] was published in Beirut in 1980.[6] In the last years of the first Gulf War he left Iraq for Paris, where he still lives.

Al-Tikirlī is not a prolific writer; he does not produce more than one short story a year. Most of them are well constructed and painstakingly written. His rather voluminous novel took over eleven years: it was begun in Paris in February 1966 and finished in Baghdad in September 1977. It is obvious from the published edition that he even made corrections during the proof-reading.[7]

The well-known Iraqi literary critic 'Alī Jawād al-Ṭāhir stated in his review of the first edition of *al-Wajh al-ākhar* that sexuality and socially deviant forms of sexuality play a considerable role in al-Tikirlī's short stories.[8] Sexuality here is not a joyous game; nor is it titillation, as found in older Arabic literature. Socially or ethically 'unusual' sexual relations (and, even more, sexual relations that are frowned on), or at least desire and its suppression, are indicative of social and individual disturbances and disorder.

Al-Tikirlī's first short story, "al-'Uyūn al-khuḍr" [Green Eyes], first published in 1952[9] in the magazine *al-Usbū'*, shocked Iraqi readers. It deals with a theme known to world literature at least since French Romanticism, but it was new at that time in Arabic: the theme of the virtuous or loving prostitute,[10] a young woman who is a victim of the harsh conditions of life, and of a patriarchal society with its male-orientated ideas of sexuality that promote the sexual exploitation of women, the weaker members of society. The story is told through the reflections and reminiscences of a young woman travelling north with her aunt by train from Baghdad via Ba'qūba: her life and the way she has been treated by men have taught her, from her youth, that a woman should live (or, better, exist) without any emotions, without even hate or disgust. She has only known one man who seemed to respect her as a human being; he did not even touch her but spoke to her gently, warning her to take control of herself and her life. This man, an official from Ba'qūba who lived there with his mother (as the young woman discovered from his friends), was the only man she had really loved: yet he deeply disappointed her.

When the train stops for twenty minutes at Ba'qūba, where she had lived and met him over a year ago (and where she could still get off the train to see him again), she remembers how she begged him to help her during his visits. Evidently she was dependent upon a pimp, an old man, in whose house she had a room. After an interval of two weeks, the official came back with his friends: one after the other they had sex with her while he looked on. Crying and yelling and at the end of her tether, she accused him of being a pimp, asking him why he did not take money for his services. After this, she never saw him again.

Here, as elsewhere in the story (and in other short stories by this author), the depiction of nature and of the surroundings is symbolic; the train leaves Ba'qūba through tender folds of darkness for a distant, unknown horizon.[11] Here, it seems to be the social conditions that make a love relationship impossible. The characterization of the prostitute as a particularly sensitive person, far more so than any of the men exploiting her, is new. It was not until some years later that Badr Shākir al-Sayyāb, the famous Iraqi poet, wrote his long poem "al-Mūmis al-'amyā'" [The Blind Prostitute] (included in his *dīwān*, *Unshūdat al-maṭar* [The Song of Rain]), which contains allusions to Greek and oriental myths and a poetic justification of woman's role as a prostitute. The poem became famous in Iraq.[12]

A recurrent topic in modern Arabic short stories and novels—at least since Ṭāhā Ḥusayn's moving short novel *Du'ā' al-karawān* [The Call of the Curlew] (1934)—is the *ghasl al-'ār* (the cleansing or washing of a family's honour by blood, i.e. the blood of a girl or an unmarried young woman, even when she is only suspected of losing her virginity). According to customary law, not to the *sharī'a* (religious law), the girl must be killed by her nearest male relative: her father or one of her brothers. Ṭāhā Ḥusayn tried to demonstrate how hatred could be overcome by love; in *Du'ā' al-karawān* the girl who wants to take revenge on behalf of her sister falls in love with her sister's seducer.

In his short story "al-Ṭarīq ilā 'l-madīna" [The Way to the City], however, al-Tikirlī depicts a young man's mood swings and despair, emotions that are intensified by his own social and personal frustrations. A young official, again in Ba'qūba, is urged more by his aunt than by his mother to kill his feeble-minded sister, whom he loves, because she has had a miscarriage after taking a strong laxative[!]. Against his inner convictions and driven only by social pressures, he beats his sister mercilessly. She does not understand anything, however, and his psychic agony seems as tormenting as her physical pain. While he is crying, 'I can't, I can't,' he hears shouting and applause for his sister's death: 'And he did not see Ḥamdiyya [his sister] as he did not see the sky.'[13] Although the theme of incest is not uncommon in al-Tikirlī's short stories, and although incest in this story would make the plot more dramatic, there would seem to be no evidence for Sabry Hafez's contention that Ḥamdiyya's brother was the father of her child: there is no basis for this assumption in 'Alī Jawād al-Ṭāhir's review of the story.[14]

A kind of incest, of cruel sexual abuse of a 13-year-old girl, is depicted in al-Tikirlī's short story "al-Qindīl al-munṭafi'" [The Dying Lamp] (1954), which has been translated into English, German and Dutch. Here a man who wants to marry his neighbour's very young daughter because of a sexual craving for her is rejected by her parents because he is already married and has children, so he forces his son to marry her. The fourth night after the marriage, while the girl is sleeping with the whole family in the same room and the young bridegroom does not dare to touch the child bride whom he never wanted to marry, his father falls on the girl in the dying light of the lamp and rapes her. The well-constructed plot is revealed through the reflections and observations of the young man, who lives in fear of his domineering father.

Al-Ṭāhir's claim in 1967 that this kind of situation is not typical for

Iraq may perhaps be explained by Iraqi national pride. Another of al-Tikirlī's short stories, first published in 1972, "al-Tannūr" [The Baking Oven], has the sub-title "Outlines of an Unwritten Self-Defence". It also deals with the theme of incest. Perhaps the author met a similar case when he was a judge. In confused words and contradictory statements, a 30-year-old policeman who is married and the father of several children tries to conceal the fact that he has killed his sister-in-law[15] because she could have provided evidence of his making love with his young half-sister. Knowing that the (false) accusation that his sister-in-law has committed adultery in the family house would be sufficient to justify his murdering her, he pretends that he had to defend the honour of the family. Of all al-Tikirlī's short stories, this shows the strongest evidence of irony, a sarcastic depiction of hypocritical ethical standards.

But al-Tikirlī not only deals with the repression caused by morally ambivalent social traditions: in the title story of his anthology, "al-Wajh al-ākhar", he portrays the psychological ambivalence of a man torn by the inner conflict between his love for his wife and sense of devotion to her (she went blind after the birth of their first stillborn child) and his longing to be free from this burden and to make love to their neighbour's young daughter, who is married to a rich old man she detests. The story, written between October 1956 and June 1957, runs to 115 pages and can therefore almost be classed as a novelette. Like other short stories of this time, such as Ghānim al-Dabbāgh's "al-Mā' al-'adhib" [Sweet Water],[16] it seems to be influenced by Sartre's *La nausée* [Nausea]. Here, however, the disgust felt by the male hero is not a fundamental principle of life, but is caused by social and sexual frustration and by a psychological ambivalence that he cannot overcome.

Inner psychological conflict caused by (traditionally forbidden) love relationships, or sexual desire between members of the same family who are not allowed to marry, are the themes of al-Tikirlī's short stories "Hams mubham" [Confused Whisper] (1951), "al-Ghurāb" [The Crow] (1962) and "al-Dummāla" [The Abscess] (1966). "Hams mubham" shows the love of a 16-year-old boy for his mother, who is tormented by her unhappy marriage and finally leaves with another man. In "al-Ghurāb", a mother of two children witnesses her husband making love with her sister-in-law. While she is telling her little daughter a fable, and at the same time remembering the sexual scene which terrified her, she is shot dead by her husband. In "al-Dummāla", a man falls in love with the daughter of his second wife. The young girl's showing her independence and emancipation strengthens his jealousy and his desire for her. But in his eyes this is an ugly abscess, a moral deviation, which he feels unable to bear. So in the end, blinded by tears and unable to find a way out, he drives his car into the cold, suffocating waters of the Tigris, where no one can find him, and drowns.

These last stories do not deal with typical Arab or Iraqi problems, but seem to be the discovery of ambivalence and pain in male–female relationships, in love and sexuality, which are not caused by social circumstances but by human psychology. Nevertheless al-Tikirlī's novel *al-Raj' al-ba'īd* is a brilliant depiction of a combination of political, social and human conditions which influence these relationships and are in turn influenced by them. The structure of the short stories is nearly identical. We come to know the plot through the reflections of the main characters in the third-person singular, not in flashbacks, but through the natural sequence of events. This structure, which may be interrupted by external actions, the dialogue (in Iraqi dialect) with other characters, the hero's observations, and so on, is so simple that when al-Ṭāhir heard that al-Tikirlī had begun a novel in 1966, he warned him against writing a bigger work, because obviously he did not believe him capable of it![17]

In my view, *al-Raj' al-ba'īd* is one of the best novels written in Arabic during the last fifteen years. It is a panorama of bourgeois Baghdad society, shown through three generations of a family who all live in a house in the Bāb al-Sharqī, one of the oldest neighbourhoods of Baghdad. The last months of 'Abd al-Karīm Qāsim's regime in 1962–63, with their political terrorism, the social and intellectual frustration of the middle classes and the opportunism and resignation of some of its members, seem to be an allusion to similar or even worse phenomena in the years to come. Flashbacks and reflections by the main characters widen the time-span. At the centre of the novel is the love of three men, the brothers Midḥat and 'Abd al-Karīm, and 'Adnān, a member of the next generation, for Munīra, the cousin of the two brothers and the aunt of 'Adnan. Munīra has been a middle-school teacher in (boring) Ba'qūba and has now come with her mother to work and to live as a guest of this family in Baghdad. The novel is divided into twelve chapters, narrated in the third-person singular from different points of view. The main characters reveal their personalities not only by their own reflections and inner emotions, but also by being defined in relation to others and the reflections of some of the other people about them.

One of the central scenes, 'Adnān's rape of Munīra, is first related by Munīra in the first-person singular.[18] Then the narration changes to the third-person singular, but again from Munīra's point of view. The incident degenerates from a merry, innocent game, as seen by Munīra (the older of the two), into bitter, humiliating violence meted out to her by her nephew, whom she had regarded as a younger friend, a younger brother, and over whom she had authority. Immediately after the rape, Munīra tells of her inner emotions, seeing her blood on the ground and 'Adnān trying to hide his polluted genitals. She feels him leave her world for ever and expresses her pain and humiliation:

> I broke down, and plunged to the very depths. But then came a throbbing of the heart, dividing life from death, a slight pulse beat followed by a gush of blood flowing through my veins, and I returned to this dark world for the second time. It was a patch of sky shining tenderly above my head that brought back a sense of place and time to me. I took a breath so as not to suffocate.[19]

Munīra's love for Midḥat and her desire for him are depicted again and again from Midḥat's point of view[20] after she marries him without telling him the reason for her not being a virgin on their wedding-night. He at first only senses that she does not hate sex, or even fear it like him. In spite of his love for her, Midḥat feels torn by the force of tradition, a tradition that demands a man kill his wife or at least leave her when he finds out on the wedding-night that she has already lost her virginity. He does not understand why she has never told him the reason and is tormented by a (Freudian) nightmare in which he is killing her with his dagger:

> This dream and what was hidden behind it were the hereditary disposition which connected him with all the impurities of his ancestors, with their trivialities, their complexes and their crazy obsession with honour and killing. It was, after all, the imagined realization of their will, the act they required from him, and perhaps it was his act . . . What do they want from a woman? What did they want from her? All the time, during all the centuries, deep-rooted in antiquity, since this male beast—man—was created and saw her? Would that she had informed him! . . . His dear wife! His beloved woman! The spouse of his heart![21]

But then he realizes that had she told him the truth before the wedding, he might have left her and she perhaps knew this. But what if she had not told him because she trusted in him, because she loved him? The Qur'anic verse *Wa idha 'l-mawlūdatu su'ilat 'an ayyi shay'in qutilat* (And when the new-born girl is asked why she has been killed)[22] comes to his mind, expressing the idea of the injustice done to females in Arab society in an unbroken line from pre-Islamic times to the present.

Munīra does not analyse the reasons for her silence. It is unlikely that she wants to protect 'Adnān and his parents, because they have avoided her since the rape (about which she did not even tell her mother). But like Midḥat—or perhaps even more than him—she knows the traditions and the position of a girl in Arab society, even in the 1960s. *A-lastu fatāt hādhā 'l-balad al-mu'allaqa dawman bayn al-mawt wa 'l-'ahr* (Aren't I a girl shaped by this country, always suspended between death and fornication?),[23] she says, reflecting on her situation after the rape and noticing the attention that both 'Abd al-Karīm and Midḥat are paying her. She feels that she has to act, to do something: but in the end she does nothing, justifying her inaction with the sentence quoted above.

In a long painful process of thinking and isolating himself, just as Munīra isolated herself after the rape, Midḥat first wants to commit suicide but then decides to live and to forgive. His decision is taken against the backdrop of the start of turmoil in Baghdad, with shooting and street-fighting. After Midḥat has taken the decision to live, however, he is killed by a stray bullet. This is the end of the novel, but in a previous chapter, entitled "al-Zakhm wa 'l-baqā'" [Rebuff and Survival], the author interweaves Midḥat's inner strife with the riots in Baghdad, Munīra's pain in feeling that she has lost Midḥat, and 'Abd al-Karīm's timid and pressing courtship of Munīra, who refuses him, while consoling him, when he complains of his weakness:

> You're not weak, you're like me and everybody else here: you're sick, a mutilated person . . . I don't fear anybody, because I know your real existence: you're cowards. You don't know who needs help, who is sincere, who is unlucky and what's going on in the world. You're all cowards and fools who don't want to understand, don't want to distinguish between the criminal and the person who's innocent![24]

The novel is a radical settling of accounts with the outdated moral and ethical standards and traditions concerning male–female relations and women's position in the family and society. This is carefully interwoven with a critique of an unloved and corrupt political system which seems to be both connected with and caused by a society that does not question its own social standards. Political pressure leads to social and sexual frustration: as in the case of 'Adnān, this merely turns into aggression.

The themes of love, marriage and sexuality in the narrative work of Fu'ād al-Tikirlī underwent a clear progression from the 1950s to the early 1980s. After first expressing a severe criticism of the typical Iraqi

Arab forms of male-female relationships in their social manifestations, the author moved in the 1960s to a study of the psychologically and socially determined ambivalence in the male psyche concerning relations with women. In his best and longest work so far, the novel *al-Raj' al-ba'īd,* al-Tikirlī focuses on the Arab moral and ethical traditions which have dominated male-female relations for centuries, causing pain and suffering for both sexes, but particularly for women as the socially 'weaker' sex. It is these traditions that the author wants to question here. He links these relationships and emotions to his depiction of the repressive socio-political conditions that end in an uprising and the overthrow of the ruling authority. Al-Tikirlī—like the reader—knows that this overthrow will not result in any real change in the circumstances of life. Both the author and the reader are conscious of the fact that genuine changes in deep-rooted traditions and moral standards need more time, perhaps even generations. The author's conclusion is that outdated social standards are connected with intolerable political conditions and that both can destroy the individual. As long as a society is unable to free itself from its obsolete social traditions, it will be unable to organize a life of political freedom.[25]

13

Sexuality in Jabrā's Novel, *The Search for Walīd Mas'ūd*

Mattityahu Peled

Al-Baḥth 'an Walīd Mas'ūd [The Search for Walīd Mas'ūd] is unique among the novels of Jabrā Ibrāhīm Jabrā in many ways. That it was indeed meant to be so we learn from an interview given by the author to the Iraqi writer Mājid al-Samarrā'ī.[1] There he explains that he had meant it to be a polyphonic novel, as defined by Mikhail Bakhtin[2] in his book on the poetics of Dostoevsky. Since Bakhtin analysed Dostoevsky's polyphonic novel in great detail, Jabrā's statement leaves no room for ambiguity. There are two questions that need to be investigated here. First, is this novel indeed polyphonic? And second, what is the significance of this fact?

As for the first, it is clear that Jabrā has indeed structured the novel along the lines highlighted by Bakhtin, who writes:

> A plurality of independent and unmerged voices and consciousnesses, a genuine polyphony of fully valid voices, is in fact the chief characteristic of Dostoevsky's novels. What unfolds in his works is not a multitude of characters and fates in a single objective world, illuminated by a single authorial consciousness; rather a plurality of consciousnesses, with equal rights and each with its own world, combine but are not merged in the unity of the event.[3]

Such a concept eliminates the author as the dominant narrative voice and raises the question of his position. According to Bakhtin, 'the issue here is not an absence of, but a radical change in, the author's position'.

And he goes on to explain that 'this new "objective" authorial position . . . permits the characters' points of view to unfold to their maximal fullness and independence. Each character freely (without the author's interference) reveals and substantiates the rightness of his position'.[4] Not to be misunderstood, Bakhtin elaborates:

> The consciousness of the creator of a polyphonic novel is constantly and everywhere present in the novel, and is active in the highest degree. But the function of this consciousness and the forms of its activity are different than in the monological novel: the author's consciousness does not transform other consciousnesses (that is, the consciousnesses of the characters) into objects, and does not give them second-hand and finalizing definitions.[5]

Thus, the emphasis is on the dialogic nature of the novel, which is the foundation of polyphony. When considered superficially, it may be argued that a novel like Jabrā's *al-Safīna* [The Ship] is no different to the one we are discussing. However, the basic difference lies in the absence of the dominant narrative voice in the latter. This structural difference is dictated by the nature of the novel as well as moulding it. Again we have a clear statement by the author[6] to the effect that *al-Baḥth 'an Walīd Mas'ūd* was written to raise or deal with a problem, or an issue. This, too, is considered by Bakhtin as an essential element of Dostoevsky's polyphonic novel:

> It is given to all of Dostoevsky's characters 'to think and seek higher things'; in each of them there is a 'great and unresolved thought'; all of them must, before all else, 'get a thought straight'. And in this resolution of a thought (an idea) lies their entire real life and their own personal unfinalizability . . . In other words, the image of the hero is inseparably linked to the image of an idea and cannot be detached from it. We see the hero in the idea and through the idea, and we see the idea in him and through him.[7]

The nature of the idea, as explained by Bakhtin, lies in its dialogicality: 'The idea is a *live event*, played out at the point of dialogic meeting between two or several consciousnesses.'[8] Thus we see that by choosing to write a polyphonic novel, Jabrā indeed meant to write 'a novel of idea' or an ideological novel. This is not to be taken as meaning that his novel is dominated by an idea, however, for this would have turned it into a monological novel. The novel of idea, according to Bakhtin, is a novel where the various consciousnesses confront each other with ideas in an open-ended argument. It should be stressed once again that for Dostoevsky the image of an idea is inseparable from the image of a person, the carrier of that idea. It is not the idea that is the hero of his works but rather the person born of that idea. The hero in Dostoevsky is a man of the idea.[9] Therefore a confrontation of ideas would mean a confrontation of consciousnesses which cannot be end-determined and which are not subjected to the author's arbitration. His may be one of those ideas represented in the novel, provided he participates in it and does not reserve for himself the right to impose from the outside his own idea, thus turning it into a monological novel.

There is yet another characteristic of Dostoevsky's polyphonic novel which needs to be mentioned:

> He saw and conceived the world primarily in terms of space, not time . . . [He] attempted to preceive the very stages [of some unified development] in their *simultaneity*, to *juxtapose* and *counterpose* them dramatically, and not stretch them out into an evolving sequence. For him, to get one's bearings on the world meant to conceive all its contents as simultaneous, and *to guess at their interrelationships in the cross-section of a single moment.*[10]

With the elimination of the sequential plot, we may justifiably ask if the spatial form does away with plot in the accepted sense. As we have learnt from E. M. Forster, a plot requires causality. The sentence 'The King died and then the Queen died' is a story but 'The King died and then the Queen died of grief' is a story with a plot.[11] The difference is that in the second version there is the element of causality. As explained by Joseph Frank in his seminal study of spatial form,[12] that form does away with seqential development and hence has no use for causality. Instead it presents the readers with elements of narrative in fragments scattered through the book which they can fit together 'spatially' until, by what Frank calls 'reflexive reference', they are linked together. The result is that the reader discovers *a situation, not a narrative*. The technique of structuring the novel is that of knitting the chapters together 'not by progress of any action—either narrative or, as in a stream-of-consciousness novel, the flow of experience—but by the continual reference and cross-reference of images and symbols that must be referred to each other spatially throughout the time-act of reading'.

Formulated differently, but to the same effect, Bakhtin explains that:

> Plot in Dostoevsky is absolutely devoid of any sort of finalizing functions. Its goal is to place a person in various situations that expose and provoke him, to bring people together and make them collide in conflict—in such a way, however, that they do not remain within this area of plot-related contact but exceed its bounds. The real connections begin where the ordinary plot ends, having fulfilled its service function.[13]

By comparison we can see that *al-Safīna* is a sequential plot with causality forming the main link between its phases.

Having described the major elements of the polyphonic novel, it can clearly be seen that Jabrā has indeed moulded his novel strictly in accordance with its principles. It behoves us next to to see the significance of this structure. Since dialogue is the corner-stone of the whole edifice of the polyophonic novel, launching *al-Baḥth 'an Walīd Mas'ūd* with what Bakhtin describes as 'a dialogue on the threshold' must be considered particularly fitting.

Walīd's recorded message, found in his deserted car near the border station of Rutba on the way leading to Jordan and Syria, sums up his life history in the form of *Anacrisis*, one of the two devices of the Socratic dialogue. As explained by Bakhtin, this device 'was understood as a means for eliciting and provoking the words of one's interlocutor, forcing him to to express his opinion and express it thoroughly'.[14] The threshold here is the point beyond which Walīd disappears. He never explains his decision to disappear, which leaves everyone guessing: why did he leave and where has he gone? His recorded message, which some critics refer to as farewell message, gives no indication of his motive, nor does it provide anything in the nature of a will or last words of wisdom. His voice is heard against the irritating background noise of Purcell's music accompanied by the sound of the roaring engine. All it contains are rambling recollections of a lifetime, uttered as if under a hypnotic spell. Its language is too polished for a stream-of-consciousness utterance and too vague to make clear sense. In fact, Walīd's friends, gathered to listen to it, take it as a riddle to be solved rather than as an explanation of his disappearance. The many allusions to people present or absent from the scene and to personal secrets and episodes of Walīd's early childhood, unknown to his Baghdadi friends, without divulging any reasons for his disappearance, provoke strong emotional reactions. Nevertheless, the message forces the listeners to speak frankly and reveal their innermost thoughts and feelings. As a result, several people independently put on record their experiences with Walīd as remembered at the moment of recording, in the style of a confession. Confession, as observed by Michel Foucault:

> is a ritual of discourse in which the speaking subject is also the subject of the statement; it is also a ritual that unfolds within a power relationship, for one does not confess without the presence (or virtual presence) of a partner who is not simply the interlocutor but the authority who requires the confession, prescribes and apreciates it and intervenes in order to judge, punish, forgive, console and reconcile . . .[15]

The story does not reveal why the friends speak out or at whose instigation and whether they know of each other's confessions. It is clear that all of them wish to be exculpated but it is not clear who is there to administer them absolution. Common to all of them is the disregard for the time sequence. Things past are related by means of *anachrony*, whereby a series of *analepses*—or flashbacks—are utilized in order to sustain the sentiments of the moment of recording. The past is not recalled for its own sake but for the sake of describing the present. As one of the protagonists puts it, 'I want the past in the present'.[16] The end result is an accumulation of spatial images as revealed in the narrators' stories, together forming a montage of pictures.

As these individual stories unfold, various suggestions are made concerning the reasons for Walīd's disappearance and his fate, with the author, true to his principles, leaving the mystery unresolved—that is, open-ended. The one suggestion which concerns us here is that of Dr Ṭāriq Ra'ūf, a medical psychologist who, on the basis of the message, states that Walīd was a Don Juan suffering from a mother complex, as defined by Carl Jung. This is specific enough to give us an idea of Walīd's personality according to a professional diagnosis. The basis for this diagnosis, as can easily be understood, is the fact that the recorded message alludes to numerous love-affairs, beginning in childhood and continuing throughout adult life. The message ends with the following utterance:

> O mother how would you save your children this time except by your admirable pride which you have passed on to them artlessly fearing no excessiveness since pride was your sole domain and your stubbornness could crush a stone and dry up the sea and fill the hills with springs no matter what I said and how I said it and Jawād was concealing his amazement at the many women I had known searching for the one who

would have my mother's stubbornness and pride and he claimed that he could not understand me but it was I who could never understand anyone.[17]

Dr Ra'ūf reaches this conclusion only after Walīd's disappearance, but it accords well with a perception of Walīd he has formed earlier. According to Jung, Don Juanism is one possible effect of the mother complex in the son.[18] Prior to hearing Walīd's recorded message, and while Walīd is still around, Dr Ra'ūf is persuaded that, being a Capricorn, Walīd has the qualities attributed to his kind by the fourth-century scholar, Fermicius. This scholar claimed that Capricorns are afflicted by an irresistible sexual passion which they manage to hide under a saintly guise and that they have a tendency to commit suicide because of their uncontrollable passion. This information is provided by Walīd himself, evidently as a witty jest at the expense of the psychologist. But the doctor is so convinced of the truth of the horoscope that he concludes that Walīd has in fact committed suicide. The additional information, gleaned from Walīd's message, confirms his prior astrological diagnosis.

We are not told a great deal about Walīd's attitude towards Dr Ra'ūf but he clearly shows him no warmth of feeling. The doctor, on the other hand, has the strongest resentment of Walīd, whom he envies for his great success with women. He collects information, both oral and written, on Walīd's exploits among the women of Baghdad, all of which convinces him that Walīd is indeed a Don Juan. And when one of Walīd's former mistresses, the beautiful Maryam, comes to the doctor for treatment after a nervous breakdown, he takes advantage of her and has sexual intercourse with her (with her consent) in his clinic. Although he desires her passionately, his desire to emulate Walīd clearly plays a role in his conduct. Thus, though not a Capricorn himself, he personifies the type in his own conduct. Dr Ra'ūf's greatest disappointment comes when he discovers that his own half-sister, Wiṣāl, has become Walīd's mistress. He tries to dissuade her but she tells him bluntly that he is driven not by concern for her but by jealousy of Walīd.

Ra'ūf's story illustrates what Bakhtin describes as the 'carnivalization'[19] of literature, arguing that carnival has worked out an entire language of symbolic, concretely sensuous forms and that this language has given expression to a unified carnival sense of the world. This language cannot be translated into a verbal language, but it is amenable to a certain transposition into a language of artistic images that has something in common with its concretely sensuous nature; that is, it can be transposed into the language of literature.

Several individual aspects and characteristic features of carnival can be demonstrated. Maryam is a typically liberated Arab woman and her confession is one of the novel's centrepieces. Exquisitely beautiful and highly educated, she is married against her will to an unsuitable husband, a man of enviable social position, whom she constantly betrays until she finally divorces him. After obtaining a higher degree in literature in England, she returns to a university post in Baghdad, but remains a lonely woman with racked nerves. The treatment she receives from her psychiatrist is not particularly helpful. His passion for her remains only partially satisfied and a strange incident causes a complete rupture between the patient and her lover doctor. He calls very late one night, asking to come to her. She agrees to receive him. (He has secretly left his wife's bed.) But when he is about to enter her home he hears Walīd's voice asking if Dr Ra'ūf has arrived. He runs away believing that Maryam and Walīd are conspiring to expose him. It is nothing but a hallucination, however, and Maryam, deeply offended by the doctor's strange conduct, accuses him of humiliating her.

Maryam's story of her romance with Walīd is another example of Jabrā's carnivalistic writing. Before meeting Walīd, Maryam has been the mistress of 'Āmir 'Abd al-Ḥamīd, an architect of note and a family man, married to an English woman. With the help of a woman friend, she contrives to meet him alone in her friend's home and throws herself into his arms. He desires her but never loves her. Eventually they agree to meet in Beirut for a holiday, but when Maryam arrives she discovers that 'Āmir has left for London without her. Walīd, who is a close friend of 'Āmir's and happens to be spending some time in Beirut staying at his house, invites her to a party that evening. After the party, she stays on. Her mood, as she admits in her confession, is that of a prisoner set free. She regards Walīd and 'Āmir as two faces of the same coin. So when all the guests have left, she tells us:

> We went into the house, which was in chaos, with chairs, cushions and glasses all over the place and went straight into the bedroom, which was similarly chaotic, and dropped onto the bed. We did not get up until the following evening . . . We heard the birds singing in the morning while we were in bed. They were followed by the chirping of the cicadas at noon and we were still in bed. The telephone rang several times and we stayed in bed. The evening's silence spread over the trees and the house and the entire world and we were still in bed.[20]

She does not end the story before testifying to Walīd's sexual prowess, saying that he possessed her for the tenth time as if was the first.

The other great love-affair in the novel is that between Walīd and Wiṣāl. She is a very independent young woman who falls in love with Walīd while she is still a schoolgirl. When she decides to court him she does so without any inhibitions. One morning—after a garden party at which she has her first alcoholic drink—she phones him and suggests a ride in his car. As they are driving along, she suggests reading him a poem she has written. But she somehow allows her breast to fall out of her bra. Walīd pays no attention to the poem and asks her to expose both her breasts. Eventually they go to his apartment. Afterwards he breaks with Maryam in an emotional letter telling her he loves her but loves another woman more. Wiṣāl soon discovers that while professing to be very much in love with her, when she is not available Walīd is making love to another woman. Thus we see that Dr Ra'ūf's suspicion is well founded.

Many more—though lesser—love-affairs are described in the novel, all in the same carnivalistic vein. They all follow a similar pattern: educated men and women, considering themselves free of old-fashioned prejudices, aspire to find happiness in life but settle for something less. Even those who are married and have a profession and a family are no exception. Unhappy and unsatisfied, they search for sexual satisfaction, depicted here as a paradigm of human passions. This is seen in the wide-ranging discourses of the various protagonists, who admit their frustrations and shattered hopes along with their sexual adventures. According to Foucault, the peculiariarity of modern Western societies is 'not that they consign sex to a shadowy existence, but that they talk of sex *ad infinitum* while exploiting it as *the* secret.[21] In Jabrā's Baghdadi society sex is not a secret at all. It is discussed freely by people, both men and women, who have failed to gratify their desires. This is a novel about unfulfilled desire, the distinctive trait of the world created by the author.

The novel as an art form, says Wolfgang Iser,[22] has always been directly concerned with social and historical norms that apply to a particular environment, and so it establishes an immediate link with the empirical reality familiar to the reader. In dealing with social and historical norms, the novel may well be critical of them and in any case presents them as the subject of discussion which frequently ends in a questioning rather than a confirmation of their validity. This is the challenge offered to those whose familiar world is made up of the norms that have been questioned.

The world depicted by Jabrā is one of worldly values, where the way of life of a milieu, and its system of values, shape a personal consciousness which prizes the fulfilment of desire above all, though in most cases people cannot possibly attain that goal. Frustration is therefore universal, since desire, as observed by Leo Bersani, 'is an activity within a lack; it is an appetite stimulated by an absence . . . it is an appetite of the imagination . . . The activity of desiring is inseparable from the activity of fantasizing.'[23] This, Jabrā tells us, is the world of the bourgeoisie, whose value is worldliness, or *mondanité*. As defined by Peter Brooks,[24] worldliness is 'an ethos and personal manner which indicate that one attaches primacy . . . to life within a public system of values . . . that further this life and one's position in it'. Jabrā's evaluation of this world has been succinctly stated in the interview quoted earlier. Speaking of the failure of the Arab bourgeoisie, when compared to the Western bourgeoisie, to develop an urban civilization he says:

> The power of this bourgeois class to create the city and expand it has somehow produced groups which I see from within: they have failed to realize any kind of intellectual eminence in spite of their great material achievements because they embraced appearances and neglected the essence. For this reason they have lost, in my opinion, their right to be regarded as leading the civilizing thinking of this city.

And he goes to say:

> I observe the contradictions in the life of the Arab bourgeoisie, I ponder over this and I am trying to put it all in my novels . . . I have seen the collapse of the bourgeoisie as it failed miserably. But I have also seen the ambition of the bourgeoisie (which has been replenished by groups coming from the countryside and rising up both materially and in influence), constantly growing and engendering democracy or demanding it, and engendering freedom for this nation and demanding it. But that ambition often engenders none of these for the nation and in that sense the bourgeoisie has failed in its historical mission which I believe the Europeans were much more successful in accomplishing for their societies until now.[25]

When we read a novel that is so directly engaged in valorizing the society it depicts, our interpretation of it is bound to be studded with problems concerning context more than text. Background knowledge has a direct bearing on our interpretation of the text.

Depicting the Baghdadi bourgeoisie as an affluent society devoid of the ability to orient itself towards a loftier value system need not necessarily place sex at the centre of the plot. But sex is no doubt the most telling aspect of that society's predicament. As observed by 'Abdelwahāb Bouḥdība in his book *Sexuality in Islam*, the Arab bourgeoisie, being the bearer of modernity, has been responsible for making modernity, from the very beginning, synonymous with the emancipation of women and for arriving at the stage where modernity has become synonymous with sexual emancipation.[26] And the emancipation of women also means a restoration of sexual intiative.

> The emancipation of Arab women [writes Bouḥdība] is now situated on the only valid terrain, that of sexuality. I give love, therefore I am. *Coeo ergo sum*. Thus the Arab woman is rediscovering, but to her own advantage, that ethics of experienced pleasure, that sensation of existing through love, that the Arab language admirably terms *wijdān*.[27]

It therefore makes sense to examine the worldliness of the Arab bourgeoisie, as Jabrā does, by focusing on the sexual aspect of that society. Seen through his eyes, it is clear that with all the progress made by women they are still far from turning their liberty into a source of happiness. The only happy women described in the novel are those of the traditional type, who may play a significant but always secondary role at home. The liberated, independent woman has still not reached equality with men; she is very much the weaker party in the male-female equation and therefore she is unhappy. The interesting question is why Jabrā should highlight this situation by planting a Palestinian refugee into that society and making him the touchstone of its system of values. The answer is probably that Jabrā is employing sex in two different ways. As far as Baghdadi society is concerned, sex is shown by means of the personal stories recorded in the confessions of the various protagonists. But in the case of Walīd, sex is also employed as a means of raising another issue. Walīd's function in the novel is to personify an ideal. Ibrāhīm Nawfal, the eccentric intellectual in the novel, sums up Walīd's personality in glowing terms:

> But Walīd is that unaccepting Palestinian, the explorer, the builder, the unifier (if my nation is destined ever to be unified), the scholar, the engineer, the technologist, the innovator, the stern mover of the Arab conscience . . . His important role was to sustain the new spirit which is based on science, on liberty, on love, on rebellion against reaction—realizing the all-embracing Arab revolution. And the

> revolution for him was not merely changing the ruling class in the system of government, or replacing the Right with the Left, or the other way round. For him the revolution meant placing the Arab in the middle of the vast world and proving his capability to resist as well as to offer. Had I not scrutinized Walīd's life in this way I would never have understood him.[28]

A man with these qualities can indeed become a source of inspiration, as most of the confessors admit that Walīd had actually been for them. But his very presence among them could cause resentment as well, as some felt towards him, for exposing their own shortcomings. What is the significance of making him a sex symbol? Three chapters of the book (three personal stories, two by women who were Walīd's lovers and one by a man who was jealous of him) are devoted to that aspect of his personality. For others, his sexual exploits are taken as part of his personality that does not interfere with their appreciation of him as an unusual and admirable man.

In order to understand his role, his story must be further looked into. His personal history is presented in three autobiographical chapters, telling of his childhood, his adolescence and a traumatic experience he had under the Israeli occupation of the West Bank, when he was arrested, interrogated and deported. Additional information is provided by a relative who remembers Walīd's childhood. A fifth chapter is told by Walīd's son, Marwān, from his Palestinian wife. This son, who joined the Palestinian fighters, recounts an armed attack on an Israeli village in which he died. This is an interesting piece of existential writing, attempting to condense a life-span into the last moment of existence, an attempt not dissimilar to Walīd's own recorded confession. Only this time the 'dialogue on the threshold' elicits no response—as if symbolizing the world's indifference to the Palestinian struggle.

As far as people surrounding Walīd are concerned, they knew him either before emigrating to Iraq or since then. These two phases constitute two separate, unconnected parts in his life. In Baghdadi society his Palestinian chapter is unknown, as they all admit. They were even unaware of any activity he was engaged in as a Palestinian within the ranks of the Palestinian national movement. The only link to that part of his history is his Palestinian wife, Rīma, who goes mad after a few years in Baghdad and is sent back to Bethlehem for hospitalization. Deprived of his wife and son, the Palestinian hero now symbolizes hopelessness. But as seen by his Baghdadi friend Ibrāhīm, Walīd is transformed after the departure of his wife:

> Rīma's collapse proved to be an amazing boost to Walīd. He continued to follow her treatment in a sanatorium at Bethlehem, but he began to live the day with an impetuosity that makes no distinction between despair and hope, between a wedding and a funeral. It became clear to him that Rīma would never recover: she was in a state of total mental lethargy. And her lethargy behind the hospital walls released in Walīd a riotous demon.[29]

Here we see the fundamental contrast between the two phases of Walīd's life. Whereas there are no descriptions in the novel of Walīd's sex life with his Palestinian wife, or at any time prior to his arrival in Baghdad, his life after Rīma's disappearance is presented as one revolving almost entirely around sex. We are told that he is intellectually active, that he is a successful businessman, that he is engaged in underground Palestinian activities. But none of this is actually shown. Only his sex life is described in great detail. The narrators of his sexual activities are his Baghdadi friends, particularly the women he has loved. By contrast, his Palestinian chapters show almost no awareness of this aspect of his life. So sex in the case of Walīd must be seen as a *trope*, a foreground experience directly linked to his being a stranger in his new society. And there his love-affairs, though numerous, are all barren; the possibility of a permanent union with any one of his women is clearly excluded; he is always dissatisfied. All his experiences—including the sexual—are written down in a disjointed, episodic style that obscures both temporal sequence and the causal connection.

Since the structure of the novel does not show the causes for his conduct we are obliged to look elsewhere. This means having to read the text as a 'writerly' (or 'scriptible') text, to use Roland Barthes' expression. Such a reading not only reveals that sex in exile has become for Walīd a way of compensating for the absence of wife and motherland, which is self-evident. It also shows that Walīd is fully conscious of the futility of the search, that it involves a degradation of the missing values which he cannot ignore. In Freudian terms his erotic life can be seen as a failure to maintain a fully normal attitude in love. Of the two currents whose confluence is required to attain normalcy in erotic life, according to Freud,[30] namely tender, affectionate feelings and sensual feelings, the first alone is directed towards his Palestinian wife, with the resultant psychical impotence. Towards the women of Baghdad, he directs the sensual current alone, exhibiting the degradation of his erotic relations with them. This is why his leaving them is so abrupt and unforgiving. His departure is a protest. The last mark he leaves is located at a road junction: one branch leading to Lebanon and the other to Palestine.

But having suggested that sex in his experience is a trope, we must point to another matter which makes Walīd's protest more universal, as speaking also for native Baghdadis. Although not much is revealed of his intellectual activity, this aspect of his life is sufficiently stressed to give it a universal significance. In this respect his disappearance assumes the nature of an escape. Again, the context is important. In a conversation with Alain Robbe-Grillet[31] during the Baghdad Poetry Festival of 1988, the French writer expressed amazement at an Iraqi professor's saying that a creative artist should place his pen at the service of his country. Jabrā's reply was:

> It is true that the writer in progressive societies is almost a government unto himself . . . and I mean by that that the writer can become a power opposing the existing government just as he can be in harmony with it . . . But in our world, the writer is still a part of society . . . and he is forced to be in harmony with it . . . otherwise he would be repudiated . . .

The political aspect of life in Iraq is conspicuous by its absence in the novel. It is vaguely alluded to by mentioning that Walīd was put in prison together with Ibrāhīm, where their friendship was reinforced. Occasionally there is some reference to Walīd's secret political activities. The only explicit statement made about political power is uttered by a retired politician who claims that he learned his most important lesson in life from Voltaire, who taught him that the best thing for a man is to tend his own garden. For Walīd, the free thinker, the sceptical intellectual as he is shown throughout the novel, submitting to the dictates of political power is an ordeal he has to escape. Very early in the novel he is quoted as having said:

> When I noticed for the first time, early in my life, a group of men talking, constantly glancing around asking, 'Has anyone heard us?' I was appalled. Are we so afraid of others knowing what we say? But over the years this fearful look and nervous question have been repeated so often that they have become normal. Fear has become part of our lives, we live with it, we pretend as far as possible it's not there, we get used to thinking like conspirators, we are always fearful, seeking shelter against people's evil. Under the pressure of this state of mind, you are expected to create, to produce dazzling pearls of originality before the eyes of those who have become blind a long time

> ago. I would rather search for the eye of the hurricane and escape all of this.

This he clearly does by disappearing from Baghdad, leaving behind a group of friends and a bewildered mistress wondering why he has abandoned them. But where can he go? The region described by 'Abd al-Raḥmān Munīf as 'East of the Mediterranean' leaves no real alternatives. Walīd simply has to disappear.

14

Women's Narrative in Modern Arabic Literature: A Typology

Sabry Hafez

This essay[1] investigates the relationship between language, gender and identity as an introduction to the study of the literary discourse of women writers in modern Arabic literature. It offers a triadic typology of the development of feminist awareness in the Arab world and posits a homological relationship between this typology, the changes in class background of the writers and their perception of national identity. Like any typology, particularly those concerning a body of discourse developed in a relatively short period of time, there are areas of overlap and coexistence. The essay illustrates its theoretical claims by a close reading of three novels. In its practical part, it demonstrates the coexistence of the three distinct phases of female consciousness by deliberately selecting novels written in one decade, the 1980s, yet representing three different discourses.

Patriarchy and Logocentrism

Arabic narrative discourse has long been recognized as a reflection of the many political, national and social issues of the Arab world, but it has rarely been studied as a battleground for the war of the sexes that has been waged through narrative since the rise of its various genres at the turn of the century. The persistent neglect of this issue has helped to consolidate the status quo and posit it as the unquestionable norm. Modern Arabic narrative discourse has therefore played a significant role in shaping, influencing and modifying the existing power relations between men and women in society. In a patriarchal society the literary discourse reflects a social structure whose dynamics are based on a power relationship in which women's interests are subordinated to those of men. Patriarchy in general is a social order which structures norms of behaviour, patterns of expectations and modes of expression, but in Arabic culture it has acquired a divine dimension through the religious ratification of the supremacy of men enshrined in the Qur'an.

The divine is masculine singular and enforces the patriarchal structural order which permeates all forms of social interaction. The divinity bestowed on men also encompasses the masculine language of the Qur'an and slights the feminine language of everyday life. The gender vision inherent in the diglossia of the Arabic language has not been studied nor has the equation between the written and the literary and the system of connotations inherent in the linguistic canon. The logocentrism of the written language is closely related to the patriarchal nature of society on the one hand, and the masculine character of the traditional establishment on the other. Classical Arabic literature, whether in its pure literary form—poetry—or in its other scholarly, linguistic and theological guises, has been predominantly male-controlled and male-oriented.

The patriarchal nature of both Arab society and its traditional literary establishment has made it extremely difficult for women's discourse to emerge within the tradition. Although there are exceptions, such as the poetess al-Khansā' (575–664?), her poetry was sanctioned by the establishment because she devoted her powerful elegiac talent almost entirely to immortalizing men, her two brothers, Mu'āwiya and Ṣakhr, and urging her tribe to revenge them. The other major work which is presumably composed by a woman or largely from a female perspective, *The Arabian Nights*, has been excluded from the literary canon and banished into the marginal domain of folk and oral literature, and even banned on occasions. It is ironic that such a rich and sophisticated literary work has been omitted from the literary canon for centuries, yet survives and continues to play a significant role throughout the Arab community from Iraq to Morocco and from Syria to Sudan.

In their seminal book, *The Newly Born Woman*, Hélène Cixous and Catherine Clément have emphasized the solidarity between logocentrism and patriarchy which they call phallocentrism in the Christian tradition,[2] but the condition in Arabic is even stronger for such an association is enshrined in the scriptures. The emergence of modern narrative discourse in Arabic literature spelt the end of this association and of the male monopoly of literary discourse. It is therefore not surprising that women were among the most active pioneers in this field. At the turn of the century, 'Ā'isha al-Taymūriyya (1840–1902), Zaynab Fawwāz (1860–1914), Farīda 'Aṭiyya (1867–1918), Zaynab Muḥammad, Labība Hāshim (1880–1947) and Malak Ḥifnī Nāṣif (1886–1918) were among the founders of narrative fiction. This tradition has continued throughout the twentieth century until the contribution of women writers has gained currency and prominence in contemporary Arabic narrative and ended in effect the old male monopoly on literature.

Another factor which has undermined the sacred alliance between patriarchy and logocentrism is the diglossic nature of Arabic narrative. From the early stages of the genesis of modern Arabic narrative discourse, diglossia has been one of the major topics of controversy concerning the language of narrative fiction.[3] The dichotomy between the formal literary language and the vernacular has only been debated and explained in literary terms. It is more than a mere linguistic or even literary issue, for it involves a major restructuring of ideological and cultural representations. It is therefore no coincidence that the strongest opposition to the use of the vernacular in literary texts was waged by the traditional establishment, who perceived it as a threat to both the social order and the literary canon. They were aware that the acceptance of the vernacular in the literary canon amounted to relinquishing the monopoly of the male over the literary realm. They may also have suspected the secular nature of narrative discourse and by extension its democratic and liberating force.

Yet the emergence of modern narrative discourse as a new mode of literary expression has been effectively employed to consolidate the status quo and enhance the solidarity between patriarchy and logocentrism. Like its Western counterpart, Arabic narrative has been used to enforce the patriarchal social order by enshrining its values in the major works of its genres. The *Trilogy*, *Bayn al-qaṣrayn* [Palace Walk] (1956), *Qaṣr al-shawq* [Palace of Desire] (1957) and *al-Sukkariyya* [Sugar Street] (1957),[4] by Najīb Maḥfūẓ is the patriarchal novel *par excellence*. Its hero, the charismatic Aḥmad 'Abd al-Jawwād, is both the father of the family and the pivot of the narrative world. From his loins all the protagonists emerge, and from his social and business activities other characters are brought into being. He is the prime mover of the text and the source of its life and every character in the novel is hierarchically placed in relation to him. Narrative structure, characters' motivation and spatial presentation are all mobilized to reflect and enforce the patriarchal order. Although the novel contains a detailed and vivid account of everyday life and the interaction between characters from the middle and lower strata of society, its long text contains no trace of colloquialism. Its concern with the linguistic purity of its *fuṣḥā* (formal and standardized Arabic) is inseparable from its interest in the immaculate portrayal of the patriarchal order.

Feminist Literary Typology

Since the early stages of the genesis of modern narrative discourse, women writers have tried to undermine the solidarity between logocentrism and patriarchy. The question of language is closely linked to both gender and identity and the female writers' attempt to express their gender difference led to the development of certain syntactic mutations. They played an important role in forging a new mode of linguistic expression which proved to be more felicitous to narrative discourse. They also exploited the secular and liberating qualities of narrative discourse to express their own views and enable feminine values to penetrate and subvert the patriarchal order that contains them. Feminist literary theory has strongly objected to the fitting of women between the lines of male tradition, and striven to free itself from the linear absolutes of male literary theory.[5] It has developed a different typology for the study of women's literature which is not dependent on systems of classification derived from male-dominated writing. In order to study the literature of women writers in Arabic, it is also necessary to develop a system of classification evolving from the study of their work and not imposed on it by expecting it to conform to the literature of their male colleagues. Since no exhaustive study of women writers' novels in Arabic has been undertaken, I shall adopt a slightly modified form of the typology developed by a feminist critic working on British women novelists.

In her study of the female literary tradition in the English novel, *A Literature of Their Own,* Elaine Showalter demonstrates how the development of this tradition is similar to the development of any literary subculture:

> First there is a prolonged phase of imitation of the prevailing modes of the dominant tradition, and internalization of its standards of art and its views on social roles. Second there is a phase of protest against these standards and values, and advocacy of minority rights and values including a demand for autonomy. Finally there is a phase of self-discovery, a turning inward freed from some of the dependency of opposition, a search for identity. An appropriate terminology for

> women writers is to call these stages: Feminine, Feminist, and Female.[6]

In her study, these three phases seem to be neatly divided into equal historical periods, each of which lasts forty years.[7] Each period is compartmentalized and socially and historically distinct as well as distinct in literary terms.[8]

Showalter's typology corresponds to Julia Kristeva's concept of the various stages of the feminist consciousness and struggle for identity. Kristeva rejects both biologism and essentialism as explanations of gender and argues for a historical and political approach that perceives the development of the feminist struggle as a three-tiered process

> which can be schematically summarized as follows: 1. Women demand equal access to the symbolic order. Liberal feminism. Equality. 2. Women reject the male symbolic order in the name of difference. Radical feminism. Femininity extolled. 3. Women reject the dichotomy between masculine and feminine as metaphysical.[9]

Kristeva's scheme is as relevant to the classification of women's narrative discourse in Arabic as is the triadic typology of Showalter. Moreover, Kristeva's is not a chronologically based system, thus allowing for a greater degree of overlap and coexistence. This overlap is particularly relevant to the experience of Arab women writers, for it explains why certain texts contain a mixture of qualities some of which belong to one phase and others to the following one. The presence of certain dominant features of a specific type does not necessarily result in the exclusion of all others. Dominance is a key word in differentiating between various types of feminist literary discourse.

Homology and Interaction

The typology of modern Arabic narrative discourse corresponds to that of its Western counterpart, but is not identical to it because it is considerably modified by a constant interaction with its socio-cultural context. Although the three types elaborated by Showalter can be identified in Arabic literature, they do not fall neatly into equal historical categories. The experience of Arab women novelists demonstrates that the condensing of these phases gives rise to an interdependence between them in a manner that makes each phase necessary for the emergence and development of the succeeding one. Even if one national literature completes one or more of these phases, another cannot omit them, even if it is aware of what the former has been through. For a long time, the marginalization of women's writing hindered the flow of their experience from one literary tradition to another. Although the first phase of 'feminine' writing in Arabic literature started after the end of its British counterpart in 1880, it was necessary for Arab women writers to go through it even if some of them were aware that the work of their British counterparts had finished with this stage and they were now engaged in the second one.

The brevity of the period in which Arabic narrative went through these three different phases created a certain overlap in presentation and literary qualities, but the phases remained as distinct and different in Arabic as they were in British and other literatures. In addition to the general continuum of any subculture, these three phases in the development of the female literary tradition in Arabic narrative were more stages of female consciousness in Kristeva's sense than autonomous periods of literary development. As such they were linked to two main factors: the change in class background of the female writers, and subsequently their formative experience; and the nature of the collective perception of the national identity. The perception of gender and/or individual identity is generally linked to the wider perception of the national self and its place in the surrounding world. This forges the individual and the social into a unitary condition which seeks to articulate its tenets in a particularized literary language capable of formulating alternatives. The change from one phase of women's literary discourse to another is both a manifestation of the wider socio-political conditions and an active force in the process of formulating them.

The correspondence and interaction between these three sets of changes, the social, the political and the literary, is part of a wider change in literary sensibility from the traditional sensibility with its metonymic rules of reference to the modernistic one based on metaphoric rules.[10] Elsewhere, I have elaborated the nature of this change in literary sensibility in modern Arabic literature, the transition from the first to the second and the different sets of rules of reference underlying each one.[11] What is relevant here is that the first two phases of the 'feminine' and 'feminist' discourse in Arabic literature took place within the rubrics of traditional sensibility in which the literary text was perceived as an extension to or a reflection of an external and largely hierarchical reality. The third phase, the 'female' discourse, by contrast, is part and parcel of the modernistic sensibility which emphasizes the autonomy and internal cohesion of the literary text and minimizes its dependence on exterior absolutes or a hierarchized reality. The two different sensibilities provide each phase with its literary context, enable the reader to react to its products with the analogous interpretative responses and explain a certain overlapping of characteristics between the two first phases. They also locate women's work within a wider framework of secular Arabic discourse and dispense with simplistic arguments of imported feminism. The relevance of Showalter's and Kristeva's schemes is that they can be used as a starting-point, then qualified and modified to suit the new context.

'Feminine' Literature of Imitation

The prolonged phase of 'feminine' writing characterized the output of upper-class Turco-Circassian women in Egypt and the Levant in the late nineteenth century. This period is distinguished by what Margot Badran calls 'invisible feminism',[12] a condition of minimum awareness of gender difference and an inarticulate demand for the bare essentials of feminine rights. The awareness of gender difference is normally confined to the areas recognized by the patriarchal order and is indispensable for the preservation of its authority and the hierarchical allocation of roles and space. The portrayal of domestic bliss and the joy of its protective enclave played an active role in enforcing the confinement of women to the harem and even raised it to the status of a desirable utopia. Women's presentation of life in the harem had the authority of first-hand experience and was more effective in communicating the patriarchal message to other women.

The books produced by women writers of this early period circulated in the harem and as a result centred around the experience of their prospective readers who fitted congenially into the patriarchal system. It is natural that the titles of these rudimentary novels were either of a highly traditional and moralistic nature or entertaining and sentimental.[13] The rudimentary narrative of these women writers was not very different from that of their male contemporaries in its social or moralistic outlook or in its language and textual strategies.

This soon changed with the nationalistic stance of Hudā Sha'rāwī and others at the beginning of the twentieth century and their articulation of the need for women's participation in Egypt's struggle for independence. They called for women to be granted certain 'essential' rights so that they could manifest their support for the patriotic cause. The female role in the nationalistic struggle, in which the polarization was between a monolithic national 'self' and a foreign 'other', was completely subordinated to that of the male. The whole period was distinguished by the idealization of the beauty of the country and the romanticization of patriotism. In this stage national interests, and with them national identity, were seen as monolithic and abstract, a vision that was totally in harmony with the prevalent patriarchal world view of the predominantly bourgeois élite. The interests of women were not distinguished from those of men, nor were the concerns of the rich from those of the poor. This shows that one of the reasons for the failure of the nationalistic project at the time was the inherent contradiction in its quest for liberation: namely, the desire to liberate the male from foreign domination but subject the female to the domination of the patriarchal system.

It is interesting that the 'feminine' literary discourse which prevailed in Egypt and the Levant in the last decades of the nineteenth century and the early part of the twentieth is currently echoed in Arabia and the Gulf. This highlights the uneven literary development of various parts of the Arab world, and the coexistence of the three types of writing in the contemporary literary scene. In this type of 'feminine' discourse,[14] women writers reproduce not only the world view inherent in the predominantly masculine discourse, but also adopt its version of the passive, docile, selfless female. In their works the value system encoded in the hierarchical social order which places the female at the bottom is adopted without questioning and is even praised for its concern and protection of the meek, helpless female.

The narrative works of this type are but a variation on the patriarchal discourse in which the nature and social role of women are defined in relation to norms which are clearly male. Gender and identity are perceived within the confines of the patriarchal order and their narrative representation is structured in a manner that serves the preservation of the prevalent hierarchy. Yet the female writers of this type, though conforming to the male views and canons, have been marginalized and their names almost purged from the history of modern Arabic literature. The marginalization of their writing is both a consequence of the gender relations which have structured women's absence from the active production of 'important' or 'serious' literature, and a direct result of their own discourse which made their writing no more than variations on the main patriarchal discourse whose strong presence renders any variation unimportant. Yet these imitative variations on the prevalent male discourse were the necessary first step without which subsequent development would not have been possible. It accustomed both the reader and the patriarchal establishment to the phenomenon of women writers. It also earned the women writers respect, a prerequisite for taking their writing seriously, and more importantly made the 'invisible woman' clearly visible. Despite its conformity, or rather because of its ability to appease patriarchal fear by adopting its vision, it took a major step towards breaking down the male monopoly on discourse.

'Feminine' Literary Discourse

The 'feminine' narrative discourse is represented in this essay by a novel by the Kuwaiti writer Laylā al-'Uthmān, *Wasmiyya takhruj min al-bahr* [Wasmiyya Emerges from the Sea] (1986).[15] In this novel we find a clear example of the internalization of the male perspective and its faithful reproduction by a female writer. Like that of the writers of the first phase of 'feminine' discourse in Egypt and the Levant, Laylā al-'Uthmān's work[16] appeared within the context of establishing a new national literature. Before 1970 Kuwait had no narrative literature of any significance,[17] and al-'Uthmān's narrative work can be seen as part and parcel of the process of establishing a new literary discourse capable of shaping a specific identity.[18] Although Kuwaiti writers started to publish when mainstream Arabic narrative had already moved away from the traditional sensibility towards the modernistic one, their work, as well as that of the rest of the Arabian peninsula, is produced within the rubrics of traditional sensibility and according to its dynamics and metonymic rules of reference.

Wasmiyya takhruj min al-bahr is no exception. It aims to reflect the reality of a changing Kuwait and the impact of this change on social interactions, roles and gender. The dominant narrative voice in this novel is not that of its heroine, Wasmiyya, whose name is enshrined in the title, which reflects a male stereotypical vision of the female as a siren emerging from the sea, but that of the hero, 'Abdullāh. The narrative oscillates between first and third person; in the former 'Abdullāh speaks of his inner feelings and anxieties and in the latter he narrates the rest of the story and presents other characters. The identification between 'Abdullāh's personal perspective and that of the third-person narrative enhances his authority and presence in the absence of his direct voice. This creates a textual equivalent of the stereotypical male whose women conform to his system of values and ideals regardless of whether he is physically present. The prevalence of his point of view throughout the narrative, and particularly when he is not involved in the narrated event, is a manifestation of the all-embracing patriarchal order whose control over the world of narrative is seen as the norm.

The prevalence of the male hero's perspective throughout the narrative is ostensibly intended to glamourize the female, but results not only in the male's manipulation of the narrative point of view, but also in structuring the absence of the female and denying her any narrative voice. The heroine is the epitome of the silent woman who has internalized the male belief that the silent female is by definition chaste, for verbal intercourse leads inevitably to sexual intercourse. The idealization of the female through the eyes of the male narrator is a strategy that allows the text to reproduce in its heroine the desired female, the one who internalizes the male perception of the 'correct' feminine code of conduct, and enables the narrator to be the active agent who inspires and controls her action. The ultimate presence of the heroine is mainly achieved through her complete absence, her death by drowning which identifies her with both the sea and the siren of the title.

Her wilful death is presented as the conclusive feat of submission at the behest of patriarchy, for she intentionally sacrifices herself in order to preserve intact the supremacy of the patriarchal code of conduct. Her death is enveloped in certain ambiguities—was it voluntary or accidental?—yet the structuring of the event which leads to her death makes it inevitable that she rather than 'Abdullāh is selected for this fate. This is enforced both by her initiative to hide under water and by her failure to cry for help when she is engulfed by the waves, to demonstrate her devotion to preserving the order that dictates her annihilation. Her reward for such selfless surrender to the patriarchal order is inscribed in every aspect of the narrative to allow her absence to prevail over the presence of 'Abdullāh's wife, who shows less than total capitulation to his vision. The absent Wasmiyya becomes the ultimate object of desire while the present stereotypical nagging wife is presented as an objectionable obstacle in his quest to satisfy his desires.

At one level the novel contains a reproduction of an inverted form of the stereotypical female who uses her beauty to snare the rich and/or powerful male, for it tells the love-story of the poor 'Abdullāh and the rich and beautiful Wasmiyya. They were brought up together as children, but their childish playfulness soon turned into an adolescent passion that was curbed by the divisive social order. But this is far from what Kolodny calls 'inversion', which occurs when the stereotyped traditional literary images of women are turned around in women's narrative works for comic purpose, to reveal their hidden reality, to expose their underlying prejudice or to connote their opposite.[19] The ostensible 'inversion' of the traditional stereotype merely has a sentimental connotation and conforms to the patriarchal conceptions. The inversion of the traditional tale serves patriarchal control, for it enables the poor male, 'Abdullāh, against the dictates of social class, to prevail over the rich female, Wasmiyya, in a manner that allows the patriarchal order to prevail over social class.

This is confirmed through the allocation of space in the novel, for while a whole variety of space is open to the male narrator, the female is confined to the limited domain of the home. This is not seen as a prison, but as a haven from the devilish heat of the outside world and the contamination of its experience. Indeed, her departure from its protective habitat exposes her to danger and leads to her death. In addition, the association of the innocent love of childhood with the nostalgic past of pre-oil Kuwait, with a simple existence of fishing and tribal life, is posited as a paradise lost. This is contrasted with the materialistic ways of post-oil society, which is strongly divided by class consciousness. The loss of innocence is seen as the cause of corruption and disharmony, but the only way to regain the lost paradise is through death. Although one can detect a Freudian implication in positing death as the ultimate object of desire—as Nirvana or the recapturing of the lost unity and the final healing of the split subject—the presentation of the action in the moment of the hero's drowning, longing to attain unity with his lost beloved, offers conflicting implications. With its emphasis on the return to the happy days of yore, nostalgia has been identified as an anti-feminist textual strategy preaching a return to the past when men were men and women were women.[20]

Another aspect of this nostalgic resistance to change in the novel is the representation of the present as degenerate, corrupt and ugly. The hero's acceptance of its rules is posited as a loss of authenticity and masculine supremacy, for the woman who calls for its acceptance is presented as the nagging, unattractive wife devoid of sympathy, love or understanding. She has no feeling for her husband and is portrayed in the text as the devil incarnate.[21] Despite her association with the present, she remains nameless, faceless and characterless; her time, the present, is depicted as the time of 'gushes of black gold which emit greed, hatred, malice and endless hostility'.[22] Her presence is purged from the text, whose core is the remembrance and glorification of the past. Her opposing character, Wasmiyya, not only has her name enshrined in the title of the novel but is also beautiful, tender, loving and understanding.

> In nostalgic writings, opposition past/present accumulates crucially important meanings. As we have seen, the term past is attached to other terms that make of it a locus of authenticity. So vivid does this constructed past become that the rhetorical strategies used to create it seem to disappear . . . The mythic past becomes real.[23]

This is what the novel aspires to achieve, to make this mythic and highly imaginative version of the past real by purging the text of any real representation of the present.

'Feminist' Inversion of Codes

The second and most prolific phase is that of the 'feminist' narrative discourse of protest against the standards and values of the patriarchal discourse and its implicit system. In this phase, which lasted from the 1930s until the 1970s, Arab women writers realized that literary discourse plays a significant part in the social and political life of their nation. They also became aware of its function as a propagator of a 'world view' and hence of its vital role in keeping the oppressed passive or inciting them to revolt against their lot. For without altering women's perception of themselves and their role, it is difficult to motivate them to undergo the required change. This coincided with the spread of education, progressive urbanization, the acceleration of social mobility and the rise of the middle class and its wide participation in the political quest for national identity. It is therefore natural that the majority of women writers of this phase are descendants of middle-class families who felt, with the euphoria of independence, that their chance had come to play a significant role in the development of their country. The old aristocratic class of female writers who perceived of literary activity as a luxury faded away, to create room for the aggressive and aspiring middle class. The end of the colonial era in the Arab world and the emergence of independent states changed the nature of nationalistic issues, and brought about a new agenda and a class and gender polarization. The romantic nature of the nationalistic cause of the past, when the monolithic national 'self' was contrasted with the colonial 'other', was over; in its place, a number of contending political visions competed for public attention and gender issues moved to the foreground.

One of the major contradictions of this phase is that the more the 'feminist' writer rebelled against the prevalent norms, the more attractive she became to the ruling establishment, which was in the habit of co-opting the propagators of change. This was so because the newly established nationalist regimes were in need of a programme of social change which attracted wide support and, as a result, identified with the 'feminist' call for reform. The main characteristic of the 'feminist' narrative discourse of this phase, namely its desire to subvert patriarchal control of the distribution of roles, was seen by the nationalistic ruling establishments as directed against the old order and hence analogous to that of the new regimes. The association with the establishment gave the 'feminist' discourse a boost and enabled it to consolidate its grip on the educational establishment in many parts of the Arab world.[24] As a result, new venues were opened for women and their place in the literary world was enhanced. The very number of women writers published in this period, throughout the Arab world and particularly in its old centres in Egypt and the Levant, confirms this.[25] Yet many of their texts reveal a peculiar tendency to invert the prevalent patriarchal order without a clear understanding of the dangers involved. The inversion of an unjust order retains the inherent contradictions of its original system, albeit in a reverse form. They are recuperating the ideology of the system which they set out to repudiate. The critique of a male-dominated vision becomes entangled in the metaphysical framework of male supremacy it seeks to dismantle.

This is evident in Nawāl al-Sa'dāwī's novel, *Suqūṭ al-imām* [The Fall of the Imam] (1987),[26] which tells the story of a woman who discovers that she is the illegitimate daughter of the Imam, a political leader who exploits religion for his own ends. The heroine, Bint-Allah, recalls the story of her problematic relationship with her father while she watches his assassination and the ceremonial preparations for his official funeral. The structure of the novel is a structure of equivocation, selective and controlled both by the account of the public assassination and by the preparations for the official funeral and the flashes of subjective memory which punctuate events and provide them with their historical dimension. The story aspires to inscribe in its subjective account both the education of the 'female' in the face of adversity and the general history of the corrupt political establishment, of patriarchy.

On one level, the novel may be seen as a female *Bildungsroman* which elects to maximize the obstacles and constraints in the path of its female protagonist in order to elaborate the process of her cultural and sexual development. The heroine is no ordinary young women, but the Imam's illegitimate daughter. She has been wronged by her father, who left her mother and married another woman who shares with him the fruits of his success and the reins of power. The heroine and her mother are relegated to poverty and persecuted if they dare to reveal their relationship with the Imam. For a 'feminist' project, the wronged woman is an appropriate point of departure and the plot enhances this by making the very identity of the heroine the problematic issue in the novel. The revelation of the heroine's identity poses a threat to her father, the Imam, and his corrupt authority. The power of the Imam, or in other words of patriarchy, is based on the suppression of the identity of his daughter, of the 'woman'.

The conflict between the woman's desire for self-expression and realization of her identity and the institution of patriarchy is given added weight by making the Imam the ultimate symbol of power and the holder of political, cultural and religious authority.

In order to posit her heroine as the counter-power in this multidimensional conflict and give her added religious significance, al-Sa'dāwī presents her heroine as a female version of Christ. The text insists on calling her Bint-Allah (literally, the daughter of God) and endows her mother, who was a combination of prostitute and belly-dancer, with martyrdom. But the fact that her father is a false God and her mother is no Virgin Mary weakens the author's argument, for in order to sustain her role as a saviour, the novel needs to sever her relationship with her father, the false God. Yet suppressing her relationship with her father is exactly what the novel's patriarchal institution seeks to achieve. The conflict between these two strands in the novel's structure undermines its potency and highlights the equivocal nature of its project. The novel's challenge to patriarchy requires a reinforcement of the heroine's bonds with her father, while the added religious significance demands the weakening of these bonds. This structural equivocation is a product of the author's imposing her ideology on her narrative. In her introduction to the novel, al-Sa'dāwī discloses her unease in naming her main character,[27] in a manner that demonstrates her imposition of certain ideas on the novel's structure. It is indeed a bright 'feminist' idea to invert the story of Christ and posit the heroine as his modern female version. It is also viable to raise abused women and prostitutes to martyrdom. But to bring this from the realm of vague intentions into solid narrative realization, capable of imparting a symbolic layer of meaning, requires a poetically creative and skilled presentation which can integrate this into the narrative structure.

Although the very orientation of the narrative makes the daughter's the prevalent voice in the text, the author fails to articulate the motivations for her war against the Imam, whose recognition she neither seeks nor respects. Setting the daughter against her father and making her a major threat to his corrupt establishment requires very sensitive treatment and an elaborate process of *éducation sentimentale*, of which there is little in *Suqūt al-imām*. The novel pays little attention to its heroine's social and cultural background, so when she launches her crusade against the Imam she lacks motivation and credibility. As a result, the political and ideological objectives of her campaign against him appear to be surgically implanted and the reader is asked to accept them as natural. Her feelings and views of her father lack the complexity of a love–hate relationship, which one expects in a situation like this. One may surmise that the author's antipathy towards the Imam, and all male characters, is designed to help her heroine justify her behaviour towards them. The text has many obnoxious men, and several less obnoxious women, but there is little interaction between all these characters to generate the dynamics of conflicting interests and clashing visions. The mere cumulative effect of the juxtaposition of situations and characters speaking in turn, dictated by narrating the selective past from the viewpoint of the present, fails to create the desired unity and the dynamics of opposing perspectives.

In addition, the Imam's despotic nature and fanatical views are portrayed as the product of an inferiority complex, for the Imam is not only vulgar, contorted, cruel and stupid, but he is also from a low and poor background. The author seems to equate poverty with immorality and wealth with good manners and solid ethical values,[28] a position that is incompatible with much of 'feminist' ideology. This hierarchical concept is not confined to the characterization of the Imam but permeates the structure of the novel. Ordering social value and status on a hierarchical scale contains implicit patriarchal connotations, despite the novel's strong attack on patriarchy. Although the feminist's ultimate aim is the dismantling of the patriarchal system, al-Sa'dāwī's thinking, in its hierarchical and binary structure, is identical to that of patriarchy. As Cixous and Clément demonstrate:

> organization by hierarchy makes all conceptual organization subject to man. Male privilege is shown in the opposition between activity and passivity which he uses to sustain himself. Traditionally, the question of sexual difference is treated by coupling it with the opposition of activity/passivity, . . . culture/nature, day/night, head/heart, intelligible/palpable, logos/pathos, man/woman, always the same metaphor.[29]

When it comes to the man/woman opposition which Cixous sees as the core of patriarchal binary thinking, she insists on putting it on the page in its vertical and hierarchic form:

$$\frac{\text{Man}}{\text{Woman}}$$

rather than in the horizontal juxtaposition which may imply opposition between equals. Hierarchy is the other side of the same coin of binary patriarchal thinking, and the two permeate every aspect of al-Sa'dāwī's novel.

On another level of interpretation, *Suqūṭ al-imām* is a political allegory based on the Sādāt era and using thinly disguised characters who lack inner motivation and have little symbolic value. In spite of his weakness and abhorrent dispositions, the Imam (for which, we can read 'man') has miraculously managed to attain power and employs a group of people who are more intelligent and better educated than he is to help him run a highly corrupt state apparatus. In addition, he has succeeded in establishing a personality cult that enables his universally hated regime to survive after his death. This is so because most characters derive their credibility neither from apt characterization, nor from the internal cohesion of the plot, but rather from their reference to real figures in Egypt's recent political history. The fictional world of the novel strives for plausibility and derives it from its constant reference to extrinsic data. For those who cannot relate its events or characters to their historical referents, it seems an ambiguous fantasy, full of repetition and cardboard characters, and marked by a burdensome authorial presence which generates a heavy sense of didacticism and reproduces one of the worst aspects of patriarchal narrative.

The author's dedication and preface suggest how the reader should perceive events in the novel, and hints at both its political and 'feminist' interpretation. Indeed, on the dust jacket of the British edition, Doris Lessing declares it to be 'a tale of women suffering under harsh Islamic rule',[30] pointing out both its 'feminist' posture and its anti-Islamic stance. However, selecting bad patriarchs does not help al-Sa'dāwī's anti-patriarchal stance: it is easy to trivialize her attack by arguing that good patriarchs do not behave in such an abhorrent manner. In this respect, the author resorts to easy solutions in supporting her argument, including the falsification of evidence. One such case is her use of the frame story of *The Arabian Nights*,[31] where she rewrites the story in a manner inferior to the original.

On the artistic level, the author allows her various characters to speak in turn in the first person, giving us their own versions of certain aspects of the story. Unfortunately, they all speak with a unified language, the language of the author and not that of the characters, which fails to take into account their different socio-psychological backgrounds and their opposing ideological stances. What unfolds in the novel is not a multitude of characters and fates in a single objective world, illuminated by a single objective consciousness, but a group of fragmentary characters who are objects of authorial discourse, not subjects of their own directly signifying discourse. This calls into question the author's motivation for using the device of first-person narrative, and the logic of using such a demanding technique for a task that could be achieved by resorting to the usual functions of characterization and plot development. Although the allegorical nature of the text and its ideological implications necessitate a rich dialogue between the various arguments and viewpoints, al-Sa'dāwī's discourse in *Suqūṭ al-imām* is of a monological rather than a dialogical nature in the Bakhtinian sense of the term.

Unlike the polyphonic narrative of Dostoevsky, which unifies highly heterogeneous and incompatible material, the compositional principle of al-Sa'dāwī's narrative is monophonic, which reduces the plurality of consciousness to an ideological common denominator that is excesssively simplistic. Al-Sa'dāwī's road to literary creativity is paved with good causes and honourable intentions. She aspires to achieve justice and wants to fight for her sisters' rights, equality and self-determination in a traditional and highly patriarchal society. But her one-dimensional approach to her data impoverishes her narrative. Introducing her new ideas to such a conservative milieu warrants certain exaggerations and didacticism which are by their very nature incompatible with literary presentation. This leaves her critics in a quandary and has led some of them to advise her to confine her writing to militant theoretical prose. Fortunately, hers is not the last word in Arab women's discourse, for there is a third group of younger, 'female' writers whose work is gradually commanding attention and respect.

The Sophisticated Discourse of Self-Realization

Our third type of narrative discourse—the 'female'—is the discourse of difference, which expresses itself in a rich variety of different techniques. It has emerged in the work of recent years as a reaction to the prevalent 'feminist' perceptions that reduced the women's movement to a bourgeois egalitarian demand for women to obtain power in the present patriarchal system. It sees the feminists as women who crave power and social legitimization that grant them respect and a place in the prevalent but faulty system. Instead, the new 'female' writers[32] are developing a fascinating narrative discourse of self-discovery. It is concerned with granting the voiceless female a mature narrative voice that is truly her own. Most of the writers of this new discourse come from a background of voicelessness, such as the poor Shi'ite community in the south of Lebanon or the working and peasant class in Egypt, Tunisia and Iraq.

Their subtle, shrewd and artistically mature techniques for subverting the prevalent order result in the most interesting 'female' discourse in the Arab world, for it develops in the context of changing national realities and is careful not to alienate the other gender. The main feature of this reality is the disintegration of the old nationalist project and the emergence of new forms of traditionalism. The rational approach is rapidly making way for a new sectarian thinking whose rising forms of belligerency use the sacred to consolidate the shaky old order and manipulate a religious discourse to serve the patriarchal system. Fundamentalism resorts to the static religious discourse and fixed 'view of the world' to avert the danger of a dynamically changing society. Narrative discourse, by its very nature, is both secular and liberal and is capable of developing counter-strategies. In the varied and highly sophisticated narrative of these 'female' writers, there are numerous textual strategies capable of undermining the rising discourse of traditionalism and furthering the secular.[33] One of these strategies is the glorification of the female, a literary strategy that aspires to break the male's monopoly on the divine and provide the sacred with a feminine aspect. This also humanizes the sacred and reflects a fundamental change in the perception of the female in the culture.

In the few works of this phase, the 'female' writer has become increasingly aware of the inability of 'feminist' discourse to disentangle itself from what Cixous calls 'patriarchal binary thought' and its hidden male/female opposition with the inevitable passive/active evaluation as its underlying paradigm. The binary oppositions are heavily implicated in the patriarchal value system; and the new 'female' writers posit a multiple heterogeneous *différence* against its scheme of thought. This is evident in Salwā Bakr's novel *Maqām 'Aṭiyya* ['Aṭiyya's Shrine] (1986)[34] in which the narrative structure itself is based on the multiplicity of testimonies that make such *différence* capable of reflecting the two categories of the different and the deferred in Derrida's work. From the very title of the novel one becomes aware of the multi-layered structure, for the word *maqām* in the title means both 'shrine' and 'status', and refers in addition to the musical structure which is inherent in the piece with its variations on the theme and final coda. The second word, 'Aṭiyya, is the proper name of the heroine (a common Egyptian female name) as well as a reference to the age-old concept of the female being created from man's rib and 'given' as a 'present' to the male. The passive meaning built into the Arabic morphology of the name 'Aṭiyya is counterbalanced by its active grammatical role in the *iḍāfa* structure in which the name, 'Aṭiyya, is the cornerstone of the grammatical structure of the title. This is enhanced by the selection of an androgynous name, 'Aṭiyya, which is used in Arabic for both men and women—a feature which the text is keen should not escape the reader's attention, for it often extends this androgynous nature to the heroine.[35]

The narrative structure uses the polyphony of narrative voices neither to establish the various facets of truth nor to demonstrate its relativity, but to defer any application of patriarchal binary thought. The text posits narrative discourse against that of the media, seen as one of the main tools of what Louis Althusser calls 'the ideological state apparatus' and jettisons all preconceived notions about the prescribed position of the female in society. The novel resorts to a significant technique which acknowledges the absence of the woman and turns it with the dexterity of narrative treatment into a sign of her overwhelming presence. The main character in the novel, 'Aṭiyya, is deliberately absent, as if to conform with the prevalent social norm, in an attempt to investigate this norm by taking its tenets as its point of departure. The novel's primary concern is to exorcise this absence and turn it into a stark form of presence, superior in quality and significance to that of the omnipresent male. By taking absence as its point of departure, the novel equates the writing of the story of the deceased 'Aṭiyya with that of realizing the potential of the narrator of the story, 'Azza, in an attempt to suggest the vital connection between 'female' writers rewriting the story of their foremothers and reshaping that of the present generation.

The recourse to the technique of the novel within the novel (which dates back to *The Arabian Nights* and is one of the oldest forms of Arabic narrative structure) establishes the strong affinity between the novel and its deep-rooted popular tradition. This narrative structure with its inherent intertextuality enhances the rich dialectics between the frame and the enframed stories on the one hand, and that of fiction and reality on the other. From the outset, the text establishes both the perspective of narrative and the function of writing as well as its ideological stance *vis-à-vis* the establishment. The story is presented as fragments of a suppressed text divided, like the body of Osiris, among various voices and scattered over a temporal plain that spans Egypt's modern history from the national Revolution of 1919 to the present. It is also seen as an attempt by its collector (the narrator and young journalist 'Azza Yūsuf, who is clearly an anti-establishment figure) to give meaning to her life after the death of her husband, the Egyptian archaeologist 'Alī Fahīm. For the piecing together of the various parts of 'Aṭiyya's story corresponds to the emerging and evolving love-story which results in her marriage to the archaeologist and bearing his son.

The multiple identification of 'Azza and 'Aṭiyya with the ancient

Egyptian goddess Isis involves the reader in the relational network of the text and its intertextual implications. Although 'Aṭiyya can be seen as Isis in relation to her own family, she can also be seen as a female version of Osiris in her relationship with 'Azza. The identification with Isis is in constant interaction with its presentation as the female version of Osiris, for the inversion of roles in the 'female' stage of writing is achieved without alienating the woman from her female self. This is enhanced on the text's ideological plane by positing popular belief (with its feminine synthesizing nature, in which ancient Egyptian creeds are blended with the tenets of Christianity and Islam and integrated in their practice) against the dogmatic male version of Islam (with its inherent fundamentalism). The shrine of 'Aṭiyya is a continuation of that of ancient Egyptian gods, while the religious opposition to it stems from the male establishment that has been stripped of its virility by the rising and more potent force of fundamentalism and the media. Yet the popular beliefs in which many religious elements blend and harmonize, and which penetrate the testimonies of both male and female characters in the text, are victorious over the discredited official ones.

The novel succeeds in creating a textual equivalent of the social conditions in which sexual politics are structured around the suppression of the female voice, yet this voice is written into the very texture of the narrative. The presentation of narrative discourse constructs the textual space in a manner reproducing the structural order of patriarchy, while at the same time subverting its very authority. It gives the male voices the function of starting and ending the story, and squeezes the females, who are outnumbered by the males, into the middle. Men start the narrative and end it, ostensibly confident of retaining control, and leave the squabbling over its middle for women. Yet by cutting up the continuity of the male voice, and giving the female the interruptive role, it is possible to achieve the real inversion of the prevalent order by turning its structure against itself. In addition, grouping the female voices in the centre of the narrative sequence assures the continuity of their voices and the centrality of their position within the hierarchy of the textual order. Unlike the 'feminist', the 'female' writer does not aspire to cancel out the male voice, or to subject it to the rubrics of feminist oppression, but rather to create a new order in which the two genders relate a different story of the female.

These three phases, or more precisely, three types of narrative discourse—'feminine', 'feminist' and 'female'—correspond to similar phases in the development of the quest for and perception of national identity. They do so in a manner that reveals the interaction between the national consciousness and the position of women in society, and the impossibility of realizing the aspirations of a nation without realizing the full potential of both genders.

15

The Development of Women's Political Consciousness in the Short Stories of the Kuwaiti Author Laylā al-'Uthmān[1]

Angelika Rahmer

Introduction

The literary works[2] of Laylā al-'Uthmān, born in Kuwait in 1945, deal with a wide range of problems in the Arab world. Many of these difficulties concern changes that have taken place in Kuwaiti society during the last fifty years, particularly the transformation from a traditional bedouin tribal society and maritime-mercantile structures to an industrialized capitalist welfare state.[3] Kuwait has now developed into a multinational society faced with increasing foreign immigration and still in quest of its own values and traditions. Al-'Uthmān describes the social environment of people who live in the old, traditional areas of towns and the loss of orientation that confronts wealthy Kuwaiti citizens. Not only does she depict her own people; she focuses some of her narratives on the Palestinian conflict.

Women play a central role in all her writing. In the patriarchal society of Arabia that she describes, they are the ones who suffer the effects of discrimination, defamation and social isolation, not to mention both physical and psychological abuse. Al-'Uthmān chooses to accompany her characters as they pursue their road towards emancipation. Provided with the necessary political awareness, women are made to appear as a symbol of their native land. Thus they are portrayed not as static, but as dynamic characters.

Submissive Woman

In "al-Judrān tatamazzaq" [The Walls Fall Apart],[4] a 14-year-old girl tells her story to a female social worker. Since her mother's death the girl has been living with her married sister. Her brother-in-law seduces her and forces himself upon her a number of times. She becomes pregnant as a result, but is able to keep the matter a secret. She eventually has the baby in the school toilet and immediately kills it. The story realistically depicts the hopelessness that confronts the girl in the face of the persecution she suffers at the hands of her brother-in-law; for she is not only inferior to him in the physical sense but also economically dependent on him. As a result she is essentially defenceless. Even her own sister deserts her, ignoring her pleas for help. Above all, the girl is well aware that, as far as society is concerned, it is she who is guilty; she has been 'tarnished' and what makes it worse is that, as she admits with some shame, the experience even gave her a certain amount of pleasure. Al-'Uthmān is anxious to draw her reader's attention to the dilemmas that women have to face. While forced into sexual relationships, every illicit contact has to be kept secret since such a situation is regarded as sinful, especially when pleasure intensifies the feelings of guilt.

In "al-Ishāra al-ḥamrā'" [The Red Light],[5] the heroine reveals to her husband's brother, Farās, how deeply she loves her husband, Rashād, who is on a visit to London. At that moment she is expecting Rashād's child, but is unaware of the fact that Farās secretly desires her. When she discovers an anonymous love-letter in her bag, she suspects nothing. However, upon Rashād's return, he accidentally discovers the letter and gives her a brutal beating, believing that she has committed adultery with his brother whose handwriting he recognizes. Yet again, women are forced to endure society's double standards. Rashād punishes his wife for infidelity, but does nothing to his brother. Moreover, he openly boasts of his own flirtations with women in England.

"Al-Thawb al-ākhar" [The Other Garment][6] fits the same pattern. A man forces his wife to have sex with his business partners. The woman, who has only acquired wealth through her marriage, suffers terribly from the disgrace involved but fulfils her obligations. Eventually she is told to meet Ḥāzim, yet another of her husband's business partners. Aware of her situation, he surprises her by declaring his love and promising to free her from her predicament. As a result she is able to find the necessary strength of mind to leave her husband. Although the story seems fairly simple and even artificial, it can be seen as illustrating the 'liberation' of the heroine as the result of external rather than internal forces.[7] She is prepared to articulate her own misery but then surrenders to passivity. In order to sustain the level of wealth and luxury to which she has become accustomed, she is forced to offer herself to other men although she runs the risk of destroying herself mentally. The author's intention seems to be focused here on a condemnation of city life under whose abuses women in particular have to suffer.

Even in the context of the modern Arab city premarital sexual relationships are regarded as a blot on women's reputation. They are also a symbol of repressive structures that predominate above all in traditional rural life. This is the theme of "Ākhir al-layl" [The End of Night].[8] Wasmiyya tells her husband about her supposed pregnancy, something she has been expecting for five years. Through a flashback we learn the reason for this misfortune. During a funeral in her village Wasmiyya stays at home alone. We see her searching through the room of her cousin, Nāṣir, who, being an orphan, lives in their house. To complicate matters further, she is infatuated with him. Entering the room unexpectedly, Nāṣir rapes her. Becoming pregnant, Wasmiyya is forced to have an abortion at the hands of the aged Umm Fāḍil. It is only because he is severely punished by her father that Nāṣir agrees to marry Wasmiyya. The couple are childless for five years, clearly as a result of the rough treatment she received at the hands of the old midwife. The reader never discovers whether Wasmiyya's hopes of being pregnant are correct or not. Following the rape, Wasmiyya remains passive during the painful abortion procedure and the forced marriage. All this is forcefully presented in the narrative. An observant narrator lays great emphasis on the depiction of the rural environment, the characters involved and the funeral ceremony. Through the limited viewpoint of the narrator, we also learn about Wasmiyya's state of mind; the reader views the outside world through her eyes and is thus directly confronted with the girl's innocence and helplessness.

Rebellious Woman

Through the image of the rebellious woman, al-'Uthmān portrays those who choose to fight against their oppression. These images play a central role in her work, particularly since she seems eager to come to terms with her own loveless childhood.[9] It is hardly surprising that her stories seem to contain a number of autobiographical features. In "Lā khabar . . . lā" [No News . . . None],[10] a wedding celebration forms the frame story within which the heroine reflects on her own sad fate. Through a flashback she recalls the tyranny of her father, the man whose hand she was forced to kiss every day and who made her drink the camel's milk she hated. From him she learns that all that women can expect from married life is oppression and submission. She tries unsuccessfully to rebel against the orders of her father, who still believes in the traditional way of doing things and refuses to allow her to marry the man she loves because he is a Palestinian and not a Kuwaiti. As a result, the man leaves the country. The heroine shares certain experiences culled from al-'Uthmān's own life: she, too, hated having to kiss her father's hand. It was her revolt against an arranged marriage to her cousin that marked the beginning of her resistance to continuing oppression.[11]

The story "Kull al-aydī mutashābiha" [All Hands Are Alike][12] deals with a completely different type of rebellion. It is set against the background of the Palestinian *intifāḍa*. The heroine attends a meeting where artists voice their solidarity with the Palestinian people. Among the audience she discovers a man of high reputation. While looking at his hands, she feels an overwhelming desire to kiss them. As she considers his possible reactions, she sees the image of her own father's hand which she was forced to kiss as a child. Nevertheless, the meaning of hands changes in the course of the story: later they come to embody the rebellion of Palestinian youths, a countless number of stone-throwing hands. Eventually these hands are transformed into Palestine itself when the heroine compares her deep desire for a man's hand with the Palestinians' aspirations for their homeland. Both acts require courage and strength. It is this that makes her afraid that the man will ridicule her commitment as a Kuwaiti woman.

Concerning her own involvement in her writing, al-'Uthmān notes, 'I cannot let go of my stories. I live with the protagonists. I love them and feel close ties towards them'.[13] A short survey of her narrative techniques will show how far this holds true. The heroines show an enlightened consciousness. In "Lā khabar . . . lā", the first-person narrator protests at social injustice. She recognizes connections which imply that her individual rebellion, even if it fails, will assume more widespread dimensions. She seems to be speaking with al-'Uthmān's voice, illustrating the author's intention of adjusting her heroine's personality to her own. The narrative thus becomes a mouthpiece for the author herself. The heroine is not an independent fictional character—this is confirmed by the story's autobiographical elements.

Such elements are particularly apparent in "Kull al-aydī mutashābiha", which is written from the perspective of a third-person narrator. Such a narrator normally stands outside the fictional world of the narration itself and the characters in it; rather s/he takes a position in between the fictitious world and the author's and reader's reality.[14] In this story, however, the narrator does not stand outside but remains close to the heroine and eventually assumes her point-of-view. The author and heroine, one might suggest, are here identical, the more so in that a switch from third- to first-person narration is quite imaginable. The heroine merely serves as the author's mouthpiece.

In "Min milaff imra'a" [From a Woman's File],[15] we see how close al-'Uthmān comes to her heroines, although this time she is not writing about personal experiences. A 17-year-old girl has to stand trial for murdering the 70-year-old husband to whom she was married against her will by her father. The disgust she felt for this old man changed into sheer hate and she eventually killed him with a hammer. The girl admits her crime. Via flashbacks, she talks constantly about her father's contempt for her needs and wishes. In recounting her tragic fate she makes use of very strong language; the mere act of talking seems to liberate her from her dreadful experience.

Woman as Oppressor

According to al-'Uthmān, men are not solely responsible for women's suffering. Women also come in for criticism. Mothers, sisters and mothers-in-law frequently appear as severe, even cruel tyrants in their particular domain—the home. "Al-Muwā'" [Mewing][16] deals with an unmarried woman who mourns her lost youth. The sight of a cat evokes memories of her childhood. As an orphan living in her married brother's house, she often cried for sheer hunger and used to sneak into the kitchen like a cat to search for something to eat since her sister-in-law refused to give her any.

The actual story involves her talking to the cat. She appears as a narrative 'I' endowed with full creative competence.[17] By using flashback the heroine comes to terms with her fate, just like al-'Uthmān herself. "Al-Muwā'" is yet another story with strong autobiographical features; the author herself says that it represents her own childhood.[18]

"Al-Qalb wa rā'iḥat al-khubz al-maḥrūq" [The Heart and the Smell of Burnt Bread][19] is set in the backyards of the old traditional quarter of a city. A widow jealously watches her son's activities, but is unaware that he is fond of Zahra, a girl from the neighbourhood. One day while his mother is out, he persuades Zahra to accompany him to his house. Unfortunately the mother comes home early and finds them exchanging caresses. As a consequence she gives the girl a severe beating.

"La'ba fī 'l-layl" [Night Game][20] deals with psychological abuse. In order to spend the night with her lover undisturbed, a married woman threatens her little stepdaughter with *zā'irat al-layl* (the night-stalker), who abducts and devours any young children who are not asleep. Needless to say, these threats generate panic in the girl's mind. One night, however, her curiosity is stronger than her fear and she sneaks into her stepmother's room. Hearing a noise, she catches a glimpse through the slightly open door of the silhouette of a stranger. 'What kind of game is the night-stalker playing with my stepmother?' she wonders.[21] Here al-'Uthmān succeeds in describing the girl's world of naive innocence. She does not seem even to be aware of her 'evil stepmother's' oppression, and the obvious naivety generates a certain dismay in the reader.

None of the above stories is seen through the oppressor's eyes, but always from the viewpoint of the victim. Reality is depicted by the victims; it is presented to the reader from their perspective, the 'inner perspective'. The clearly authentic portrayals, especially in the case of "al-Muwā'", show how al-'Uthmān lends her own voice to that of her heroines and is perhaps unable to write from an oppressor's point of view.[22] In this context al-'Uthmān's aim is not to be the mouthpiece for women, but rather to promote a more humane society for both men and women. She insists on the right and need for women to participate in public life, implying the necessity for them to leave the confined environment of the house where they not infrequently abuse their power, as preceding examples have shown. She appeals for women's liberation and emancipation within Arab society by trying to instil a sense of self-confidence and political wareness. The Syrian writer Ḥannā Mīna notes that al-'Uthmān 'neither makes peace with reality . . . nor avoids it, but rather she stands up to it and suggests another reality which is sweeter and more wonderful'.[23] In that sense she offers solutions by leaving reality and resorting to fiction.

Woman as National Symbol

"Al-Ṭāsa" [The Dish][24] is set in a bygone era in old maritime Kuwait. A woman who is anxious about her seafaring husband feels lonely. She is exhausted by the task of raising her three daughters and beats them frequently. Her mother, on the other hand, is a stable, patient and loving person who criticizes her daughter for her never-ending litany of complaints; she dislikes the way her daughter constantly keeps a wary eye on her dowry, a golden dish. One day, while they are doing the washing by the sea, the dish is swept away by a wave. The sea—the preserver and destroyer of life—here takes away the dish just as it does the lives of many seamen. The grandmother shows all the patience, love and strength of those women who in former times had to manage without their husbands for many months on end. The younger women may be seen as representatives of those Kuwaiti women of more recent times who have become more 'feminine' and are unable to fulfil their duties within society.[25] The real heroine here is the grandmother, who does not appreciate the political dimension of the way she handles the situation because it is all determined and ruled by tradition.[26] That is why the attitude of the grandmother is not reflected in that of her daughter.

The story "Riḥlat al-sawā'id al-samrā'" [The Journey of Dark Forearms][27] is an impressive example of the awakening consciousness of women. While bathing in the sea, a woman thinks that she has lost her ring. She dives down to search for it, but fails to find it; all she finds are human fingers, arms and legs. Back home, she discovers the ring lying on the table next to her husband who is reading the newspaper. Here the values of the past are contrasted with the worthlessness of the present. While close to the sea, the woman embodies the old traditional values; the ring itself symbolizes the kind of luxury and wealth that people today do not have to struggle for any more or even risk their lives for as pearl-divers did in former times; it is their remains that she sees while diving. By contrast, her husband personifies modern society because he does not really care for his wife or identify himself with the sea. He thus lacks the boldness of sailors of old.

Another richly symbolic story is "al-Jinniyya" [The Genie].[28] Here al-'Uthmān takes the description of women a step further. Not only do they come to symbolize their native country, they are also viewed as its guardians. A female demon loaded down with pearls lures a man lying on the beach into the water. In trying to grab the pearls he almost drowns. She rescues him but then shows him a terrible scenario: the sea itself is on fire, people are plunging into the water, the beach is lined with parts of human bodies and disgusting vermin, and the sky is darkened by crows and locusts. The man is panic-stricken and prepares to fight. He demands the demon's claws. After handing them to him, she vanishes beyond the crests of the waves. All alone, he suddenly feels very weak and distracted by the sight of a woman in the distance; he falls asleep and loses the claws. Here the sea is once again the major focus. In former times, pearls—the sea's great gift—were hard to obtain. Modern mankind fails to appreciate the past and, in this particular context, the enormous importance of the sea. The terrible plagues within the story itself clearly imply that the excessive production of oil will inevitably lead to pollution. Both sea and soil become scenes for political and armed conflict.[29] People are prepared to disregard the destruction taking place around them and insist on pursuing their own needs and desires regardless of the consequences.

The sea also takes centre-stage in the story "Zahra tadkhul al-ḥayy" [Zahra Enters the Quarter].[30] When the beautiful young Zahra settles in a coastal village, the women are initially afraid for the welfare of their menfolk, but they soon discover that their worries are unfounded. Zahra gains their confidence and even enchants them with her politeness and skills. The wise old Umm Muḥammad is the only one to avoid contact with Zahra. She is aware of the danger implicit in Zahra's settling down in the community. One by one, Zahra's relatives are brought in and start to buy up the villagers' houses. As a result of their efforts, the village starts to prosper. Umm Muḥammad is still worried about the soil and the sea and she continually warns her people of the dangers. The villagers, however, turn a deaf ear to her warnings. When they find out what Zahra's real intentions are, it is too late: she offends Umm Muḥammad and threatens to drive out all the villagers. From one point of view, this story can be interpreted as a comment on an internal Kuwaiti problem, the issue of alienation, involving the balance of the population between native Kuwaitis and foreigners. However, it can also be seen as a metaphor for early Zionist setttlement. Within such an interpretation, Zahra can be viewed as an embodiment of the first Jewish settlers in Palestine who, with their ambition and technical expertise, were able to develop the land. Umm Muḥammad represents early resistance by Palestinians to Jewish immigration, an effort that was weak and thus unsuccessful.

"Al-Raḥīl" [Departure][31] can be seen in the same light. A married couple decides to leave the country for a year or more. The wife, Umm Hijrān, is afraid to leave because she fears their stay abroad may be a long one. She is shocked when her husband tells her that he has asked Mūsā to look after their house while they are away. Her husband tries to calm her down, but her suspicions prove to be correct: no sooner has their car driven away than Mūsā changes all the locks on the doors to the house. Mūsā, who is described as homeless but willing to work, is once again a figurative prototype for the Jewish settler; and yet again it is the woman who recognizes the danger.

Al-'Uthmān devotes a number of stories to the fate of the Palestinians, involving both past and present perspectives.[32] She is eager for women to be transformed into politically active beings. By abandoning realism and resorting to heavy symbolism in her fictional works, she seems to be acknowledging that such political awareness has yet to be achieved.

Conclusion

In Laylā al-'Uthmān's work, the topic of sexuality is of great significance. Many of her stories deal with the subject of women as victims of brutal sexual exploitation. In this regard, her use of language is important in that she makes use of very explicit vocabulary in her depictions. The taboo of sexuality is presented in a forthright manner that often verges on the crude. Al-'Uthmān's purpose is not always to achieve absolute authenticity, however. Rather, the character named in her title comes very much to the fore, while the plot within which s/he is placed sometimes seems contrived.[33] By using the techniques of flashback and first-person narrative, al-'Uthmān manages to depict effectively the acute suffering of her heroes and heroines, who are often young girls or children. Theoreticians of narrative suggest that the use of a first-person narrative is of existential relevance to the first-person narrator.[34] Within such a narrative framework the reader is directly confronted with this existential relevance and, through a sense of deep sympathy for the protagonist, comes to condemn the social circumstances described. It is that condemnation which is part of the author's intention.

One may conclude that al-'Uthmān's literary development goes hand in hand with changes in women's status as seen in the above-mentioned images. In her early stories she assigns a central role to passive and romantic women, mostly within the context of a discussion of the problems facing her own homeland but occasionally within the context of Palestine. It is only later that political issues begin to feature more prominently.[35] Through her depiction of the suffering of women, the brutal suppression of their sexuality, the desperate attempts they make to rebel against repression, not to mention the oppressive behaviour that they themselves use towards weaker members of their immediate environment, al-'Uthmān shows that such circumstances will only be overcome when women achieve their appropriate status within society and publicly voice their anger and frustration. This demand explains, indeed necessitates, the constant presence of women in al-'Uthmān's works.

16

Death and Desire in Iraqi War Literature

Miriam Cooke

I met Daisy al-Amīr, one of Iraq's best-known women writers, in Beirut in 1980. Since before the outbreak of the Lebanese civil war in 1975, she had been working as press attaché in the Iraqi Cultural Centre. Ten years later, after a brief but brutal stint in another war, this time in the land of her birth, she came to America for a year. During her visit to Duke University, I told her of my project on war fiction in the Arab world. Soon afterwards, the postman delivered two gunny sacks filled with novels, short stories and volumes of literary criticism produced in Iraq during the last three years of the Iran–Iraq war, 1986–8. All of these books, a mere fraction of the literature and its criticism published on the war, are issued through two state-sponsored series: 'On War and Culture' and 'Qādisiyyat Saddam—Under Flames of Fire'.[1] This essay will examine the intersections of sexuality, love, marriage and death in a few of these novels and short stories.

It was Sigmund Freud who first schematized the eternal interaction of two apparently opposing principles: *eros*, or the sexual instinct as the embodiment of the will to live; and *thanatos*, or death as libidinal sublimation. Most people most of the time function as though desire and death were completely separate. Indeed, they keep the two apart lest the one threaten the other. Yet Freud has written that only 'by the concurrent or mutually opposing action of the two primal instincts—*eros* and the death instinct—never by one or the other alone, can we explain the rich multiplicity of the phenomena of life'.[2] Nowhere do these two primal instincts reveal themselves more sharply in harmony and in contrast than in war. During war, when death is a constant, lurking presence that informs every decision and every action, the continuum between desire and death is revealed and during trauma, or what Jacques Lacan has called the 'real' or 'sheer, wholly undifferentiated and unsymbolized force or impact',[3] it may be eroticized.

In *Beyond the Pleasure Principle*, Freud has written of the three reactions to death in war: anxiety, fear and fright. Anxiety, he says, 'describes a particular state of expecting the danger or preparing for it, even though it may be an unknown one'. Fear requires a definite object of which to be afraid. Fright, however, is 'the name we give to the state a person gets into when he has run into danger without being prepared for it'.[4] To these three categories we must add a fourth: denial. Denial manifests itself in two ways: a reckless embrace of danger; and a pretence that business is as usual. In both instances, denial allows the individual to function in a way that would not otherwise be possible. It is important to add 'denial of death' as an aspect of wartime behaviour because war in the postmodern era is fought other than it was in the past. It is at once distanced and total, high in the sky and everywhere down on the ground. Combat pilots deny death in war because they cannot afford to give space to fear and anxiety lest it unman them, render them impotent. For many others, war—in preparation and in metaphor—has become part of their everyday life. Civilians are increasingly experiencing war as but another, if more extreme, manifestation of systemic violence. Denial of death is a significant aspect of war and its writing of which little has been made. It is, however, an essential aspect of contemporary war and one that allows wars to flourish.

Arab literary accounts of reactions to death in war accord with these four categories: anxiety, fear, fright and denial. Iraqis like Fayṣal 'Abd al-Ḥasan Hājim write about men who have known the spectrum of anxiety, fear and fright, for they have witnessed all too much death in combat. They know war is devastating and can see no sufficient reason for its justification. These narratives do not flinch from describing pain, despair, death and the pointlessness of a venture whose necessary outcome is destruction. These graphic texts do not have to announce themselves as opposed to war. Every page, every word is imbued with a horror and a despair that makes impossible the old lie that it is sweet and suitable to die for one's country.

But war is not always and everywhere the persistent confrontation of opposing sides. War is the legitimization of violence as an appropriate instrumentality and its sporadic organization on behalf of perceived needs and worthy goals. War can thus often be war without feeling as though it were. This was the case throughout much of the Lebanese civil war. The Beirut Decentrists created protagonists who refused to function under pressure of their mortality, and acted as though they did not have to take death into account.[5] They created a meta-normality that excluded death while at each instant being informed and shaped by it. These characters were living out a plot removed from the site of confrontations. Blocking death from the horizon of their thoughts, they persisted in their resistance to the hopelessness of civil war and thus survived. However, distance from the violence does not guarantee immunity to its impact. Iraqi women's literature on the Iran–Iraq war narrates events that, although they transpire far from the heart of the fighting, none the less revolve around death. The brutal eight-year war did not allow for the establishment of a meta-normality, for the dead kept showing up.

Denial is also an essential attitude for those who are ready to fight, who anticipate that the intensity of combat will bring rewards but who have not yet confronted death. In particular, those who fight alone like combat pilots seem to find or, perhaps, have to create in the death-charged landscape an intense aliveness, a thrill rooted in the sexual.[6] Heroes obsessed with tales of virility, courage and power know that it is in war that they may actualize the ideal of masculinity, what society tells them is necessary to become a man. War provides them with the opportunity to test themselves, to demonstrate manly virtues, as they challenge death and come out either victorious or dead.

Fiction and films in both Western and non-Western cultures have made much of the fact that, for pilots, the excitement of combat is high.[7] They fight virtually alone and with the illusion of power and immortality because of their distance and situation above the enemy. They must not focus on death lest they lose their effectiveness.[8] They must suppress anxiety as cowardice, they must put the fear of death out of their heads except as an impertinent challenger to be overcome, they must deny the possibility of fright which threatens to undo them through physical annihilation or, worse, through psychological dissolution. During trauma, the combatant summons all of the body's resources so as to retain its wholeness. *Eros*—as desire for life experienced as desire for sex—is the body's most resilient resource against *thanatos*.

Desire and Death in the Iraqi Narrative

In the novels and short stories of Iraqi male writers like Ṣalāḥ al-Anṣārī and Dāwūd Salmān al-Shuwaylī, desire and death are closely interwoven. Having denied anxiety and fear, they are aroused by fright. Military men, often officers directing rather than engaging in combat, are depicted at the moment they realize that they have been mortally hit. They almost invariably hallucinate or project images of their beloved.[9] Fantasies provide a libidinal sublimation. Stanley Rosenberg quotes an American Air Force pilot describing the escalating threshold of thrill during attack:

> First, just flying the airplane is a thrill. Then, you need to be dropping bombs. Then, you have to see what you're dropping bombs on. Then, to feel the thrill, you have to see that you've hit what you're dropping bombs on. Then, you need to be getting shot at while you see what you've blown up. Then, you have to be getting hit to feel the thrill, and the last thing is to get dead.[10]

Sexual arousal is associated with risking death. War writers evoke combatants who at the instant that they experience fright conjure up erotic memories which foil the threat of disintegration, physical as well as psychological, by producing an illusory unity. In *Männerphantasien* [Male Fantasies] (1977), Klaus Theweleit attributes sexual arousal in combat to a pathological need to shore up masculinity so as to be able to withstand the threat of dissolving into the feminine. He quotes *Medusa's Head*, where Freud has written that 'becoming stiff means an erection, it offers consolation to the spectator; he is still in possession of a penis, and the stiffening assures him of the fact'.[11] Desire is good as long as it is not allowed release.

Dāwūd al-Shuwaylī's *Abābīl* [Flocks] (1988), dedicated to the heroic pilots, officers, engineers and technicians of the 29th Air Unit, 'emblems of Ṣaddām's glorious Qādisiyya', places in high relief the *eros–thanatos* construct. The novel follows a pilot on his mission over Iranian territory. The mission is preceded by preparations for take-off reminiscent of the most melodramatic, macho moments of the *Battle of Britain* film. The pilots are bonded as a body, yet always respectful of superiority conferred by rank.[12] Yāsīn is the universally acknowledged group idol. The mission is launched and the planes take off in perfect flying formation. They reach their goal, drop their payloads and then turn back. Yāsīn's plane is hit. Defying commands to bail out, he keeps his place and steers back home. Spartan warrior to the last, he refuses to risk being taken prisoner and being raped or dying on enemy land. He will return dead or a hero. The novel ends with Yāsīn's ecstatic dying utterance: 'God is Great!' This war cry, which has become symbolic of Islamic holy war, seems to mark the author's approval of death in a 'just war' such as this.

Yāsīn's inspiration for such bravery is Sawsan. This woman's words assure him not only of his masculinity but also of his potential heroism. For had he not been a hero, she says, she would not have agreed to be associated with him. Then there is Amal, who is not merely inspiration, she is also an erotic presence from the moment that he is about to drop the bomb until his realization that he is going to die. The narrative fragments into a staccato alternation between descriptions of the present operation and flashbacks to encounters with Amal that become increasingly physical. He even conflates signifieds as he interchangeably calls his plane and his fiancée *yā ḥabībatī* (my beloved). As the crisis climaxes, he hears Amal again urging him to hold her tightly: 'O, Yāsīn, embrace me . . . ! Stretch out your hands! Hold me close to you! Don't leave me like this! Without hope! Hold me to you!' There follows a frantic description of his trying to grab hold of the *'atala*. Although the reader assumes that what is referred to here is the pilot's 'joystick', its actual meaning according to the Hans Wehr Dictionary is a 'crowbar' and according to Lane's Arabic-English Lexicon is a 'large, or thick, rod of iron, having a wide head. Or, a thick staff of wood.' Since the term is left imprecise, it is difficult within this eroticized context not to assume a phallic referent. Yāsīn finally gives up, frozen with fright.[13]

Yāsīn has lost control of himself and of his plane. He swoops so low over the earth that he can see everything clearly. Then, when the intensity of fear and panic have peaked, he is overwhelmed by a sense of dissolving: 'the earth welcomes me. I see her opening her arms . . . she is calling to me . . .' The wording may not be explicit, but the orgasmic association of danger, death, desire and release in union is clear.

When Women Become Combatants

It is not only male protagonists who experience arousal in war, women do also. However, for women the stimulants are different. Wendy Chapkis has written that women in real life may be as susceptible as men to the eroticism of the military myth, but for different reasons. She writes that when women become combatants, the military myth provides 'an avenue to personally transgress gender boundaries or as a means to project the eroticism of power on to male objects of desire'.[14] How does war literature enable a woman to become a combatant? It does so by creating women who challenge gender norms by playing men's roles and wearing men's clothes or, more subtly, by refusing society's rules for proper conduct for women. This change from observer to combatant is often erotically marked.

Lebanese war literature provides examples of women's construction of new gender norms. Some heroines escape from a male controller and train to become combat-ready; others deliberately enter into zones forbidden to all, but especially to women, by the well-advertised presence of a sniper. Lebanese war literature creates a hyperspace in which women can transform themselves from passive observers to military and discursive participants. After bidding her husband farewell, Nuhā Samāra's protagonist of "Wajhān lī imra'a" [Woman with Two Faces] (1980) finds herself alone in the war.[15] It is the first time that she has ever had the opportunity to think for herself, to make her own decisions. From this new vantage point, she begins to assess her situation rather differently. It is suddenly unacceptable that her husband should have left her in this dirty war; it is suddenly evident that she is not waiting passively. She is expected to cope alone in the chaos. Although at the time she had not objected to his decision to go, people's comments make her realize that staying alone involves responsibilities and self-defence. She cuts her hair, a literary convention that marks women's assumption of control over their lives, and enrols in military training. The metamorphosis is crowned by erotism: looking at her newly masculinized image in the mirror, she masturbates. She then determines to find a lover and calls up her husband's best friend. She thus bears out Chapkis' contention that turning themselves into military personae allows women 'to project the eroticism of power on to male objects of desire'.

The heroine of Ḥanān al-Shaykh's novel *Ḥikāyat Zahra* [The Story of Zahra] is another Lebanese woman who experiences *jouissance* as she transforms herself from observer to participant. Zahra, a young woman who bears the scars of incest and rape, has inured herself to pain through psychological distancing that others call madness. She allows no one, and particularly not men, to come close to her and floats alone over the surface of life. When her neighbourhood is plunged into a violence over which a sniper reigns supreme, she begins to move out of her shell. Seeing others in pain makes her feel less alone, more willing to be touched. With time she adopts responsibility for those around her. Despite warnings, she ventures out into the menaced streets and makes her way to the building out of which the sniper is said to be operating. If she can distract him even for a while, she will have saved one innocent person's life. Crazy, alienated Zahra has decided to enter the fray, to become a combatant. Despite terrible fear that gives rise to hallucinations of her own death, she arrives at the building and climbs to the roof. He rapes her. Accustomed as she is to sexual abuse, she feels nothing, or almost nothing. Yet the experience is not so bad that she does not return. Day after day, she trudges back to the building and up the stairs for a ritual re-enactment of the first encounter. Each time she is there, and each time less reluctantly, she convinces herself that she is doing what she is doing so as to defend her neighbours. However, she is also sensing something unusual happening in her body. Finally, one day it is as though the sniper is not raping her but rather making love to her, and he gives her pleasure. Zahra, like the woman in "Wajhān lī imra'a", has become a combatant who has found erotic pleasure in that role. She has not witnessed death while being constantly in its presence. She can thus imagine that the emblem of war's senseless killing is not a death machine but rather Sāmī, a man she would like as a husband for herself and as a father for their unborn child.

It is at the moment that these two heroines recognize that participation in the war gives them freedom, self-control and the chance to affirm themselves as *other* than expected that they experience erotic desire and pleasure. Both men and women in Arabic war literature may feel erotic arousal when engaging the idea of death. However, whereas the men's desire is activated by battle participation that *confirms* gender identity, women's desire marks the assumption of a role that is *in contradiction* with social expectations of gendered behaviour. Each is in some ways overcoming the feminine condition that disables the warrior spirit.

For men, the fantasies vanish in the light of reality. As Theweleit writes about fiction describing the German Freikorps male soldiers' fantasies of women during the inter-world war period, the moment women become 'real, all of these beautiful fictions would have to die.'[16] In the short stories of *Abjadiyyat al-ḥarb wa 'l-ḥubb* [The Alphabet of War and Love], his fourth publication on the war, Ṣalāḥ al-Anṣārī portrays the opposed images of women in military men's imaginations. They are divided between the beloved and the wife, the unattainable and the unbearable, and the divide may often take place within a single body. In "Jidārān" [The Two Walls], the hero tells his wife, 'I loved a woman other than you' and it seems that this other woman was in fact her, but only when she was not who she was then.

"Jalsa 'ā'iliya" [A Family Gathering] focuses on an unbearable wife. The hero is a writer. One night as always, his wife's shrill voice shatters the silence he cherishes for reading and writing. She is calling the children to dinner. There ensues an exchange in which she accuses him of dreaming about imaginary girlfriends and he refuses to answer except in his head. He is horrified that she wants, as he puts it, to enter the pores of his skin. That may be what she wants, but he will never let her come close. He escapes into sweet memories of a fragrant childhood but also into gloomy thoughts about a horror apparently comparable to his own—the Palestinians in the Bourj al-Barajneh camp who were eating rats to survive.

Iraqi Women Writers on Love and Death

Out of the experience of war, men and women usually write of heroes and heroines in gendered spaces. Out of these spaces, men and women talk about absent women and men. When they write of men and women *together* during war, the only love they invoke is a sick love.

In Iraqi women's writings, death brings the loved men home and reveals the emptiness, the destructiveness even, of that love that had required distance to survive. 'Aliya Ṭālib's story "al-'Ināq al-muḍī'" [The Luminous Embrace] enters the deranged mind of a young woman who is being dragged towards the coffin of her martyred lover. Her life has been ruined, all that she has left are memories. In "Intiẓār jadīd" [A New Wait], the woman protagonist, who has abandoned all her education and professional training, is awaiting her husband's return. She is holding the baby conceived on the eve of his departure six years earlier. Torn between reality and her imagination, between her old and her new selves, between her missing husband and her soldier-to-be son, she pastes together a fragile façade of normality. She has turned the boy into the image of the father and will not be satisfied until she has 'made him exactly like him'—only then can the father return. The father does return, but wrapped in the national flag. If she remains true to this destructive love, she will assure her son's future. In "al-Ikhḍirār" [Greening], Ṭālib again draws a powerful parallel between the experiences of soldiers at the front and women at home. A pregnant woman is trying to prevent her foetus from being born. She has promised her husband that he will be the first to see their son. As she struggles to control her labour, he is dying inside the tank on the battlefield. Each is trying to prevent the inevitable outcome of a pain that has been considered emblematic of the major difference between women and men: the mother's pain at childbirth as opposed to the hero's pain due to combat wounds. In the end, both fulfil their destinies: the mother gives birth, but to death; the soldier becomes a hero, but a dead one. The final scene lampoons the mother's satisfaction as the dead infant's lips are placed on the dead father's brow. She at least has kept her promise that the father will be the first to 'see' his son.

Luṭfiyya al-Dulaymī's Budhūr al-Nār

The prolific, apparently pro-Baathist Luṭfiyya al-Dulaymī has written two novels on the Iran–Iraq war: *Budhūr al-nār* [Seeds of Fire] (1987) and *Man yarith al-janna?* [Who Will Inherit Paradise?] (1988). *Budhūr al-nār* is the only novel I have read to deal with both men and women and their fantasies and representations of each other out of their gender-specific spaces. It describes a year in the life of two couples against the backdrop of war. The women are artists on the home-front in Baghdad; one of the men is a poet working in the desert, a place that is not the front, yet is described in terms that always recall the front. This marking of the man's absence as being 'not at the front' allows al-Dulaymī to describe men's experience without trespassing on what is said to be male writers' terrain.[17] The other man lives mostly in Bagdad, a man on the home-front.

This parallelism between an always absent front and a corollary space runs through *Budhūr al-nār*. The war is constantly invoked: explosions can be heard in the distance; Yāsir describes plants that survive the heat and the dryness as *ṣāmida* (steadfast), a term that Palestinian usage has filled with political resonance; families are fragmented by the conscription of sons; mothers wait; martyrs are announced; aunts adopt war orphans; brothers are imprisoned; finally even the home-front is hit; above all, everyone organizes their lives around the 'end of the war'.

The novel begins from the perspective of Yāsir the pseudo-fighter in the desert mines where he has been posted for a year to take the place of someone who has been conscripted to the front. This may not be the front, but he tells his wife Laylā that she should think of it as though it were. Later, his experiences in the desert are literally compared with those of the soldiers, and he is described as though he had become part of the war and the war part of him:

> The night winds of the desert sowed seeds of fire beneath his skin and in his blood, small seeds that the hand of time had scattered over the earth of his body. Yāsir felt tiny coals burn him and enflame his griefs, his desires, his anger and his longing for the small pleasures that most people do not notice. When he feels the burning of the flames, distant and recent memories are churned up and for a while he forgets this hell that pervaded his world and left in it fires, the stench of corpses and the ghosts of the dead.

This is not the description of an experience in the mines but rather the vivid evocation of the soldier's experience in the battlefield: privation and nightmare but also oneiric escapism and heightened sensuality. Death and the war have become part of him to the extent that others recognize the incorporation.[18]

During his times of loneliness and crisis far from home, Yāsir, like the heroes of Iraqi men's writings discussed above, longs for a woman. His fevered imagination conjures up Laylā. But this is not Laylā the person he has tenderly loved and married; this is Laylā, a woman, any woman, Woman who fuels his fantasies.[19] By calling the fantasy Laylā, he can convince himself that his adventures with other women are not betrayal. He even calls one prostitute Laylayāna (a play on his wife's name, Laylā) so that he can imagine the affair as having been with his wife. His acknowledgement of his misdemeanour involves an unspoken apology to Laylā and the assurance that when he is with other women he feels himself to be with her. When he comes home, however, he predictably loses his fantasy of Laylā the lover and cannot tolerate Laylā the wife. He wants her to be devoted to him and to his needs. Any sign of independence must be quashed, any lack of respect for his achievements is counted as a sin. When he turns down a lucrative offer to work with Rashīd, he expects Laylā to praise him. She does not. Her indifference is an affront. He needs to be the centre of attention and will not tolerate a lapse in admiration.

Laylā is a graphic artist in Baghdad, plying her trade but also playing her war role as waiting woman. Pregnant, she awaits her unborn child; sister, she awaits her brother who is at the front; wife, she awaits her husband from the mines.[20] At the beginning of the novel, the waiting role predominates, though with immediate caveats as she contextualizes her fantasy within reality. When she hears an enemy bomb explode, her first thought, spurred by the baby's kick, is that of the mother waiting for her unborn child. She wants to give birth to the fruit of her love for Yāsir before dying. This saccharine moment is relieved by a political reflex: thinking of her own motherhood makes her think of other, less happy mothers 'as they awaited the return of their sons from the front'. In war, after all, women give birth to death either as a product, a killed son, or as an instrument, a son who will kill. The thought of these mothers' faces allows her to regain awareness of self and control of body. She is the waiting wife worrying about her husband's welfare as he confronts danger and death. She can talk about love as 'wanting someone for his sake and not for the sake of our happiness with him . . . Love is giving happiness and joy without counting the cost. It is then that the loved one gives us what we would never have expected.'

Then, however, Yāsir arrives home on a brief leave. His presence shatters the illusions that his absence has nurtured. He is completely preoccupied with himself and does not even notice that she is pregnant. The mirage of connubial bliss dissipates in the bright light of reality. Involuntarily, she flashes back to his pre-nuptial promises of a happy future which she suddenly remembers as punctuated by self-satisfied crows at being the possessor of so much 'beauty, femininity and gentleness'.[21] This memory helps her to plug Yāsir's attitude into a system that victimizes women, especially creative, intellectual women. She is keenly aware of the fact that men's claim to protect women actually means contempt.[22] She admonishes her girlfriend Asīla not to accept the role of victim, 'the worst role for women or for any human being', while she struggles not to be a victim herself. She is victimized by her husband's indifference to who she really is, by Asīla's need for her to suffer in love as she did, by her male colleagues' fear of the power of her painting, but also by society directly. She can never be alone in a public place without being suspected of immorality. One day, she walks out into the streets. She is briefly gratified to feel acknowledged as being independent. Then a woman silently hands her a jasmine flower (a gesture that probably has sexual connotations) and a soldier accosts her without respect for her pregnancy: she cannot walk through the streets alone without being categorized as a prostitute.

Laylā knows that she must establish her own independent space. Even if this space cannot be for herself alone, it will be for her vicarious self. She turns their son into a 'new independent island'. The future will be different if the next generation can be spared the influence of the fathers. As the novel progresses, she becomes increasingly sensitive and resistant to Yāsir's authoritarianism. His absence has given her the space to become more self-assertive, and he feels the need to rein her in. He cannot understand, or perhaps he understands too well and fears, her need for affirmation. When she again asks for his help in putting on a one-person show of her paintings, he suggests that she wait until after the birth of the baby. This retort reminds her that 'they had talked three years ago about putting on her first show and that he had written the introduction to a few of her new canvases. However, his studies were never published, her show never happened.'

In the meantime, an art critic has taken an interest in her work and published an article about one of her paintings. When she tells Yāsir the exciting news, he is annoyed and says:

I read the article. 'Abd al-'Azīz al-Qādirī didn't say anything new.

> That's what I've always thought about your style and technique because I know your background and experience. Haven't I already told you everything he repeats in his article? . . . Al-Qādirī is not an art critic. He merely flatters women painters.

Not only is Laylā remembering an unfulfilled promise, she is again confronted with his jealous possessiveness and his intolerance of her public affirmation. It should be enough for her that her husband thinks highly of her painting, and irrelevant that someone else has bothered to put into print and therefore bring to public attention what he has merely thought. Eager to put his competitor down, Yāsir loses himself in a paradoxical discourse. First, he establishes himself as the more credible critic because of privileged information; then, he turns his argument against himself by discrediting as flirtation the criticism that he has compared with his own. After delivering himself of this tirade, Yāsir cannot understand why Laylā should be pensive and sad!

The other plot of *Budhūr al-nār* revolves around the war-booty hunter Rashīd, the unrequited lover Riyāḍ and the sculptress Aṣīla. Aṣīla despises her soldier admirer and obstinately holds on to her dream of her love for Rashīd, despite his marriage to another woman. Aṣīla calls her love for Rashīd a 'sickness' and later describes his occupation of her thoughts as a 'rape'. This is no soldier in danger of his life, this is a philanderer. Yet Aṣīla is determined to love the man who jilted her as though he were a hero at the front. The loyalty she reserves for this man who has married another and who yet wants to retain control over the woman he has abandoned is truly 'madness'. Aṣīla has the choice between a conventional wartime relationship with Riyāḍ and one with Rashīd that goes against the grain: to love a non-soldier with the love reserved for the man at the front—passive loyalty. Rashīd exults in Aṣīla's misplaced love: 'I know how to manipulate the strings and make the puppet dance. I have my ways that a dreaming lover like you, Yāsir, who is satisfied with the love of one woman, does not know.' He mocks Yāsir's loyalty, which the reader has learnt is self-deceptive at best, hypocritical at worst.

Aṣīla's project is doomed to failure. Unlike her 30-year-old and still unmarried female colleagues at the museum who prefer to be educated than to be married—and if they are to marry, then it will be to richer and younger men than the divorcees and widowers who are currently presenting themselves—she pursues an old and hopeless love. She searches him out in the westernized area of town to which he has moved. Here his assistant Victoria presents her with another ideal of femininity: 'I would never have done well in my work had it not been for you, Mr Rashīd. No woman, however talented, can succeed without a man's support.' Aṣīla's life and friends are proofs of the contrary, yet because she has made her choice to love in war someone who has opted out of the war, she finds herself in an impossible situation. The last scene between Aṣīla and Rashīd suggests that had the area in which they both happen to find themselves at the same time not been bombed, they might have come together again. However, death intervenes. The independent woman artist who has adopted her nephew, a war orphan,[23] and has thus assumed the role of martyr's wife, cannot find in war a space to love a selfish man who had hoped to make of the war his fortune.

Budhūr al-nār is told from three perspectives: Yāsir's in the desert and Laylā's and Aṣīla's in Baghdad. This assigning of sections to a man on an ersatz front and to two women on the home-front allows the author to establish apparently self-evident separate spaces and roles in which men and women function. Yāsir, like the military men, is associated with spheres of death and war: the arid, life-devouring desert and the front with its risks of death and imprisonment. The women are associated with life and peace through symbolic scenes of nature that include doves and olives, and lush greenness. And then, they wait; or rather, they ripen 'like fruit on the tree of waiting'.

The novel seems to affirm the spatial and behavioural binaries proper to war. There can be no crossings lest identities and roles be threatened. Yāsir tells Laylā she cannot join him in the desert and that she should think of him as going to the front. Because his co-workers are like soldiers, they will not respect her for who she is but regard her as a body only. Laylā acquiesces.

However, the neat binary of front and home, of action and inaction is actually broken in the lives of the ne'er-do-well Rashīd and of the artist Laylā. Rashīd does not fight on any front and his only connection to the war is through the desire for gain. While family and friends are dying at the front, he convinces his brother-in-law to set him up in furniture and perfume factories. Soon, his marriage falls apart, his businesses collapse and he tries to lure Aṣīla back. Just as it seems that he is about to succeed, they are both killed by a couple of explosions. Rashīd has brought the killing home.

Laylā, on the other hand, has used the war and the consequent absence of many men from Baghdad to establish a space of action for herself. Both she and Aṣīla were revolutionaries in the late sixties. They had taken part in demonstrations after 1967 and Laylā was wounded in a police chase. They each then turned to art. Laylā seems to use graphic art to pursue her resistance agenda. She is supposed to design enticing advertisements for consumer goods that will convince people to 'do what the advertiser wants'. But she feels driven to focus on the 'aesthetics' of the message. Her director is mortified, fearing that attention to the aesthetics will draw attention to the art and to the artist. Attention to the creator of the message will highlight the message, which will then cease to be subliminal and therefore effective: when consumers buy they are not and should not be aware of the reason for their buying. The phrasing of these mandates recalls sinister definitions of propaganda: first, make people do what you want; second, do not allow them to understand why they are doing what they are doing. Laylā can only paint subversively and yet she is not dismissed, nor does she obey Yāsir who tells her to resign.

From the heart of the war machine, the producer of 'integration—status quo—propaganda',[24] and in the absence of men, Laylā is combating the system. Her methods are so subtle, so subliminal that even she does not seem to know what she is doing. The director recognizes the powerful impact of her art on women. He warns her that she will anger them; but the text tells the reader that she delights, indeed, she mobilizes, women. Her art creates an alternative for others and for herself. It gives her the courage and self-assurance to confront her boss. On one occasion, after she has shown him what he considers to be a particularly incendiary painting, he insults her. Then, in the hope of mollifying her, he invites her to be a token woman at a reception for visiting French dignitaries. To his utter incomprehension, she is furious at being reduced to an 'accessory'.

This *Künstlerroman* is reminiscent of those that women have written out of the experience of the Lebanese civil war and the *intifāḍa*. The protagonist finds release from personal crisis through artistic, and usually subversive, creation. Art allows Laylā to construct a world outside the one in which she is compelled to live. After hearing of her brother's capture at the front, Laylā returns home and starts to paint. She places his photograph on the table and begins to paint in 'hot, staccato [*mutaqāṭa'a*] colours'. Out of the colours emerge the shapes of lovers intertwined. She paints on:

> until the painting turned into a strange star freed from the bonds of existence and she hurried to give the man the features of Yāsir. When she contemplated the painting she felt the satisfaction one gets after plunging oneself into something beautiful. She felt relieved to have unloaded the weight in her head and body into the sudden, brilliant colours of her painting. Then she felt sleepy.

When reality becomes unbearable, she transforms it through art.

Budhūr al-nār ends abruptly and unconvincingly. Yāsir returns home after a year at the desert mines. He finds Laylā slaving over a hot kitchen stove, the new baby boy slumbering and delicious smells emanating out of the kitchen. Who is she expecting? Why, him! Every night, she says, she prepares his welcome. Saying which, they fall woodenly into each other's arms. This is *not* the Laylā of the preceding 260 pages, a woman who has resisted all the men who have tried to control her, Yāsir in particular. However, this ending provides the censor with a 'happy-ever-after' sense of closure. On the other hand, for those, like Rachel du Plessis and the author of the present essay who feel compelled by the disjuncture to read beyond the ending, the conclusion calls into question all those moments when Laylā expressed any form of domestic delight. Hence, we read beyond the ending to a month later when Yāsir will leave for the front, but we also return to page 1.

As long as Yāsir is far away, at the ersatz front, Laylā loves him perfectly. She can daily engage in the charade of the happy homecoming as though for the unquestionable love of her life. As soon as she finds herself face to face with this beloved, her love melts into frustration and anger. As long as he is away, Yāsir loves Laylā, but imperfectly. She becomes the pretext for fantasy, or rather, for the unbridled pursuit of erotic satisfaction lightly veiled under the pretence that if he thinks that other women are Laylā they will become Laylā. His adultery thus parades faithfulness. When he steps back into women's space, the home-front, he is annoyed at any sign of independence from Laylā. He resists her desire, her need to create a life of her own. He cannot tolerate any form of self-affirmation, but insists on her acquiescence in his desires as well as in his representation to himself of who he wants her to be.

Aṣīla's love is always a 'sickness', always a 'madness'. She does not need the return from the front for her self-delusion to be made apparent. She is always fully aware that her love is inappropriate. She loves a civilian, and a rascal at that, with the love reserved for the soldier. However, when the 'soldier' is shown not to be in danger of death, but rather to be exploiting a situation of danger for others, such a love becomes destructive for both subject and object. Yet even under such perverse circumstances, the man in war is shown to be redeemable. Aṣīla's love earns Rashīd the title of martyr when he dies in the explosion. For he did not die (*māta*), he died as a martyr (*istashhada*). Aṣīla, of course, also died; however, as a woman she could only die (*mātat*).

Conclusion

In Iraqi literature of the last years of the Iran–Iraq war, love thrives only when men and women retain their gender-specific spaces as mandated by the exigencies of war. In men's literature, women exist as Spartan Mother, castrating wife or erotic fantasy. In women's literature, on the other hand, men at the front are heroes-in-the-making, the love of whom is a national, nay, a natural mandate. However, when these men come home alive, notions of heroism give way to the reality of tension. When they come home dead, the absurdity of the meaningless death—for that is how it is often described—strikes at the heart of patriotic constructions of masculinized militarism.

What we are witnessing in this late Iraqi war literature is a struggle over the interpretation and definition of the war. Was it a manly war? Or did the war unman its men? For most writers, the answers to these two questions fall along gendered lines. For some, like Luṭfiyya al-Dulaymī, the questions are more complex and are posed along the fault line that segregates men from women in war. As long as men and women do not cross into each other's space, the *eros–thanatos* construct holds. When they do cross into each other's zone, which by being the other's is forbidden, they disturb what are seen to be 'natural' social arrangements. And although it is not mentioned explicitly (in patronized, patriarchal literature it cannot be), their crossing into that forbidden zone shows how fragile are the foundations on which that segregated society is based. If men discover that during their absence women have entered public, i.e. male, space and are there negotiating power relations that the men thought to be essential and unchanging, then the reasons and motivations for going to war are destabilized. How manly is the soldier whose wife is independent and therefore perhaps stronger than he? And if an unpatriotic man can elicit the same devotion in a woman as can one who is prepared to die for his country, of what value is that love? Once notions of militarism as the quintessential domain of masculinity, and of this masculinity as inherently superior to femininity, are questioned, the stable gender relations so necessary to the peaceful waging of war are undermined. Since the reason for the disturbance is the war, it is the war itself which threatens the very fabric of a society it had been fought to defend.

17

Nizār Qabbānī's Autobiography: Images of Sexuality, Death and Poetry

Stefan Wild

Nizār Qabbānī is one of the most famous and at the same time one of the most popular poets in the Arab world today.[1] His *dīwāns* are sold in many thousands of copies[2] and many of his poems have become popular songs sung by the best-known singers of the Arab world. Qabbānī has earned a reputation as the *enfant terrible* of Arab literature and society. This reputation rests mainly on three features of his work: first, his flippant and bantering style with its studied disrespect for many symbols of the Arab-Islamic heritage, and its identification with heterodox, heretical personalities and movements; second, his outspoken and harsh criticism of Arab society, Arab mentality and Arab political leadership; and third, his unusually frank and unconventional approach towards love and sexuality.

This essay will deal only with the third aspect. It is not, however, primarily concerned with Qabbānī's large poetical *œuvre*. Instead, we shall start from his autobiography *Qiṣṣatī ma' al-shi'r* [My Story with Poetry][3] and try to analyse the self-image of an author—subjective, biased, but still the author's own image, one he wants to transmit to posterity as the image of the true Nizār Qabbānī.

It should be mentioned in passing that Qabbānī's poetic and other works show a marked predilection for the *yawmiyyāt* (diaries) and *mudhakkirāt* (memoirs) title. The report-like, subjective quality of a day-by-day diary which such titles suggest and create seems to be an important feature of the poet's work.[4]

Qabbānī's autobiography can be read in different ways: as a fight against censorship, as the success story of a self-made poet, as the *chronique scandaleuse* of an Arab Don Juan and possibly a variety of other readings. It can also be read as an invitation to a layman's crash course in the basic tenets of psychoanalysis. When we speak of Nizār Qabbānī in the following, we are referring to the first-person narrator of the autobiography, who, needless to say, is not necessarily identical with the real person Nizār Qabbānī. *Qiṣṣatī ma' al-shi'r* gives the reader a literary self-creation—as do all autobiographies.

Some biographical details may be useful at this point. The son of a pastry-maker, Nizār Qabbānī was born on 21 March 1923 in French-governed Damascus. He entered the Kulliyya al-'Ilmiyya al-Waṭaniyya (National College of Science) in Damascus and later praised his father for this prudent choice: it was neither a purely foreign missionary school like the École des Frères nor a purely Arabic one like the Madrasat at-Tajhīz al-Rasmiyya (Tajhīz State School). His second language is French, and at school French was the language of his teachers and his schoolbooks.[5] French was, for Qabbānī, the entry ticket to European thought—and French colonialism could not change this fact. Renoir was not responsible for the follies of Napoleon, the author explains to us, and the eyes of General Gouraud, the French conqueror of Syria, were not the eyes of Isabel of Aragon.[6] After his successful study of law, the young Qabbānī entered the Syrian diplomatic service in August 1945 when he was barely 22 years old. His career as a diplomat led him as cultural attaché to Cairo (1949–51), London (1952–5), China (1958–60) and Madrid (1962–6). He left the diplomatic service in 1966 and settled in Beirut as an editor, journalist and poet. During the civil war in Lebanon, he had to leave Beirut and decided to move to Geneva. At present, he lives in London. He is a frequent contributor to the critical Arabic-language monthly *al-Nāqid* based in London.

There are three main features to the self-image which Qabbānī creates in his autobiography and which we shall analyse briefly: Nizār Qabbānī the rebel, Nizār Qabbānī the eternal child and Nizār Qabbānī the Don Juan.

Nizār Qabbānī, the Rebel

In his autobiography, Qabbānī quotes an example of what he considers a revolutionary attack on conventional Arabic love poetry:[7] a passage from "Ilā ṣāmita" [To a Silent Woman] from his *dīwān*, *Qaṣā'id mutawaḥḥisha* [Savage Poems]:[8]

Speak, my beloved, of what you did today.
Which book did you read before going to sleep?
Where did you spend the weekend?
Which film did you see?
At which beach did you swim?
Have you become tanned the colour of tobacco and roses like every year?
Tell me, tell me.
Who invited you to dinner this Saturday?
In which dress did you dance?
Which necklace did you wear?
For all your news, my queen,
Is the queen of news.

Qabbānī explains the easy flow of the poem:

> I pondered long before this language. I wondered whether people would forgive me this deliberate aggression against the history of Arabic rhetoric with all its pride, magic and majesty. This was more, this was an aggression against my own poetic history . . . My questions led me to other questions: Why should simplicity be an aggression against history? Why should the naivety of a poem be a reason to condemn it?[9]

Qabbānī neglects to say that, of course, the subject-matter of this poem is as scandalous as its form. The image of the woman evoked portrays a Westernized woman, Westernized at least as far as her consumer and social habits are concerned: she is free to go dancing, free to spend a weekend somewhere, free to swim and sunbathe at the beach, free to be invited to dinner.

But the studied simplicity of Qabbānī's poetic language, its closeness to the colloquial, was indeed one of the characteristics which invited the criticism of poets and those critics who considered themselves to be more 'serious'. At the same time, this language was one of the ingredients of Qabbānī's immense success. He—and others—call this simple, unforced Arabic 'the third language' (*al-lugha al-thālitha*).[10]

Qabbānī is proud of this rebellion against poetic norms. Rebellion against the literary tradition is at the same time rebellion against the moral norms of his society. He advocates the 'smashing of the glass of legality' (*kasr zujāj al-shar'iyya*),[11] and smashing literary convention is the same process as smashing the traditional model of male–female relations.[12]

Nizār Qabbānī as the righteous rebel, as a Robin Hood of love,[13] is an important feature of the autobiographical Nizār Qabbānī. Qabbānī's view of the unity between linguistic and sexual rebellion is omnipresent in his poetry. He calls one of his poetic collections explicitly *Ash'ār khārija 'alā 'l-qānūn* [Illegal Poems] and another *Ashhadu an lā mra'ata illā anti* [I Swear that there Is no Woman but You], using the *shahāda*-formula in which woman takes the place of God in a mildly blasphemous way. The poet invites the reader to move out into the 'wilderness of poetry' (*barriyyat al-shi'r*). This iconoclastic self-image is dear to his heart. In many places, Promethean allusions force this perspective on the reader. One of his chapters begins:

> The stealing of the fire has been my passion since I started writing poetry. I did not steal the fire of heaven like Prometheus. Because heaven did not interest me. The fire of earth was my aim. The lighting of fires in the consciousness of men and in their clothes was my fixed idea.[14]

Rebellion is also what makes the first-person narrator of his autobiography come out into the open with his love-affairs:

> In a country like ours, where the double standard kills and where love is made behind the curtains, which clings to the principle of *taqiyya* in its emotional behaviour, a poet like myself cannot ride with his beloved on a horse and go around in the streets of the city and be safe. People in our country can neither distinguish between the book and the writer, nor the poetic form from the person of its author. Abstraction, a purely intellectual approach, is not practised in this region of the world. In the East, the discussion of love refuses love and considers it an illegitimate child, or a merchandise like forbidden drugs . . .
>
> In a society like this, the poet becomes an outlaw, the poems which treat the fiery relations between man and woman become an open scandal. So the poet of love in our country walks on a knife-edge; his pictures are stuck to the walls of the cities with the legend, 'Wanted, dead or alive.'[15]

And his literary models are clear:

> The poets of sensual love in Europe, the novelists and dramatists, do not wage a crusade against their societies like the Arab writers have to do. This is because the view of their societies towards love and sex

> has taken its natural form and is not a cancerous swelling as it is in our society. D. H. Lawrence, Oscar Wilde, Henry Miller, Alberto Moravia have gone much further in their writings than we did. But they did not have to pay the price which we paid and they were not exiled outside the walls of their cities like we were.[16]

Nizār Qabbānī, the Eternal Child

Within most rebels, there lurks a conservative mind, and Qabbānī is no exception. There have been only five women, he confesses, with whom he has been really in love, and these five had to satisfy (and in fact did satisfy) three conditions. First, each had to resemble him; second, Qabbānī says, each one had 'to be my mother' (*an takūna ummī*); and third, his poetry had to be part of their lives.[17]

The first point means, explains Qabbānī, that he could never seriously love a foreign, in other words a non-Arab, woman:

> I felt that to love a foreigner or to marry her would be signing a marriage contract in hieroglyphs. The husband of a foreign woman will serve all his life as an interpreter. By my very nature, I cannot love a woman in which I do not smell the smell of mint, of wild thyme, of basil, of genista, of jasmine, of gilly-flower and dahlias which fill the fields of my country.[18]

This poetico-physical geography is taken very far:

> I am very Arab in this respect. I cannot be close to a woman whose body does not resemble in detail the map of my country: with its forests and rainfalls, its canals and minarets, its love-songs, its cups of *raki* and the cooing of its doves.[19]

This is conventional and suggestive imagery: conventional, because the equation home-country = beloved woman is a fertile symbol in modern Arab, especially Palestinian poetry; and suggestive because the erotic allusions in Arabic poetry are rarely as frank and passionate as in Qabbānī's work.

The second condition is that the woman he loves should be his 'mother'. Not that he suffers from an Oedipus complex, Qabbānī hastens to add. But, he explains:

> I live in a constant condition of childhood—in my behaviour, in my

actions, in my writing. Childhood is the key to my personality and to my literature.[20]

Qabbānī's mother as she appears in the autobiography is made out to fit every stereotype of the Arab mother:

My mother was the spring of emotion, giving without reflection. She considered me her favourite son and bestowed on me favours which she did not grant my brothers. She satisfied my childish demands without complaint or grumbling. I grew up, but in her eyes I was always her weak and helpless child. She gave me her breast till the age of seven and fed me with her hand till my thirteenth year.[21]

The following passage is typical for Qabbānī's frank juxtaposition of sexuality and death, a recurrent leitmotiv in his autobiography:

A woman who takes a kleenex out of her handbag and rubs my forehead while I am driving the car owns me. A woman who takes away with her hand the ash of my cigarette while I am drowned in smoke kills me from jugular vein to jugular vein [*tadhbaḥunī min al-warīd ilā 'l-warīd*]. A woman who puts her hand on my shoulder while I am writing gives me the treasures of King Solomon.[22]

The third condition is that his beloved should be as interested in his poetry as Qabbānī himself:

I cannot bear to see a woman at my side who tries to separate me from my alphabet. Who tries to kill my poetry so that she can survive. This type of woman dies at once in front of me.[23]

He continues:

These three conditions make love possible as far as I am concerned. These are childish conditions, as you see. But it seems that only few women tolerate children and bear with them. However, most of my relationships were wrecked because one of these conditions was not met . . . So I turned from one woman to another, looking for the martyr [*fidā'iyya*] who would accept dying on my breast and on the breast of my poetry as Pandora did in the story of the Flying Dutchman.[24]

Nizār Qabbānī, the Don Juan

Qabbānī devotes a whole chapter to a refutation of the reproach that he is a Don Juan.[25] Defence against misunderstanding and apology are time-honoured aspects of autobiography. But, paradoxically, Qabbānī's autobiographical first person does everything to convince us that he is, in fact, a Don Juan, even in a very old-fashioned and trite sense:

> The logic of love is different in Damascus, different in Hong Kong, different in Soho, different in Düsseldorf, different in Granada, different in Shanghai, different in Hamra-Street and Garden City . . . Each woman in these cities was a continent in itself with its serenity and rain and change of weather . . .[26]

Qabbānī's constant quest for a woman who could be his mother and his beloved at the same time seems to be linked to the ultimate impossibility of finding such a woman. The poet goes one step further: his autobiographical ego is not only a Don Juan but a Shahriyar, the king in *The Arabian Nights* who makes love to a virgin every night and then kills her:

> Like Shahriyar, the multitude [of women] struck me with disgust and loathing. When the number of women in my life increased, my feeling of exile and isolation increased.[27]

And he closes the chapter by asking his reader:

> Do you understand now how deep Shahriyar's wounds were?

Qabbānī must have known to what extent his self-presentation as the eternal child and the Don Juan makes him vulnerable to the simplest kind of hostile psychoanalytical analysis. The poet plays with the relevant vocabulary: 'Oedipus complex', 'narcissistic', 'Don Juan syndrome', 'Freudian approach', and so on. Is there perhaps a twinkle in his eye when he does everything to lay himself wide open to a blistering condemnation? Whether this is true or not, the reader is struck from the outset by Qabbānī's apologetic tone. The writer's self-assertion is a defensive act. Why is he writing this autobiography? The very first sentences answer this question:

> I want to write my story with poetry [*qiṣṣatī ma' al-shi'r*] before

someone else writes it. I want to draw my face with my own hand because there is no one who can draw it better than I can. I myself want to remove the veils from myself, before the critics tell my story and sum me up according to their whim, before they re-create me . . . This is the notebook of my recollections. In it, I have written down all the details of my journey into the forest of poetry.[28]

The Arabic word *rihla* (journey) is throughout the book a powerful symbol for Qabbānī's development. The poet changes places as he changes loves. Apology is never far away: the author defends himself against being called a Don Juan; he insists he is not narcissistic; Freud and the Oedipus complex are evoked only to be dismissed. But on the metaphorical level, the link between sexuality and poetry is pressed on the reader time and again:

> The poet's head is like the woman's belly: unknown regions locked up, full of creatures of undefinable essence, origin and sex.[29]

To write is to make love:[30]

> The relation of the poem with the sheet of paper I am writing on is a relation which shares many of its pecularities with sex. It begins like all physical relations with the desire to occupy a space which we do not know, in a country which we do not know. The sheet of paper in front of me is a body which I do not know. A cold emptiness in search of someone to cover it, a harbour for every hunter, and pearls for each sailor. A sheet of paper—like any woman—has to master the rules of the game and the fundamentals of hunting and the catching of the prey. The coloured sheet of paper is for me a trap into which I easily fall. The rose-coloured sheet arouses me as the Spanish bull is aroused by the savageness of the colour red. The existence of the poem, then, depends on the shrewdness of the paper, on the preparedness of its body and soul to receive passion. Sometimes I feel that the paper is ready and I make love with it successfully. And often I feel that the paper does not want me, so I put on my clothes and depart.[31]

The same metaphor is used to compare poetic production with the sensual pleasure or frustration of making love:

> For thirty years I have tried to surprise poetry in its underwear or naked . . . But every time it wore a cap of invisibility.[32]

One is tempted to translate the title, *Qiṣṣatī maʿ al-shiʿr*, not so much as 'My Story with Poetry' but rather as 'My Affair with Poetry'.

Conclusion

Love between a man and a woman is portrayed in Qabbānī's autobiography as an adventure. But it is an adventure with very uneven risks. A man usually survives this adventure: a woman runs the risk of death. The poet tells us that he comes from a family in which everybody is an expert on love. For the poet's father, for his grandfather, for all his ancestors, love has always come naturally and early. All members of the Qabbānī family love to the point of self-sacrifice (*yuḥibbūna ḥattā 'l-dhabḥ*). And Qabbānī tells us that his elder sister committed suicide because she was not allowed to marry the man she loved. The poet turns this tragedy into literature:

> In the history of our family there is a moving instance of death for love's sake. The martyr is my elder sister Wiṣāl. She killed herself in all simplicity and in unparalleled poeticalness (*bi-shāʿiriyyatin munqaṭiʿati 'l-naẓīr*) because she could not marry her lover.[33]

The 'poeticalness' of this suicide lends poetry as a kind of indelible quality not so much to the sister, but to the author himself. At this point, Qabbānī's autobiography ceases to be autobiographical and becomes like a novel. The matter-of-fact tone changes into heavy symbolism when he continues:

> When in my fifteenth year I walked in my sister's funeral procession, love walked beside me in the procession, seized my arm and cried. When they had lowered my sister into the ground and we came back the following day to visit her we could not find the grave. Instead we found in its place a rose . . .[34]

Qabbānī sees the condition of many Arab women: fettered by age-old traditions, and sacrificed to a double standard of morality and the tribal ethics governing the relations between the sexes. He is at his best when he denounces male hypocrisy, when he savagely attacks values which he feels suppress women. He does not give us a solution, nor should we expect a poet to solve the questions which society poses. In the imagery of his autobiography, Qabbānī and his first-person narrator let us see the intimate link between sexuality and poetic production, the endless and ever-failing quest for the beloved as the mother and the almost brutal fusion of the metaphors of passion, violence and death. There are many ambiguities in the autobiographical metaphors: Nizār Qabbānī the rebel is at the same time Nizār Qabbānī the eternal child. The woman who wants to be loved by him must liberate herself from all the fetters of traditional Arab society but must at the same time play the role of his mother; she must be completely Arab but in many ways resemble a caricature of an emancipated Western woman. Compassion for the plight of many Arab women, the process of poetic creation and a certain machismo in Qabbānī's poetical expression are inextricably interwoven.

Qabbānī has tried his hand at writing something like a woman's poetic autobiography in a small *dīwān* called *Yawmiyyāt imra'a lā mubāliya* [Diary of a Reckless Woman].[35] There are striking similarities and differences between his *Qiṣṣati ma' al-shi'r* and the real autobiographies of contemporary Arab women. An interesting contrast is marked by the Palestinian poet Fadwā Ṭūqān's autobiography, *Riḥla jabaliyya riḥla sa'ba. Sīra dhātiyya* [A Mountainous Journey. The Life of Palestine's Outstanding Woman Poet].[36] It would be fascinating and productive to compare the growing corpus of Arab women's autobiographies with all their anger, frustration and bitterness, on the one hand, with Nizār Qabbānī's frank and iconoclastic but at the same time slightly flashy bravado on the other.

18

Love and the Body in Modern Arabic Poetry

As'ad E. Khairallah

In Arabic poetry, passionate love has rarely concerned the body in an outspoken manner. It is generally sublimated into a chaste love, leading to the denial of sensual pleasures and ending in divine love. Sexual intercourse seemed the surest way to abolish the magical charm of the beloved. Thus to let the lovers 'enjoy' each other has commonly been prescribed as the only antidote against 'love-melancholy'.

The interesting phenomenon in modern Arabic poetry is the extent to which the poet is able to 'enjoy' his beloved, and yet cultivate not only a relatively passionate love for her, but often a mystical relationship with her body, or even with the totality of Being as condensed in her body. This poetry does not isolate the body from the rest of the person. Instead of the hedonism of Imru' al-Qays (d. *c.* 540) or 'Umar Ibn Abī Rabī'a (d. 719), or the Platonism of *'udhrī* poets like Jamīl (d. 701) and the legendary Majnūn (d. *c.* 700), some modern poets yearn passionately for the body, without this being a sheer physical or particular end in itself. It is, rather, a window to the Infinite, the focus of a total experience, and a means of spiritual, not only physical ecstasy. The body is thus the place of all questioning, all exploration of the self and the other, all doubt and fascination, hope and despair, tenderness and violence. For the first time, the body of the beloved (similarly to the poet's own body) seems to be neither transcended nor used as sex-object, but as an object of sustained passion, verging on mystical *'ishq* (passionate love).

The present essay will investigate the new attitude towards the beloved's body and what it implies in the poet's imagination and expression, as well as some of its ramifications on the social and moral levels. We shall focus on texts by poets like Nizār Qabbānī, Tawfīq Ṣāyigh, Unsī al-Ḥājj and Adūnīs, and also refer to some short stories by Edwār al-Kharrāṭ.

Post-war Arabic poetry was largely dominated by ideological commitments to the renovation of nation and culture or to the struggle for socialist justice at home and in the world. Little space remained for the private concerns of the individual, except when these happened to symbolize the collective situation of rare exultation and of frequent failure and frustration. Celebrating one's joys in love did not seem revolutionary enough. This is poignantly rendered by Buland al-Ḥaydarī (b. 1926)[1] in his poem, "Muttaham wa law kunt barī'an" [Guilty even when Innocent], where two lovers are watched by a secret agent, who reports:

Sir, I heard her
Asking him about his marvellous love
About a body —
I beg your pardon, Sir —
She told him: it burns like fire
It burns me like fire
. . .
I beg your pardon, Sir
They were insistent in their innocence.

But their insistence was to no avail, bodily pleasure being suspect. Moreover, 'All people are criminals / Even the innocent love in their eyes.'

And when daylight awoke in my city
The news broadcast mentioned
The story of a room on the seventh floor
The moment of vengeance
The anger of the revolutionaries
And they had a noose round their necks and a nail
In their hands.[2]

Many of the modern revolutionary poets, dedicated almost exclusively to the collective utopia, were themselves psychologically and ideologically inhibited as regards sexual enjoyment, let alone indulgence. This is well expressed in Ṣalāḥ 'Abd al-Ṣabūr's verse drama, *Laylā wa 'l-Majnūn* [Laylā and the Madman],[3] where Laylā insists on being recognized in her bodily existence, whereas her lover, the revolutionary poet Sa'īd, is practically impotent and unable to approach her sexually. He is inhibited by his negative childhood's memories (having frequently witnessed the legitimate 'rape' of his mother). He sublimates his problems by struggling for the coming ideal, the just state. Only then, he thinks, will love be possible.

Fortunately, not all modern poets are like this Majnūn. The other type, known in the Umayyad period—in other words the Don Juan type, 'Umar Ibn Abī Rabī'a—is well represented by the most popular modern poet, Nizār Qabbānī (b. 1923).[4]

Not only has Qabbānī championed the freedom of women from male despotism (father, brother, husband) and from the harem mentality; he has also had the courage to celebrate women in love and their full right to sexual pleasure. He even breaks some of the most sacred taboos, as in his wonderful description of an adolescent girl's first menstruation,[5] or in his joyful and positive rendering of a love scene between two lesbians.[6] He adopts an exceptionally accessible, playful style in describing his erotic relationships. This has given him the widest public, mainly among young people, and provided a counterbalance to the rather earnest tones of the Arabic New Poetry.

Yet Qabbānī remains a self-centred Don Juan, often betraying a rigid masculine outlook.[7] He is not open to discoveries, since he claims to know everything about women.[8] His beloved must remain true to a certain ideal type of feminine beauty. He is often insulting towards older women[9] or those who show intellectual tendencies.[10] He sees himself as the creator of his women. This motif, found in his early poetry,[11] becomes a tedious leitmotiv in his later work.

More important for our purpose is that in Qabbānī's text, the woman's body is so present in its details that one wonders if it is not an object in itself, before and beyond the person of the woman. Indeed, the woman is somewhat absent under the heap of her parts, her toiletry, her jewelry and her perfumes, or under the details of the poet's belongings, his coffee, cigarettes, wine, cognac, newspaper, coat, and so on. For some five decades Qabbānī has been repeating these same elements to which he often dedicates full-length poems, such as 'The Long Earring', 'The Bra', 'Buttons', 'Nipple', 'To a Yellow Dress', 'To a Red Shawl', 'Manicure', 'The Blue Bathing Suit' and 'Christian Dior'.[12]

In short, Qabbānī remains at the surface of love's fire and deep waters. Love for him is a game, and he is elated to be the one who sets the rules. He is against the old oriental harem, but is proud to use his poetry as bait for his new liberal harem. A narcissistic Don Juan, he is never constant except in his self-love. Relatively few poems describe the act of love, and then only through hints and quick allusions. Love does not seem a serious matter; it is a game between tom-cat and pretty mouse. And this tom-cat is boastful of his conquests:

There is no black nor white breast
over which I haven't struck my flag
There's no corner in a beauty's body
Over which my chariots haven't passed
Out of women's bodies I made a gown
And built a pyramid out of nipples.[13]

In contrast to this public, declamatory poetry, bent on self-aggrandizement, a few first-rate poets present an often tragic yearning to make love a way for permanent unity with what is beyond the beloved's body. Edwār al-Kharrāṭ's *Amwāj al-layālī* [The Waves of the Nights][14] is of such exceptional intensity and dynamic tension that many of its passages could be counted among the best prose poems in Arabic. We shall use this outstanding work as a starting-point for discussing what one may call the metaphysics of sex in modern Arabic poetry.

Al-Kharrāṭ's narrative is made up of episodes that can be read either as separate entities or as parts of one organic whole. The text is interspersed with pure poetic moments of ardent cantos, conjuring away the absence of the beloved. It moves lightly between past and present, reality and dream, mixing genres and levels of thought and language, citing popular as well as Ṣūfī (mystic) sayings, shifting without transition between narration, poetry and reflection. It thereby offers us enough discursive material for an exposition of our main subject: art, time, love and death; the mad struggle to unite the finite with the Infinite, and to blow up the fleeting moment to the dimensions of Eternity; the mad longing of the drop of human flesh to become definitively one with the Ocean of Being.

These themes are recurrently treated in al-Kharrāṭ's book in different combinations and perspectives, but here we shall quote extensively from the second episode entitled "Majānīn Allah" [The Fools of God], where physical and metaphysical ecstasy is presented in two simultaneous but opposite movements. In the first case, mystical ecstasy is compared to sexual orgasm. In the second, it is orgasm that leads to mystical ecstasy.

Before daybreak, the speaker lies in bed with his beloved, while outside in the empty square a mystical musician, of the Orpheus type, has a sort of spiritual intercourse with God. This musician is the epitome of the artist. His first appearance in the text leads to a reflection on the nature of art as an existential struggle to conquer time, having its climax in divine madness. The musician is:

> bent on his warm lute which rests in his lap like an intimate part of himself, being at the same time the source of ecstasy, its medium, and where it finally pours . . .
>
> His music has become a day and night inspiration, a dream, running like the very blood of life . . .
>
> Did he ever dream of fame and glory? Of richness and women?
>
> Or of art, of art alone? . . .
>
> Why is then this perfect perfection in the performance of his music? This self-annihilation?
>
> Does his existence have any meaning outside this self-annihilation?[15]

Here we have art as source, medium and recipient of mystic ecstasy, cast in the physical and rather sexual description of the lute. And the speaker goes on recalling their reflections:

> The ultimate madness in love. Divine madness.
>
> A madness without reward, except through itself and in itself.
>
> I told her: The transience of perfection; the performance that will never be repeated; lost after being realized for a single time; which has no antecedent, has nothing like it, and can never have. For, here, the immortality of perfection is impossible.
>
> She said: Eternal, fixed, petrified perfection is a copy and not an original, a ghost, that has no reality . . . Life, my love, is like a performance—it does not tolerate mummification.
>
> I said: How I wish the moment—with all its vitality—would not pass away.[16]

This is exactly the central point: the poet's craving to eternalize the fleeting moment of his erotic or artistic ecstasy. But each poet has his own way of recovering this lost eternity or quenching his thirst for it.

> Outside, the musician suddenly screams his mystical trance:
>
> 'It is not I, it is not I, it is He . . . !
>
> O my Love . . . O my Love . . .'

> I heard it, says the speaker, in sounds and melodies of imploration and suffering, distress and desire, sounds of peace and defiance, of ecstasy and obedience, pain and aching happiness, resembling the ultimate moment of ejaculation.[17]

Orgasm as a metaphor for the closest emotional and spiritual intimacy with God, far from being coincidental, is at the centre of al-Kharrāṭ's vision. Similarly, the opposite process, the sense of perfect unity with God obtained through sexual orgasm, is recalled as follows:

> I still feel the pressure of her lips around 'it'. I feel her tasting it, indeed its spreading into her whole body, so that 'it' becomes 'she'. The warmth of her breathing into the well-guarded sanctuary, the wet and hot dampness, the ecstasy of a unity exempt of the utility of pleasure. A unity which at the recurring peaks of pleasure is inevitable.
>
> In those days, I called out . . . in the vehement ardour of my perfect ecstasy:
>
> — I don't want anything from You now. Neither from You, nor from Your angels. I don't fear anything from You, neither from You nor from Your devils. Now all is perfect. Life won't bring me anything more, because I have experienced unity with You.
>
> No, I was not exaggerating at all.
>
> This is exactly what I meant.
>
> . . .
>
> She said: Why do you insist that sex be divine, or metaphysical at least? Sex is sex. Nothing else. Really enjoyable, great and linked with an enriching love . . . yet it is nothing but a sexual act.
>
> I said briefly and firmly . . .
>
> — Not true.
>
> Everyone becomes mad about God in his own way.
>
> It is true that everything has a touch of God in it.
>
> But *this* is the *divine itself*, I have no doubt.[18]

Al-Kharrāṭ's text sums up the whole point. It is striking, though, that it is the woman who regards sex as simply sex, whereas the man insists on giving it a metaphysical dimension.

A similar situation to that presented by al-Kharrāṭ, but much more tragic in nature, is found in the poetic world of Tawfīq Ṣāyigh (1923–71).[19] There the poetic persona resembles al-Kharrāṭ's musician, yet he is enraptured by a treacherous woman and a seductive god. In his exile from the paradise of motherhood and homeland, this persona is lured by a lighthouse. When he enters, he discovers that he is in the belly of a cyclops. The trouble is that he is in love with that cyclops and feels miserable when he is thrown out of its belly.[20]

Ṣāyigh's is the most private and hermetic poetry in Arabic; it all focuses on his obsessive passion for Kay,[21] his whimsical, despotic cyclops, who, like al-Kharrāṭ's woman, regards sex as sheer sex, but who has a voracious appetite for it. 'Touching her hand,' says Ṣāyigh, 'seeing her eyes . . . leads to the ultimate sexual act. She expresses her emotions, her thanks, her anger, pain, feelings and revolt through the ultimate sexual act.'[22] Kay is the female counterpart of Don Juan. Ṣāyigh knows that, but cannot help being literally obsessed by her. After she disappears, all his writings are but 'substitutes for her'[23] and he prays God to help his poetry be worthy of their past love.

Defending himself, Qabbānī says, 'Men usually talk about their victories in love and keep quiet about their defeats.'[24] But Ṣāyigh does not hide his weakness and defeats. His openness in confessing his own physical and psychic failures is, to say the least, very rare in Arabic poetry. He is helped, perhaps, by mingling the erotic realm with the religious, since, like al-Kharrāṭ's musician, Ṣāyigh holds Christ responsible. Christ too is a Don Juan, a seducing fisher of men, who promised to return and seems to have disappeared for ever.[25] 'Help me! Help me!' cries Ṣāyigh, addressing Christ:

> Don't leave me to dry up, to end
> To be led to darkness, defiled, far away from you;
> Don't let the ugly angel
> Undress me, ravish me,
> And brand me with his seal;
> Not to vanquish me,
> But (my God, my God) to vanquish *You*![26]

Obtaining no response, he yields to his death-wish, shouting, "Min al-a'māq ṣarakht ilayk yā mawt" [Out of the Depths I Cry unto You, O Death!], the title of a poem in which he invites the white mare of death to let him ride her to his end:

> So gallop with me
> You modern Sheherazad
> Who deflower every night a Shahriyar
> And suck him out of existence

Gallop!
You gaping womb,
Wet with sweat,
Which makes the organs soft and castrated
Gallop with me
And I'll gallop with you
. . .
We'll pant together
Together we climb, and we descend
We get to the last horizon
And to the dewy abode of pleasure. [27]

Sexual intercourse with Death, ecstatic death, and artistic trance are the axis around which another poetic world revolves, that of the Lebanese Unsī al-Ḥājj (b. 1937), who is also a *poète maudit* (an accursed poet) like Ṣāyigh, but whose surrealist vision allows him a more explosive discourse against the inhibitions imposed on the body and the subconscious by religion, morality and reason.

Unsī al-Ḥājj, the *enfant terrible* of this poetic movement, is particularly interesting if one considers his development. A *poète maudit* by choice, his first poems were the most violent and denigrating frontal attack on the foundations of sexual taboos anchored in both patriarchal and religious tradition. 'To be free,' says al-Ḥājj, 'a *poète maudit* shatters every standing rule and norm. He is a prophet, a God.' This statement is included in the introduction to his first work entitled *Lan* [Never].[28] 'The particle *lan* . . ., construed with the subjunctive of the imperfect . . ., is a very strong negation of the future, *not at all, never*.'[29] Used without specifying any verb, it seems to imply the pure negation of all acts or statements for ever, in other words, absolute negation. 'Subversion' is too mild a word for this project. This is a pure will to destruction. Al-Ḥājj adopts a very personal language in an excessively private sphere. His inaccessible surrealist style goes to extremes in this first work, which embodies a radical rejection of traditional poetic diction, rhythm and subject-matter. Few of his poems have been analysed by the critics, let alone read or understood by the public at large. This may have been the shield that has protected him from being declared blasphemous and being lynched.[30]

If Tawfīq Ṣāyigh laments his unrequited love (or more precisely his short stay in the belly of the cyclops), Unsī al-Ḥājj is particularly relevant as a contrast because he does not present us 'a weak character'[31] as Kay calls Ṣāyigh, but a volcanic one, full of dynamism and rage, full of contradictions, not haughty and aloof, but aggressive and consciously destructive. There are no reminiscences about a lost country, a lost virgin mother, a lost, beloved Mary Magdalene. Al-Ḥājj's poetic persona is totally engulfed in carnal pleasures and offensively declares it, though not without the guilt of an accursed person who feels he is hurting himself while hurting others. Yet he remains true to his project, and the best strategy of his war-machine against a repressive society is a devastating parody of its sacred, religious, moral, intellectual and literary values. His technique is well illustrated in a poem entitled "al-Ghazw" [The Invasion], where he mocks the prevailing political and religious discourse. In a surrealistic scene, his breaths 'kick him in his axis . . . Yet this one rises to the level of the event and says: "He who hit me on my left testicle is right, because I lost the right one . . ."'[32] The parody of Christ's words is obvious.

In another poem, al-Ḥājj says, 'I saw a child being castrated because he was naked, while the sun was seeing him. God and His hands are a tattoo on his waist. God is his buttocks.'[33] In yet another poem, al-Ḥājj's persona describes his first wet dream in highly sarcastic terms, then his first masturbation. He personalizes the first droplet of sperm, calling it 'Charlotte', and describes his adventure with her at home and at work.[34]

But al-Ḥājj's passionate mind was bound to sway from one extreme to the other. After three more works where his first fury is relatively tempered, we find him at last in a long poem entitled, "al-Rasūla bi-sha'rihā al-ṭawīl ḥattā al-yanābī'" [The Apostle with her Hair Long until the Sources] (1975), where he returns to God through the woman he loves. Here the poet of violence and destructive rage becomes a man of faith, spreading the message of love and calling on all people to celebrate life, because his beloved has converted him to an affirmation of the glory of existence. Whereas *Lan* was full of sexual violence and the sarcastic interplay of sex and sacred tradition, in "al-Rasūla", he barely mentions the body. Only such symbolic parts are mentioned as the eyes, the hands, the voice, as well as the hair, symbol of the reaching back to the sources of existence. His woman resembles a Holy Virgin (for whom he is ready to give up his life, so she will live a thousand years!). She is tenderness and forgiveness. She is the prisoner of this rude, oppressive male, who casts her out of the paradisiac unity of the one body, takes the place of God in the garden of Eden, and follows his lust for power and destruction. Her generosity, patience and forgiveness ultimately dawn upon him, bringing him back to her and to his faith in life and its Creator. The whole poem is a passionate hymn celebrating this awakening and reunion. It is written in the style of the *Song of Songs*, but with the fervour of Christian prayers to the Virgin Mary.[35] Perhaps the most interesting aspect is that al-Ḥājj was formulating, in 1975, many of the ideas that we find in the current feminist discourse about men's aggressiveness and their being the source of violent dominance and destructiveness.

Whereas the 'ideological years' largely avoided the term *jasad* (body), this term has become a password for the younger generation of poets who have flourished since the seventies and is hardly equalled by any other general term.[36] It becomes the matrix of a whole new poetic imagination. This is almost a new ideology, attending the fragmentation in the political, social and psychological make-up of Arab society. The shattered socio-political, national and democratic Arab project has left the way open to another dream: the Islamic empire. But fundamentalism is puritanical. In this new atmosphere, to declare the kingdom of the body is heresy, a revolutionary act. Those who go to extremes in liberating the body (in its instincts and dreams) are the Arab surrealists, who, naturally enough, are outcasts, when not exiled by force or by choice. For these surrealists, whose main periodical was *al-Raghba al-ibāḥiyya* [The Libertine Desire] and is now *Farādīs* [Paradises],[37] the basic revolutionary battle is that of sexual liberation. All else will follow. Compared with their texts, those of Nizār Qabbānī seem bourgeois and extremely docile, almost puritan, adolescent stuff.

Unsī al-Ḥājj is among the Arab surrealists' main spiritual fathers. But if he sees God as the buttocks of an innocent child, they see Him as the buttocks of a lesbian.[38] And if he ends up affirming the metaphysical dimension of the fatal, sexual experience, they still indulge in conscious sex-exhibitionism, coupled with a savage attack on religious tradition, starting with the belief in God. This makes them celebrate the body, especially the sexual aspect of it, in a violent revolutionary vein which rarely encourages them to see much beyond this particular aspect. Indeed, it often sounds more like physical nihilism rather than a way into communion with something beyond. Indulging in the body, its instincts and dreams does not seem to have led them yet to any real union with the absolute. For most of them, this absolute can only mean the total liberation of the individual.[39]

Our last poet, Adūnīs (b. 1930),[40] combines the surrealist and the mystical visions with Nietzsche's basic injunction to remain true to the earth. Adūnīs presents us with his very distinctive voice, expressing a vision that is not far from that of al-Kharrāṭ. Yet instead of attempting to retrieve the past, and craving the eternity of the moment, our poet is totally thrown into the future. He has quite early embraced the phenomenon of permanent change and fully consented to the transience of all things. What remains is the belief that, through poetry, one can write the future:

O Poetry, O our mad coachman, take me
Take us to run ahead of our death
To see, to write what will come,
And to be the Opening of the Book.[41]

But poetry, our mad coachman, can have only one vehicle: the body. This gives Adūnīs much freedom and serenity to celebrate the act of love in itself and as a creative act, in both the literary and physical senses of the term. Love is creative of the self as well as of a new life. Furthermore, the body is the place of all questioning and, by extension, of all poetry: it is our immediate scene of the stream of Becoming (the permanent metamorphosis of Being), and as such it has its sacredness. That is why there can be no basic difference between male and female, whether in the erotic relationship, or in the whole poetic process of discovering the secret of life, hidden in their living, dying and ever-metamorphosing bodies:

In sexual ecstasy
Man and woman are equal —
Each of them feels
He/She is born from the other's rib.[42]

Woman—the beloved, the wife and the mother[43]—is man's fully equal partner in the dangerous adventure of exploring the secrets of life and death, at that sharpest edge of the sword, the highest climax of sexual intercourse. Some of Adūnīs' best poetry is erotic poetry, where love and death seem to be two sides of the same experience and move with the same dynamism. Suffice it here to quote some verses from a wonderful poem entitled "Taḥawwulāt al-'āshiq" [Transformations of the Lover], which, in Kamāl Abū Dīb's words, 'explores the ritualistic moment of unison between the bodies of two lovers, declares the total purity of the body, and reveals the affinities between the moments of love and death':

. . .
I branch out around you
And I fall, between you and me, an eagle with thousands of wings

I hear your hallucinating limbs
I hear the sighs of the waist and the peace of the hips
I see the light of wonder, and everything about me gets intoxicated.
Thus speaks the body—the master.
. . .
After this we sit in the shade of the pavilion of the pelvis
Where the star of sex revolves
The metamorphosis is completed
Your breasts become day and night.
The world suddenly walks out to us
Saying:
The tree of the soul has grown in the earth.
Thus speaks the body—the master.
. . .
I ask: is love alone a place which death doesn't reach?
Can the immortal learn love? And what do I call you, death?
Between me and myself a distance
within which love casts its eye upon me,
death casts its eye upon me.
And the body is my baptism.[44]

No other Arab poet has done as much to rehabilitate the word and the subject-matter: *jasad* (body). 'I do not write, I declare an interpretation of my body,' says Adūnīs and goes on humming his incantations through this magic word.[45]

From passing hints or short poems in Adūnīs' early poetry, the presence of body and earth grows to be the dominant theme of his "Mufrad bi-ṣīghat al-jam'" [Singular in the Plural Form],[46] a symphonic poem of four movements, the longest of which is called "Jasad", and where poetry is the language of the body in love:

Let my body be fixed on paper:
An alley, and your steps are the trees
A scene, and your body is the actor and the story
A shadow, and your body is the signs and the gestures
A surface and your body is the depth
Letters and your body is the writing.[47]

Here the body of the lover is fixed on paper, and that of the beloved is the way, the drama, all signs, depths and writing. Furthermore, the earth (i.e. all nature) and poetry (i.e. all writing) are again and again metaphorically intermingled within body, desire and the sexual act. "Mufrad bi-ṣīghat al-jam'" begins with 'Not a body was the earth / it was a wound' and ends with 'And now is the beginning of the earth.' The poet, as a child, makes love to the earth: 'Thus he welcomes you, Earth, and spreads your thighs wide apart.'[48] Earth and body are created anew through the fire of poetic vision that burns all abstract tradition and memory, while affirming the body as the source of writing. Thus writing is a mystical union with the body and, through it, with all nature:

I do not write / I hallucinate my mystical states
I say what overcomes me
what my body attracts me to
I do not write /
I declare an interpretation of my body
. . .
I do not write /
I invent joys and things of pleasure
I throw my lashes forwards
And forget my memories
There is no good, nor evil
Nothing but these movements, difficult and easy
slow and fast
Movements that shine from my limbs,
One piece of clay at its will.[49]

This is in line with the poet's basic principle:

Let language be the form of the body
And let poetry be its rhythm.[50]

Yet the poetic resurrection of the body, here and now, sometimes takes place at the expense of non-physical love:

And I said:
The body not love is the skin of time the pores of the earth
The body not love is the arc of the horizon the muscle of the wind.[51]

This physical, organic unity between the bodily microcosm and the widest cosmic horizons was bound to make this poet of permanent change ever more conscious of death. But our poet remains defiant: 'From the depths of ephemeral things / I declare love / *Liber libera phallus*.'[52] It is the fire of love that challenges death while consuming the lovers, the same fire which generates that mad coachman called 'Poetry':

> He listened to her body (her body is his language and with it he speaks)
> . . .
> He speaks of the body's revolt and establishes its authority
> He speaks in order to found the system of blood between their two bodies
> He speaks to produce a writing equivalent to her body
> To remain high on one level with death . . .[53]

The mystical motif of the moth enraptured by the burning fire is not new. What is new in Arabic poetry is the consciousness that this fire is not necessarily transcendental. On the contrary, the mark of some of the finest New Poetry has been the strong desire to eternalize the great moments of physical ecstasy as much as those of creative perfection. Adūnīs says, 'For the body, the present / Is the form of time.'[54] The same idea is expressed differently by al-Kharrāṭ:

> My other time, other dream, other body.
> Everything is other.
> There never was, nor will be anything here and now . . .
> Except the moment of love.[55]

In modern Arabic poetry there is a new mysticism of the Earth, centred in the body, itself tense as an electric wire at the moment of love. At that moment, the body is no longer the matter of transitory, earthly pleasure. It is the medium for unity with all existence in its burning presence.

Notes

Introduction

1. Ghālī Shukrī, *Azmat al-jins fī 'l-qiṣṣa al-'arabiyya* (Cairo, 1971); Jūrj Ṭarābīshī, *Sharq wa gharb, rujūla wa unūtha* (Beirut, 1977); Jūrj Ṭarābīshī, *Ramziyyat al-mar'a fī 'l-riwāya al-'arabiyya* (Beirut, 1981); Charles Vial, *Le personnage de la femme dans le roman et la nouvelle en Egypte de 1914 à 1960* (Damascus, 1979); Ṭāhā Wādī, *Ṣūrat al-mar'a fī 'l-riwāya al-mu'āṣira* (Cairo, 1980); and Miriam Cooke, *War's Other Voices: Women Writers on the Lebanese Civil War* (Cambridge, UK, 1988).

Chapter 1. Love and the Birth of Modern Arabic Literature

1. The term literature was used for the first time in 1800, in the School of Jena's journal *Athenaeum, Ideen 95*. It was taken up again in the same sense and used by Schlegel in his lectures at Berlin University in 1801–2. At about the same time, Mme de Stael, who was a specialist in German literature, wrote her *De la littérature*, in which she introduced the term into France. See P. Lacoue-Labarthe and J.-L. Nancy, *L'absolu littéraire, théorie du romantisme allemand* (Paris, 1978), pp. 263–5.

2. F. Schlegel insisted, especially in *Ideen*, on the absolute need for heterosexual love in order to attain 'religion', that 'nostalgia of unity and of a desire for fusion' as Lacoue-Labarthe and Nancy put it (*L'absolu littéraire* . . ., p.196). They continue: 'The initiation [to religion] is only achieved by the mutual penetration of poetry and philosophy' (p. 198), in other words of man and woman.

3. See, among other definitions, that given by Buṭrus al-Bustānī in his encyclopedia *Dā'irat al-ma'ārif*, which began to appear in Beirut in 1875.

4. See the article *adab* in E.I., 1960 edn.

5. Transl. into French by A. Louca under the title, *L'or de Paris* (Paris, 1988).

6. The *relations indiennes* are a group of letters addressed by missionaries, especially Jesuits, living in India to Christians in Europe for their edification. They describe the progress made in evangelization and the sacrifices it entails. They are often in the form of a diary or travel account. Examples may be found in: *Lettres édifiantes et curieuses, écrites des Missions Etrangères* (Lyons, 1819), vols 6, 7, 8; *Correspondance de Saint François Xavier 1535–1552: lettres et documents*, ed. and transl. by H. Didier (Paris, 1987).

7. Originally published in Paris in 1855 by Benjamin Duprat's Librairie de l'Institut, the book has recently been translated into French by R. Khawam under the title, *La jambe sur la jambe* (Paris, 1991).

8. We refer to the terminology developed by Greimas in his *Sémantique structurelle* (Paris, 1966) and subsequent works, and rendered more precise and accessible by Josep Courtès, especially in *Analyse sémiotique du discours, de l'énoncé à l'énonciation* (Paris, 1991).

9. See in particular part 3, chs 6, 11, and part 4, chs 6, 7, 10, 11 of 'Imād al-Sulh's edn (Beirut, 2nd edn, 1987).

10. The author decides to devote the 13th chapter of each part (the book has 4) to a pastiche of the *maqāma*, giving it an ironic slant and for the sheer fun of it. See ibid., pp. 70, 90, 96 for his justification of this partisan view.

11. See, for instance, ibid., pp. 78, 93.

12. See ibid., part 1, ch. 5, and part 3, ch. 19.

13. From the very first years of the twentieth century al-Rayḥānī was expressing quite daring ideas about literature in the context of his suggestions about poetry in prose.

14. Muṭrān was probably the first person to give serious reflection to what poetry is, and thus to the specific nature of literature, in his periodical *al-Majalla al-miṣriyya*, founded in 1900 and regarded as the first literary magazine in the strict sense of the term.

15. See *al-Majmū'a al-kāmila li-mu'allafāt Jibrān al-'arabiyya* [Jibrān's Complete Works in Arabic] (Beirut, n.d.), in particular the chs *al-Shā'ir*, p. 316, *Nāshid al-insān*, p. 343, *Ṣawt al-shā'ir*, p. 344. See also the piece *Anā gharīb* in *al-'Awāṣif* and his famous manifesto *Lakum lughatukum wa lī lughatī* which, curiously, is not included in his complete works.

16. See J.-M. Schaeffer, *La naissance de la littérature, la théorie esthétique du romantisme allemand* (Paris, 1983), ch. 3 entitled 'Roman et romans'.

17. The reference is to his poem "al-Nafs".

18. This aspect is brought out well in K. Hawi, *Khalil Gibrān, his Background, Character and Work* (Beirut, 1973).

19. Schaeffer, *La naissance de la littérature . . .*, pp. 26–31.

20. To such an extent that almost any of Jibrān's short stories will only reveal its hidden meaning when this fact is taken into account. *Yuḥannā al-majnūn* is the most revealing example.

21. Al-'Aqqād relates in his *Murāja'āt fī 'l-adab wa 'l-funūn* (Cairo, 1925), p. 17, that, 'The teachers of Arabic were unanimous in giving their students this advice: "Read al-Manfalūṭī and try to imitate his style." This stand was justified by al-Manfalūṭī's tendency to a certain lyricism which forced writers to stop trotting out hackneyed ideas and images.' Al-Zayyāt, for his part, writes in *Waḥy al-risāla*, vol. 1 (Cairo, 1956), p. 391: 'As young students, they would position themselves in the 'Abbasid corridor of al-Azhar University. There they recited poems to each other . . . while on the look-out for the appearance of the Thursday issue of *al-Mu'ayyid*, when they would read al-Manfalūṭī's article up to six or seven times. Ṭāhā [Husayn] was there, all ears, al-Zanātī listened with his eyes shut and al-Zayyāt, dazzled by the beauty of the style, didn't speak a word or dare to make any movement. All had a burning desire to become friends of this al-Manfalūṭī who by divine choice had received the mission to create this entirely original literature.'

22. See the introduction in vol. 1.
23. Boutros Hallaq's essay was translated by Hilary Kilpatrick.

Chapter 2. The Figure of the Lover in Popular Arabic Drama of the Early Twentieth Century

1. Among twentieth-century studies (both general and specific) in this field, the reader is referred to: H. Reich, *Der Mimus* (Berlin, 1903); G. Horowiz, *Spüren griechischer Mimen in Orient* (Berlin, 1905); T. Menzel, *Meddah, Schattentheater und Orta Oyunu* (Prague, 1941); F. Rosenthal, *Humour in Early Islam* (Leiden, 1956); F. Bowers, *Theatre in the East* (New York, 1960); M. Rezvani, *Le théâtre et la danse en Iran* (Paris, 1962); C. Pellat, 'Seriousness and Humour in Early Islam', *Islamic Studies*, 2: 2 (1963), pp. 353–62; J. M. Landau, *Etudes sur le théâtre et le cinéma arabes* (Paris, 1965) [English edn: *Studies in the Arab Theater and Cinema* (Philadelphia, 1958)]; A. R. Ṣāliḥ, *al-Masraḥ al-'arabī* (Cairo, 1972); M. Aziza, *Les formes traditionnelles du spectacle* (Tunis, 1975); A. S. al-Hajjaji, *The Origins of Arabic Theatre* (Cairo, 1981); M. A. el Khozai, *The Development of Early Arabic Drama (1847-1900)* (London, 1984); M. Eliade, *Mito e realtà* (Rome, 1985); and M. M. Badawi, *Early Arabic Drama* (Cambridge, 1988).

2. See P. Della Valle, *De' viaggi di Pietro della Valle il Pellegrino, descritti da lui medesimo in lettere familiari all'erudito suo amico Mario Schipano* (Rome, 1650); C. Niebuhr, *Travels through Arabia and Other Countries in the East* (Edinburgh, 1792); A. Russel, *The Natural History of Aleppo* (London, 1794); and E. W. Lane, *The Manners and Customs of the Modern Egyptians* (London, 1966) (4).

3. See E. Welsford, *The Fool* (London, 1968), p. 51; and Badawi, *Early Arabic Drama*, pp. 11–19.

4. S. D'Amico, *Storia del teatro drammatico*, vol. 1: *Grecia e Roma* (Milan/Rome, 1940), pp. 34–9.

5. A. Mazahery, *La vie quotidienne des musulmans au Moyen Age* (Paris, 1947); C. Pellat, *Le milieu basrien et la formation de Jāḥiẓ* (Paris, 1953); C. E. Bosworth, *The Mediaeval Islamic Underworld. The Banū Sāsān in Arabic Society and Literature* (Leiden, 1976); A. Bouhdiba, *Sexuality in Islam* (London, 1985) (2); and E. Weber, *Imaginaire arabe et contes érotiques* (Paris, 1990).

6. Weber, *Imaginaire arabe . . .*, pp. 46–56.

7. Badawi, *Early Arabic Drama*, p. 10; L. Veccia Vaglieri, 'Costumanze odierne del mese di ramadan in vari paesi musulmani', *Annali dell'Istituto Universitario Orientale di Napoli*, 10 (1937–8), pp. 191–201; and G. Cerbella, 'Il Garāgūz in Libia e nell'Oriente. Il Ramaḍān nelle tradizioni popolari libiche', *Libia*, 7 (1955), pp. 1–43.

8. See, for example, Della Valle, *De' viaggi . . .*, pp. 110–11.

9. Weber, *Imaginaire arabe . . .*, p. 56; and S. Moreh, 'The Background of the Mediaeval Arabic Theatre', *Jerusalem Studies in Arabic and Islam*, 13 (1990), pp. 294–329.

10. Badawi, *Early Arabic Drama*, p. 10.

11. Weber, *Imaginaire arabe . . .*, pp. 57–64.

12. Ṣāliḥ, *al-Masraḥ . . .*, pp. 41–2; and Badawi, *Early Arabic Drama*, p. 11. For 'folk sexuality', see Bouhdiba, *Sexuality in Islam*, p. 197: 'This [sexual] folklore contains an immense wealth of meaning. It is a veritable battery of safety valves in a rather enclosed social system, a permanent determination to correct sclerosis and to circumvent prohibitions in one way or another.'

13. There is an obvious comparison with Harlequin; see D'Amico, *Storia del teatro . . .*, pp. 90–114, on Italian masks. It is interesting to note that Cerbella, 'Il Garāgūz . . .', p. 30, says that Arlecchino speaks Venetian dialect with a marked Arabic intonation.

14. On sexuality and buffoonery see D'Amico, *Storia del teatro . . .*, pp. 138–43 (Commedia dell'Arte and popular buffoons); and A. Amīn, *Qāmūs al-'ādāt wa 'l-taqālīd wa 'l-ta'ābīr al-Miṣriyya* (Cairo, 1953), p. 288.

15. Landau, *Etudes sur le théâtre . . .*, p. 21; and Cerbella, 'Il Garāgūz', pp. 28–9.

16. F. Durrenmatt, 'Jak pisat' zle, kolyž se nam dobře žije?', *Divadlo* (Dec. 1968), p. 68.

17. This is also confirmed in the detailed studies by A. Abū Shanab, *Masraḥ 'arabī qadīm: Karākūz* (Damascus, 1964) and S. Qaṭāya, *Nuṣūṣ min Khayāl al-ẓill fī Ḥalab* (Damascus, 1977).

18. Landau, *Etudes sur le théâtre . . .*, p. 22, also notes this peculiarity: 'People love this buffoonery, especially when the body of the puppet is afflicted with an abnormal phallus.'

19. See M. And, *Karagöz. Turkish Shadow Theatre* (Istanbul, 1979), 2, pp. 84–6. E. Zachos-Papazahariou, 'Les origines et survivances ottomanes au sein du théâtre d'ombre grec', *Turcica*, 5 (1975), p. 38, remarks that: 'The original shape of the popular Karagöz, which was born in Anatolia and spread throughout most large towns of the Mediterranean, was phallocratic.'

20. Examples are A. Taymūr, *Khayāl al-ẓill* (Cairo, 1957) and A. Ḥ. Yūnus, *Khayāl al-ẓill* (Cairo, 1965).

21. See the important works by G. Jacob: *Bibliographie ueber das Schattentheater* (Erlangen, 1902); *Geschichte des Schattentheaters im Morgen und Abendland* (Berlin, 1907); and 'Bibliographie berichte. Neue Karagos Literatur', in *Mitteilungen des Seminars für Orientalische Sprachen zu Berlin* (Berlin, 1925), pp. 3–6. See also: E. Littmann, *Arabische Schattenspiele* (Berlin, 1901); C. Prufer, *Ein Aegyptisches Schattenspiel* (Erlangen, 1906); P. Kahle, 'Islamische Schattenspielfiguren aus Aegypten', *Der Islam*, 2 (1911), pp. 142–95; P. Kahle, *Das Leuchtturm von Alessandria* (Stuttgart, 1930); J. M. Landau, 'Shadow Plays in the Near East', *Edoth*, 3 (1947–8), pp. 135–73; and M. M. Badawi, 'Mediaeval Arabic Drama', *Journal of Arabic Literature*, 13 (1982), pp. 83–108.

22. Qaṭāya, *Nuṣūṣ min Khayāl al-ẓill . . .*, p. 16, for example, mentions a rich group of puppeteers in Aleppo who were very famous in the first decades of the twentieth century. See also R. Dorigo Ceccato, 'Il teatro d'ombre a Damasco', *Quaderni di Studi Arabi*, 2 (1984), pp. 127–54.

23. M. Kayāl, *Ramaḍān wa taqālīd dimashqiyya* (Damascus, 1973).

24. Landau, *Etudes sur le théâtre . . .*, pp. 21–50.

25. See Badawi, *Early Arabic Drama*, p. 10; and Landau, 'Shadow Plays . . . ', pp. xxv–xxviii.

26. For the Syrian shadow theatre, see Landau, *Etudes sur le théâtre . . .*, pp. 41–4; and Dorigo Ceccato, 'Il teatro d'ombre . . . ', pp. 134–6. In some countries, such as Syria—the second most important country after Egypt with regard to the presence and diffusion of this type of entertainment—it is still possible to find unpublished documents, even though the art of the shadow play can be said to have disappeared by now in this region too.

27. Zachos-Papazahariou, 'Les origines . . . ', p. 36.

28. For Algerian shadow theatre, see Landau, *Etudes sur le théâtre . . .*, p. 45.

29. It must not be confused with the Egyptian *masraḥ Arā'oz*, a type of theatre performed with glove puppets and whose principal hero is a man called *Qarāqūs* (*Arā'oz*), which recalls the name of Saladin's famous minister in the thirteenth century. In Egypt today, *Qarāqūs* is still a synonym for a clown. See Badawi, *Early Arabic Drama*, pp. 12–13; and Dorigo Ceccato, 'Il teatro d'ombre . . . ', p. 129.

30. See M. Nicholas, 'Karagöz: le théâtre d'ombres turc d'hier à aujourd'hui', *Quaderni di Studi Arabi*, 5–6 (1987–8), pp. 581–600.

31. For the Tunisian shadow theatre, see Landau, *Etudes sur le théâtre . . .*, pp. 45–50.

32. This is particularly true in Syria: see Qaṭāya, *Nuṣūṣ min Khayāl al-ẓill . . .*, p. 45, where the writer asserts that shadow plays from Aleppo have no obscene words or situations. A perfect example of a moral play is a text known as *al-'Āshiq wa 'l-ma'shūq* (pub. by J. G. Wetzstein under the title, *Die Liebenden von Amasia*, Damascus, 1857/Leipzig, 1906). See S. Moreh, 'The Shadow Play in the Light of Arabic Literature', *Journal of Arabic Literature*, 18 (1987), pp. 46–61; S. Moreh, 'Live Theater in Medieval Islam', in *Studies in Islamic History and Civilization* (Leiden, 1986), p. 608.

33. Landau, *Etudes sur le théâtre . . .*, p. 44, underlines that, while in most shadow plays the physical grotesque prevailed, in Syria character anomalies were preferred.

34. Like the indecent behaviour of the opium-smoker: see ibid., p. 43.

35. See W. Hoenerbach, *Das nordafrikanische Schattentheater* (Mainz, 1959), pp. 76–8.

36. Ibid. The scholar gives a summary of the text and only a German translation of the dialogues, in which we read: 'Karakus goes home and takes pleasure in Fatma' (p. 77).

37. Aziza, *Les formes traditionnelles . . .*, pp. 50–8.

38. Here the text is reported in Arabic, with a French translation. We read: 'Je me paierai auprès de cette jolie femme' (p. 58).

39. This text can be found in M. Kayāl, *Yā Shām* (Damascus, 1986), pp. 179–80; see also Dorigo Ceccato, 'Il teatro d'ombre . . .', pp. 147–54.

40. Dorigo Ceccato, 'Il teatro d'ombre . . .', pp. 148–9.

41. Hoenerbach, *Das nordafrikanische Schattentheater*, pp. 78–80.

42. See Dorigo Ceccato, 'Il teatro d'ombre . . .', pp. 142–4.

43. Ibid., p. 143.

44. Taymūr, *Khayāl al-ẓill*, p. 29.

45. The joke against Karākūz in the play *'Urs Karākūz*, is typical, in which the hero thinks he is going to be married to a lovely girl, whereas his wife-to-be is actually an ugly old woman.

46. On satyrical elements in shadow plays, see Landau, *Etudes sur le théâtre . . .*, pp. 50–2.

47. Hoenerbach, *Das nordafrikanische Schattentheater*, pp. 82–5.

48. J. M. Landau, 'Popular Arabic Plays', *Journal of Arabic Literature*, 17, pp. 120–5.

49. Ibid., p. 122.

50. Ibid., pp. 122–3.

51. Ibid., p. 123.

52. Taymūr, *Khayāl al-ẓill*, pp. 23–4.

Chapter 3. The Romantic Imagination and the Female Ideal

1. Most of these opening remarks are taken from my chapter 'The Romantic Poets' in M. M. Badawi (ed.), *Modern Arabic Literature* (Cambridge, 1992).

2. A. H. Hourani, *Arabic Thought in the Liberal Age* (Oxford, 1962), pp. 164–70.

3. M. M. Badawi, *An Anthology of Modern Arabic Verse* (Oxford, 1969), pp. 21–3.

4. P. J. Vatikiotis, *A Modern History of Egypt* (London, 1969), pp. 306–7.

5. R. Christiansen, *Romantic Affinities* (New York, 1969), p. 103.

6. R. Williams, *Culture and Society* (London, 1987), pp. 87–109.

7. K. Muṭrān, *Dīwān al-Khalīl* (Cairo, 1908), p. 171.

8. M. M. Badawi, *A Critical Introduction to Modern Arabic Poetry* (Cambridge, 1975), p. 32.

9. A. R. Shukrī, *Dīwān 'Abd al-Raḥmān Shukrī* (Alexandria, 1960), pp. 99–100.

10. Ibid., p. 257.

11. Ibid., pp. 142, 159–60.

12. Badawi, *Critical Introduction . . .*, pp. 116–45.

13. A. Z. Abū Shādī, *Andā' al-fajr* (Cairo, 1934), p. 34.

14. A. Z. Abū Shādī, *Zaynab* (Cairo, 1924), p. 16.

15. A. Z. Abū Shādī, *Aṭyāf al-rabī'* (Cairo, 1933), pp. 23–6.

16. Abū Shādī, *Zaynab*, pp. 38–40.

17. M. M. Badawi, 'Convention and Revolt in Modern Arabic Poetry', in G. E. von Grunebaum (ed.), *Arabic Poetry, Theory and Development* (Wiesbaden, 1973), p. 196.

18. A. Q. al-Shābbī, *Aghānī al-ḥayāt* (Tunis, 1966), p. 185.

19. Badawi, *Critical Introduction . . .*, pp. 129–37.

20. I. Nājī, *Dīwān Nājī*, ed. by A. Rāmī, Ṣ. Jawdat, A. A. M. Haykal and M. Nājī (Cairo, 1961), pp. 344–5.

21. Ibid., p. 56.

22. Ibid., p. 39.
23. Badawi, *Critical Introduction . . .*, pp. 137–45.
24. A. M. Ṭāhā, *Layālī al-mallāḥ al-tā'ih* (Cairo, 1943), pp. 2–9.
25. Ibid., pp. 10–11.

Chapter 4. Love and Beyond in Mahjar *Literature*

1. They are Anjal 'Awn (b. Lebanon; d. 1983, São Paulo), Salwā Salāma Aṭlas (b. 1883, Lebanon; d. 1949, São Paulo), Jibrān Khalīl Jibrān (commonly known as Gibran) (b. 1883, Lebanon; d. 1931, New York), Mīkhā'īl Nu'ayma (b. 1889, Lebanon; d. 1988, Lebanon), Najīb Quṣṭanṭīn Ḥaddād (who published a novel on this subject in 1939 in São Paulo) and Shafīq Ma'lūf (b. 1905, Lebanon; d. 1976, São Paulo).

2. It was first published in the magazine *al-Funūn* in 1916, and then in book form in 1917.

3. All information on Anjal 'Awn is based on N. Ḥarb, *Anjal 'Awn. Kātiba wa adība wa shā'ira (al-Barāzīl)* [Anjal 'Awn. Writer and Poet (Brazil)] (Damascus, 1985). This book consists of a short biographical sketch plus a selection of 'Awn's writings. The author gives no dates except the year of 'Awn's death. The selected writings are presented without further information about the original sources or the dates of their first publication. As regards the life of 'Awn, Ḥarb mentions that she was born in Lebanon (the daughter of a clergyman), studied in Beirut and was a teacher in Ḥasbiyya and Rashiyya. After the death of her father, her brother took her and her mother to Brazil, where she was married to a merchant who was her senior by 25 years. The author does not indicate how long this marriage lasted, but he does tell us that her husband eventually became semi-paralysed and that 'Awn was his personal nurse for fifteen years. After her husband's death she took various courses and was then nominated juridical translator by the Brazilian government in Rio de Janeiro.

4. This story was published in the volume *Arā'is al-murūj* [Nymphs of the Valley] in 1905. The quotations have been translated from the Arabic edn (Beirut, 1964) in *al-Majmū'a al-kāmilah lil-mu'allafāt al-'arabiyyah li Jibrān Khalīl Jibrān* [Complete Works in Arabic of Jibrān Khalīl Jibrān], pp. 58–68.

5. Ibid., pp. 75–99.

6. Ibid., pp. 167–239.

7. Published in the volume *Hams al-Jufūn* [Eyelids' Whispering] (Beirut, 1945), pp. 75–9.

8. See C. Nijland, 'A "New Andalusian" Poem', *Journal of Arabic Literature*, 18, pp. 102–20.

9. *'Abqar*, quoted from the 4th edn (São Paulo, 1949), p. 173.

10. A. Sa'āda, *al-Ṣirā' al-fikrī fī 'l-adab al-sūrī* [The Intellectual Struggle in Syrian Literature] (Buenos Aires, 1943), p. 76.

11. Salwā Salāma (1883–1949) married Jūrj Aṭlas in 1913. He set up the women's magazine *al-Karma* for her in 1914. Salwā Salāma Aṭlas was the editor of this magazine, which existed for more than thirty years. In 1939 it celebrated its

quarter-century. In 1941 Salwā Salāma Atlas published a collection of articles and stories from *al-Karma* and other sources under the title *Amām al-mawqid* (São Paulo, 1941); the short story "Ya'qūb al-Sharrāt" (written originally by her late husband) was published anew in this selection (pp. 62–82).

Chapter 5. The Four Ages of Ḥusayn Tawfīq . . .

1. See the title of one of al-Ḥakīm's early collections of essays, *Min al-burj al-'ājī* (1941). For al-Ḥakīm as *'aduw al-mar'a* (the enemy of women), see, for example, P. G. Starkey, *From the Ivory Tower: A Critical Study of Tawfīq al-Ḥakim* (London, 1987), pp. 153–8, 177, etc. An essay entitled "Kun 'aduwan li 'l-mar'a" appeared in the collection *'Ahd al-shayṭān* (Cairo, 1938).

2. For a general discussion of these novels in English, see: H. Sakkut, *The Egyptian Novel and its Main Trends from 1913 to 1952* (Cairo, 1971), pp. 85–97; H. Kilpatrick, *The Modern Egyptian Novel* (London, 1974), pp. 41–51; A. B. Jad, *Form and Technique in the Egyptian Novel 1912-1971* (London, 1983), pp. 38–42, 50–6, 73–7, etc; and Starkey, *From the Ivory Tower*, pp. 53–8, 84–92, etc.

3. On this, see, for example, P. Cachia, 'Idealism and Ideology: The Case of Tafīq al-Ḥakīm', *Journal of the American Oriental Society*, 100: 3 (1980), reprinted in P. Cachia, *An Overview of Modern Arabic Literature* (Edinburgh, 1990), pp. 152–70.

4. N. Barbour, "'Awdat al-rūḥ", *Islamic Culture*, 9 (1935), p. 488.

5. T. al-Ḥakīm, *Return of the Spirit*, transl. by W. M. Hutchins (Washington, D.C., 1990), p. 67. All quotations from *'Awdat al-rūḥ* have been taken from this translation.

6. Ibid., p. 63.

7. Ibid., p. 79.

8. Ibid., p. 123.

9. Ibid., p. 253.

10. Ibid., p. 269.

11. For this theme, see, for example, I. J. Boullata, 'Encounter between East and West: a Theme in Contemporary Arabic Novels', *Middle East Journal*, 30 (1976), pp. 49–62.

12. *'Uṣfūr min al-sharq* (Cairo, 1988), pp. 144–5.

13. *Return of the Spirit*, p. 85.

14. Ibid., p. 151.

15. Ibid., p. 47.

16. Ibid., pp. 88–102.

17. *Yawmiyyāt nā'ib fi 'l-aryāf* (Cairo, 1988), p. 41.

18. Ibid., p. 141.

19. Ibid., p. 23, etc.

20. Ibid., p. 134.

21. Ibid., p. 92.

22. For plays inspired by the position of women in Egyptian society see, for example, *Urīd hādhā al-rajul* (*Masraḥ al-mujtama'*, pp. 35-62), *al-Nā'iba al-*

muhtarama (ibid., pp. 63–84), and, from an earlier period, *al-Mar'a al-jadīda (al-Masrah al-munawwa'*, pp. 533–635). These plays, and others on similar themes, are discussed in Starkey, *From the Ivory Tower*, pp. 56–7, 153–9.

23. On this, see Starkey, *From the Ivory Tower*, pp. 45–6, 207–20, etc.

24. *Al-Ribāt al-muqaddas* (Cairo, 1988), pp. 136ff.

25. Ibid., pp. 211ff.

26. Starkey, *From the Ivory Tower*, p. 227.

Chapter 6. Erotic Awareness in the Early Egyptian Short Story

1. Transl. into English by M. M. Badawi under the title, *The Saint's Lamp* (Leiden, 1973).

2. Arabic text: *fa-huwa farīsa mumazzaqa bayna quwā dāfi'a wa-ukhrā jādhiba. Yahrabu min al-nās wa-yakādu yujannu fi wahdatih* (Cairo, 1975), p. 71.

3. *The Saint's Lamp*, p. 8.

4. H. A. R. Gibb, *Studies on the Civilization of Islam* (Princeton, N.J., 1982), p. 264.

5. See: J. Brugman, *An Introduction to the History of Modern Arabic Literature in Egypt* (Leiden, 1984), p. 86; and R. Fakkar, *L'influence française sur la formation de la presse littéraire en Egypte au XIXe siècle* (Paris, 1973), pp. 94, 135.

6. For an analysis of both stories, see C. Vial, *Le personnage de la femme dans le roman et la nouvelle en Egypte de 1914 à 1960* (Damascus, 1979), pp. 81–3.

7. See A. Jad, *Form and Technique in the Egyptian Novel* (London, 1983), pp. 57ff.

8. Arab specialists on the short story, such as Sabry Hafez, Sayyid Hāmid al-Nassāj and 'Abbās Khidr, have described the New School's literary production within the larger framework of their studies on the Arabic short story. Abdel Meguid's book on the same topic does not even mention the existence of such a school. I have tried to explore the beginning of the Modern School in my own study on Muhammad Taymūr. We all owe a further debt to Yahyā Haqqī for having enhanced the discussion of this avant-garde movement in modern Arabic prose. See: Sabry Hafez M. Abdel-Dayem, 'The Rise and Development of the Egyptian Short Story 1881–1970' (unpub. dissertation, University of London); Sabry Hafez, *The Genesis of Arabic Narrative Discourse* (London, 1993); Sayyid Hāmid al-Nassāj, *Tatawwur fann al-qissa al-qasīra fī Misr 1910–1933*, 4th edn (Cairo, 1984); 'Abbās Khidr, *al-Qissa al-qasīra fī Misr* (Cairo, 1966); Abdel Aziz Abdel Meguid, *The Modern Arabic Short Story* (Cairo, n.d. [1956]); Ed C. M. de Moor, *Un oiseau en cage. Le discours littéraire de Muhammad Taymūr* (Amsterdam, 1991); and Yahyā Haqqī, *Fajr al-qissa al-misriyya*, 2nd edn (Cairo, 1975; 1st edn, 1960).

9. Muhammad Taymūr, *Mu'allafāt* I (1973), p. 276; and Muhammad Taymūr, *Mā tarāhu al-'uyūn* (1990 edn), pp. 75–6.

10. *Mā tarāhu al-'uyūn*, pp. 45–51.

11. Ibid., pp. 53–8.

12. Arabic text: *fa-yā lil-'ajab mimmā tarāhu al-'uyūn fī zalām hādhihi al-hayāh* in *Mā tarāhu al-'uyūn*, p. 58.

13. See Khiḍr, *al-Qiṣṣa . . .*, pp. 215–27.

14. *Majallat al-Funūn*, 1 Sept. 1924, pp. 14–17; see al-Nassāj, *Taṭawwur*, p. 210.

15. *Al-Fajr*, 27 Jan. 1925.

16. Khiḍr, *al-Qiṣṣa . . .*, p. 224.

Chapter 7. The Arabic Short Story and the Status of Women

The author would like to thank Gregory Bell for his help in tracing the texts of several of the stories cited.

1. The negative side of this larger family structure is described and discussed by E. Accad, *Sexuality and War: Literary Masks of the Middle East* (New York, 1990), p. 29.

2. Ḥanān al-Shaykh, "Ḥammām al-niswān", in *Wardat al-ṣaḥra'* (Beirut, 1982), pp. 9–18. The figure of the grandmother also appears in the titles of the Egyptian Suhayr al-Qalamāwi's early collection of short stories, *Aḥādīth jaddati* (Cairo, 1935), and of Marilyn Booth's recent collection of short stories written by Egyptian women, *My Grandmother's Cactus*, transl. by M. Booth (London, 1991).

3. Yūsuf Idrīs, "Naẓra", in *Arkhaṣ layālī* (Cairo, n.d.), pp. 11–12; transl. by T. Le Gassick as 'A Stare', in R. Allen (ed.), *In the Eye of the Beholder* (Minneapolis, 1978), pp. 3–4; also P. M. Kurpershoek, *The Short Stories of Yusuf Idris* (Leiden, 1982), pp. 98–100.

4. Yūsuf Idrīs, "La'bat al-bayt", in *Ākhir al-dunyā*. See *al-Mu'allafāt al-kāmila: al-qiṣaṣ al-qaṣīra* (Cairo), pp. 378–89; transl. by R. Allen as 'Playing House', in *In the Eye of the Beholder*, pp. 79–87.

5. Muṣṭafā al-Fārisī, "Man yadrī . . .? Rubbamā", in *al-Qanṭara hiya al-ḥayāh* (Tunis, 1968), pp. 87–102. Henry James' comment is as follows: 'A distribution of the last of prizes, pensions, husbands, wives, babies, millions, appended paragraphs and cheerful remarks.' See H. James, 'The Art of Fiction', in J. E. Miller Jr (ed.), *Theory of Fiction: Henry James* (Lincoln, Neb., 1972), p. 32.

6. Salwā Bakr, "'An al-rūḥ allatī suriqat tadrījiyyan", from *'An al-rūḥ allatī suriqat tadrījiyyan* (Cairo, 1989), pp. 19–25.

7. Yaḥyā Ḥaqqī, *Qindīl Umm Hāshim*, Iqra' Series no. 18 (Cairo, n.d.), pp. 74–87; transl. by M. M. Badawi as 'The Three Orphans', in *The Saint's Lamp and Other Stories* (Leiden, 1973), pp. 50–8.

8. See Ḥaqqī: *Qindīl . . .*, pp. 81–2; and *Saint's Lamp*, pp. 55–6. See also Miriam Cooke's comment on this description in *The Anatomy of an Egyptian Intellectual* (Washington, D.C., 1984), p. 70.

9. Zakariyyā Tāmir, "al-Thalj ākhir al-layl", in *Rabī' fī 'l-ramād* (Damascus, 1973), pp. 7–20; transl. by M. Shaheen as 'Snow at Night,' in M. Manzalaoui (ed.), *Arabic Writing Today: The Short Story* (Cairo, 1968), pp. 269–75.

10. May Muẓaffar, "Awrāq khāṣṣa", in *al-Baja'* (Baghdad, 1979), pp. 17–26; transl. by S. Fattal as 'Personal Papers', in M. Badran and M. Cooke (eds), *Opening the Gates* (London/Bloomington, Ind., 1990), pp. 180–5.

11. Khalīl Jibrān, *'Arā'is al-murūj* (Beirut, 1908); transl. by H. N. Nahmad as 'Martha'. in *Nymphs of the Valley* (New York, 1968), pp. 3-9 (abridged); Dhū al-Nūn Ayyūb, *al-Āthār al-kāmila*, vol. 1: *al-Qiṣaṣ* (Baghdad, 1977), pp. 95-103 (from the collection, *al-Ḍaḥāyā* [1937]). The most infamous quotation on this theme is that of Yusuf Wahbi, the famous Egyptian actor: 'A girl's honour is like a single match.' Quoted by G. al-Sammān in E. Warnock Fernea and B. Qattan Bezirgan (eds), *Middle Eastern Muslim Women Speak* (Austin, Tex., 1977), p. 395.

12. Maḥmūd Taymūr, "Najiyya ibnat al-shaykh", in *al-Shaykh 'Afā' Allāh* (Cairo, 1936), pp. 115–22. See R. Wielandt, *Das erzählerische Frühwerk Mahmūd Taymūrs: Beitrag zu einem Archiv der modernen arabischen Literatur* (Beirut/Wiesbaden, 1983), pp. 381–4.

13. Maḥmūd Taymūr, "Fatāt al-jīrān", in *'Amm Mitwallī* (Cairo, 1925), pp. 69–82; see Wielandt, *Das erzählerische . . .*, pp. 239–40.

14. Zakariyyā Tāmir, "Wajh al-qamar", in *Dimashq al-harā'iq* (Damascus, 1973), pp. 95–103; transl. by H. al-Khaṭīb as 'The Face of the Moon', *Journal of Arabic Literature*, 3 (1972), pp. 96–100.

15. "Ḥādithat sharaf", in *Ḥādithat sharaf* (Cairo, 1971), pp. 94–123.

16. Ḥanān al-Shaykh, "Bint ismuhā Tuffāḥa", in *Wardat al-ṣaḥrā'*, pp. 121–6; transl. by M. Cooke as 'A Girl Named Apple', *Translation*, vol. 11 (fall 1983), pp. 4–8; reprinted in Badran and Cooke (eds), *Opening the Gates*, pp. 155–9.

17. This can also be gauged from recently published anthologies in English: see S. K. Jayyusi (ed.), *The Literature of Modern Arabia* (London, 1988); and *Assassination of Light*, transl. by A. Molnar Heinrichsdorff and Abu Bakr Bagader (Washington, D.C., 1990).

18. Khalīl Jibrān, *al-Arwāḥ al-mutamarrida* (Beirut, 1908); transl. by H. N. Nahmad as *Spirits Rebellious* (New York, 1969), pp. 3–28, 47–64.

19. Alīfa Rif'at, "Fī layl al-shitā' al-ṭawīl", in *Fī layl al-shitā' al-ṭawīl* (Cairo, 1985), pp. 5–14; transl. by D. Johnson-Davies as 'The Long Night of Winter', in *Distant View of a Minaret and Other Stories* (London, 1983), pp. 55–9.

20. Dhū al-Nūn Ayyūb, *al-Āthār al-kāmila*, vol. 1: *al-Qiṣaṣ* (Baghdad, 1977), p. 181 (from the collection, *Ṣadīq* [1938]).

21. Yūsuf Idrīs, "al-Martaba al-muqa''ara", in *al-Naddāha* (Cairo, 1969"), pp. 70–1; trans. by R. Allen as 'The Concave Mattress', in *In the Eye of the Beholder*, pp. 119–20. See also Kurpershoek, *Short Stories of Yusuf Idris*, pp. 161–4.

22. Maḥmūd Taymūr, "Inqilāb", in *Fir'awn al-saghīr* (Cairo, 1939), pp. 101–14; transl. by G. M. Wickens as 'Revolution', *Nimrod*, 24: 2 (spring/summer 1981), pp. 129–34.

23. Yūsuf Idrīs, "'Alā waraq sīlūfān", in *Bayt min laḥm* (Beirut, n.d. [1971]), pp. 37–58; trans. by Roger Allen as 'In Cellophane Wrapping', in *In the Eye of the Beholder*, pp. 169–89.

24. 'For the Arab man, women exist in various personifications: virgin, girl, wife, mother. There is no room for the woman friend or lover . . . There is no love, only sexuality . . . Marriage is a sexual pleasure on the one hand and a means of procreating on the other; the image of the wife is thus identified with that of the mother.' A. Khalīlī quoted in M. Salmān, 'Arab Women', *Khamsīn*, 6 (1978), p.

26; quoted in Cooke, *Anatomy of an Egyptian Intellectual*, p. 163, n. 4. Najīb Maḥfūẓ puts the following comment into the mouth of Khadīja in his novel, *al-Sukkariyya*: 'If a bride doesn't get pregnant and have children, what use is she?' See Najīb Maḥfūẓ, *al-Sukkariyya* (Cairo, 1957), p. 349; transl. by W. Maynard Hutchins and A. Botros Samaan as *Sugar Street* (New York, 1992), p. 274.

25. Mīkhā'īl Nu'ayma, "Sanatuhā 'l-jadīda", in *Kāna mā kāna*; transl. by J. Perry as 'The New Year', in Mikhail Naimy, *A New Year: Stories, Autobiography and Poems* (Leiden, 1974), pp. 23–32.

26. Laylā al-'Uthmān, "al-Raḥīl", in *al-Raḥīl* (Beirut, 1979), pp. 47–59; transl. by L. Kenny and N. Shihab Nye as 'Pulling Up Roots', in Jayyusi (ed.), *Literature of Modern Arabia*, pp. 483–8.

27. Laylā Ba'albakkī, "Safīnat ḥinān ilā 'l-qamar", in *Safīnat ḥinān ilā 'l-qamar* (Beirut, 1963), pp. 179–90; transl. by D. Johnson-Davies as 'Spaceship of Tenderness to the Moon', in *Modern Arabic Short Stories* (London, 1967), pp. 130–6. For a transcript of the trial at which Ba'albakkī was accused of obscenity, see Fernea and Bezirgan (eds), *Middle Eastern Muslim Women Speak*, pp. 273–90.

28. Daisy al-Amīr, 'The Newcomer', in Y. T. Hafidh and L. al-Dilaimi (eds), *Iraqi Short Stories* (Baghdad, 1988), pp. 283–8.

29. Edwār al-Kharrāṭ, "Ḥīṭān 'āliya", from *Ḥīṭān 'āliya* (Cairo, 1968, private circulation; Beirut, 1990); and Tawfīq Yūsuf 'Awwād, *al-Ṣabī al-a'raj* (Beirut, 1963), pp. 175–89.

30. Yūsuf Idrīs, "Bayt min laḥm", in *Bayt min laḥm* (Beirut, n.d. [1971]), pp. 5–13; transl. by M. Mikhail as 'A House of Flesh', in *In the Eye of the Beholder*, pp. 191–8; and by D. Johnson-Davies as 'House of Flesh', in *Egyptian Short Stories* (London/Washington, 1978), pp. 1–7. See also F. Malti-Douglas, 'Blindness and Sexuality: Traditional Mentalities in Yusuf Idris' "House of Flesh"', *Literature East and West* ['Critical Pilgrimages'] (1989), pp. 70–8.

31. Suhayr al-Qalamāwī, "Imra'a nājiḥa", from *al-Shayāṭīn talhū* (Cairo, 1964), pp. 147–56.

32. Najīb Maḥfūẓ, *al-Marāyā* (Cairo, 1972), pp. 268, 353; transl. by R. Allen as *Mirrors* (Chicago, 1977), pp. 180, 239. See also Yūsuf Idrīs' novel, *al-'Ayb* (Cairo, 1962), which provides a rather superficial view of the situation in the workplace, showing the way in which the first woman employee in an office that thrives on corruption is herself gradually corrupted both financially and sexually.

33. "Mawt ma'ālī al-wazīr sābiqan", from *Mawt ma'ālī al-wazīr sābiqan* (Cairo, 1980).

34. Daisy al-Amīr, "Marāyā al-'uyūn", in *Wu'ūd li-al-bay'* (Beirut, 1981), pp. 17–20.

35. Zaynab Rushdī, "Taṭābuq al-muwāṣafāt", in *Yaḥduth aḥyānan* (Cairo, 1975), pp. 38–42.

36. Salwā Bakr, "Zīnāt fī janāzat al-ra'īs", from *Zīnāt fī janāzat al-ra'īs* (Cairo, 1989), pp. 19–25.

37. Khayriyya Ibrāhīm al-Saqqāf, *An tubḥira naḥwa 'l-ab'ād* (Riyadh, 1982); transl. by A. M. Heinrichsdorff and Abu Bakr Bagader in *Assassination of Light*, pp. 47–51.

38. Ghāda al-Sammān: *Bayrūt 1975* (Beirut, 1975); and *Kawābīs Bayrūt* (Beirut,

1980); Emily Nasrallāh: *al-Yanbū'* (Beirut, 1978); and *al-Mar'a fī 17 qiṣṣa* (ibid., 1983). Several of Naṣrallāh's stories about the war are translated in the collection, Emily Nasrallah, *A House Not Her Own*, transl. by T. Khalil-Khouri (Charlottetown, Prince Edward Island, 1992).

39. See M. Cooke, *War's Other Voices* (Cambridge, 1988) and Accad, *Sexuality and War . . .*

40. Nuhā Samāra, "Wajhān lī imra'a", in *al-Ṭāwilāt 'āshat akthar min Amīn* (Beirut, 1981), pp. 93–112; transl. by M. Cooke as 'Two Faces, One Woman', in *Opening the Gates*, pp. 304–13.

41. Booth, *My Grandmother's Cactus*, p. 6. For Virginia Woolf's views on the subject, see Accad, *Sexuality and War . . .*, p. 39.

42. R. and L. Makarious (eds), *Anthologie de la littérature arabe contemporaine: le roman et la nouvelle* (Paris, 1964), p. 330.

43. Colette Khūrī, *Ayyām ma'ahu* and *Layla wāḥida* (Beirut, 1961).

44. Ghāda al-Sammān, *Hubb* (Beirut, 1973).

45. Ḥalīm Barakāt [Syr.], *Visions of Social Reality in the Contemporary Arab Novel* (Georgetown, 1977), p. 24; and Ḥ. 'Awwād, *Arab Causes in the Fiction of Ghāda al-Sammān 1961-1975* (Sherbrooke, Canada, 1983), p. 19.

46. Nawāl al-Sa'dāwī, *Mudhakkirāt sijn al-nisā'* (Cairo, 1983); transl. by by M. Booth as *Memoirs from the Women's Prison* (London, 1986).

47. Laylā al-'Uthmān, *Fī 'l-layl ta'tī al-'uyūn* (Beirut, 1980), p. 9.

48. Y. al-Shārūnī (ed.), *al-Layla al-thāniyya ba'd al-alf* (Cairo, 1975), pp. 14–15.

49. H. Bloom, *Ruin the Sacred Truths* (Cambridge, Mass., 1987), p. 3.

50. With regard to Laylā Ba'albakkī, this view is shared by Muḥyī al-Dīn Ṣubḥī, *al-Batal fī ma'zaq* (Damascus, 1979), p. 206.

51. 'Īsā 'Ubayd, "Mudhakkirāt Iḥsān Khānum", in *Iḥsān Khānum* (Cairo, 1964), pp. 1–8; Maḥmūd Taymūr, "Inqilāb", in *Fir'awn al-ṣaghīr* (Cairo, 1963), pp. 127–42. See also Wielandt, *Das erzählerische . . .*, pp. 393–4.

52. Yūsuf Idrīs, *Bayt min laḥm*, pp. 7–8.

53. Nawāl al-Sa'dāwī, *Mawt ma'ālī al-wazīr* (Cairo, 1980).

54. Laylā al-'Uthmān, "al-Maqhā", in *Ḥālat ḥubb majnūna* Mukhtārāt Fuṣūl no. 68 (Cairo, 1989), pp. 101–11. The same process occurs in "'Alā safar", except that the narrator emerges as a male; Laylā al-'Uthmān, *Fatḥiyya takhtār mawtahā* (Beirut, 1987), pp. 51–8.

55. Laylā al-'Uthmān, "al-Ru'ūs ilā asfal", in *al-Ḥubb la-hu ṣuwar* (Beirut, 1983), pp. 52–63.

56. Salwā Bakr, *al-Majālis*, 27 June 1987; quoted by F. Ghazoul, "Balāghat al-ghalāba", in Salwā Bakr, *'An al-rūḥ allatī suriqat tadrījiyyan*, p. 103.

Chapter 8. Love and the Mechanisms of Power . . .

1. Conversations with al-Ghīṭānī, 1984, 1986, 1988.

2. In *al-Zaynī Barakāt*, echoes can be traced of Ibn Iyās, al-Tanūkhī, and *Tharthara fawq al-Nīl* and *Qaṣr al-shawq* by Maḥfūẓ.

3. I have used the following editions: *Bayn al-qaṣrayn* (Cairo, 1975); *Qaṣr al-shawq* (Cairo, 1975); and *al-Sukkariyya* (Cairo, 1975); published in English as: *Palace Walk* (transl. by W. M. Hutchins and O. E. Kenny, New York, 1990); *Palace of Desire* (transl. by W. M. Hutchins, L. Kenny and O. E. Kenny, New York, 1991); and *Sugar Street* (transl. by W. M. Hutchins and A. B. Samaan, New York, 1992).

4. I have used the following edition: *al-Zaynī Barakāt* (Cairo, 1985); transl. into English by F. Abdel Wahab as *Zayni Barakat* (London, 1988).

5. M. Foucault, *Discipline and Punish: the Birth of the Prison* (New York, 1979).

6. See, for instance: M. Hussein, *Class Conflict in Egypt 1945–1970* (New York, 1973); S. Somekh, *The Changing Rythm* (Jerusalem, 1978); S. Mehrez, 'Al-Zayni Barakat: Narrative as Strategy', *Arabic Studies Quarterly*, 8: 2 (1986); and I. Gershoni, 'Between Ottomanism and Egyptianism: the Evolution of National Sentiment in the Cairene Middle Class as Reflected in Najib Mahfuz's *Bayn al-Qasrayn*', *Asian and African Studies*, 17 (1983).

7. Besides *Discipline and Punish*, see also M. Foucault, *Power/Knowledge; Selected Interviews and Other Writings, 1972–1977* (New York, 1980).

8. See the proceedings of the spy conference in *al-Zaynī Barakāt*, pavilion five, pp. 221ff.

9. Ibid., pp. 94, 147–8, 233.

10. See especially *Bayn al-qaṣrayn*, various chs.

11. *Al-Zaynī Barakāt*, pp. 78, 109–10, 208–10.

12. Ibid., pp. 74, 109–10; and *al-Sukkariyya*, pp. 257–8.

13. This concept has been developed in particular by Jacques Lacan; see, for instance, M. Bowie, *Lacan* (London, 1991).

14. *Al-Zaynī Barakāt*, p. 255; and *al-Sukkariyya*, pp. 229, 308, 335, 338–9.

15. See *Qaṣr al-shawq*, ch. 31.

16. *Al-Zaynī Barakāt*, p. 232.

17. Notice especially the arrest of Aḥmad and 'Abd al-Mun'im in *al-Sukkariyya*, ch. 52.

18. For a discussion of the growth of the historical novel, see G. Lukacs, *The Historical Novel* (Harmondsworth, 1969). For a discussion of concepts of history and the representation of history, see H. White: *Metahistory: the Historical Imagination in Nineteenth Century Europe* (Baltimore, Md., 1973); and *The Content of the Form; Narrative Discourse and Historical Representation* (Baltimore, Md., 1987).

Chapter 9. Fathers and Husbands . . .

1. In an interview given in Paris in March 1988.

2. E. G. A. A. Ṣāliḥ, "Markaz thaqāfī wāḥid am 'iddat marākiz", *al-Sharq al-Awsaṭ*, 15 June 1990 (this article is one in a series on Arabic literature by the same author all published between June and August 1990).

3. H. Kilpatrick, 'The Arabic Novel—A Single Tradition?', *Journal of Arabic Literature*, 5 (1974), pp. 93–107. See also: W. Walther, 'Identitätssuche—

Identitätsfindung durch Literatur. Literaturentwicklungen im arabischen Raum', *Der Deutschunterricht*, 44 (1992), pp. 8–36, esp. p. 17; and 'Neue Entwicklungen in der zeitgenössischen arabischen narrativen und dramatischen Literatur', in W. Fischer (ed.), *Grundriss der Arabischen Philologie*, vol. 3 (Wiesbaden, 1992), pp. 209ff.

4. Kilpatrick, 'The Arabic Novel . . . ', p. 97.

5. Printed in the collection *Kāna mā kān* (Beirut, 1937; 8th edn, n.d.), pp. 39–51. See C. Nijland, *Mīkhā'īl Nuaymah, Promotor of the Arabic Literary Revival* (Istanbul, 1975), pp. 60–2.

6. Printed in the collection *Mā tarāhu 'l-'uyūn* (Cairo, 1927; reprint, 1990), pp. 9–16. See W. Ende, 'Sollen Fellachen lesen lernen? Muḥammad Taymūrs Kurzgeschichte Fī 'l-Qiṭār', *Die Welt des Islams,* 28 (1988), pp. 112–25.

7. The terminology used in this essay tries to differentiate between literature written in the Arab world or by Arabs (Arab literature) and literature written in Arabic (Arabic literature).

8. A. Laābi, *Le chemin des ordalies* (Paris, 1982).

9. J. Wolf, 'Interview avec Abdellatif Laabi', *Présence Francophone*, 5 (1972), pp. 35–8; quote on p. 36.

10. Laābi, *Le chemin des ordalies*, p. 41.

11. M. Zahiri, 'La figure du père dans le roman marocain', *Présence Francophone*, 30 (1987), pp. 107–26 (esp. p. 108).

12. D. Chraïbi, *Le passé simple* (Paris, 1954).

13. See I. Yetiv, 'L'évolution thématique du roman maghrébin d'expression française (1945–1962)', *Présence Francophone*, 1 (1970), pp. 54–70 (esp. p. 61).

14. See L. Mouzouni, *Le roman marocain de langue française* (Paris, 1987), ch. 2: 'Critique de l'ordre social et révolte dans *Le passé simple*' (pp. 34–70).

15. E. Accad, 'La longue marche des héroines des romans modernes du Machrek et du Maghreb', *Présence Francophone*, 12 (1976), pp. 3–11 (esp. p. 6).

16. D. Chraïbi, *Succession ouverte* (Paris, 1962).

17. D. Chraïbi, *La civilisation, ma mère!* (Paris, 1972).

18. A. Serhane: *Messaouda* (Paris, 1983) and *Les enfants des rues étroites* (Paris, 1986).

19. R. Boudjedra, *La répudiation* (Paris, 1969).

20. See S. Kebir, 'Rachid Boudjedra—ein Potrait des algerischen Schriftstellers', *Zeitschrift für Kulturaustausch und internationale Solidarität*, 27 (Oct. 1985), pp. 18ff.

21. Mouzouni, *Le roman marocain* . . ., ch. 6: 'Le roman picaresque au Maroc (1re partie): Mohamed Choukri, Cherhadi et Merabet' (pp. 149–81).

22. First published in Paul Bowles' English version under the title *For Bread Alone* (London, 1973; new pb edn, London, 1993), then in Tahar Ben Jelloun's French translation: *Le pain nu* (Paris, 1980); the Arabic original appeared in Morocco in the 1980s with no indication of the date; it was later published in London and Beirut in 1988.

23. Mouzouni, *Le roman marocain* . . ., p. 172.

24. M. Dīb: *La grande maison* (Paris, 1952), *L'incendie* (Paris, 1954) and *Le métier à tisser* (Paris, 1957). On the 'missing father', see J. Déjeux, 'Mohammed

Dib—romancier et poète algérien', *Présence Francophone*, 8 (1974), pp. 60–77 (esp. p. 68).

25. Published in Arabic in 1929 and 1940, respectively. On this work, see F. Malti-Douglas, *Blindness and Autobiography*. Al-Ayyām *of Ṭāhā Ḥusayn* (Princeton, N.J., 1988) and F. Dawwāra, *Ayyām Ṭāhā Ḥusayn. Madkhal li-fahm adabih* (Cairo, 1990). In the English translation, the titles of the three volumes are as follows: vol. 1: *An Egyptian Childhood*; vol. 2: *The Stream of Days*; vol. 3: *A Passage to France*.

26. Published in 1964, this work has also appeared under the title *Ḥayātī*. For Tawfīq al-Ḥakīm and his work, see: R. Long, *Tawfiq ak-Hakim: Playwright of Egypt* (London, 1979); and P. Starkey, *From the Ivory Tower: A Critical Study of Tawfīq al-Ḥakīm* (London, 1987). Both authors make ample use of al-Ḥakīm's autobiography.

27. For a detailed discussion of this expression, see Malti-Douglas, *Blindness and Autobiography* . . ., pp. 19ff.

28. E. al-Kharrāṭ, *Turābuhā za'farān* (Cairo, 1986).

29. See C. Nijland, *Mīkhā'īl Nu'aymah: Promotor of the Arabic Literary Revival* (Istanbul, 1975). On the father-and-son topic in particular, see H. Fähndrich, 'Gesellschaft als (veränderbares) Schicksal in Mīhā'īl Nu'aimas Drama Väter und Söhne (al-Abā' wal-banūn)', in J. C. Bürgel and H. Fähndrich (eds), *Die Vorstellung vom Schicksal und die Darstellung der Wirklichkeit in der zeitgenössischen Literatur islamischer Länder* (Berne, 1983), pp. 117–39.

30. M. Nu'aima, *Sab'ūn—ḥikāyat 'umr*, vols 1-3 (Beirut, 1959-60). On this work, see F. Gabrieli, 'L'autobiografia di Mikhail Nu'aima', in his *Arabeschi e studi islamici* (Naples, 1973), pp. 197-207.

31. A helpful collection for a first orientation in the jungle of literature about autobiographies is G. Niggl (ed.), *Die Autobiographie. Zu Form und Geschichte einer literarischen Gattung* (Darmstadt, 1989).

Chapter 10. The Foreign Woman in the Francophone North African Novel

1. R. Wielandt, *Das Bild der Europäer in der modernen arabischen Erzähl- und Theaterliteratur* (Beirut, 1980), pp. 489-553.

2. J. Déjeux, *Image de l'étrangère. Unions mixtes franco-maghrébines* (Paris, 1989), pp. 13-67.

3. Wielandt, *Das Bild* . . ., p. 492.

4. Déjeux, *Image de l'étrangère* . . ., p. 65 and *passim*.

5. This does not exclude a certain conservatism with regard to the relationship between the sexes, to which two of the three examples (Feraoun and Memmi) bear witness, while the third author (Boudjedra) is considered to be either a provocative feminist or a provocative sexist by different critics (see M. Aldouri-Lauber, 'Zwischen Defätismus und Revolte. Die postkoloniale "conscience collective" Algeriens im Lichte des Romanwerks von Rachid Boudjedra', unpub. PhD dissertation, University of Vienna, 1984, pp. 267-9). In fact, he does not seem to be a feminist, for he often refers to women as '*femelle*' instead of '*femme*', displays rather violent sexual fantasies and invents dreadful metaphors for the female sex.

6. Thanks to numerous translations these authors are also well known outside French-speaking countries. All the three above-mentioned novels are, for instance, available in a German version, though two of them appeared only recently. M. Feraoun, *Die Heimkehr des Amer-U-Kaci* (2nd edn, Würzburg, 1956); A. Memmi, *Die Fremde* (Mainz, 1991); and R. Boudjedra, *Die Verstossung* (Zurich, 1991).

7. Feraoun comes from a village situated in the Kabyle mountains, while Memmi grew up in the Jewish community of Tunis.

8. The 1950s and 1960s are held to be the formative period of the present Maghrebi literature.

9. Feraoun, an untiring defender of Algerian-French reconciliation until his death, links up with those authors of the 1930s and 1940s who pleaded for assimilation, integration or synthesis. From the 1920s up to the 1940s a number of novels appeared whose aim was to depict a happy Arab-European marriage as a symbol for the possible coalescence of both cultures. Later, authors became more reluctant and even negative with regard to mixed marriages and inter-cultural relations. See Déjeux, *Image de l'étrangère* . . ., pp. 20ff, 54ff.

10. M. Feraoun, *La terre et le sang* (Paris, 1950), p. 93.

11. A psychoanalytical study of the North African novel has pointed out that many of the heroes' fathers are dead, absent or play no vital role. The authors seem to be more interested in the love between mother and son than in the rivalry between father and son. See C. Montserrat-Cals, '*Questionnement du schema oedipien dans le roman maghrébin*', *Psychanalyse et texte littéraire. Etudes littéraires maghrébines*, 1 (Paris, 1991), pp. 49–59.

12. Childlessness is a frequent theme in North African literature. See E. Accad, 'The Theme of Sexual Oppression in the North African Novel', in L. Beck and N. Keddie (eds), *Women in the Muslim World* (Cambridge, Mass., 1980), p. 624.

13. A. Memmi, *Agar* (Paris, 1955), p. 44.

14. Ibid., p. 64.

15. Ibid., pp. 68ff.

16. Feraoun's Marie is 'an amiable fairy' (*une aimable fée*, p. 44) and Memmi's Marie 'a fragile puppet' (*une fragile poupée*, p. 46). Boudjedra's Marie, on the other hand, is of a quite different kind: 'We observed each other like two boxers, willing not only to fight, but to bite until bloodshed' (. . . *nous observant comme deux boxeurs prêts non pas à se battre mais à se mordre jusqu'au sang*, p. 10).

17. R. Boudjedra, *La répudiation* (Paris, 1969), pp. 273ff.

18. I shall not enter into Kateb Yacine's mythological creation *Nedjma* (Paris, 1956), since it is not in contradiction with my results. Goddesses and whores, as represented by Nedjma, usually go well with mothers. What *Nedjma,* like most novels of this time, lacks is the non-emblematic woman.

19. See M. Mammeri on the segregation of the sexes: 'Men's and women's worlds are like the sun and the moon; they may see each other every day, but they will never meet' (*Le monde des hommes et celui des femmes sont comme le soleil et la lune: ils se voient peut-être tous les jours mais ils ne se rencontrent pas*) in *La colline oubliée* (Paris, 1978), p. 149. See M. Dib on male ignorance with regard to the inward life of women: 'A painful thought touched me: I know nothing of her'

(*Une pensée douloureuse m'effleura: je ne sais rien d'elle*) in *Qui se souvient de la mer* (Paris, 1962), p. 62. And see again M. Mammeri on the absence of women in literature: 'This corresponds to reality and to the insignificant role men grant them in the life of the country' (*Cela correspond à la réalité et à la faible place que les hommes leur laissent dans la vie du pays*) in *el-Moudjāhid*, 10 Dec. 1967.

20. See N. Khadda, 'Sur le personnage féminin dans le roman algérien de langue française', in *Visions du Maghreb* (Montpellier, 18–23 Nov. 1985; 'Cultures et peuples de la Méditerranée' series, no. 142).

Chapter 11. The Function of Sexual Passages in some Egyptian Novels of the 1980s

1. M. J. al-Qalyūbī, "Ḥikāyat al-jins 'inda ahl al-adab" *al-'Arab* (London), 9 Jan. 1991, p. 10.

2. In a collection with the same title (3rd edn, Cairo, 1984 [1st edn, 1979]), pp. 145–91.

3. Ibid., pp. 146ff.

4. He remembers, for example, the storm of protest against a Latin American novel that had been translated into Arabic and published by al-Hay'a al-Miṣriyya al-'Āmma lil-Kitāb. It is true, al-Qa'īd says, that this novel was full of *mawḍū'āt jinsiyya wa ibāḥiyya* (sexual and licentious settings or topics). Nevertheless, *salafī* circles had, in his opinion, no right to attack it, for two reasons: first, the so-called ugly, dirty, disgusting sexual passages were meant not to stimulate the readers sexually but as an expression of the hero's inner crisis; and second, the Arab-Islamic heritage is full of *mashāhid ṣarīḥa* (unconcealed, frank scenes), and it was Islamic publishers that had reissued those works at the end of the nineteenth century—and at that time there were no objections. Another incident occurred when the first chapters of al-Qa'īd's own novel *al-Qulūb al-bayḍā'* had just been serialized in the *Rūz al-Yūsuf* magazine. Here, the author recalls, the Minister of Public Transport, Sulaymān Mitwallī, had been angry to find his daughter reading *kalāman ibāḥiyyan ṣārikhan yukhaddish al-ḥayā' al-'āmm* (flagrantly licentious words, encouraging a general feeling of shame). He therefore applied to the Cabinet and in consequence the Prime Minister, Kamāl Ḥasan 'Alī, demanded that the remaining parts of the novel should never see the light of day. But Fatḥī Ghānim, editor-in-chief of *Rūz al-Yūsuf*, wanted to continue the serialization. In the end, a compromise was reached: the novel could be published in a 'cleaned-up' version. Al-Qa'īd comments bitterly: 'The *salafīs* in Egypt and the Arab world want to convince us that art is *ḥarām* (sinful, a sin), that the novel is *ḥarām* and that the short story is an evil for which Satan is responsible' (see al-Qalyūbī, "Ḥikāyat al-jins . . . ", col. 4).

5. Beirut. The edn used here is Cairo (1982). For reviews and analyses of this and the other novels discussed here, see S. Guth, *Zeugen einer Endzeit. Fünf Schriftsteller zum Umbruch in der ägyptischen Gesellschaft nach 1970* (Berlin, 1992) (= *Islamkundliche Untersuchungen*, vol. 160).

6. Cairo (1982). According to p. 171, the novel was written between Feb. 1977 and Dec. 1979. The meaning of the Arabic title *Taḥrīk al-qalb* is ambiguous: it could be the heart that moves something or the heart that is moved (emotionally) by

something. The author explicitly wanted the title to be understood in both ways.

7. Cairo (= *Riwāyāt al-Hilāl*, no. 482).

8. For an attempt to summarize recent research about literary developments in Egyptian literature from the mid-1960s onwards, see Guth, *Zeugen einer Endzeit . . .* (see n. 5), ch. III.A.

9. In the interview with al-Qalyūbī quoted in n. 1 above, Ṣun'allāh Ibrāhīm seems very impressed by the psychological implications of the words of a *Sa'īdī* whom he happened to meet on a boat from Aswan to Abu Simbel when he was starting his novel *Najmat aghusṭus*. In a night gathering on the boat, the Upper Egyptian told his listeners the story of a king who feared that his friend would commit adultery with his wife when he (the king) was away on a mission. So, the *Ṣa'īdī* said, the king 'had his [i.e. the friend's] personality/identity cut off' (*qaṭa'a shakhṣiyyatah*). When Ibrāhīm asked what this meant, he was told, 'his personality, that is his penis'.

10. For Yūsuf al-Qa'īd, for instance, sexuality is *juz' min al-tajriba al-insāniyya al-'arīḍa* (part of the broad human experience) and should not be subjected to any kind of taboo. If it continues to be taboo, this will produce the same kind of distorted personalities as we have now, and the future will be no better (see also al-Qalyūbī, "Ḥikāyat al-jins . . . ").

11. Al-Qalyūbī, "Ḥikāyat al-jins . . . ".

12. For details, see Guth, *Zeugen einer Endzeit . . .*, pp. 262–6.

13. Al-Qalyūbī, "Ḥikāyat al-jins . . . ".

14. The passage in question is on p. 45 of the Khartoum (1986) 1st complete edn. Yaḥyā Ḥaqqī's comments on that scene are quoted by Ṣun'allāh Ibrāhīm in his *'Alā sabīl al-taqdīm*, on p. 7 of this same edn.

Chapter 12. Distant Echoes of Love in the Narrative Work of Fu'ād al-Tikirlī

1. Anwar Shā'ūl, *al-Ḥiṣād al-awwal* (Baghdad, 1930), p. 7.

2. Ibid., p. 5.

3. See the review in 'Alī Jawād al-Ṭāhir, *Fī 'l-qiṣaṣ al-'irāqī al-mu'āṣir*, (Beirut, 1967), pp. 12–35; and 'Umar Muḥammad al-Ṭālib, *al-Qiṣṣa al-qaṣīra al-ḥaditha fī 'l- Irāq* (Mosul, 1979), pp. 337–62.

4. See two very critical articles by 'Alī Jawād al-Ṭāhir in the newspaper *al-Jumhūriyya* in February 1985, published in 'Alī Jawād al-Ṭāhir, *Min ḥadith al-qiṣṣa wa 'l-masraḥiyya* (Baghdad, 1988), pp. 511ff.

5. French translation: *Les voix de l'aube* (Paris, 1985).

6. See al-Ṭāhir, *Fī 'l-qiṣaṣ . . .*, p. 524; and *al-Nakhla wa 'l-jīrān and* [sic] *al-Qurbān* (by Ghā'ib Ṭu'ma Farmān, who had been living as a refugee in Moscow for many years and was married to a Russian).

7. See, for example, pp. 302 and 307.

8. Al-Ṭāhir, *Fī 'l-qiṣaṣ . . .*, pp. 20ff.

9. According to ibid., p. 12.

10. See E. Frenzel, *Motive der Weltliteratur*, 3. Aufl. (Stuttgart, 1988), s. v. 'Die selbstlose Kurtisane'.

11. *Al-Wajh al-ākhar* (Baghdad, 1982), pp. 310–29.

12. Badr Shākir al-Sayyāb, *Dīwān*, vol.1 (Beirut, n.d. [1986]), pp. 509ff.

13. *Al-Wajh al-ākhar*, pp. 163–87.

14. Al-Ṭāhir, *Fī 'l-qiṣaṣ* . . ., pp. 17ff. (Sabry Hafez's statement was made during the 1992 EMTAR symposium held in Nijmegen, The Netherlands, in April 1992.)

15. *Al-Wajh al-ākhar*, pp. 263–72. German translation by W. Walther in W. Walther (ed.), *Erkundungen. 28 irakische Erzähler* (Berlin, 1985), pp. 25ff.

16. German translation by R. Karachouli in W. Walther (ed.), *Erkundungen* . . ., pp. 61ff.

17. Al-Ṭāhir, *Fī 'l-qiṣaṣ* . . ., pp. 29ff.

18. Fu'ād al-Tikirlī, *al-Raj' al-ba'īd* (Beirut, 1980), pp. 193ff.

19. Ibid., p. 201.

20. Ibid., pp. 242, 250ff, 256ff.

21. Ibid., pp. 303ff.

22. Ibid., p. 308.

23. Ibid., p. 207.

24. Ibid., p. 350.

25. The only critical review I have found in Arabic is Muḥsin Jasīm al-Musāwī, "al-Insān wa 'l-zaman fī 'l-Raj' al-ba'īd" in Muḥsin Jasīm al-Musāwī, *al-Riwāya al-'arabiyya, al-nash'a wa'l-taḥawwul* (Baghdad, 1986), pp. 245–67. Al-Musāwī does not really enter into the contents of the novel, but analyses, as the title of his article shows, the different ways in which the author depicts his characters' acting in time. Turad al-Kubaisi's "Mashrū' ru'ya naqdiyya 'arabiyya fī 'l-riwāya 'l-'arabiyya", *al-Adāb* (2 March 1980), pp. 87–93, is highly critical of all Iraqi novels up to 1979, claiming that no good Iraqi novel was written before that date. Muhsin Jassim Ali, in his article 'The Socio-Aesthetics of Modern Arabic Fiction', *Journal of Arabic Literature*, 14 (1983), pp. 67ff., esp. pp. 72ff., gives a short but good analysis of the literary techniques used by the author.

Chapter 13. Sexuality in Jabrā's Novel, The Search for Walīd Mas'ūd

1. J. I. Jabrā, *Ta'ammulāt fī bunyān marmarī* (London, 1989), pp. 138–9.
2. M. Bakhtin, *Problems of Dostoevsky's Poetics* (Minneapolis, Minn., 1987).
3. Ibid., p. 6.
4. Ibid., p. 67.
5. Ibid., p. 68.
6. Jabrā, *Ta'ammulāt* . . ., p. 139.
7. Bakhtin, *Problems* . . ., p. 87.
8. Ibid., p. 88.
9. Ibid., p. 85.
10. Ibid., p. 28.
11. E. M. Forster, *Aspects of the Novel* (Harmondsworth, 1972), p. 93.
12. J. Frank, 'Spatial Form in Modern Literature', in R. Castelanetz (ed.), *The Avant-Garde Tradition in Literature* (Buffalo, 1982 [first pub. in *The Widening Gyre*,

Rutgers University Press, 1963]), p. 50 and *passim.*

13. Bakhtin, *Problems . . .*, pp. 276–7.

14. Ibid., p. 110.

15. M. Foucault, *The History of Sexuality*, vol. 1 (New York, 1980), p. 61.

16. *Walīd Mas'ūd* (Beirut, 1981), p. 331.

17. Ibid., p. 34.

18. See C. G. Jung, *Four Archetypes* (Princeton, N.J., 1969), p. 19.

19. 'We are calling this transposition of carnival into the language of literature the carnivalization of literature' (Bakhtin, *Problems . . .*, p. 122).

20. *Walīd Mas'ūd*, p. 224.

21. Foucault, *History of Sexuality*, p. 35.

22. W. Iser, *The Implied Reader* (Baltimore, Md., 1974), p. xi.

23. L. Bersani, *A Future for Astyanax* (London, 1978), p. 10.

24. P. Brooks, *The Novel of Worldliness* (Princeton, N.J., 1969), pp. 4–5.

25. Jabrā, *Ta'ammulāt* , , , pp. 140–1.

26. A. Bouhdiba, *Sexuality in Islam* (London, 1985), p. 234.

27. Ibid., p. 239.

28. *Walīd Mas'ūd*, p. 322.

29. Ibid., p. 321.

30. S. Freud, 'The Most Prevalent Form of Degradation in Erotic Life', *Collected Papers*, vol. 4 (London, n. d.), pp. 203–16.

31. *Al-yawm al-sābi'*, 16 Jan. 1989, p. 34 (recorded by Ḥasūna al-Miṣbāḥī).

Chapter 14. Women's Narrative in Modern Arabic Literature

1. Feminist literary theory has aptly shown that gender is not merely a biological difference but a more comprehensive concept inscribed into all aspects of humanity from everyday language to the subconscious. Gender is both a socially constructed concept and an ideological force which is at work in various types of discourse.

2. H. Cixous and C. Clément, *The Newly Born Woman*, transl. by B. Wing (Manchester, 1986), p. 65.

3. For details, see S. Hafez, *The Genesis of Narrative Discourse: A Study in the Sociology of Modern Arabic Literature* (London, 1993).

4. The *Trilogy* is now available in both English and French translations. In English: *Palace Walk* (1990), *Palace of Desire* (1991) and *Sugar Street* (1992), transl. by W. M. Hutching and others (London). In French: *Impasse des deux palais* (1985), *Le palais du désir* (1987) and *Le jardin du passé* (1989), transl. by P. Vigreux (Paris). R. van Leeuwen has recently translated the *Trilogy* into Dutch.

5. E. Showalter, 'Towards a Feminist Poetics', in E. Showalter (ed.), *The New Feminist Criticism: Essays on Women, Literature and Theory* (New York, 1985), p. 131.

6. E. Showalter, *A Literature of Their Own: British Women Novelists from Brontë to Lessing* (Princeton, N.J., 1977), p. 13. The quotation is taken from T. Moi, *Sexual/Textual Politics: Feminist Literary Theory* (London, 1985), p. 56.

7. Showalter's book was published in the 1970s and although the last phase was open to the present and the future, it seems from the works studied that it covers approximately forty years.

8. Showalter, 'Towards a Feminist Poetics', pp. 138–9.

9. Moi, *Sexual/Textual Politics . . .*, p. 12.

10. For a detailed discussion of the difference between metonymy and metaphor in the typology of literature, see D. Lodge, T*he Modes of Modern Writing: Metaphor, Metonymy and the Typology of Modern Literature* (London, 1977), pp. 73–124.

11. See S. Ḥāfiẓ, *al-Qiṣṣa al-'arabiyya wa-l-ḥadātha: dirāsa fī aliyyāt taghayyur al-ḥassāsiyya al-adabiyya* (Baghdad, 1990), pp. 116–83.

12. See M. Badran, 'Hudā Sha'rāwī and the Liberation of the Egyptian Woman', unpub. DPhil thesis, Oxford University, 1977; and also M. Badran (ed.), *Opening the Gates: A Century of Arab Feminist Writing* (London, 1990), p. xxi.

13. Examples of traditional and moralistic novels are: *Natā'ij al-aḥwāl fī 'l-aqwāl wa 'l-af'āl* (1888) and *Mir'āt al-ta'ammul fi al-umūr* (1893), two *maqāma*-type narratives by 'A'isha al-Taymūriyya; *al-Durr al-manthūr fi ṭabaqāt rabbāt al-khudūr* (1895) and *Husn al-'awāqib* (1899), both autobiographical narrative works by Zaynab Fawwāz; and *al-Faḍīlah sirr al-sa'ādah*, one of the titles in a 7-vol. narrative work by Zaynab Muḥammad. Examples of entertaining and sentimental works are: *al-Hawā wa 'l-wafā'* (1897?) by Zaynab Fawwāz, and *Mudhakkirāt waṣīfa miṣriyya* (1927), another in the series by Zaynab Muḥammad, who was probably one of maids in the Khedival Court. Her texts all appeared in around the 1920s, the last part of the work in approximately 1927. Some of the volumes had sensational titles such as *Bārīs wa Malāhīhā*, *'Ashiq ukhtih*, *Ḍaḥāyā al-qadar*, *Akhirat al-malāhī*, *'Awāṭif al-ābā'*, etc. Nor was Zaynab Muḥammad afraid to exploit nationalistic feelings. Vol. 6 was entitled *Ilā raḥmat Allāh yā za'īm al-sharq*, in a clear reference to Sa'd Zaghlūl.

14. Authors include: Warda al-Yāzijī, Warda al-Turk, Zaynab Fawwāz, Farīda 'Atiyya and Labība Hāshim (in Lebanon) and 'A'isha al-Taymūriyya, Malak Ḥifnī Nāṣif (Bāḥithat al-Bādiya) and Zaynab Muḥammad (in Egypt at the turn of the century). More recent exponents include: Laylā al-'Uthmān and Thurayyā al-Baqṣamī (in Kuwait), Fawziyya Rashīd and Munīra al-Fāḍil (in Bahrain), Salmā Maṭar Sayf (in the UAE) and Ruqayya al-Shabīb, Maryam al-Ghāmidī and Laṭīfa al-Ṣālim (in Saudi Arabia)

15. L. al-'Uthmān, *Wasmiyya takhruj min al-baḥr* (Kuwait, 1986).

16. Al-'Uthmān started her career as a journalist in 1965 and then turned to the short story in 1974. Her first collection was *Imra'a fī inā'* [A Woman in an Urn] (1976). Then came *al-Raḥīl* [Departure] (1979), *Fī 'l-layl ta'tī 'l-'uyūn* [At Night Sirens Appear] (1980), *al-Ḥubb lahu ṣuwar* [Love Has Many Forms] (1982) and *Fatḥiyya takhtār mawtahā* [Fatḥiyya Choses Her Death] (1984). Her first novel, *al-Mar'a wa-l-qiṭṭa* [The Woman and the Cat] appeared in 1985 and was followed by *Wasmiyya takhruj min al-baḥr* in 1986.

17. A few rudimentary forms of narrative writing appeared in periodicals in the late 1940s and early 1950s, particularly the work of Khālid Khalaf, Ḥamad

al-Rujayb, Fāḍil Khalaf and Fahd al-Duwayrī. But these early pioneering work did not develop into mature narrative work and the 1960s witnessed the dwindling of these early attempts.

18. The group of Kuwaiti writers who participated in this process all started their work in the 1970s, such as Sulaymān al-Shaṭṭī, Sulaymān al-Khalīfī, Ismā'īl Fahd Ismā'īl, Laylā al-'Uthmān and others. For a detailed historical account, see: M. H. 'Abdullāh, *al-Ḥaraka al-adabiyya wa-l-fikriyya fī 'l-Kuwayt* (Damascus, 1973); I. F. Ismā'īl, *al-Qiṣṣa al-'arabiyya fī 'l-Kuwayt: qirā'a naqdiyya* (Beirut, 1980); and I. A. Ghallūm, *al-Qiṣṣa al-qaṣīra fī 'l-Khalīj al-'Arabī: al-Kuwayt wa-l-Baḥrain* (Baghdad, 1981).

19. See A. Kolodny, 'Some Notes on Defining a "Feminist Literary Criticism"', *Critical Inquiry*, 2: 1, pp. 75–92.

20. For a detailed study of this, see J. Doan and D. Hodges, *Nostalgia and Sexual Difference: The Resistance to Contemporary Feminism* (London, 1987).

21. Al-'Uthmān, *Wasmiyya . . .*, p. 8.

22. Ibid., p. 52.

23. Doan and Hodges, *Nostalgia . . .*, p. 9.

24. This reached its peak in Tunisia in the 1960s where it was translated into legislation and succeeded in institutionalizing many of the gains of the women's movement, thanks to the strong support of Bourguiba's regime.

25. See, for example, Suhayr al-Qalamāwī, 'A'isha 'Abd al-Raḥmān, Laṭīfa al-Zayyāt, Ṣūfī 'Abdullāh, Jadhibiyya Ṣidqi and Nawāl al-Sa'dāwī (in Egypt), Samīra 'Azzām, Laylā Ba'albakki, Imīlī (Emilie) Naṣrallāh, Laylā 'Usayrān, Kūlīt (Colette) Khūrī and Ghāda al-Sammān (in the Levant) and Nāzik al-Malā'ika and Dīzī (Daisy) al-Amīr (in Iraq).

26. Nawāl al-Sa'dāwī, *Suqūṭ al-imām* (Cairo, 1987). This novel is available in English as: Nawal El-Saadawi, *The Fall of the Imam*, transl. by Sherif Hetata (London, 1988).

27. Al-Sa'dāwī, *Suqūṭ al-imām*, p. 9.

28. Here the text perpetuates the worst kind of backward morality, which sees the poor as despicable, sleazy and the source of all evil, and associate good values with the rich.

29. Cixous and Clément, *Newly Born Woman*, pp. 65, 64.

30. See El-Saadawi, *Fall of the Imam.*

31. Al-Sa'dāwī, *Suqūṭ al-imām*, p. 53.

32. Such writers include: Ḥanān al-Shaykh [in her novels, *Ḥikāyat Zahrah* (1980), *Misk al-ghazāl* (1988) and *Barīd Bayrūt* (1992)] and Hudā Barakāt [in her novel, *Ḥajar al-ḍaḥik* (1990)] in Lebanon; Raḍwā 'Ashūr [in her novels, *Ḥajar dāfi'* (1985), *Khadījah wa-Sawsan* (1989) and *Sirāj* (1992)], Salwā Bakr [in her novels, *Maqām 'Aṭiyya* (1986), *al-'Araba al-dhahabiyya lā taṣ'ad ilā al-samā'* (1991) and *Waṣf al-bulbul* (1993)], Iqbāl Baraka [in her novels, *Wal-nazall ilā l-abad asdiqā'* (1971) and *Laylā wa-l-majhūl* (1981)], I'tidāl 'Uthmān [in her two collections of short stories, *Yūnis wa-l-baḥr* (1987) and *Wash al-shams* (1992)] and Saḥar Tawfīq [in her collection, *An tanḥadir al-shams* (1985)] in Egypt; 'Alyā al-Tābi'ī [in her novel, *Zahrat al-ṣabbār* (1991)] in Tunisia; and 'Aliya Mamdūḥ [in her novel,

Habbāt al-naftālīn (1986)] in Iraq. It should be mentioned that there are several other Egyptian writers such as Hāla al-Badrī, Ni'māt al-Biḥayrī and Sihām Bayyūmī, to name but a few.

33. The limited scope of the present essay does not allow a detailed study of the richly diverse contribution of this group; only one example serves to give the reader a feel for their attainments. Their work deserves a more detailed investigation which I have attempted elsewhere and continues to be the subject of subsequent work. In Arabic, I have written several articles on their work, particularly that of Radwā 'Ashūr, Ḥanān al-Shaykh, 'Alyā' al-Tābi'ī and Salwā Bakr.

34. S. Bakr, *Maqām 'Aṭiyyah* (Cairo, 1986).

35. The text refers several times (e.g. pp. 21, 22, 27, 36, 40) to the various characters, from her father to her husband, who perceive her as a man and to the different incidents in which she acts like one.

Chapter 15. The Development of Women's Political Consciousness in the Short Stories of Laylā al-'Uthman

1. This essay deals only with publications from 1978 until 1987, except for one story (see n. 12 below). It does not cover the period immediately before the Gulf War of 1991.

2. Laylā al-'Uthmān's complete works consist of: (a) a collection of poems: *Hamasāt* (Kuwait, 1972); (b) seven anthologies of short stories: *Imra'a fī inā'*, 2nd edn (Kuwait, 1981); *al-Hubb lahu ṣuwar*, 2nd edn (Beirut, 1983); *al-Raḥīl*, 2nd edn (Kuwait, 1984); *Fī 'l-layl ta'tī 'l-'uyūn*, 2nd edn (Kuwait, 1984); *Fatḥiyya takhtāru mawtahā* (Beirut, 1987); *Ḥālat ḥubb majnūna*, 2nd edn (Kuwait, 1992); and *55 ḥikāya qaṣīra* (Kuwait, 1992); and (c) two novels: *al-Mar'a wa 'l-qiṭṭa* (Beirut, 1985) and *Wasmiyya takhruju min al-baḥr* (Kuwait, 1986).

3. 'Until the beginning of the oil boom, Kuwait had been poor and undeveloped. Its inhabitants earned their living as fishermen, pearl divers, animal herders, and carrier traders.' Kamla Nath, 'Education and Employment among Kuwaiti Women', in L. Beck and N. Keddie (eds), *Women in the Muslim World* (Cambridge, 1978), pp. 172–88.

4. In al-'Uthmān, *al-Ḥubb lahu ṣuwar*, pp. 45–51.

5. In al-'Uthmān, *Imra'a fī inā'*, pp. 57–64.

6. In ibid., pp. 65–72.

7. See W. Abū Bakr, "al-Ṣawt al-thānī fī 'l-qiṣṣa al-kuwaytiyya", in *Qirā'āt fī 'l-maḍmūn* (Kuwait, 1985), p. 33.

8. In al-'Uthmān, *al-Raḥīl*, pp. 36–46.

9. Al-'Uthmān is recorded as suffering greatly from the strict, cold atmosphere of her parental home; she calls her mother particularly hard and even cruel. See A. 'Abd al-Raḥmān, "al-Qāṣṣa al-kuwaytiyya Laylā al-'Uthmān li al-taḍamun 'lā astaṭī'u al-'aysh illā janāḥ rajul", *al-Qabas*, no. 160 (9 May 1986), p. 58. See also A. 'Abdallāh al-Fattāḥ, "Ṣūrat al-mar'a fī qiṣaṣ Laylā al-'Uthmān", *al-Bayān*, no. 61 (1987), p. 63, and A. M. Ṣumāliḥ (ed.), 'Laylā al-'Uthmān', in *Adab al-mar'a fī 'l-Kuwayt* (Kuwait, 1978), p. 238.

10. In al-'Uthmān, *al-Ḥubb lahu ṣuwar*, pp. 64–9.
11. See 'Abd al-Raḥmān, *'al-Qāṣṣa al-kuwaytiyya Laylā al-'Uthmān . . .'*
12. In al-'Uthmān, *Ḥālat ḥubb majnūna*, pp. 93–101.
13. In al-'Uthmān, "Anā al-ūlā fī Albāniyya", *al-Qabas*, no. 190 (6 April 1986), p. 67.
14. See F. K. Stanzel, *Theorie des Erzählens* (Göttingen, 1985), p. 71.
15. In al-'Uthmān, *al-Raḥīl*, pp. 31–5.
16. In al-'Uthmān, *Imra'a fī inā'*, pp. 21–5.
17. Stanzel, *Theorie des Erzählens*, p. 113.
18. When the author was still an adolescent, her sister-in-law punished her by refusing her food and even called her a 'stray cat' (extract from an interview with the author in 1989 in Berlin).
19. In al-'Uthmān, *Imra'a fī inā'*, pp. 97–104.
20. In al-'Uthmān, *al-Ḥubb lahu ṣuwar*, pp. 111–19.
21. In ibid., p. 119.
22. An impressive example is to be found in her novel, *al-Mar'a wa 'l-qiṭṭa*. See A. al-Ra'ī, "al-Kātiba al-kuwaytiyya Laylā al-'Uthmān wa riwāyatuhā al-nābiḍa 'al-Mar'a wa 'l-qiṭṭa'", *al-Qabas*, no. 3199 (31 Sept. 1986).
23. H. Mīnā, "Ṭāli'a min baḥr azraq, azraq", in al-'Uthmān, *Fī 'l-layl ta'tī 'l-'uyūn* (Kuwait, 1984), p. 9.
24. In al-'Uthmān, *al-Ḥubb lahu ṣuwar*, pp. 101–10.
25. 'They no longer have any real function; they can't even tolerate their own children's crying.' L. al-'Uthmān, "Min al-sīra al-dhātiyya wa 'l-tajriba al-qaṣaṣiyya wa 'l-riwā'iyya", *al-Adāb*, vol. 38 (Jan. 1990), pp. 46–52.
26. See Abū Bakr, *'al-Ṣawt al-thānī . . .'*, p. 11.
27. In al-'Uthmān, *Fī 'l-layl ta'tī 'l-'uyūn*, pp. 39–45.
28. In al-'Uthmān, *al-Raḥīl*, pp. 116–21.
29. The Gulf War of 1991 showed just how accurate these visions were.
30. In al-'Uthmān, *Fatḥiyya takhtāru mawtahā*, pp. 135–49; see also *Ibdā'*, vol. 5 (1985), pp. 86–90.
31. Al-'Uthmān, *al-Raḥīl*, pp. 116–21; transl. as 'Pulling up Roots', in S. K. Jayyusi (ed.), *The Literature of Modern Arabia: an Anthology* (London, 1988), pp. 483–8.
32. It is worth noting in this context that al-'Uthmān is married to a Palestinian.
33. This can be seen in the adoption of names such as 'Umm Fāḍil', 'Zahra', 'Umm Hijrān' and 'Mūsā'.
34. See Stanzel, *Theorie des Erzählens*, p. 133.
35. For example, she has written about the Iraqi occupation of Kuwait in: al-'Uthmān, *'Min yawmiyyāt al-ṣabr wa 'l-murr'*, *'al-Hawājiz al-sawdā'"* and *al-Mughanniyya, al-mawt, al-aṣdiqā'* (forthcoming).

Chapter 16. Death and Desire in Iraqi War Literature

1. Qādisiyya is where the seventh-century Arab Muslims won their first victory over the Persians. Ṣaddām Ḥusayn's adoption of this name for his war against the

modern Persians indicated how significant he wished this war to become in future Muslim history.

2. R. Boothby, *Death and Desire. Psychoanalytic Theory in Lacan's Return to Freud* (NY/London, 1991), p. 4.

3. Ibid., p. 19.

4. S. Freud, *Beyond the Pleasure Principle*, transl. by J. Strachey (New York, 1961), p. 6.

5. The Beirut Decentrists were a group of Arab women who wrote about the war while it was being being waged between 1975 and 1982. See M. Cooke, *War's Other Voices. Women Writers on the Lebanese Civil War* (Cambridge, 1988).

6. I am not referring here to the countless stories men have written of passionate love affairs played out on the battlefield or in the lands of the enemy; dashing young men allowing themselves to be seduced just long enough so that they can repair tattered energies and return refreshed and restored to the fray. These romances are post-bellum fictions of home as haven of love and safety. Combat, rather, is the site of the clash of primal instincts, a clash which is raw and visceral, with little of love about it.

7. Wendy Chapkis calls the military myth 'a highly gendered erotic fantasy built around images of masculinity'. She describes the language that men use in the film *Top Gun* as erotic and she quotes one as saying that viewing training films of F-14s in action gives him a 'hard-on'. Another pilot remarks that the enemy aircraft 'must be close, I'm getting a hard-on'. W. Chapkis, 'Sexuality and Militarism', in E. Isaksson (ed.), *Women and the Military System* (New York, 1988), pp. 109–10.

8. Stanley Rosenberg writes that pilots' narratives from the Second World War evince neurosis which was combated with 'such mechanisms as splitting, denial, projection, compartmentalization and reversal of affect. These processes of distortion and self alienation permitted the participants to live with death (their own potential death, their comrades' deaths, the deaths of the victims of their bombs, cannon and napalm) as if death were not real.' S. Rosenberg, 'The Threshold of Thrill: Life Stories in the Skies over Southeast Asia', in M. Cooke and A. Woollacott, *Gendering War Talk* (Princeton, N.J., 1993), p. 60.

9. For example, S. al-Anṣārī's "Maqṭa' min ḥayāt baḥḥār" [Episode in the Life of a Sailor]: as his ship sinks, the hero thinks of the woman who had wanted him to propose to her (*Alphabet of Love and War*, Baghdad, 1988, p. 13).

10. Rosenberg, 'Threshold of Thrill', pp. 62–3. What is less known, because more recent, is the story of the 1991 Gulf War pilots. For these young men (the number of women pilots are too small to signify in this connection), the experience of combat was greatly distanced. More than their predecessors, they were spared the sight of the human results of their actions. What they saw was a burst of fireworks on a screen. More, because their missions were so closely monitored, their bombs so 'smart' and their opponent so weak they were in general spared the 'anxiety'. Without anxiety and little possiblity of fright, they lacked the possibility of cathexis. They felt no thrill, were not aroused. They might be less effective. Since it was not possible or advisable that they should be artificially frightened, they were artificially aroused. On 5 Feb. 1991 J. Ledbetter reported in *The Village Voice* (p. 80) what has

now become common knowledge: 'pilots aboard the USS *John F. Kennedy* told AP that they'd been watching porn movies before bombing missions'.

11. K. Theweleit, *Male Fantasies* (Minnesota, 1987), vol. 1, p. 198.

12. The men are constantly in competition with each other, for example when playing chess, but at the moment of victory outside of war, the victor must pull back lest the defeat undermine the *esprit de corps*.

13. Freud describes fright physiologically as 'a lack of hypercathexis of the systems that would be the first to receive the stimulus. Owing to their low cathexis those systems are not in a good position for binding the inflowing amounts of excitation and the consequences of the breach in the protective shield follow all the more easily . . . [T]he mechanical violence of the trauma would liberate a quantity of sexual excitation which, owing to the lack of preparation for anxiety, would have a traumatic effect.' Freud, *Beyond the Pleasure Principle*, pp. 25, 27.

14. Chapkis, 'Sexuality and Militarism', p. 111.

15. M. Badran and M. Cooke, *Opening The Gates. A Century of Arab Feminist Writing* (London/Bloomington, 1990), pp. 304–13.

16. Theweleit, *Male Fantasies*, vol. 1, p. 139.

17. M. Higonnet, 'Not So Quiet In No Woman's Land', in Cooke and Woollacott, *Gendering War Talk*.

18. Laylā tells Yāsir that she has seen 'seeds of fire' in his eyes (*Budhūr al-nār*, Baghdad, 1987, p. 143).

19. In 'Did You Measure Up? The Role of Race and Sexuality in the Gulf War', A. Farmanfarmaian discusses an attempt to exploit this process that occurred during the Gulf War. The eroticization of wives served as a kind of familial presentation of fantasy to American military men. 'Operation Desert Cheer' took photographs of 'soldier's wives half nude, lace-clad, and sent the pictures to the husbands in the Gulf. For a military more than ever made up of family people, this can uphold fantasies without leaving the parameters of the family.' He does not say what happened when these men returned home: see C. Peters (ed.), *Collateral Damage: The New World at Home and Abroad* (Boston, Mass., 1992), p. 133.

20. She tells her friend Aṣīla that women's lives are devoted to 'waiting in which there is pleasure at combating death.' The possibility of combating the threat of death gives pleasure and feeds love.

21. This remembering of a man's possessiveness once he has gone can be found in other women's writings on war; see, for example, Nuhā Samāra's "Wajhān li imra'a" [Woman with Two Faces] in *al-Ṭāwilāt 'āshat akthar min Āmīn* [The Tables Lived Longer than Amin] (Beirut, 1980).

22. Her director tells Laylā that she should have asked him to intercede on her behalf so that Yāsir was not sent to the mines. He is not interested that Yāsir may have actually chosen his job posting.

23. 'Son of my soul and foster son of the sorrows of the war . . . Had God and the war not granted this beautiful boy to me, I would have dried up like a tree whom poisoned winds had scorched'.

24. A. P. Foulkes, *Literature and Propaganda* (London/NY, 1983).

Chapter 17. Nizār Qabbānī's Autobiography: Images of Sexuality, Death and Poetry

1. For a general overview of Qabbānī's earlier life and work, see Z. Gabay, 'Nizar Qabbani, the Poet and his Poetry', *MES*, 9 (1973), pp. 207–20. For a psychological study, see K. Najm, *an-Narjisiyya fī adab Nizār Qabbānī* [Narcissism in Nizār Qabbānī's Work] (Beirut, 1983), p. 453. In a similar vein, see J. al-Mukhkh, "al-Firāsh al-bārid. Al-Wahan al-jinsī fī shi'r Nizār Qabbānī" [The Cold Bed. Sexual Weakness in Nizār Qabbānī's Poetry], *al-Nāqid*, 65 (Nov. 1993), pp. 36–8. A sometimes angry attack on Qabbānī's political poetry is J. Fāḍil, *Fatāfit shā'ir. Waqā'i' ma'raka ma' Nizār Qabbānī* [Crumbs of a Poet. Encounters with Nizār Qabbānī] (Beirut, 1989). See also A. Wannūs, "Mādhā fa'al Nizār Qabbānī bi 'l-shi'r?" [What did Nizār Qabbānī Do to Poetry?], *al-Nāqid*, 30 (Dec. 1990), p. 80, and the ensuing discussion: A. Qūbī, "al-'Auda ilā Nizār" [Back to Nizār], *al-Nāqid*, 40 (Oct. 1991), p. 66, and M. M. 'Allūsh, "Wa lanā kalima fī mauḍū' Nizār Qabbānī" [We Also Have Something to Say on the Subject of Nizār Qabbānī], *al-Nāqid*, 51 (Sept. 1992), p. 81.

2. Nizār Qabbānī himself claims to have sold 10 million 'legal' copies of his collected works, not counting the illegal reprints (*Muḥākamat Nizār Qabbānī* [Judgement on Nizār Qabbānī], Ramallah/al-Bira, n.d., p. 7).

3. Nizār Qabbānī, *Qiṣṣatī ma' al-shi'r. Sīra dhātiyya* [My Story with Poetry. An Autobiography], 1st edn (Beirut, 1972); I use the 5th edn (Beirut, 1979). This source is quoted in the following as *'Qiṣṣatī'*. Qabbānī has often written about himself, but as far as I know, never again in a systematically autobiographical form. I have, however, not seen his *al-Shi'r qindīl akhḍar* [Poetry is a Green Lamp] (Beirut, 1963), which is said to contain 'essays on his poetic art and view of literature': see I. J. Boullata (ed.), *Modern Arab Poets 1950–1975* (London, 1976), p. 140. In 1990—marking the fiftieth anniversary of his poetic activities—Qabbānī wrote a personal 'testimony' for the London-based Arabic monthly *al-Nāqid* entitled *Khamsūna 'āman min al-shi'r, al-sukna 'alā ḥāfat al-burkān* [Fifty Years of Poetry. Abode on the Edge of a Volcano], *al-Nāqid*, 21 (March 1990), pp. 4–9. This could be seen as a completion of his autobiography. See *Man yastaṭī' an yuḥāwir qaṣīda?* [Who Can Converse with a Qaṣīda?] in *al-Nāqid*, 25 (July 1990), pp. 32–3. Six volumes of his collected poetry have been published by his own publishing house: vol 1: *al-A'māl al-shi'riyya al-kāmila* (Beirut, n.d.); vol. 2 (2nd edn, Beirut, 1980); vol 3: *al-A'māl al-siyāsiyya al-kāmila* (2nd edn, Beirut, 1983); vol 4 (Beirut, 1993); vol. 5 (Beirut, 1993); vol. 5 (Beirut, 1993); vol. 6: *al-A'māl al-siyāsiyya al-kāmila* (Beirut, 1993).

4. *Al-Yawmiyyāt al-sirriyya li-Bāhiyya 'l-miṣriyya* [The Secret Diary of Bāhiyya, the Egyptian] (Beirut, 1979), a violent poetic diatribe against Anwar al-Sādāt and his Israeli policy; *Yawmiyyāt madīna kāna smuhā Bayrūt* [The Diary of a City whose Name was Beirut] (Beirut, n.d. *c*. 1978), a prose account of the nightmare situation in Beirut during the civil war written in the first person: *Anā Bayrūt . . .*; *al-Sīra al-dhātiyya li-sayyāf 'arabī* [The Autobiography of an Arab Hangman] (London, 1987), a long poem containing the confessions of an Arab hangman, symbolizing corrupt and oppressive Arab political leadership in general;

Yawmiyyāt imra'a lā mubāliya [Diary of a Reckless Woman] (Beirut, 1965 = *A'māl*, 1, pp. 575–640). A *dīwān*, *al-Awrāq al-sirriyya li-'āshiq qurmuṭī* [The Secret Notes of a Karmatian Lover] was published in *A'māl*, 5, pp. 13ff.

5. Anyone who spoke a single word of Arabic at school received the notorious badge (called 'signal' by the students) to wear all day and was made to learn by heart fifty verses by Racine or Corneille (in French) as punishment (*Qiṣṣatī*, p. 43).

6. Ibid., p. 44.

7. A typical case of censorship of a poem of Qabbānī's occurred as late as 1990. On 8 March 1990 the Egyptian Minister of Education, Aḥmad Fatḥī Surūr, issued a decree to ban or suppress Nizār Qabbānī's *qaṣīda, Inda 'l-jidār* [At the Wall] from the newly edited schoolbook of Arabic reading material for the First Class of High Schools (*i'dādī*), because 'it contradicted the values of education and instruction'. The poem describes in nostalgic retrospect the first love and secret kisses of two children. This decision to ban the poem was welcomed by, and probably taken under pressure from, the Jordanian Council of Islamic Organizations and the Egyptian fundamentalist newspaper *al-Nūr*. Qabbānī had written this *qaṣīda* in 1950 in his *dīwān*, *Anti lī* (*al-A'māl*, 1, pp. 205–6). *Al-Nūr* explained: 'The poems of Nizār Qabbānī were among the causes of the Arab defeat of June 1967. These poems spoiled great parts of the young generation in the Arab world, male and female.' At the same time *al-Nūr* attacked the people responsible at the Ministries of Education and of Waqf, the Azhar scholars and the teachers at Egyptian universities in general, because they had kept silent at this 'devastation which menaced the mind of the student by being taught poems of this sort' (*al-Nāqid*, 24 (June 1990), pp. 36ff).

8. Beirut, 1970, *A'māl* II, p. 687; see *Qiṣṣatī*, p. 52.

9. *Qiṣṣatī*, p. 52.

10. Qabbānī gives a vivid description of the problems which Arabic bilingualism poses for the Arab poet, who suffers what he calls linguistic alienation (*ghurba lughawiyya*, p. 119): 'The Arab reads, writes, composes, lectures in one language and sings, jokes, fights, plays with his children and flirts with the eyes of his beloved in a second language' (*Qiṣṣatī*, p. 119). The way to end this alienation is the third language employed by Qabbānī. A hostile critic once said about Qabbānī's poems: 'If Nizār Qabbānī dropped a paper in the bus containing writing by him and signed by him, then the first passenger who picked it up would bring it to his house' (*Qiṣṣatī*, p. 120).

11. *Qiṣṣatī*, p. 122.

12. The same attitude is to be found throughout his recent self-descriptive *qaṣīda* called "Innī aqtarif al-shi'r . . . wa hādhā tawqī'ī" [I Perpetrate Poetry . . . and This Is My Signature] in *al-Nāqid*, 22 (April 1990), pp. 4–6.

13. See the title of one of his more recent poems, "Uḥāwil inqādh ākhar unthā qubayl wuṣūl al-tātār" [I Try to Save the Last Female before the Arrival of the Tatars] in *al-Nāqid,* 17 (Nov. 1989), pp. 4–5.

14. *Qiṣṣatī*, p. 77.

15. Ibid., pp. 132ff. Qabbānī adopts a purely Western point of view when he says, 'I never felt that sex was a wild beast devouring everything which came near

it. On the contrary, I was convinced that sex is a tame house cat. It is us who made it terrible and frightening, we made it loiter in narrow alleys and sleep in the ruins. I always thought that the shame was on us, not on love . . . Only in societies of magic, astrology and backwardness does the idea of sex become inflated like an inflamed appendix' (*Qiṣṣatī,* p. 134).

16. Ibid., p. 135.
17. Ibid., p. 142.
18. Ibid., p. 143.
19. Ibid.
20. Ibid., p. 144.
21. Ibid., p. 73.
22. Ibid., pp. 144ff.
23. Ibid., p. 145.
24. Ibid., p. 146.
25. Ibid., pp. 147ff. *Anā wa 'l-dunjuwāniyya.*
26. Ibid., p. 151.
27. Ibid., p. 155.
28. Ibid., pp. 9ff.
29. Ibid., p. 186.
30. This seems to be one of the basic Qabbanian metaphors. See the verses in "Hawāmish 'alā daftar al-shi'r", *al-Nāqid*, 14 (Aug. 1989), pp. 4–10: 'the sheet of paper is female/and to approach a sheet which does not want us / is the act of rape'; 'the *qaṣīda* sleeps with a thousand men/ and remains a virgin'.
31. *Qiṣṣatī,* p. 191.
32. Ibid., p. 22. As another example: 'Fame has killed me . . . How can I sleep with 200 million Arabs[!] in one room in one bed?' (*Khamsūna 'āman*, 8, no. 18).
33. Ibid., p. 71.
34. Ibid.
35. Beirut, 1968.
36. Amman, 1985. Transl. by O. Kenny as *A Mountainous Journey. The Life of Palestine's Outstanding Woman Poet* (London, 1990). See also N. Odeh, *Dichtung als Brücke zur Aussenwelt. Studien zur Autobiographie Fadwa Tuqans* (Berlin, 1994).

Chapter 18. Love and the Body in Modern Arabic Poetry

1. Buland al-Ḥaydarī is one of the Iraqi pioneers of the New Poetry. At present he lives in London. For more information about the poets mentioned here, as well as translations from their works, see: M. A. Khouri and H. Algar, *An Anthology of Modern Arabic Poetry* (Berkeley, Calif., 1974); M. M. Badawi, *A Critical Introduction to Modern Arabic Poetry* (Cambridge, 1975); I. Boullata, *Modern Arab Poets* (Washington, D.C., 1976); S. Moreh, *Modern Arabic Poetry, 1800–1970* (Leiden, 1976); S. K. Jayyusi, *Trends and Movements in Modern Arabic Poetry* (Leiden, 1977); I. Boullata (ed.), *Critical Perspectives on Modern Arabic Literature* (Washington, D.C., 1980); A. al-Udhari, *Modern Poetry of the Arab World* (London, 1986); M. A. Khouri, *Studies in Contemporary Arabic Poetry and*

Criticism (Piemont, Calif., 1987); S. K. Jayyusi (ed.), *Modern Arabic Poetry: An Anthology* (New York, 1987); and M. M. Badawi, *Modern Arabic Literature* (Cambridge, 1992).

2. From the Arabic, *muttaham wa law kunta barī'an* (accused even if you are innocent), in B. al-Ḥaydarī, *Aghānī al-ḥāris al-mut'ab* [Songs of the Tired Guard], 2nd edn (Beirut, 1974), pp. 19–23. Transl. by al-Udhari, *Modern Poetry* . . ., pp. 43ff.

3. Ṣalāḥ 'Abd al-Ṣabūr (1931–81), the pioneer of the New Poetry in Egypt, made a fundamental contribution to the development of poetic drama. His *Laylā wal-Majnūn* was first published in 1970. See the Arabic/German *Laylā wal-Majnūn/Laylā und der Besessene*, ed. and intro. by A. Neuwirth (Bamberg, 1991). See also A. E. Khairallah, 'The Individual and Society: Ṣalāḥ 'Abdaṣṣabūr's Laylā wal-Magnūn', in J. C. Bürgel (ed.), *Gesellschaftlicher Umbruch und Historie im zeitgenössischen Drama der islamischen Welt* (Wiesbaden/Beirut, 1994).

4. The Syrian poet Nizār Qabbānī is the most popular love poet in Arabic. At present he lives in London. (See chapter 17 in the present work.)

5. See N. Qabbānī, *al-A'māl al-shi'riyya al-kāmila*, vol. 1 (Beirut, 1971), pp. 598–9.

6. "Al-Qasīda al-shirrīra" [The Evil Poem], in ibid., pp. 351–3.

7. In "Urīduki unthā" [I Want You a Female], he says:

I want you a female in the hands
Female in the hissing of earrings
Female in your voice . . . female in your silence
Female in your weakness . . . Female in your fear
Female in your purity . . . Female in your cunning
Female in your wonderful walk
Female in your ninth authority
And female I want you from head to toe

See N. Qabbānī, *Hākadha aktub tārīkh al-nisā'* [Thus I Write the History of Women], 3rd edn (Beirut, 1981), p. 27.

8. Ibid., pp. 147, 142.

9. See "Ilā 'ajūz" [To an Old Woman], in *al-A'māl al-shi'riyya* . . ., p. 74; and "Hiwār ma' imra'a 'alā mashārif al-arba'īn" [Dialogue with a Woman Approaching her Forties], in *Hākadhā* . . , p. 149.

10. See "Ayyatuhā al-sayyida allatī istaqālat min unūthatihā" [You, Lady Who Resigned from her Femininity], in *Hākadhā* . . , pp.135–48, esp. pp. 140–1.

11. See his *al-A'māl al-shi'riyya* . . , *passim*; and *Hākadhā* . . , p. 141.

12. All from his *al-A'māl al-shi'riyya* . . ., vol. 1. They are, respectively: "al-Qurṭ al-ṭawīl" (pp. 65–6), "Rāfi'at al-nahd" (pp. 67–8), "Azrār" (pp. 93–4), "Ḥalama" (pp. 129–31), "Ilā ridā' asfar" (pp. 137–8), "Ilā wishāḥ ahmar" (pp. 154–5), "Mānīkūr" (pp. 219–20), "al-Māyyūh al-azraq" (pp. 230–1), "Krīstiyān Diyūr" (pp. 268–9).

13. "Al-Rasm bil-kalimāt" [Drawing with Words] in ibid., pp. 464–6.

14. *Amwāj al-layālī* (Cairo, 1991). Edwār al-Kharrāṭ (1926-) is a leading Egyptian modernist (novels, short stories, criticism), who shows unusual vigour and

experimental daring in both language and form. Some of his works are translated into various European languages. One of his major novels, *Turābuhā za'farān* (Cairo, 1986), has been published in English as *City of Saffron*, with an introduction by F. Liardet (London, 1989). For a discussion of his works, see: R. Allen (ed.), *Modern Arabic Literature* (New York, 1987); R. Ostle (ed.), *Modern Literature in the Near and Middle East, 1850-1970* (London, 1991); and M. M. Badawi (ed.), *Cambridge History of Arabic Literature*, vol. 4 (Cambridge, 1992). (See also chapter 9, pp. 113–14, of the present work.)

15. The quotes are taken from *Amwāj al-layālī*, pp. 17, 18, 19, respectively.

16. Ibid., pp. 19–20.

17. Ibid., pp. 22–3.

18. Ibid., pp. 25–6 (italics mine).

19. The Palestinian poet Tawfīq Ṣāyigh, one of the most original poets of this generation, has not received the critical attention he deserves, owing perhaps to the difficulty of his poetry. See, in this respect: I. J. Boullata, 'The Beleaguered Unicorn', *Journal of Arabic Literature*, 4 (1973), pp. 69–93; and M. A. Khouri, 'The Paradise Lost in Ṣāyigh's Poetry', in Khouri, *Studies in Contemporary Arabic Poetry . . .*, pp. 139–47. For a well-documented literary biography of Ṣāyigh, see M. Shurayḥ, *Tawfīq Ṣāyigh: Sīrat shā'ir wa manfā* (London, 1989).

20. See Shurayḥ, *Tawfīq Ṣāyigh . . .*, pp. 99–100.

21. Kay Shaw was an artist in her twenties when Ṣāyigh first met her in January 1957. See Khouri, 'The Paradise Lost . . .', p. 146; and Shurayḥ, *Tawfīq Ṣāyigh . . .*, p. 77.

22. Shurayḥ, *Tawfīq Ṣāyigh . . .*, p. 86.

23. Ibid., p. 83.

24. N. Qabbānī, *Qiṣṣatī ma' al-shi'r* [My Story with Poetry] (Beirut, 1973), p. 153.

25. Shurayḥ, *Tawfīq Ṣāyigh . . .*, p. 84.

26. Transl. by I. Boullata in 'The Beleaguered Unicorn', p. 91. See T. Ṣāyigh, *al-A'māl al-Kāmila* (London, 1990), pp. 322–3.

27. The translation is mine, from Ṣāyigh, *al-A'māl al-Kāmila*, pp. 240–1. For a translation of the whole poem, entitled, 'Out of the Depths I Cry unto You, O Death!', see Jayyusi (ed.), *Modern Arabic Poetry . . .*, pp. 420–5.

28. U. al-Ḥājj, *Lan* (Beirut, 1960)

29. W. Wright, *A Grammar of the Arabic Language*, 3rd edn, reprint (Cambridge, 1986), vol. II, p. 300, § C.

30. This may explain why, to my knowledge, none of his major works has yet been translated.

31. See Shurayḥ, *Tawfīq Ṣāyigh . . .*, p. 78.

32. Al-Ḥājj, *Lan*, p. 24.

33. Ibid., pp. 35–6.

34. Ibid., pp. 53–7.

35. See U. al-Ḥājj, "al-Rasūla bi-sha'rihā al-ṭawīl ḥattā al-yanābī'" (Beirut, 1975), pp. 16–32.

36. Incidentally, another term that opens a whole new metaphorical horizon is

ar-rūḥ (the spirit).

37. The Iraqi poet 'Abd al-Qādir al-Janābī (b. 1944) first published *al-Raghba al-ibāḥiyya* in Paris in 1973, then replaced it in 1982 by *al-Nuqṭa* [The Point]. At present he publishes *Farādīs* in Germany, with the collaboration of another Iraqi poet, Khālid al-Ma'ālī (b. 1956).

38. See *Farādīs*, 3 (1992), the picture after p. 124.

39. My very sketchy presentation of this trend does not imply a value judgement regarding this group of poets, many of whom are worthy of serious attention.

40. As poet, critic, and editor of major avant-garde reviews, the Syro-Lebanese poet Adūnīs has had the greatest influence on Arab poetic modernism. Many of his works are translated, mainly into French, but also into English and most European languages. The best all-round reference, including essays both on Adūnīs and by the poet himself, is the special issue of the French review, *Détours d'écriture*, no. 16: *Adonis* (Paris, 1991). For a free translation of some erotic poems, see Adonis, *Transformations of the Lover*, transl. by S. Hazo (Pittsburgh, 1982).

41. Adūnīs, *Kitāb al-ḥiṣār* (Beirut,1985), pp. 194–5.

42. Adūnīs, *Iḥtifā'an bil-ashyā' al-wāḍiḥa al-ghāmiḍa* [Celebrating the Clear, Vague Things] (Beirut, 1988), pp. 61–2.

43. It is very rare in Arabic to find a poet describing the love act with his own wife. This is practically a taboo. To transgress it is to violate one's own sacred *'irḍ* (honour), which is particularly connected with the female members of the family. Besides, making love to one's own wife is no big 'conquest'; for, in a macho tradition, one may be boastful only about successful raids on forbidden fruits in forbidden gardens.

44. The quotes are taken from K. Abu Deeb, 'The Perplexity of the All-Knowing: A Study of Adonis', in Boullata (ed.), *Critical Perspectives . . .*, pp. 305–23, here pp. 311–12. For the Arabic text see Adūnīs, *Kitāb al-taḥawwulāt wa 'l-hijra fī aqālīm al-nahār wa 'l-layl* (Beirut 1965), pp. 111–66.

45. See, for instance, "Ughniya" [Song], in *Kitāb al-taḥawwulāt . . .*, pp. 162–3.

46. Adūnīs, "Mufrad bi-sīghat al-jam'" (Beirut, 1977). A fragment from this poem is translated in Boullata, *Modern Arab Poets*, pp. 67–9.

47. "Mufrad . . .", p. 170.

48. Ibid., p. 16.

49. Ibid., pp. 336–8.

50. Ibid., p. 233.

51. Ibid., p. 145.

52. *Kitāb al-taḥawwulāt . . .*, p. 142.

53. Adūnīs, *Kitāb al-qaṣā'id al-khams, talīhā al-muṭābaqāt wal-awā'il* (Beirut, 1980), p. 95.

54. *Iḥtifā'an bil-ashyā' . . .*, p. 53.

55. *Amwāj al-layālī*, p. 77.

Index

Dumas, Alexandre (père) 67

East–West relations: alienation 22; dichotomy between 59, 93
Egypt, literature in 11, 12, 13, 27, 29, 34-40, 41-5, 48, 62-4, 66-76, 91, 111-14, 123-30, 160
emancipation, women's 11, 12, 34, 35, 36, 43, 44, 63, 135, 149, 177-9, 209, 219
Enlightenment 34, 35, 36
eroticism 9, 12, 18, 24, 25, 30, 31, 66, 70, 74, 76, 125, 151, 186, 189-90, 199; in drama 25, 31; in poetry 10, 41, 45, 212, 216, 220

Fajr group (of writers) 67-76 *passim*
al-Fajr (journal) 67, 74
Farādīs (periodical) 219
al-Farāfiṣa, Nā'ila bint *see* Nā'ila bint al-Farāfiṣa
al-Fārisī, Muṣṭafā 79
  "Man yadrī . . .? Rubbamā" (short story) 79
Faṣl al-ḥammām (Tunisian comedy) 28
Faṣl sarāyat 'Aywāẓ (Syrian shadow play) 29
Fatimid period 27
Fawwāz, Zaynab 156
Fawzī, Ḥusayn 67, 70, 74-5
  "Ḥikāya qadīma" (short story) 75
  "Nustāljiyā" (short story) 75
  "Qiṣṣat marīḍa" (short story) 75
  "al-Shaykh 'Awda" (short story) 74
feminism 34-5; feminist discourse 218-19; *see also* women: writers
Feraoun, Mouloud 116-19 *passim*
  La terre et le sang (novel) 116, 117, 118
Flaubert, Gustave 75
  Madame Bovary 75
Forster, E. M. 142
Foucault, Michel 92, 95-8 *passim*, 144, 147
  Discipline and Punish: the Birth of the Prison 92, 95-6
Frank, Joseph 142
French Revolution 35-6
Freud, Sigmund 102, 129, 137, 151, 164, 184-5, 187, 206, 207
  Beyond the Pleasure Principle 185
  Medusa's Head 187
al-Funūn (journal) 52

gender 160, 161
ghazal: *see* love poetry
al-Ghīṭānī, Jamāl 12, 91-105 *passim*, 125, 126-7, 129
  Risālat al-baṣā'ir fī 'l-maṣā'ir (novel) 125